Booked
FOR THE
Holidays

CHELSEA CURTO

To the book lovers and the go-getters: never stop chasing your dreams.

This book is an **open-door** romance with a handful of explicit scenes. In addition, within these pages you'll also find language, a car accident (not depicted on page and mentioned briefly), parental abandonment (off page and mentioned briefly) and relationship abandonment (off page and mentioned briefly).

This story has a Happily Ever After with just a touch of angst and lots of holiday fun!

No matter what holiday you celebrate or with whom, I hope you have the best season with those important to you. And, if you ever feel you don't have anyone to celebrate with, my messages are always open.

You are loved.

Happy holidays.

ONE

BRIDGET

NOVEMBER 1ST ARRIVES with little fanfare. It's not circled in red ink on a calendar to denote it of any significant importance. No multi-colored leaves fall from the trees or litter the pavement, marking the onslaught of late autumn. The only indication as to what the date might be are the mutilated pumpkins and melted Twix bars left behind from last night's Halloween festivities, chocolate and nougat bleeding onto the gray pavement. Ziggy, my rescue pit bull, eagerly sniffs the forgotten candy and whines when I give him a gentle tug to resume our walk, denying him a stolen treat.

The first sunrise of the new month peeks through tree branches as we make our way down the quiet sidewalk, refusing to bring with it a dip in the high temperatures that exist almost year round in central Florida. A bead of condensation rolls down my forehead, and I bat it away with the back of my hand. It feels less like the unofficial start of the festive season and more like the Fourth of July.

I hate it.

We get the occasional cold front, a blast of freakishly arctic air for three days when everyone scrambles to pull out jackets buried deep in their attics for the last eleven and a half months. The weather folks panic, strongly advising parents to not let their children stand outside in the positively frigid fifty degree temps without a hat and scarf.

The Northerners must think we're lunatics.

The Sunshine State is far from a winter wonderland, and just *once* I'd love for the impending holidays to be authentic. Like what you'd find in a classic Hallmark movie and not the swampy humidity I'm currently trudging through.

Dodging a particularly dismembered gourd vaguely resembling Chris Evans in *The Avengers,* I slow my stride as I approach my shop. It's empty out front, save for a figure looming there, to the left of the door. A man. Tall. Somewhat broad shouldered with his arms crossed over his chest. I snort when I recognize who it is.

Theo Gardner, the manager of the hardware store next door.

He's the textbook definition of cantankerous, a frequent scowler and an all-around prickly human. Even from here, half a block away, I can sense the waves of indignation rolling off of him. It's a steady stream, ebbing away from friendly and moving toward profoundly annoyed.

I pause, my gaze raking over him. He's wearing dark brown leather work boots with a drop of black paint on the toe of the left shoe. Jeans hug his thighs, molding over the muscles hidden beneath the denim. A red flannel shirt is unbuttoned over a simple white tee, the outer layer rolled to his elbows. Tattoos of various shapes and colors are visible on both arms. The artwork is intricate; an inky collage covering every inch of tan, tawny skin it can find.

"Bridget," he says. "You're late."

"Good morning, neighbor," I answer, cheerily lacing the greeting. "How are you? It's November 1st and we're officially in the holiday season, my friend!"

His response is a scoff.

Next, a grunt.

Then, in dramatic conclusion, as the epitome of Perpetually Disappointed, he frowns.

Creases form deep between his eyebrows, creating a valley of disgruntlement. The downward slope of his lips suggest I hurled a barrage of lethal words his way instead of merely saying hello. His arms flex, drawing attention to the tendons and cords of muscle sharpened and toned from years of what I assume is manual labor.

Jesus.

Those forearms have *veins*, sneakily disappearing under his sleeves in a way I've definitely never noticed before. Now it's all I can focus on.

"You're three minutes late," he clarifies.

The chastising snaps me out of the momentary trance and appreciation of his body, pointing out the extent of my apparent transgression. He pushes his thickly framed glasses up his nose with his pointer finger, waiting. The glance he gives me is cool, bordering on frosty, glacial indifference.

"What time is it?" I ask.

Confusion crosses Theo's face. After a check of his phone, he answers. "Seven o' three."

"Really? In that case, I'm sorry to tell you, you're wrong."

"Wrong?" he repeats, as if I've spoken a verbose monologue in a foreign language. "Wrong how?"

"You never stand outside the shop before 7:07. I'm not late. You're early."

Seconds tick by without a response. A car door slams. A train horn blares faintly in the distance, approaching the station up the street. Above us, a bird sings from a branch. Still, he says nothing.

I wait with bated breath. A thousand different scenarios run through my head, but I don't anticipate the response he gives me that will certainly, without a doubt, go down in the books under literary refinement.

"Are you fucking with me?" he asks.

Surprise and irritation pepper the words. Cautious curiosity hides behind the question and weariness, perhaps, to hear the answer.

"I can assure you, Theo, I am definitely *not* fucking with you. You don't strike me as the fucking around type."

"You'd be surprised," he draws out sardonically.

I haven't got a damn clue how I'm supposed to respond to that joke. Comedy is not a talent I've known Theo to employ. Frequently peeved? Without a doubt. Quick-witted and humorous? This is a new development.

"Every Wednesday morning at exactly 7:07 a.m., rain or shine, you walk through this door." I gesture to the entrance, a piece from the original construction I painted bright red. "It's different from the other days, when you order your drink off the website, head straight in, and pick it up without any interaction. I'm not sure what compelled you to be ahead of schedule today, but *you're* the one throwing us off. Not me."

I'm proud of myself, if we're being honest, for standing up to him. For calling him out on the underserved reproach. This might be the first time anyone's ever put him in his place. I dig into my pocket and find my keys, a distraction from the expected verbal lashing soon coming my way. My first attempt at opening the door results in the key clanging, upside down, against the unforgiving lock. On my second hurried attempt, I miss the lock entirely.

"Oh." Theo ponders my rebuttal. Out of the corner of my eye, I see him nod, which is followed by a half-shrug. "I'm... I'm sorry, Bridget."

Before I can think twice or process the sincerity behind his apology, he's reaching around my waist and taking the keys out of my hand. He unlocks the barrier, foot propping the door open as a rush of air conditioning hits my face.

"I forgive you," I whisper.

It comes out breathier than I intended, a puff of words and syllables catching in my throat. At that, Theo's expression softens. His eyes lighten and his shoulders fall away from his ears. He looks relieved, happy, maybe, if you stare long enough to sift through the negativity to find a hint of joy.

I cut our interlude short and hurry inside. I unhook Ziggy from his leash, watching as he trots to his favorite spot near the window under a perfect stream of sun rays, optimal for maximum relaxation. Lights illuminate the shelves of books and the shop springs to life as I flip a switch, and I smile at the sight.

Books have always been my happy place. As the one true joy and a constant fixture in my life, they've loved me back unconditionally and unwaveringly over the years. Creating a place to share my infatuation with reading was always a far-off dream of mine, forged as a young girl who spent many an hour with her nose buried in the pages of *The Babysitter's Club* and *Magic Treehouse*. The child who grew up thinking dragons were real and that she'd go to a magic school, too.

When I reached adulthood, I knew I wanted an occupation revolving around books. Becoming a librarian was a possibility, and clerking at a major retailer was another idea. Either would have scratched the itch for a little while, but I craved *more*. A place where I wasn't just another employee clocking in and out of work. I wanted something that was mine. Something I could create and help build from the ground up, contributing a fundamental part in each step of the process.

One day, it finally clicked.

I was going to own a bookstore.

The books themselves, I knew, would attract a wide following. After the initial design of shelf placement and seating areas, a component was still missing. It was incomplete, an *almost there* vision lacking a special touch I couldn't quite put my finger on.

My best friend from high school, Chandler Armstrong, suggested a café inside the space with handcrafted beverages and fresh pastries. Her reasoning was simple: there aren't many things in life better than a coffee and a good book on a cloudy afternoon.

On any afternoon, really.

She agreed to join me as head barista if I handled the baking and the books, a deal I knew would be ludicrous to pass up.

We found a sunny space on the corner of Cove Avenue, the bustling road running straight through the heart of our small town, Park Cove. Located on the edge of Orlando, we're just past the brink of theme parks buzzing with tourists and sports centers housing mediocre home teams. Our city, though, never feels like it's three miles from a major metropolis.

It's peaceful here, a location you'd find in a magazine or movie. People walk their dogs and ride their bikes up and down the street. They wave hello to folks who have lived in the same zip code for five decades, content to put up with the heat over snow shovels and frozen pipes. There are farmers' markets with fresh kettle corn and locally grown squash and peppers. We have sidewalk festivals on the weekend and parades featuring Girl Scout troops. Boutiques, art galleries and restaurants with waiting lists a month long sit under the tree-lined stretch of brick. Shoppers fill the pavement at all hours of the day, bags tucked under their arms and wallets a little lighter from frivolous spending.

The property was a steal for its location, sold to us cheaply by the previous owner who was ready to start his retirement aboard a yacht off the coast of Sarasota.

On an April morning three years ago my dream became a reality.

A Likely Story bookstore was born.

Business has been going well–better than I could have ever imagined–and we've been lucky to stumble into some recent mega-success. Earlier this year, a college cheerleader with a massive internet following walked into the store in search of a fudge brownie after an argument with her boyfriend. She browsed around, gushing endlessly over the small touches we had added to make the place welcoming and personal.

Cute coffee mugs line the shelves behind the bar.

A bright, circular rug designates the story time area where kids gather to hear favorite books read aloud.

A plush, blue velvet loveseat nestles cozily near the bay window, the perfect spot to curl up, read, and people watch.

The woman snapped dozens of photos and promised to share them online. The next morning I woke up to find our low four digit follower count on social media had catapulted to the stratosphere, surpassing six figures. Requests and messages poured in from all corners of the world, inquiring about shipping books and our online store.

Sales aren't showing any signs of slowing down, which is a good problem to have. I'm proud of our hard work. Starting a business isn't easy. Oftentimes people only see the end result; the culmination of months and months of sleepless nights and risky gambles finally coming to fruition.

They don't see when you take out a loan and sink yourself into debt for a *maybe*. They aren't there as you walk down the winding path of the unknown, standing at the edge of a cliff, wondering what comes next and if the hours you've poured into a passion project are worth it. They shy away from the daunting possibilities of an unguaranteed success, content to stay on the ground and away from the ledge.

I've always been a risk taker, and life feels *so good* when you take the leap and soar. When the wind whips through your hair on the plunge to the pools of your dreams, fears cast aside for the screams of delight tumbling from your mouth.

Taking a risk is when I feel most alive, and these last three years have breathed a fresh excitement into me. A renewed vigor and appreciation of how *lucky* I am to do what I love. I get to spend my days working alongside one of my best friend, helping customers pick out books that might change their lives, and making tasty treats in the rare spare moments I can find.

"Are we mixing it up today, or going with your usual?" I ask now, striding to the coffee corner. Theo follows behind, his heavy boots scratching a melody on the wide-plank hardwood floor.

The question is superfluous. It's been three years and I know exactly how he operates–always the same drink, never any deviation. A vanilla cappuccino, consumed every day, even when it's one hundred and two degrees outside.

"Usual, please."

He yawns and settles onto the leather barstool opposite me. His chin drops into the palm of his hand, eyes closing. I watch him, puzzled by his sedentary state. It's rare he hangs around for longer than a handful of seconds. His preferred method of coffee retrieval is grabbing his beverage and departing as expeditiously as possible, keen to remove himself before a swarm of squawking parents enter the building after high school carpool duty.

"Late night?"

"You could say that," Theo answers.

Even with weekly interaction, we don't know much about each other. He's never offered me any insight into his personal life and I never ask, adhering to his desire of keeping our communication to strictly surface-level pleasantries. We teeter between loose acquaintances and strangers, never tipping fully to the side of friends.

It's weird to exist in the same space as someone for a prolonged period of time and only learn minor details about them. I know his coffee order, sure. And that the pair of jeans he's wearing–the dark denim ones frayed at the bottom–are his favorite. There are three pairs of boots in his rotation, and the paint drip ones are his most frequently worn footwear. That concludes my limited knowledge of Theo Gardner. On a whim, I take the chance to dig a little deeper.

"Vague and elusive as always, Collector," I say.

Theo lifts his chin from his hand, intrigued. "Collector?"

"Yeah. Your arms are like the freaking Louvre. It's fine. Keep your secrets. I respect your privacy, so I'll stop subtly fishing for information."

"Not subtle at all, Brownie. Doesn't get more blunt than that."

This early in the morning, when the world is quiet and no one is around, I can better appreciate his sleep-fogged voice, husky and rich like decadent chocolate. It's deep and a little rough around the edges. Low... manly. A tone I could pick out anywhere. It sounds nice echoing against the hanging porcelain mugs behind me, a more relaxed timbre than the fighting tone from before.

And *Brownie.*

The nickname is new, a surprising twist of personalization he's enacting for the first time in our neighborly existence.

I like it.

I hum as I fix his drink: A pump of vanilla. Piping hot espresso. Steamed milk. A heavy dash of cinnamon on top of foam. I place the caffeinated goodness on the polished counter in front of him and smile.

"Anything else?"

His brown eyes drift longingly to the pastry display case. "A muffin. It was a very long night, and I'm going to need sustenance to get through the day."

"I could make you an egg sandwich or something else instead. It would probably be more filling."

Theo's attention drags back to me, puzzled. "That's not on the menu."

"So? I have eggs. I have bread. It wouldn't be hard to combine the two."

"Why would you do that for me?"

I pause. It's a valid question for him to ask. I've never offered a non-menu item before, and I can't pinpoint why this morning, of all the mornings, I decided to. So I shrug and say, "Why not?"

Absentmindedly, he runs a thumb along the curve of his jaw, from his cheekbone to his chin. I see the temptation there, the desire to say yes. I think he's about to give in and let someone do something nice for him until he answers.

"A muffin is plenty."

"Okay." I grab a pair of tongs and stuff a blueberry muffin–his favorite–into a to-go bag and hand it over.

His long, decorated arm stretches over the counter as he pays with the tap of his credit card. "Tip jar choices?"

"*Stranger Things* versus *Game of Thrones*."

"It's not even a fair competition." The one-dollar bills I didn't see him pull from his pocket fall into the *Stranger Things* bucket. "You should play some Kate Bush over the speakers next week. Thanks for the coffee and food, Bridget. I'm sorry again for earlier."

"It's okay. I hope you get some good sleep tonight."

Theo slides off the stool, taking his cappuccino and muffin with him. I'm awarded his signature parting nod as he treks toward the exit, shoulders beginning to curve in. The stoic facade is back in place, nicknames and apologies a thing of the past. His eyes remain on me as he retreats, focus unshakable. I answer his meager farewell with a dramatic salute of my own.

When he finally turns away and breaks our staring contest, just as he reaches the door, I notice his lips tugging up in the corner. A hint of a smile–small, but *there*–briefly brightens his weary face.

It's the most beautiful thing I've ever seen.

TWO

BRIDGET

"HEY." Chandler pops up from behind the counter as I enter the store on Friday morning. I free Ziggy from his leash and he bounds over to her, ready for one of the dog bones she keeps hidden in her pocket.

"Hi," I say through a yawn.

"Are you okay?"

"Just tired. I stayed up way too late last night."

"Let me guess. A good book?"

"Guilty." I grin. "He's the captain of the hockey team. She's a figure skater. The tension was *so good*. I couldn't put it down until they kissed for the first time."

"Color me shocked. Well, your morning isn't going to get much better. A shipment was dropped off an hour ago."

"What? They told me it wouldn't be in until tomorrow. It's barely eight."

"Yeah, and I've already been verbally accosted for accidentally giving someone whole milk instead of skim. Don't even get me started on the pretentious asshat who spent ten minutes complaining about the chocolate chip-to-muffin ratio. Sometimes, I want to tell people to fuck off."

"Chan, sweetie, you always want to tell people to fuck off."

She waves away my interruption, on a roll and not stopping anytime soon. "Lawrence? Luke? Lyle? The guy from next door said the boxes were sitting outside the hardware store when he got in. Guess they had the wrong address. Theo brought them over when he saw I was struggling to wrangle them on the dolly."

"He did?" I ask.

"It's not like he was going to let them sit there and block their entrance. Remember when he moved our outside tables two inches to the left because they were, and I quote, 'encroaching on his domain'? Isn't it weird the guy carries a ruler in his pocket?"

"It's also weird he knows the property line down to the millimeter. It was thoughtful of him to help you this morning."

"I didn't think thoughtful was in his repertoire."

"He's plenty thoughtful. He just has a unique way of showing it."

"You're hiding something," Chandler says. She scrutinizes me, the defensiveness on Theo's behalf a rare occurrence.

"Am not!" I answer, doing my best to convey neutrality.

It wouldn't do me any good to make it obvious I *am* hiding something. Maybe I don't want people to know that when Theo's lips pull upward, he favors the right side of his mouth, instead of the left. A lopsided smile, but beautiful nonetheless. Maybe I don't want anyone to know his eyes crinkle slightly behind his glasses and a faint splash of pink paints his cheeks, the hue you would find during sunset on a clear summer night.

And maybe, most alarmingly, I'm afraid to admit, even to myself, I enjoyed seeing that ephemeral happiness. A fleeting display of wondrous delight, and the sneaking suspicion it's not awarded to everyone.

I'm sure it's pathetic to care about such a meager, insignificant gesture, or consider myself honored or flattered. But I do, and I am, so I'm going to marvel in the secret no one else is privy to.

Theo Gardner is breathtaking when he smiles.

"How do you feel about adding a few holiday drinks to the menu early?" I ask. A change in conversation to escape a likely interrogation is necessary.

My best friend narrows her eyes, but accepts the diversion. "One step ahead of you. I brainstormed a couple of ideas last night. They'll be finalized by next week, right in time for the holiday craziness to unfold."

Chandler lasted three days at the Culinary Institute of America, deciding she prefers slinging beverages over sautéing steaks or onions. She became an aficionado at mixing frappuccinos and flavored teas. Each new season, people line up outside, covering two blocks of sidewalk to see what her drinks of the month are going to be. She has the creative ability to take four random ingredients and create flavors that seamlessly fuse taste and originality to a delicious blend in paper cups.

"Have I told you today you're the best?" I laugh.

"You haven't, but I know I am." Full of sass, she tosses her strawberry blonde hair over her shoulder. "Don't forget I'm going out of town this weekend and won't be back until Tuesday."

"Your camping trip to the mountains of North Carolina doesn't make me jealous at all, by the way."

"Are you forgetting I invited you?"

"I'm not intruding on your solo adventure, Chan. So go forth, my wilderness woman, and enjoy bonfires under a star-filled sky. Sleeping bags with no pillows. Jacket potatoes roasted over an open fire. Hiking the Appalachian Trail. Please, just don't get eaten by a bear. I'd miss you too much, and I can't operate the fancy espresso machine without your help. I have to use the old one."

"You're so freaking weird sometimes." The smile on her face betrays the snarky quip. "For the record, I'd miss you too."

I grin, heading for the large delivery waiting for me. At the start of every month, we receive large packages from various publishers, distributors, and authors themselves. The shipments include upcoming releases, a replenished stock of best-sellers that fly off the shelves like hotcakes, and independently published novels from authors who might not be on someone's radar yet.

That's what makes literature so wonderfully beautiful and poetic. There's quite literally something for everyone. What one person considers a two-star read with little purpose and merit might be someone's most prized possession. A book they return to because it offers solace in times of great need or a friend they long for on a lonely day. It's a subjective love affair that varies from person to person with enough sub-genres and obscure branches to satisfy even the most hard-to-please readers.

I do my best to accommodate a wide variety of topics from an array of different sources, so no one leaves the shop empty-handed. It's not about the sales or the money. Financial success is a goal, yeah, but it's more important to me to help people find a series or story that will become their favorite work of fiction. The scenes, characters and passages they'll think about daily, profound words sticking with them long after they read the last line.

It's what makes this job worthwhile.

I drag the first of ten boxes toward the book section, ready to get to work.

Chandler and I agreed on an open floor plan when designing the shop. We considered where each piece of furniture would go, taping the ground and walking through the room hundreds of times to get the layout perfect.

The bakery and café are in the far right corner of the space. A long, laminate counter with a cornflower blue surface forms a large L-shape. Eight stools flank the bar. The white leather on the chairs is a little worn, where patrons have spent long hours deep in conversation over drinks and pastries. Smells of lemon and nutmeg drift from the ovens, a sweet and spicy fragrance duet left behind from my baking.

To the left, a wall-to-wall bookshelf stretches from the floor to the ceiling. Painted a rich navy blue and stocked with books on every subject—from native Florida bugs to monster romance series—the piece is a focal point and where everyone's eyes are naturally drawn. A rolling ladder is the only missing element, the final piece and a dream addition I hope to add somewhere down the road.

Across the floor, chairs, couches and beanbags are scattered. Some are pushed away, against the perimeter, to allow a free-flow of foot traffic. Others are nestled between two smaller shelves, an opportune place to sit and flip through the pages of a home design magazine, searching for a new renovation project to tackle. Blankets cover the arms of recliners, quilted patterns creating a palette of color.

There's a cozy, inviting ambiance to the environment. Muted, filtered lighting. A speaker playing soft rock through the store: Lou Reed, T. Rex and Queen, the artists of choice. It's a place you might spend several hours getting lost in the pages of a fantasy world or heartbreaking love story, reality passing you by. We wanted it to feel like *home*, familiarity and a blissful content-ment welcoming you every time you walk through the door.

I think we've done a good job creating a place people want to visit. The store is always busy, a mix of familiar faces and people stopping by for the first time, our bright chalkboard sign beckoning them inside. They come for the books; they stay for the drinks and snacks, and leave with a full heart of time well spent in a place they know they'll return back to soon.

"Do you hear that?"

I look up at Chandler's question. A stack of holiday romances I plan to swap out with the thrillers we displayed throughout October sit by my side, ready to be shelved.

A sound lances through the walls, drawing nearer. It becomes more distinct; a shrill, continuous beep piercing the air. Her eyes meet mine from across the room, my grin mirrored on her face.

"Greta," we say in unison. I hurry to join Chandler at the café.

The town's busybody, a ruthless, humorous woman named Greta, retired from the Secret Service in the 90s. Always on the hunt for the latest scandal, gossip is now her weapon of choice. You can hear her horn a mile away whenever she catches a whiff, determined to scour for details of a developing story. A honk is the only warning she gives innocent pedestrians, lest they get mowed down by her motorized wheelchair. She received a citation last winter for running a stroller off the sidewalk, an incident she vehemently denies.

I'm surprised when she stops outside our shop and shifts the ECV to park. She climbs off the contraption with more grace and poise than someone who's had two hips replaced should. She flings open the door and ambles inside, a bright yellow flyer clutched to her chest.

"Ladies." She nods and makes her way over to us.

Resting her cane against the counter, she slowly climbs onto an empty stool. Once comfortable, she slams the colored paper down with ferocity, rattling the dirty silverware sitting in the sink I've yet to clean, plagued by other tasks and to-do items.

"What is this?" I ask.

"Read it and find out."

I look down at the document, bold words catching my attention. My attendance is **required** at a **mandatory town hall meeting** this evening at **6 p.m. sharp.**

"Another meeting?" I ask. A bubble of annoyance builds as I process the words and what's being asked of me. "We had one six days ago. It ended with an argument about whether the recycling bins should be blue or green."

"They should be green," Greta interjects. Opinionated and blunt, she's never afraid to share exactly what's on her mind. "Blue is far too garish."

"The two hours of discussion last week was enough, so we don't need to rehash this same debate. Calling a random meeting that's not plotted on the city calendar is a bit out of the ordinary. What if I have plans tonight? A date? Can they really make it mandatory?"

Chandler attempts to cover her laughter with an unconvincing cough. "Are we counting spending an evening on the couch with a bowl of popcorn and your favorite romance novel a date now?" she asks.

"So I'd rather be home with an Emily Henry book than listening to another man tell me about the fishing trip he took with his friends, Brad and Chad," I say. "Big deal. What's your point?"

"My point is, even though real men suck, at least they can get you off. They let you sit on their face and–"

Face-sitting, it appears, is the perverse line Greta won't let us cross. "Stop it. Both of your love lives are a travesty," she says firmly.

"Mine isn't a travesty," I counter. "I haven't dated anyone in months."

"Years," Chandler corrects.

"Non-existent can still be a travesty. We have more pressing matters to deal with."

The older woman's posture straightens, spine turning so rigid, it could rival a steel rod. A smug smile appears, wrinkles prominent on her weathered cheeks.

Oh.

She knows something.

Something really, really good.

"I've heard a rumor about monetary compensation," Greta continues.

"For attending a meeting?"

"There's been rumblings about a contest of sorts."

"What kind of contest?"

"Guess you'll have to show up to the meeting to find out." She shrugs.

The ambiguity, ironically, makes me think of Theo. He's the least involved owner on the avenue, rivaling an investor you never see or hear from. He sends an enthusiastic proxy to town hall events in his place, a carousel of rotating hardware store employees popping into various meetings. Never one for chatty conversations or story swapping, he's not usually inclined to cancel Friday night plans to accommodate someone else.

I doubt he'll be there tonight, delegating the task to some poor college kid who will be bored to death while listening to another riveting lecture on trash days and window cleaning.

When I'm expected to alter my schedule for others, I think life would be less stressful if I took a more callous approach. I'm not the type of person to tell someone to fuck off. Considerate to a fault, empathy and compassion are my downfall. I'm the one who says yes, yes, and yes to *everything*, because *no* is too difficult. I'm the first to volunteer, to ask what needs to be done, always willing to sacrifice my time and energy for people who might not return the favor.

I hate it sometimes, this overwhelming need to make sure the world is content and satisfied. I wish I had the gall to be more outspoken. I wish I could put myself first instead of last. But I don't, and I know despite my grumbling, I'm going to go to this meeting. I'm going to put a smile on my face, and do my best not to be annoyed by another meaningless presentation on sprinklers.

"Bridge? Do you want me to go?" Chandler asks.

"What?" I shake my head. "No way. You have your trip. I'll find out what the fuss is about. Must be pretty important if they're printing notices on colored paper. How long until we have a meeting on budgets?"

"Mark my words: you won't want to miss this," Greta says.

Her parting shot sounds like an ominous warning, a battle cry we'd be smart to listen to. As soon as she leaves the shop, horn blaring once more, I look at my best friend, completely bewildered.

"What the hell?" I ask Chandler.

"I don't know, B. The only takeaway from this is you *have* to be at that meeting. It's going to be important."

"As long as I don't have to sit through an hour-long discussion on the size of flower beds, I'll consider it a success."

"Text me the minute you know what's going on. I don't care if I don't have service. I'll hold my phone above my head on the side of a mountain if I need to."

"I highly doubt it's going to be *that* important, Chan, but I will. I promise."

THREE

THEO

I'M NOT sure who I've pissed off in life—plenty of people, I assume—but running late for an event I do not want to go to is torture.

I'm not in the mood to be surrounded by chatty business owners who keep their shop doors propped open with rocks reciting inspirational quotes, *Live, Laugh, Love* etched on the sandstone. They're the same people who greet patrons like they're long-lost friends, offering a bottle of water and a bowl of chocolate candy as rewards for spending lots of money.

Kiss-asses.

I stop at an intersection, impatiently tapping my foot as I wait to cross the road. The faster I get to this damn meeting, the faster I can get home. And, *fuck*, I want to go home. Having a gathering sprung on me when I was halfway out the door was not an ideal way to end my day. I was dreaming about the beer I was going to crack open and the steak waiting for me when a flyer got shoved in my hand by a passing pedestrian who didn't offer any insight into the cryptic event. With the rest of my team clocked out and heading to their cars, I knew the responsibility of attendance would fall to me.

Others whisper about me behind my back enough. I don't need to give them more ammunition, so I step off the curb and continue on my way, a scowl on my face and disdain boiling in my blood.

"Oh. Hey, Theo," someone says.

I reluctantly look to the right and find I've fallen in step with Bridget Boylston. Her voice is light and airy, like a wisp of long-awaited autumn breeze. The free hand not occupied by a dog leash waves in my direction, greeting me like we're best friends. Her companion, a medium-size dog with a light brown coat–the same one who roams around her store–sniffs my leg and wags his tail.

Dozens of adjectives pop into my mind when I think about the pastry-making, book-loving brunette by my side.

Bubbly. Lively. Perky. Sparkling. Kind.

Really happy, all the damn time.

Even now she's smiling, not a glimmer of annoyance to be found.

Seeing her brings back the memory of Wednesday. The whole morning was bizarre. Me, apologizing for wrongly calling out her tardiness. Her, offering to cook me an egg sandwich.

Who offers to cook someone a random meal, unprovoked?

Bridget Boylston, apparently.

The dark circles under my eyes were probably a dead give-away to my state of exhaustion, fatigue now a permanent fixture on my face. When I trudged back to my office, I realized she had given me a large drink instead of the usual medium I order. A small gesture, it threw me off balance and I was swept away by her thoughtfulness.

The sucker punch to my gut was the extra dash of cinnamon I know she sprinkles in the beverage on my behalf. She's done it every time since I offhandedly mentioned liking the flavor a couple years ago.

For a second, everything felt manageable.

For a second, everything was brighter.

For a second, I could *breathe*.

"Are you excited for the meeting?" Bridget continues, engaging in a one-sided conversation I've yet to participate in.

She's either ignoring my *I really don't want to talk to you* glare, or she's oblivious as hell. Anyone else on the end of that look normally mumbles an apology and leaves me blessedly alone.

Because that's my thing, I guess.

People leave me. They never stick around.

Bridget Boylston has other plans, it seems.

"No." I acknowledge her for the first time, interaction no longer avoidable as we stop at the next crosswalk. "I'm not."

"I'm curious what it could be about. And irritated, too. There are so many things I'd rather be doing tonight. I'm sure–"

I don't give her the opportunity to share *what* she's sure about, because my hand reaches out and grabs her arm, abruptly ending the conversation. I yank her toward the sidewalk, out of the path of a car running a red light. Another step closer, and she would have been hit by the speeding vehicle.

"Are you trying to get yourself killed?" I seethe. My grip on her bicep is tight and bruising, fingers curling around her muscle to keep her safely upright and not in a heap on the brick road. I scan her from head to toe, heart racing as I check for any signs of injury. A sigh escapes when I find her unharmed, and my shoulders sag in relief.

"I wasn't paying attention."

"Clearly," I scoff. "You could have been hurt. Who gives a fuck about the meeting? Open your eyes, Bridget, so you don't die before you get there."

The mocking tone and condescending words register in my head. They're far too harsh for someone like her to hear. I'm shocked there's no retaliation against my aggressive reprimand.

Instead, her eyes move to my fingers, possessively wrapped around her arm.

"Ow" hasn't been said yet, and she hasn't asked me to let her go, either. It's a request she should've demanded several seconds ago. Except she hasn't, so we stand here, motionless, my hand cemented to her bicep while traces of vanilla and caramel waft from her hair to my nose.

She's warm under my touch, like the sand on the beach in the middle of July. Her skin is soft, *so fucking soft*. And it feels like goddamn heaven.

"Thank you."

Her words, grateful and hushed, settle the deep rumble in my chest. The tension abates, and I breathe out again, steadier than before.

"Sorry." My fingers peel back and release her from their protective hold, a reddish hue left in their place.

"You didn't hurt me."

My molars grind together. Her approval isn't needed, yet here I am, eager for it anyway. "Good to know."

"I'm glad we share similar sentiments about our required attendance," Bridget continues. "If I have to hear anything about street lamps or shrubbery, I'm starting a riot."

My lips purse, the ghost of a rare grin forming at the thought. There's not a mean bone in her body. She once spent thirty-five minutes ushering a bee out of her shop rather than killing it because it was "beneficial to the environment." This is the same woman who, when a customer yelled at her for giving them a chocolate chip cookie instead of a scone, she comped the pastry with a smile.

Her inciting a riot would be hysterical.

Central Park, the expansive green space situated in the middle of downtown Park Cove and the location of our meeting, comes into view. I halt at the sight. It's crawling with people.

Lawn chairs are set up. Blankets are laid out. Charcuterie boards are spread across picnic tables. Groups have formed. The volume of chatter increases my crabbiness to a new level.

I *hate* large groups of people. There's always the fear someone's going to approach me, asking questions I don't want to give the answers to. A jackass who wants to dive deep into my personal life when I want to tell them to fuck off. The more people around, the greater the chance someone brings up memories I do my best to forget.

"Hey. Are you all right?"

A gentle hand taps my elbow, pulling my focus away from the buzzing crowd.

Bridget's watching me. Her eyebrows are pinched and her smile has faltered. Her hair, almost copper in the light of the setting sun, shields a portion of her face before she brushes the pieces away, looking concerned.

"Fine," I say, the word coming out more like a raspy affirmation than an assured declaration. "I'm fine."

I haven't convinced her because her attention stays on me for a second, two, three too long before darting away for good. Her hand disappears from my arm as she surveys the scene in front of us.

Suddenly, I miss her steadying touch.

I brush off the thought and follow her eyes, noticing the stage at the edge of the landscaped square is set up with a microphone. A hoard of people stand on the elevated platform, milling about with hushed voices.

"Holy cow," Bridget exclaims. "This isn't what I was expecting."

"What were you expecting?"

"Six people and a rowdy argument about menial topics. Some wild gesturing and a cane used as a pointing device. Oh, and the line 'back in my day' used at least eleven times."

"A menial topic like the size of mannequins in the windows of the clothing stores?" I supply. "I heard about that one."

She snorts and nods. "Yeah, or birdseed on the sidewalk. God forbid the squirrels eat the dropped leftovers."

"My favorite was the discussion about the brightness of the stoplights on the avenue. How the yellow wasn't yellow enough. Are there varying shades of yellow I should know about?"

"Wait, you weren't even at that meeting."

I try not to dwell on why she noticed my absence. I also try not to dwell on how easy it is to talk to her, words slipping out unintentionally, continuing on and on.

"No, I wasn't. But people talk. Is there a reason you don't want to be here? Seems like your kind of scene," I say. "Socializing and whatnot."

"Ah, yes, I forget you're a strict anti-socializer. My feet hurt. These shoes are new and I haven't broken them in yet. There's a long list of things I need to do at the store. Books I need to catalog and inventory I need to restock. I'm starving. All I want to do is eat a goddamn cheeseburger and French fries from Shake Shack. Is that too much to ask?"

It's different from her usual demeanor of *positive* and *optimistic*. A damn menace of a question hangs on the tip of my tongue. I want to ask her what else is on this long to-do list, and if she needs any help in completing it.

"Excuse me. This is a family friendly event. Language like that is inappropriate. And from a woman, too. Such a shame."

I glance over my shoulder, finding a woman sitting in a lawn chair. She tuts, manicured nails tapping against her wine glass. Warmth flares behind my ribs at the demeaning lob tossed Bridget's way. I know I was an ass to her a short while ago, but this is different. This feels intentionally cruel, and someone like Bridget doesn't deserve that kind of childish temperament.

"Cheating on your husband with your son's science teacher

is also inappropriate, but you don't hear us talking about it," I snap impulsively.

My palm lands on the small of Bridget's back, a pathetic attempt at a shield as I lead us away, scouting out a less busy area of the lawn. When we stop, she stares at me, shell-shocked.

"Did you just–how do you know about her cheating on her husband? That's top notch gossip, and you don't strike me as someone who cares about that sort of thing."

"The perk about not talking to people is that they don't have a problem with oversharing around me."

"Oh my god, Theo, thank you. You're my hero."

FOUR

THEO

MY CHEST PUFFS out at her praise. I stand up straighter, the warmth growing to a heat that flicks the base of my spine, a fire beginning to burn. Slow at first, then steady. Bridget looks up at me, a slight tilt of her chin and a grin sitting on those full, pink lips. Understanding dawns. Her elation is brought on by *me* and what *I* said. The heat intensifies, giving way to a blazing wildfire that starts to burn out of control.

Her eyes–not quite green, not quite brown, a color stuck somewhere in the middle–are creased around the edges, laugh lines indicating years of pure euphoria. Her smile stretches from corner to corner.

I'm not sure I've seen a more stunning sight.

I thought I had a good read on my neighbor, learning small pieces about her the last couple of years. They haven't taken much digging, easily spotted by anyone paying a lick of attention to her. Nothing overly profound, but still important.

She doesn't drink caffeine, her personality and cheerfulness fueled by natural spunk and fiery ambition.

She hates marshmallows in her hot chocolate. I heard her ranting about the fluffy pillow of gelatin once, a ten-minute passionate monologue arguing why they don't belong anywhere near desserts.

Her favorite color is blue, mentioning to a customer the shade of the large bookshelf in her store is the one she loves the most.

Of all the meaningless details I've gathered, watching her be happy–in a real, unfiltered, hell, yeah kind of way–takes the whole damn cake. I seize her admiration greedily, filing it away for safekeeping. It gets tucked inside the short catalog of other acknowledgements I hold close.

"Not a problem," I say.

I don't know why I jumped in, inserting myself into gossip I don't want to be a part of, but something compelled me to... *protect* her, almost. Defend and keep out of harm's way. It's the same something that ran through me when she almost got hit by the car, *safe, safe, safe,* chanting in my head until she *was*.

I have no clue what it means.

Her rant comes back to me, and I discover there's one thing I can help with. I fumble with the pocket of my jeans, extracting a pack of crackers and handing it her way.

"What's this?" she asks.

"A snack. You said you were hungry."

Her gaze breaks from the food to stare at me. It's obvious she was just glancing at me before, and now I have her complete, undivided attention. *Shit*, it's kind of overwhelming in a good way.

A counter normally separates us, but this close I'm able to notice features I haven't seen before. Eyes leaning closer to green now that I'm looking at them more carefully. Irises flecked with specks of gold. A freckle just below her left eyebrow. Sharp cheekbones. A parted mouth inhaling tiny breaths of air. Another cluster of freckles on the bridge of her nose, spilling across her face like splatter paint on a canvas, a million stars in the night sky.

I kind of want to trace them with my fingers, discovering what I could write. A poem? My name?

Dark brown hair cascades down her back, and jagged, uneven, windswept bangs cover her forehead. She's tall, close to five foot ten, which isn't far from my height of six foot three. Slim upper body. A trim waist. Hips jutting out in a pear shape figure that gives way to long legs under a plaid skirt.

She's really fucking pretty.

I knew she was good looking, but I never paused to stare at her from head to toe, appreciating the stops along the way. I'm so close to asking what the hell I can do to fix her day. How can I help? What else does she need?

"Don't you want them? You're probably hungry, too."

"I'm fine."

"Let's share them," Bridget decides.

"I don't–"

"Take the damn food, Theo."

I realize I no longer have a choice in the matter.

I also realize my name on her lips sounds nice, *really, really nice,* even with impatience behind it.

That's distracting, and not good at all.

Her hand knocks into mine, a nudge of knuckles as she transfers over my portion of the snack. The tips of her fingers tickle my outstretched palm, gliding over the callouses. Bridget doesn't bat an eye at the rough, raised patches of skin.

"Thanks."

"Do you want to sit together?" she asks. "Hopefully people won't chastise our choice of curse words."

I huff out something that could maybe, if I tried hard enough, be considered a laugh. "Yeah. We can sit together."

Bridget takes a seat on the ground and gestures to the spot

next to her. I crouch down and join her on the patch of grass, stretching out my legs and exhaling a sigh.

"This is Ziggy." Her hand runs along the fur of the mutt who's made his home near my hips.

"Ziggy? As in–"

"Ziggy Stardust and the Spiders from Mars?" She dips her chin and smiles. "Yeah."

I blink, thrown off by this new uncovering. She doesn't strike me as a fan of glam rock, and I add it to the small list of things I know about her. The small list of things I think I *like* about her.

"You're a fan of Bowie?"

"He's my favorite musician. I have his lightning bolt tattooed on my finger."

"Huh. I have the same bolt on my shoulder."

Her face brightens at the tiny piece of personal information I've shared, and I think I won her approval through an unintended test. "Really? Look at us. Tattoo twins. You learn something new every day. How many do you have in total, Collector?"

I stop another smile from forming. When I wander in the store on Wednesday mornings–when she's the one opening and the only day I don't order online–I always look forward to hearing what nickname she comes up with. It's like a language designed only for us.

Collector is her best one yet, a uniquely personal attribution to my physical appearance and not a generic bundle of words to check a box.

I hope she keeps using it.

"Lost track after thirty," I say.

"I only have one. I passed out during the appointment and I don't have the guts to go back."

"Maybe one day you will."

"Yeah," she says, a resolute nod in agreement. "Maybe I will."

"Good evening!" A man taps the microphone. His voice

booms through the speakers, and I wince at the static. "Can everyone hear me? I'm Jamie Mulligan, deputy mayor of Park Cove. Sorry to call everyone here on such short notice. We received word a few days ago from an important publication about an exciting opportunity. *Travel Living*, the critically acclaimed magazine published throughout the states and in ten countries, recently ranked our town the top U.S. travel destination to visit during the holiday season!"

Jamie beams at us like we found the cure for cancer and won a Nobel Peace Prize. I resist the urge to roll my eyes and settle back on my elbows, getting comfortable for the snoozefest.

"In honor of the national ranking, they're bestowing on us a prize," he continues.

What kind of toolbag uses *bestowing* in casual conversation like we're summering in regency London?

I really hate this dude.

"The prize is $100,000," he concludes.

A ripple of excitement makes its way through the crowd. People scoot to the edge of their seats. Wine glasses pause mid-sip, Chardonnay and Bordeaux forgotten. Even I sit upright, making sure I heard him correctly.

A hundred thousand dollars?

That's a big price tag. Life-changing money that could go to so many projects. Already, my mind goes into planning mode.

"It's a contest created to foster camaraderie and unity," the dude says. "The best decorated, most festive shop will be crowned the winner. You won't be working alone, though. You'll be randomly paired with another store. Between you and your employees, the two shops will have the chance to wow judges and take home the grand prize."

Oh, fuck no.

There's no way in *hell* I'm participating in this inevitable fiasco. Working with a group of strangers where we have to agree on shit and take time out of our day to hang up stockings stuffed with toys?

Absolutely not.

"The deadline for entry submission is Monday. The drawing for pairs will be on Tuesday. Judging will commence on December 22nd, and winners will be announced at a town-wide celebration on Christmas Eve!"

"Wow," Bridget breathes out. "How exciting! I'm definitely entering our names. You are too, right?"

"No," I answer curtly.

Her smile wavers, splintering in the corners. "What do you mean 'no'?"

"I mean, we're not participating. It's not mandatory, and it sounds like my idea of hell." The thought of tinsel and twinkling lights makes me grimace with distaste.

"Do carolers haunt your nightmares, too?" she presses. "You're going to give up the chance to win a lot of money because you're afraid of Frosty the Snowman?"

Damn her for being funny.

Damn her for being kind instead of cold.

Why the hell can't she leave me alone? Everyone else does. They do it gladly, too, and here she is, stretching out a conversation with me when we have nothing meaningful to talk about.

I've had too much interaction with her in the last forty-eight hours, and I'm becoming... *fuck*. I can't define the word. Agitated. But it's not the usual contempt for my surroundings. The new concept buzzes my brain and makes my skin itch with... disappointment? Regret?

It's like I'm letting her down in some way, crushing her hopes and dreams. I haven't done anything wrong, yet the feeling is there, yelling loudly in my ears about how much of an asshole I am for making her upset.

I hate it.

I stand and brush away the blades of grass from the back of my jeans before this gets any worse. "Good luck, Bridget. I'm sure you'll create a lovely winter wonderland experience. We won't be joining."

I turn and walk away from the sea of people and the beams of sunshine she tossed my way, like they were hand-picked just for me, a present from the goddess of the sky. Away from the reminder about my least favorite time of the year. Away from the eyes watching me as I leave, whispering behind my back. As I near the parking lot, I scrub my hand over my face and pull out my phone, hitting the name of one of my listed favorites. It rings twice.

"Finally!"

I smile at her voice, tension melting to a puddle on the ground. "Hey, sweetie." I climb into my truck and buckle my seatbelt. "Sorry I'm late. I'm headed home."

"Sounds good. Don't stop for food! There's some here. Love you."

"Love you too," I answer, tossing the device into the cup holder and shift to drive.

I try not to reminisce on how it's my fault Bridget's mood changed, bringing her from excited and animated to sad. The recognition is sour as I peel out of the parking spot and head away from the pretty woman who didn't run from me.

Not good at all.

FIVE

BRIDGET

"ALL WE HAVE to do to win \$100,000–holy shit, Bridget, that's so much money–is hang up some lights, put out fake snow, and sing fa-la-la-la-la until our throats are sore?" asks Chandler. There's a patch of dirt on her elbow, left behind from her weekend camping trip, and I'm filling her in on what she missed while she was gone. "I can't believe you waited until I got home to let me know what was going on."

"I thought it would be better to tell you in person since this is a big deal. You're okay with us entering, right?"

I grab a mug and pour myself a cup of fresh hot chocolate, spooning a dollop of whipped cream on top. It's pushing eighty outside today, and the scent of sunscreen assaults my nose with each customer who enters the store. I've been in a festive mood since the competition announcement, dreaming of presents under a tree and mistletoe hanging in the doorway. Of paper snowflakes dangling from the ceiling and garland framing the windows. A million ideas came to mind, potential shop layouts and themes among the slew of decorating designs I've been mulling over.

"Of course I'm okay with us entering. We're partnering with another store, right?"

"Yeah. Jamie only gave us dates about entry submission and the day of judging. Once everyone heard about the prize money, they kind of tuned him out."

"Poor Jamie. What a plight for our hardworking deputy mayor who holds a made-up position with zero power. Maybe you can make him feel better."

"Shut up. You know he's a friend. *Just* a friend," I emphasize.

"A friend who wants to get in your pants. Do you think he wears socks in bed? Oh my god. Or a belt. And not in a hot, 'I'm going to use this on you' way, but rather to keep his trousers up."

I sputter, hot chocolate traveling down the wrong pipe. "What is wrong with you? I have never in my life pictured Jamie holding a belt and telling me he was going to use it on me, and I don't want to start."

"You're no fun," she says, pouting.

Chandler is allowed to joke with me because she knows nothing would ever happen with the guy we sat next to in high school economics. Jamie's cute, a polite man whose personality is similar to mine. Kind and thoughtful, positive and bright. I've entertained the thought briefly when I've felt a particular nasty bout of loneliness linger in my chest. It dredges up more frequently during the holidays, a prevalent pain noticeable when I see a couple walk down the sidewalk, hand-in-hand, completely infatuated with each other.

Each time I try to envision a relationship with him, the idea never becomes more defined than a hazy outline. We don't have any chemistry. There's no fire, no passion. No sexual tension or desire to rip off his tie and wrap my legs around his waist. There are no pinky grazes or flirting. We don't exchange passing smiles, secretly grinning because we know what the other looks like naked, painted by the light of the moon.

When I find a man to settle down with, I don't want someone totally compatible or perfect on paper. I want someone flawed who shows me their messy parts and accepts mine in return. Someone who will challenge and push me to be the best version of myself, and support me in my wildest dreams. A guy who keeps me on my toes and surprises me every day. I want my hair pulled, wrapped around his wrist like a bracelet. I also want to be called *beautiful* and *perfect*, sweet, heart-piercing words of adoration whispered in my ear as his body hovers over mine in the late night hours, no one existing in the world except us.

I want butterflies, leaps of faith. The fairy tale and happily ever after. Some epic love story, the movie kind of romance that sweeps you off your feet with a crashing wave. I've never come close to those sensations, but I know they exist.

They have to, right?

Some people are destined to be alone and live a life of solitude. As each year comes and goes without someone by my side, I think I might be one of them. The thought keeps me up at night, a deep sadness puncturing my heart.

"Daydreaming about suspenders and loafers over there, Bridge?"

"Shut up. For the record, suspenders are hot."

"Agreed. Who are you hoping we're paired with? Bryson at the men's store would be fun."

"You want to work with him because he looks good in a suit."

"Hell, yeah, he does. He probably looks even better out of it." She grins, a wicked glint in her eyes. "I heard he spends two hours at the gym every morning."

"I've always admired your lack of filter, Chan." My phone dings, and I dive toward the counter, opening my inbox. "It's here!"

To: Bridget Boylston

From: City of Park Cove
Date: November 7
Subject: Travel Living Holiday Contest Pairing

Good afternoon, Bridget,

Thank you for your participation in the *Travel Living* holiday contest! In the following weeks you will have the opportunity to transform your store into a festive space demonstrating your decorating skills. In addition to your creations, the owners from each pair of stores will be interviewed and photographed for a spread in the special-edition late December issue of the publication. Upon completion of the contest, the winners will be featured in a full-length article in the January issue.

Guidelines and Rules:

1. Both stores must be decorated, and will be judged cumulatively for the final score.
2. There is no budget or spending limit. All purchased items and display pieces must not be offensive, derogatory, or vulgar.
3. You may include any and all holidays in your designs.
4. Switching partners will result in disqualification.
5. The stores must showcase what the holiday season means to them.
6. The stores must have decorations, whether handcrafted or store bought.
7. The stores must be accessible and functional for patrons during business hours and a judging walk-through on December 22nd.
8. Decorations are not to block your retail space.
9. Day-to-day operations must not cease at the hands of the competition.

10. Bullying, lobbying for votes, or harassing judges and city officials will not be tolerated. Blatant misbehavior violating the Park Cove Code of Ethics will be documented and result in immediate disqualification.

Your pairing is:

A Likely Story and Gardner's Hardware

For any additional questions, please reach out to Jamie Mulligan by phone or email. Winners will be announced on December 24th.

Sincerely,

Council of Park Cove and *Travel Living*

"WHAT'S WRONG? YOU LOOK PALE." Chandler pries the phone from my hand and reads the message for herself. "Wait, what? *Theo*? I thought you said he wasn't going to participate."

"Guess he had a change of heart and now we're the ones who get to work with the man who grimaced–Chan, he literally acted like he drank sour milk–when he heard what the competition entailed."

I rub my temples and sigh. All weekend I eagerly wondered who our partner might be, brainstorming ways to deck the store out in holiday glitz and glamor. What color lights would be best on the awning outside? Should we put a snowman in the window, or would a reindeer make more sense?

The prize money is an incredible perk, yeah, and I'm sure that for most of the entrants it's the driving force behind tossing their name in the ring. The other components of the contest excite me, too. Spending time with new people. Laughing as we wipe sweat off our brows, trying to find the perfect Frasier fir at a

Christmas tree farm. Wearing Santa hats as we carol, off-key, down the avenue, having a blast.

I can't imagine Theo Gardner, the man with a hundred and one tattoos up and down his arms and a scowl that probably gives small children nightmares, in a Santa hat. I giggle at the thought of him muttering under his breath as I shove a red cap on his head.

"What's so funny?" Chandler asks.

"Nothing. It could be worse, I guess."

"Worse than the Grinch himself? Doubtful. Maybe he's not joining in, and it'll just be his employees. There's no way that man will actively participate."

"Wait a second. This could be perfect. We could create a joint design that spans across both shops. A cohesive theme. They're right next to us so it could flow smoothly. Do you think we should call a meeting? We need to start planning right away."

"Why would we call a meeting? We don't have to actually work together, Bridge. We can do our own thing."

"That's no fun. It's the holidays. A time to spend with loved ones and create memories."

"Are you implying the employees of Gardner's Hardware, who you've talked to a handful of times at best, are your loved ones?"

I sigh, frustrated. "I'm trying to say we should take advantage of these next six weeks and look at it as a chance to get to know the people we share a wall with."

"Winning $100,000 would be so cool, but the last thing you need to do is run yourself into the ground. And why? To prove something to an ogre of a guy who would save himself in a fire then find a way to blame everyone else for the disaster, even if it was his fault? I say we decorate our shit, let them figure out theirs, and tell Theo to fuck off in the process. You know he's probably saying the same thing about us."

I open and close my mouth, but the words to insult him don't come out. Perhaps it's because I always try to find the good in people, even when they don't see it in themselves. Perhaps I'm holding onto a feeble shred of hope Theo might find some cheer of his own during the competition.

I don't know his story or what he's been through. I don't know if he's been hurt, or the one who inflicted the pain on someone else. It just seems like he needs something to remind him of all the good parts of life, because I think someone along the way only allowed him to see the bad parts of himself.

A flutter, persistent and tumultuous, wanes in the crevice of my chest, under my heart. The sensation is relentless, refusing to let me give up on him.

I can't force Theo to join in or participate in an event he obviously loathes. What I *can* do is continue to reach out. Continue being someone who's not afraid of the walls he's trying to construct. He attempted to ward me off the other night at the meeting. I saw the scowl, the fierce look in his eye, determined to push me away. His confusion when I didn't give in, and the acceptance of my presence. Those thirty minutes–hell, it might not have even been that long–allowed me to glimpse through the fissures of his iron-clad facade.

I don't hate what I found, either.

I kind of like it.

And I've always liked a challenge.

I would never attempt to change someone. Take Chandler for instance: although she might lash out, she's not innately mean. Her disdain is deep-rooted and stemming from a traumatic life event that's given her no choice but to snarl at the world and everyone in it. I'm starting to pick up on the same traits in Theo, too. I can tell there's a different side of him hiding. Buried under the pain, the hurt, the rubble from the past.

It might be weak.

It might be snuffed out.

It might be dim and dull, but it's *there*, and that's what matters most.

That's what the holiday season is about, right? Not presents or winning money. Not who can have the most lights in their store windows, the biggest tree, the brightest menorah.

It's about peace. Joy, comfort.

It's about love.

Gifts even the most broken people and fractured souls deserve to receive.

"I promise I'm not going to overextend myself. I already drew a sketch of a basic idea for the floor."

I pull out the folded piece of paper from my pocket, the one I stayed up late to work on last night when creativity struck, and place it face up on the counter. Chandler leans over and studies the renderings.

"Bridget. This drawing is horrible."

"What did you expect? I got my degree in business, not art."

"Yeah, and it shows. What the hell is that supposed to be?"

"A chair, obviously. I spent three hours on this!"

"*Three hours*? We need to get you out more. Or, at the very least, you need to get laid."

"My vibrator works just fine, thanks."

"Amen to that. Alright, time for me to head home, Picasso. Are you good until Brooke gets in after class?"

Chandler wipes her hands on her apron and unties it from her waist. She takes the early shifts on Mondays, Tuesdays and Fridays while I take Wednesdays, Thursdays and Saturdays, alternating who gets up with the sun and who gets to sleep in.

I wave her off. "Totally fine."

"Stick to brownies. The horrific drawings of chairs are close to rock bottom," she calls over her shoulder, leaving me alone.

I grin and listen to her advice, grabbing the piping tube

waiting for me. The brownies–double fudge with walnuts–were pulled out of the oven an hour ago, sufficiently cooled and ready for the homemade buttercream frosting I whipped up last night.

Some of my earliest memories involve books. The Scholastic Book Fair I looked forward to at school every year. The Accelerated Reader tests I passed with flying colors in fourth grade, winning pizza parties for my class. Attending midnight launch parties at Borders for my favorite new releases. Writing fan fiction online and scouring message boards, hypothesizing what might happen to a beloved favorite character. I've fallen in love with hundreds of fictional men and traversed through dozens of fantasy realms, imagining myself wielding a sword.

Baking, however, is a more recent hobby that came to me after a breakup in college. I had been dating the guy for two years, my first serious relationship. Young love. Adoring eyes and a thriving sex life. The pathetic assumption you'll be together forever. The naivety of believing we would never experience heartache.

Until I found out he was cheating on me.

A week of tissues and tears later, I crawled out of bed, yelled "fuck him!" then made my first batch of cookies as a coping mechanism. I also started going to therapy, but pastries are more fun to talk about.

Baking is cathartic to me. I like to study a recipe and figure out ways to alter it and make it better. I like to work with my hands, preferring to stand over an oven rather than sit behind a desk in a skyscraper towering over the city. I like watching people try my creations for the first time, and experience joy when they devour them, leaving nothing but crumbs behind.

Fusing my two passions together has been a literal dream come true, and I wouldn't have it any other way. I don't need promotions or an office with my name on the glass. Give me a stack of books, some flour, chocolate and a whisk, and I'll be content until the end of time.

The bells chime above the door and interrupt my work. I look up and am surprised to find Theo approaching me. A young girl walks beside him as they make their way to the counter. I put the piping bag down and give the pair a smile.

"Hey," I say.

"Hey," answers Theo. It's curt, more so than normal, nerves and discomfort hedged behind the salutation.

My eyes wander to the lanky girl with light blonde hair. She can't be more than an early teenager, if I had to guess. Her head inclines to the side, and she offers me a grin.

"You're pretty," she says. It's a matter-of-fact statement, not an opinion that's up for debate. Her elbow jabs Theo's side, below his ribs, and he flinches slightly.

"Bridget."

My name is silky and commanding coming from his mouth, a polite ask mingled with a determined demand.

"Yes?" I answer. The syllable is shaky, uneven.

"I'd like you to meet Mackenzie." A pause, a clearing of his throat. A splash of red on the tips of his ears. "My daughter."

SIX

BRIDGET

"YOUR DAUGHTER," I repeat, weighing the word.

"My daughter."

"You have a daughter. And this is her."

"Yup." Amusement laces the confirmation, followed by the upward tip of his lips. Relief, it seems, at sharing the news.

The resemblance between the two is uncanny.

Mackenzie has Theo's cheeks. There's a mischievous tinge of joy to the dark brown of her eyes, making them a shade lighter than her father's. Her mouth quirks up to the right, too, just like his. She has the same nose wrinkles when she smiles, and her body has the same tall stature, arms crossed over her chest.

Holy *shit*.

Theo is a dad.

"You can call me Mac," she supplies. "No one calls me Mackenzie unless I'm in trouble."

"Hi. I'm Bridget. Bridget Boylston."

"Mac, why don't you check out the young adult section and see if Bridget has the book you're looking for?" Theo suggests.

"My dog is over there if you want to say hi," I add. "His name is Ziggy, and he's very friendly."

"Awesome. Nice to meet you Bridget. Can I call you BB? That's a cool nickname."

"Sure. Yeah. BB sounds great."

"Cool." Mac grins, skipping to the bookshelf in the back corner of the store.

When she's out of earshot, I turn to Theo. "You have a daughter?" I hiss. "Why would you hide your kid? You aren't ashamed of her, are you? If that's the case, I'm going to kick your ass."

Something shifts. In the air, in him.

Theo steps to the counter, the distance feeling less substantial than before. An electric charge occupies the small gap between us, a crack and spark in intensity as it builds and rises to the surface. His nostrils flare and his hands land on the laminate. Large palms bracket either side of my arms, splayed out and covering half the countertop. His shoulders sink to my height, bringing us almost nose to nose. Eyes blazing, he takes a deep breath.

I see you, Theo Gardner.

I'm not afraid.

"Ashamed?" he simmers. Venom and disgust outline the edges of the adjective. "I'm not ashamed. I'm so goddamn proud of Mac and all she's accomplished. I'm a private person who hates when people butt into my personal life, and she is my *entire* personal life. My employees know about her. My friends know about her. Now you do, too, because all she talked about this weekend was a book about teenagers with magic powers who can fly. I haven't seen her this excited about something in ages. So here we are. Me, revealing a part of my life to you that not many people know about, and freaking the fuck out in the process."

I inhale. To be granted the honor of joining a small inner

circle–intentional or not–and learning another slice of Theo's story is discombobulating.

I also feel so *lucky*.

Lucky that he trusts me with this precious information. Lucky that I get to witness a part of him he doesn't broadcast to the world. Lucky that I get to hear the prideful tone his voice takes when he says how thrilled he is with his daughter.

Small beads of perspiration gather on his forehead and his chest heaves. I watch his throat bob as he swallows, attempting to compose himself. This isn't the same stoic, detached man who walked through the door a few minutes ago. He's passionate, wild. Ready to go to war. A man *alive*.

I step forward tentatively. Nearer and nearer I inch, until my hips press against the counter and I invade his space.

"Theo." My voice stays steady. A rock standing firm against the raging river of uncertainty around me. "You're a *dad*. That's so awesome. Five seconds of interacting with her and I can already tell she's wonderful. She also has a good head on her shoulders because she likes to read. I'm guessing she didn't get the coolness from you, you big fucking numpty."

He huffs out a sound, barely discernible. A laugh, I think. He glances over at Mac, and the effect she has on him is instantaneous. A smile forms. It starts on his lips, working up his face to the apple of his cheeks and the crinkles by his eyes. A quiet, resistant jubilation shows itself. For the first time, I see him in his full, magnificent splendor.

Shit, he's beautiful.

And hot as hell.

He resembles Paul Rudd, a timeless handsomeness to his features. He looks a decade younger than he probably is. It's unfair, honestly, how effortlessly attractive he is.

Amber eyes, half-hidden behind his glasses, have cooled, settling to a shade reminiscent of whiskey, neat. The kind of drink you sip slowly to savor the taste, the bite of liquor strong and worth the wait. His mop of hair falls to the side in a natural, laissez-faire style. Sprinkles of sawdust are caught in the waves, glittering in the natural light of yellows and oranges coming through the window, the room their blank canvas. The smell of cedar and pine surrounds him, manly and clean.

Behind the classic attractiveness is a hint of trouble. A splash of bad. I shiver at the intoxicating amalgamation. I've always considered Theo good looking, but watching him exhibit delight so openly about someone he loves more than life itself? Seeing him smile boldly, purposefully?

It's devastating.

The kind of destruction you welcome with open arms.

I'd do a lot of things for just one more glimpse of his joy. I want to capture this moment on film and carry it with me, stored in the back pocket of my jeans. I'd hold onto the majestic sight a little while longer and treasure it on a rainy day.

"Yeah," he finally answers. My reverie breaks. "She does."

"What else does she like to read?"

"Anything she can get her hands on. She's fast, too, which isn't great for my bank account."

"How have I worked next to you for three years and never seen her?"

"I'm careful. You know how nosy the people in this town are. One strand of hair out of order and the gossip starts. The rumor mill runs wild. She's a *kid*, and that isn't fair. She goes to school. She socializes, plays sports, and has tons of friends. I don't flaunt her around because I'm disappointed or *want* to keep her hidden. I just... Sometimes I think the less people she meets, the safer she'll be. And all I care about is her safety."

I nod, placated by his answer. "Okay. I understand."

His smile–that big, emphatic smile–changes to a mirthful smirk. I make a mental note to mark today down in my calendar as The Day Theo Gardner Grinned. It's a momentous occasion, one I doubt I'll ever forget.

"So few words, Boylston?" he asks. "That's unusual for you. If I had known this is how you'd react, I would have introduced you two years ago. It's quite entertaining."

I grab the rag draped over the dishwasher handle and swat him, nicking his arm above his elbow. He barks out a chuckle at the slap of terrycloth. I freeze, processing the noise.

It's deep. Not quite a full and complete laugh, but close. Close enough. It matches the baritone of his voice, loaded and vivacious, ringing in my ears. That's a sound I want to bottle up. To replay again and again. One I want to hold onto forever.

"You should do that more," I whisper. His eyes, cautious and guarded, meet mine.

"Do what?"

"Be happy."

"Not many people give me a reason to be happy." A pause, then, "But I think you might. Maybe."

It's shy, soft. I don't know if he meant to say it out loud, but it's in the world now, and he's not taking it back. So I tuck the confession away too, right next to his smile and laugh, a perfect trifecta, my heart quivering in the aftermath of discovery.

"Are you married?" I ask. A question I should have put forward earlier, before I got greedy. Before I wanted to take and take and take whatever Theo was willing to give me. My eyes dart to his hand, discovering his finger is void of any ring or symbolic piece of jewelry.

"No," he answers. "Not married. Are you married?"

"No. Girlfriend?"

"Nope."

"Boyfriend?"

"Also no."

"Something complicated with her mom?"

His smirk drops, turning fraught and tight around the edges of his mouth. The previous displays of glee crash to the floor, and he steps back.

"No." One word, so full of hurt, so full of pain. "She's not..." He shakes his head. "It's just me and Mac."

I want to ask why. By choice? By accident? Has he had his heart broken, scuffed up, and bruised by a former love? Is she in the picture? Was she *ever* in the picture? Has Theo gone through life so alone, he thinks no one could care about him?

As if on cue, Mac walks over, arms full with a half-dozen books. I can barely see the top of her head over the stack. "BB, I found so many books I want to read! You have a great selection. Can I get these, Dad? I know there's a bunch, but I couldn't pick just one. I promise I'll read them all."

Theo doesn't hesitate. He doesn't stop to think or argue. His wallet is out of his pocket before she can finish the question, credit card at the ready. "Of course you can, sweetheart." *Oh, hell, he calls her sweetheart.* "What's the damage, Boylston?"

My mouth works faster than my brain. "Nothing. It's free. On the house," falls out before I can think twice.

"What?" He shoves the card under my nose. "No. Don't do that."

"I'm not taking your money. I want her to have the books. Also"–I cut a large chunk of brownie and place it on a paper plate, handing it over to him–"this is for Mac. Not you, because otherwise I'd have to charge you for one too many scowls thrown my way. That's what we call the jerk tax."

Mac bursts out laughing. "Oh my god, Dad, I like her. No one's ever said that to your face before, even if it's deserved. I told you we needed to come here sooner. Thanks, Bridget!"

"You should listen to her, Theo. She's smarter than you. Mac, you're welcome whenever you want. No father required."

"I think I'm being ganged up on," Theo grumbles, pulling

out a crisp ten-dollar bill, "and I don't like it. Thank you, Bridget. That was very kind."

"Don't mention it."

"Jar choices?"

"*The Jetsons* versus *The Flintstones*. You were alive in the 50s, right? Should be an easy pick for you."

His eyes narrow and the paper flutters into *The Flintstones* jar with a flourish. He leans forward and keeps his voice low as he whispers, "Careful, Brownie. That mouth will get you in trouble one day."

The implication sends a flood of heat down my spine. Warmth inundates my body, skin prickling with awareness at our close proximity. His eyes fixate on the seam of my lips and I wonder what it would be like if his mouth met mine. Demanding? Gentle? Soft and slow?

Demanding, probably. Theo seems like a man who takes what he wants and leaves nothing behind.

And I think right now, buried under that threat, he might want to take *me*.

Holy hell.

I inhale a jagged breath. "Maybe I like trouble," I whisper back.

His mouth curls up, a braggadocious smile in place. "Noted."

I blink, looking away from the man who's making me feel like I'm flying down the slope of a roller coaster. Nervous, excited. Anticipating what might come next, and the thrill of the free fall to the ground.

"Thanks, BB," says Mac. "See you soon!"

Shit.

Finding out Theo has been hiding a literal *kid* from the world caused me to forget about asking why there was a sudden interest in joining the competition. He was so against the idea before. What the hell changed between then and now? Was Mac the reason behind the decision? Does he plan to be difficult and challenging? Is he willing to tread forward amicably, all in the name of holiday fun?

As they leave, voices growing softer the further away they walk, the store turns desolate and lonely. Quieter without their laughter and cooler without the heat of temptation. I watch Mac look up at Theo and grin. He holds the door open, scans the sidewalk, then motions for her to exit first. His eyes meet mine a final time before the pair disappears around the corner and I'm all alone.

This kind of changes everything, doesn't it?

He let me in. He didn't run away. He admitted I make him happy.

Maybe.

I've noticed over the years, the Wednesday mornings he shows up and spends more than two seconds collecting his pre-made drink and darting away are better–significantly, monumentally better–than the days I don't see him at all.

I think that means he might make me happy, too.

SEVEN

THEO

THE WINTER HOLIDAYS were my favorite time of year when I was growing up.

The season officially kicked off the Friday after Thanksgiving in the Gardner household, and not a minute before. We had lots of traditions I looked forward to, counting down the days until we could start to celebrate. As a kid, my parents and I would drive around town, searching for the houses with an over-the-top display of decorations. We'd pick out the family Christmas tree–always real–and adorn it with ornaments collected over the years. A combination of handmade projects courtesy of my elementary school art class and expensive glass-blown nutcrackers and bearded Santas hung from the branches while white lights twinkled through the living room, a kaleidoscope of colors.

We sipped hot chocolate topped with marshmallows out of personalized matching mugs and watched holiday movies in the park with other townsfolk, lounging on blankets and indulging in Mom's famous peppermint bark, the recipe handed down from her grandmother. Our three stockings hung from the mantle above the fireplace, complete with knitted initials.

It was never about the presents. Yeah, I got a basketball hoop and cool bikes, but it was about the time we got to spend together. My parents were busy entrepreneurs, running the business my great-grandfather started nearly a century ago. Even during a hectic time of year, when people were stress buying nails to hang wreaths and paintbrushes to finish the guest bathroom before their in-laws came to visit, they always made me a priority.

We had so many good days. When the weather was cooler, we'd spend all morning at the theme parks, screaming on roller coasters until our throats were sore. On the warmer days, we'd drive over to the beach for the afternoon. We'd grab subs from our local grocery store along the way for lunch, the sun beating down on our skin. Our annual family Christmas photo was captured by Kodak, in front of historic landmarks at Kennedy Space Center. Memories and snapshots I wish I could preserve, forever immortalized in the Beautiful Before.

Life was wonderful. Life was good. Life was perfect.

But perfection can't last forever.

Worried replaced wonderful. Anxious overpowered good. The world of *happiness* and *forever* changed, two events rocking my world in ways I never knew imaginable.

Mac's unplanned arrival was first. Born on December 23rd, she was the best kind of surprise and my greatest Christmas gift to date. One glance at her, eyes that looked so much like my own blinking at me from a hospital crib, and I realized how utterly clueless I had been at understanding what true, selfless love really was.

I was infatuated, a blubbering mess of emotions, and I made a vow the very first time I held her in my arms. I would do whatever it took to keep that tiny bundle of joy swaddled in a pink blanket safe, healthy and so damn happy for the rest of my days.

Before Mac, I often pictured life as a revolving door; always moving. A dozen different possibilities, each as good as the last. That's what I expected my thirties to be–a time to figure out and learn what I want to get out of my time here on Earth. Maybe I'd buy a house. Move to a different city for a while. Buy a motorcycle and do a cross-country road trip in the fall.

After her birth, I saw a different, more vivid vision of my future; the love of my life of three years and our precious new baby girl by my side. It was a future of new traditions, of matching pajamas, of Season's Greetings cards. More kids, maybe, if we wanted them, and playdates with other couple friends who had little ones Mac's age. I'd exchange texts with my wife (a ring would be coming soon) about why I was late to the parent-teacher conference or if she could grab a carton of milk from the grocery store.

Those dreams–the ones full of love and aspirations–never manifested. Life took a different turn, a sharp right off the highway to a destination I didn't know how to navigate. I was without a map, without direction, without a guiding light. The only beacon of hope, the thing that kept me going every day, was Mac. The two of us alone, trying to figure out how the hell to move on.

Parenthood was–is–an adjustment, one that probably took me longer to figure out than some people, but I don't regret it. I wouldn't go back and undo Mac's birth. Sometimes, she's the only thing keeping me sane in a world that feels more and more uncontrollable with each passing week. Most times, she's the only good part of my day, her giggle slightly deeper, height a smidge taller, but still my little girl.

In an alternate timeline full of redos and rewinds, the one thing I would erase is event number two: Christmas Eve five years ago. The abnormally cold Friday night that changed everything.

When I think about the evening for longer than a heartbeat

—the blinding headlights, the screams of pain, the wail of a siren in the distance, approaching, but still too far away— nausea and bile work their way up my throat. Sweat soaks my clothes. My insides constrict, becoming a tight spool of guilt, of sadness, of regret.

A pressure forms behind my eyes, pain radiating across my temples. It's a merciless game I never win. Discussing and processing the events in therapy has helped. It's an outlet for my anger. A place to unload all the dark thoughts no one should be plagued by. Every day gets easier. A touch more bearable. A degree less painful.

But it doesn't mean I want to listen to "Silent Night" every day from now until December 25th.

"Boss. Are you good?"

I blink and I'm transported back to the present.

Lucas, my best friend and one of the store's supervisors, is giving me a curious look.

"Hey," I say. My shoulders roll back, and I crack my neck to the side. "I'm fine."

"We've been friends for decades and you still think you can lie to me?" he muses. "Bullshit."

Red-headed and six foot five with a dimpled smile, he's been in my life for as long as I can remember. His family owned the flower and garden shop that used to sit adjacent to our building. We'd spend our afternoons on the sidewalk out front, drawing hopscotch squares with chalk and dirtying our knees in the grass. We bonded over sports and growth spurts that hit far sooner than anyone else in our grade. A real-estate office show-casing multi-million dollar listings took over the space a decade ago when Lucas's parents decided to retire, the smell of hydrangeas and roses no longer permeating through the thin walls.

My parents offered him a job after the sale, and he happily

accepted. In the last five years he's helped me navigate the rapid transition from *guy who helps out at his family's business on the weekends* to *manager who still knows jack about shit and pays people's salaries.*

No matter how much of a dick I try to be, Lucas never gets frustrated. He's my closest confidant, a diligent knobhead who grins at everything and won't ever leave me alone. I've never been one to believe in soulmates, chance encounters, or any other astronomical bullshit, but this man has saved me repeatedly. Pulled me out of my darkest hours, a hand clamped on my shoulder without asking for any details, helping however he can. He's on a lifelong quest to make sure I'm not a completely miserable prick.

It's working.

Kind of.

"It's not bullshit," I counter.

"I know you're pissed about the contest. They did it with good intentions."

His large body folds into the seat across from me, looking comfortable in the puny, pathetic chair only he ever occupies. I purposely picked the smallest piece of furniture to stop any conversations from happening in my office, but this fucker is lounging like he's sunbathing at the beach. His arms cross over his chest. He kicks his shoes up on the edge of the wooden desk, leans back like he's going to stay a while. Smiles and waits.

I hurl a scathing look his way, the most menacing one in my arsenal. I show my teeth. I scowl. The man blinks, unaffected. There's a twinkle behind his green eyes, and he knows it's only a matter of time before I'm going to fold.

Dammit.

"I'm pissed because someone went behind my back, Lucas. And lied about it. How the hell are those good intentions? I didn't enter us on purpose, and then I get an email confirming our participation? Do you know how this is going to affect our daily schedule? In addition to the busiest time of year for us, and the eight million things I have on my plate including calculating bonuses, now I have to put up strands of garland and memorize all the verses of 'Deck the Halls'?"

"Theo," Lucas says on an exhale. Exasperation fuels the heavy sigh. "We both know this isn't just about the contest. This time of year is hard for you. You harbor a lot of justified resentment. You also don't think you're allowed to celebrate anything good that happens in your life, especially around the holidays. It makes sense. I'm in your corner."

My friend has always been a helper. An avid problem solver determined to offer aid to anyone who needs a hand, he doesn't ask for accolades or recognition. He's just a kind man with a soft heart who does things because he wants to, not because he has to.

Including putting up with my shit and telling me why we need to enter a stupid contest that's going to give me a permanent migraine.

"You're in charge, man," he continues. "And you know I'd never step on your toes. I'll remind you, however, you're not the only one who works here. The rest of us want to participate. Look at the amount of money we could win. We want to have fun and wear tacky sweaters and eat candy canes. We want to spend time together, with some new people, and with you, too, you idiot. You might be a pain in my ass, but we all love working here."

Dammit.

Lucas and his kind words make me feel guilty. It would be an absolute douchebag move to not let the employees try to win the significant cash prize. I'm already doing what I can to make sure their holiday bonuses are substantial. My personal opinions about this time of year shouldn't hinder their chances to double the monetary benefits.

"Okay," I sigh. "I understand your point. For the record, I'm not happy about this. I'm not going to hold hands and belt out Christmas songs at the top of my lungs."

"God, that would be the day."

"Speaking of new people, I introduced Bridget to Mac."

Lucas's eyes widen. A slow grin spreads over his mouth. His feet drop to the floor and he props his elbows on his knees, interested in hearing more. "No shit. How'd that go?"

The spontaneous encounter slingshotted past every boundary I'd previously established. With Mac's constant badgering and threat to march over to the store herself, I was out of choices except to let them meet.

The panic Bridget showed was cute in a "let me give you six books for free because I don't know what else to say" kind of way. Her cheeks turned pink and she gnawed on her bottom lip. It probably makes me an ass that I enjoyed watching her spiral a bit.

And then she challenged me. She met me toe-to-toe and said if she found out I was ashamed of my kid she'd be pissed as hell. Hearing those words, the protection over someone she just met, sent all rationality flying out the window. There was passion painted on her face. Fierce eyes with an ember of a spark daring me to say the wrong thing. Determined, strong jaw ready to launch into a tirade if necessary. The exhale escaping her lips as she tried to compose herself. The tip of her chin, bringing her gaze to mine, showing me she was unafraid.

It was hot as sin.

I kind of wanted to grab her cheeks, yank her to me and kiss her, right there, in the middle of the store on a Tuesday afternoon, just to see how she would react.

I think she would have liked it.

I would have liked it, too.

Shit.

I shrug at Lucas now, feigning nonchalance. My hand fiddles with the corner of a faded file folder, the inventory of a hammer order, my most recent purchase. "Fine. Good. She didn't run away. Only a mild freak out that ended with her shoving a brownie in my hands."

"Of course she didn't run away."

"Yeah, well, other people do. Other people have."

"Other people aren't Bridget Boylston."

No, I think bitterly, gratefully, a tarnished mix of the two. *They are not.*

"I should... I should probably go and talk to her about logistics, right? Figure out a schedule for all of this nonsense. She can take the lead on plans. I guess we're lucky to be paired with them. I bet she already has some ideas."

I pause, thinking about A Likely Story covered in illustrations. Sketches of wreaths and snowflakes tacked to the walls. A table of candles and a questionnaire to complete, asking you to pick your favorite holiday scent. It's going to look like the Situation Room. I snort.

"Something funny?" asks Lucas.

"No. I'm just... No. Nothing's funny."

His smile broadens. "I haven't heard you talk about a woman in a while. Jesus, probably close to a decade now, huh? Nothing besides a date or two here and there. You've certainly never introduced your kid to a woman, either."

"I'm not *talking* about a woman. I'm talking about the person we're working with for a project. We aren't going to dinner. She's not sitting at my kitchen table, eating pancakes. There's a big difference."

"What did Mac say about her?"

"She said she was nice and pretty. Then she gave me shit for avoiding the bookstore for so long."

Lucas hums and stands, walking to the door. "Interesting. Kids sure are intuitive, aren't they? Go talk to Bridget. I'll let the troops know we're clear to begin Operation Holiday Cheer. And tell your pretty woman I say hi."

I scowl and launch a red pen at his back. I throw a middle finger up for good measure as he leaves me alone to think about...

Her.

The irritation from earlier lessens, chilling to hesitant excitement.

I let myself picture a life full of hope. Good tidings and cheer. The things I so desperately wanted all those years ago. The desire, the imagination never fully dissipating. It's always been there, waiting in the shadows for an opportunity to exist without burden or pain. Only joy.

The positivity–and the shift in my thinking–is brought on by the brunette next door. Her warm smile, encouraging eyes. That goddamn mouth and the way she looks at me not like I'm someone to toss to the side, but like I'm someone to keep around.

No one's looked at me like that for a long time.

I'm a glutton for punishment, I guess, because I don't hate the daydreams.

"Not my woman," I grumble to the empty room. "Not my anything."

She is pretty, though. Lucas got that part right.

I think I might have known that for a while.

EIGHT

THEO

I'M PATHETIC.

I've prioritized pointless tasks all day, going out of my way to do anything but have a conversation with Bridget.

I reorganize my file folders from alphabetical order to color-coordinated. I text Mac and ask for her Christmas list, not understanding what half the items are that she sends back. I schedule a tattoo appointment for the end of December, scratching an itch I have to add another piece to my body. A soccer ball, I think, in honor of Mac's favorite sport.

At six on the dot, I trek next door, shuffling my feet the ten steps down the sidewalk until I reach the entrance to the bookstore. After a grumble, a sigh and three minutes of loitering on the pavement, I pull open the front door, wood slamming shut behind me.

"Hello?" My voice carries through the empty room and I stride toward the counter, our usual meeting spot. As I pass the nonfiction section, I freeze. Bridget's tucked away between two waist-high shelves topped with paper Christmas trees and dreidels.

Her back is turned toward me, large, black headphones

covering her ears. She's bopping along to a song I can't hear. I wonder if it's Bowie. Maybe The Clash? There's a pep in her step as she puts a book in place, briefly pausing her work to play an invisible air guitar. I lean against a recliner to my right and watch her, selfishly indulging, just for a second.

How can I not?

She's mesmerizing.

Free. Long limbs, fluid movements. Cheeks with splotches of color. Her hair catches in the fading sunlight, a cross between melted milk chocolate and a spiraling tornado. She glides over the floor effortlessly. Her hips wiggle in her jeans, denim hugging her ass in a way that leaves little to the imagination. Tight around the globes of her backside, I can see the creases of her cheeks before they fan out further down, looser around her calves.

I want to feel the material under my palm as I run my hand up the inside of her thigh. Play with the stitching as I graze higher and higher toward the zipper, tugging it down while she watches with a content–and satisfied–smile on her face.

Her eyes are closed and her chest bounces as she spins, the tiny straps of her pink tank top doing little to conceal her breasts. She circles around, around, and around, not a care in the goddamn world.

She's pretty, yeah, but this woman is also sexy as hell in a sneaky way that could get me in trouble. Soft curves, smooth lines. And when she bends over to grab something off the floor, I almost combust at how badly I want to sink my fingers into her flesh, littering her skin with little pink marks.

I haven't been with a woman in... Shit. Three years? Or is it four? Time moves faster the older I get. The lack of physical interaction is catching up to me; I'm half tempted to drag her up to the counter, pull her ass to the edge, and bury my head between her thighs while her legs wrap around my neck.

Does she smile when she comes? Does she let out a little giggle, a breathy moan when she's touched in just the right spot? What's her favorite part of her body? Does she know she has a patch of freckles on her left shoulder? Could those jeans be any tighter?

And that *ass*.

I want to drop to my knees and worship it.

I want to make her dinner, too.

My mind works on overdrive and I slam the heel of my palm against my forehead, determined to dispel the image of her naked. I know I'm not supposed to, I know I shouldn't, but I can't help it.

Here on the counter, paper cups and packets of sugar substitute careening to the floor.

In my room, jostling the lamp on the bedside table as we stumble to the mattress in the dead of night.

Bridget's loud laugh slants through the air, fantasy shifting to reality. It's a siren's song; hypnotic and making me want to draw nearer. Her shoulders shake and her laughter grows, a building crescendo. Every book on every shelf is subjected to the bright sound that could probably, most definitely, end world wars. A paradigm of peace.

There's still time for me to leave. I can walk out the door and pretend like I never came by, never saw her dance or laugh until tears leaked out of her eyes. Lucas can stop in tomorrow and let them know our plans for involvement. Better yet, I can send a formal email, outlining how we'll be doing our own decorating, but we look forward to cordially supporting A Likely Story in any way we can. That's the safest bet.

Minimal interactions, with less chance for her to—

"Theo? What are you doing here?"

Ah, shit.

Bridget spotted me. Her hands have fallen to her hips. Her

hair is matted to her face, bangs sticking to her damp forehead. She's looking at me like I'm positively insane, as if *I'm* the one who was just laughing maniacally in an empty room. Time to jump into this head-fucking-first, I suppose.

"Hey," I say.

"What's up?"

"I was stopping by."

"Are you looking for a book?"

Double shit.

I didn't think this far in advance.

Just tell the truth and get it over with, Gardner.

Competition.

Working together.

See you later, have a nice night.

"Um. Yes. I was looking for a historical fiction book," I say instead.

I'm a goddamn idiot.

She laughs again, and you'd think I told the world's funniest joke. "Good thing I have a whole section of those. Want me to show you some options?" Rocking on her feet, I can tell she's excited by the possibility of chatting about literature choices. Can I really be the one to deny her?

"Sure. That would be great."

Nope. Guess I can't.

"Come on, Collector."

I follow her through the maze of shelves, not looking at the ass that's taunting me with every sway of her hips. It's a goddamn feat keeping my eyes on the ceiling until we reach the far side of the store and she's a safe distance away.

"Anything in particular you're looking for?"

"Any book will do," I answer.

"That really helps narrow it down." Bridget turns, focusing on the wall of books. I watch her contemplate the spines. Scan the options. From this angle, I can see her fingers tap her cheek. Her tongue is caught between her teeth, deep in thought. "Permission to pick something for you?"

I must have nodded, I think, because she rises on her tiptoes and reaches for the second highest shelf on the large built-in. The hem of her tank top rides up with the motion, revealing a patch of skin I haven't seen before. I try to avert my eyes, I really fucking do, but I still get a peek. Smooth. Creamy white. Divots in the small of her back.

Horrible, stupid things I wish I could unsee.

Her hand misses the book on the first attempt, centimeters short. I watch her reach again, straining and stretching, and I frown.

"You don't have a step stool?" I ask. "How did you get the books up there in the first place?"

"Chandler sits on my shoulders. I'd love a rolling ladder. It's on my list. One day."

"I could, uh…" I pause, hand rubbing the nape of my neck. The skin is warm, flared with heat. "I could make you one," I blurt out before I can think twice.

Carpentry is not in my skill set. I'm shit with a saw. Yet here I am, suggesting it and watching her face grow brighter with the idea.

And now I have to–*want* to–build her a ladder because I need to see that look again.

"Really? You could?"

"Yeah," I say, shrugging my shoulders like making a fifty-pound piece of furniture involving metal rods and wheels is as easy as putting together a peanut butter and jelly sandwich. "I could."

It earns me her biggest smile yet. I'm not normally a smiler, but I answer it with one of my own. Because when Bridget smiles at me–with her eyes, her cheeks, her teeth, her entire being–for some inexplicable reason, I'm inclined to smile back.

"That would be so cool!"

She drops a book into my hands, and I notice pen marks on the inside of her fingers and–is *that* where her Bowie tattoo is hidden? On her pointer finger, the lightning bolt running from just below the nail to her second knuckle?

This woman is an anomaly.

"Women fighter pilots during World War II. How does that sound?" she asks.

"Like an astute choice."

"Wow, good word. Maybe when I grow up like you my vocabulary will expand, too."

"Has anyone ever told you you're a smartass?"

She laughs, the sound echoing around us. "No, but you can start if you'd like."

"What were you listening to when I came in? I hope I didn't interrupt anything."

"Oh! My favorite comedian. Farley Jones. Shit. Wait. No, she got married, so I think it's Farley Harrigan now. She's a genius. There's this diarrhea joke she tells and–never mind. I'd butcher it."

"Never thought we'd be talking about diarrhea when I walked in here. I haven't heard of her. I'll make sure to check her out."

"You should. I love women who are unapologetically themselves, you know? The women who don't let society tell them what they can and can't be. It's refreshing."

"The world needs more people like that, who aren't afraid to tell others to shut up and live life how they want," I agree.

"You're a fan of loud women then?"

"Of course I am. I'm trying to raise Mac to think that way, too."

"So if she wanted to be a Formula One driver, you'd be cool with it?"

"Are you kidding? That would be awesome. Doctor. Teacher. Stay-at-Home Mom. Boxer. I don't give a crap. I want her to speak her mind, yell loudly about the things that make her happy, and not let anyone push her around."

"That is... astute parenting right there." Bridget says it jokingly, using my word back to me, but I hear the sincerity behind the compliment. I see her face soften away from humor to a degree more appreciative. Like she's *proud* of me in a way. And, fuck, if that doesn't make me feel good. "Are you here for comedian and book recommendations, or is something else going on?"

I sigh and pinch the bridge of my nose. "It's about the holiday competition. I know I originally said I wasn't interested. One of my employees entered us and things have changed. So, I uh, came over to let you know we'll be working together."

"I wondered how we were paired up after you were *thrilled* with the announcement. This is so exciting!" Bridget squeals and claps her hands together.

"There's one condition, though," I say. "I'm not reenacting any scenes from 'The Twelve Days of Christmas.' No turtle doves. No French hens. It's going to be an avian-free collaboration. And no Santa hats, either. Okay?"

"Aversion to birds?" she asks.

"No. More like, what the hell do you do with them after you're finished?"

She gives me a solemn nod, but I get the feeling she's holding back laughter as her lips twitch. "I can agree to that compromise. No reenactments. No hats. Got it. Do you need to leave, or do you have a few minutes? There's a questionnaire the owners are supposed to answer for the magazine. It shouldn't take long. We could knock that out and maybe pick a time for all of our people to get together and start planning?"

I check my watch. Mac spends time at my parents' house after soccer practice, and I'm normally well on my way to pick her up by now. No matter what kind of shit is going on at work, it's a priority of mine to be home for dinner every night. Making a split second decision, I pull out my phone.

"My parents watch Mac, and I'll just tell them I'm going to be a little late."

"Shit. Of course. I'm so sorry. I don't want to take you away from any family plans. It was stupid of me to assume you had tons of free time."

"It's okay," I assure her. "Hey. Bridget. Look at me."

I've found I like to say her name. I like it even better when she listens, raising her chin, eyes meeting mine. Her lip is caught between her teeth, worry painted on her scrunched brows. Ink-stained hands twist together, fingers intertwining. I want to reach out and hug her, to let her know she hasn't done anything wrong.

And I'm not a hugger.

"What?" she asks, hesitant, unsure.

"You're not stupid."

"I assumed you could drop everything and–"

"I *am* dropping everything. I'm an adult and I can make my own decisions. I'm here with you because I want to be here with you. Alright?"

"You promise? Because you can go. I can send you an email or something. Maybe a fax if it's more your speed."

I nudge her shoulder with mine as I pass. "Yeah, Brownie. I promise. Give me five minutes, and I'm all yours."

NINE

THEO

"HEY, DAD. WHAT'S UP?"

Whenever Mac answers the phone, she never sounds like a girl who's almost thirteen or the kid who got her braces off six months ago. She sounds like a college freshman, one foot out the door, on her way to a party I'm not supposed to know about.

It trips me up every time.

"Dad? Helloooo?"

"Sorry. I'm here. Did you finish your homework?"

"Homework is complete and we're doing a puzzle now. Will you be here soon? We're having chicken and mashed potatoes."

"I'm going to be a little late tonight."

Her gasp is so loud, I have to pull the phone away from my ear. "Do you have a *date*?"

"It is not a date. I'm working on a holiday thing."

"What kind of holiday thing?"

"Something for a magazine I'm doing with Bridget. Don't ask."

"I want to hang out with Bridget! She was so cool when I met her the other day. Will you tell her I said hi?"

"Sure thing. I'll pick you up later, okay?"

"Sounds good. And Dad?"

"What's up?"

"I've never seen you with a girl... or a guy, and... well, you know you're allowed to date people, right? It's not like I'll be mad. Justine's mom downloaded Tinder and she's having a great time."

"I am *not* downloading Tinder."

"Okay, but if you *did* want to start something with someone who, maybe, like, owns a bookstore, I'd be fine with it. Really. Think of all the free books!"

"Jesus." I rub my temples and shake my head. "No points for subtly on that one. I'll keep your approval in mind."

"Alright, Dad. Don't forget to tell Bridget hi."

"I will. Love you, punk."

"Love you too."

I take a second after I hang up the phone, replaying her words. We haven't talked about why I don't bring women around, and she hasn't asked. I don't think it's necessary to dole out introductions for people I can tell right away aren't going to be a permanent, lasting addition to my–our–life.

It's not about jumping at the chance to get with the first woman who looks my way or tosses me a flirty smile. It's not just about me, and it hasn't been for a long time. I have another person I have to think about when it comes to these decisions. Another person's wellbeing to consider. It's important shit, and I can't afford to be selfish.

I'm most afraid of letting my kid see my insecurities. My fear of whoever I seriously date next might leave me like the last one did: Alone. Confused. Picking up the pieces and wondering what the hell I'm doing wrong.

I don't want the next one to run.

I want them to stay.

"Are you okay?" asks Bridget.

It's tender, a soft caress over my taut muscles. The tension loosens, a slight uncoiling of the invisible weights that sit there. The spool unravels. The block of dread lightens.

"I'm good. Sorry about that," I answer.

"Please don't think you need to apologize for talking to your daughter."

"I'm just used to apologizing for it, I guess."

"That's shitty."

"People are shitty," I counter.

She hums in agreement. "Yes. They are."

We walk to the counter and pick two stools side by side. Should I have left one in between us? Is this too close? She would have moved over if she was uncomfortable, right?

Why the hell am I overanalyzing it?

Her foot taps against mine as she gets settled. Unbothered by my proximity, she pulls out her laptop. A press of a button, and music starts from the speakers mounted to the wall above the coffee machines. I expect some popular Christmas song to play, rocking around trees or building snowmen. Instead, I hear the opening notes of "Janie Jones" and I smile at her stellar song choice.

Impressive tattoo. Impressive playlists. Impressive, Impressive, impressive.

A woman full of surprises.

"Ready to get started?" she asks.

"Go for it, Boylston."

"*Travel Living* wants to know what your company would do if you won the contest. How would you spend the prize money?"

The question is predictable and I can't hold back the eye roll. "You'd think an internationally published magazine could ask something more original. What about what charities we donate to? What unique skills do our employees have? Do they honestly care to hear about trust funds and shopping sprees?"

"Look," Bridget says, "I know you're not super jazzed about this, but sometimes as business owners we have to do things we don't enjoy. Sometimes that includes answering questions you *know* are stupid. But a hundred thousand dollars is a shit ton of money, so you're going to keep your complaining to a minimum and we're going to knock this out. Got it?"

"For clarification purposes, is a shit ton more or less than a crap ton? I'm unfamiliar with the measuring unit. If we're going to be working together, I should learn your terms."

"More, but less than a fuck ton. Does that help? Should I spell it out on a Lite-Brite so your boomer ass can comprehend it better?"

I blink at her once, twice, a third time. I throw in a fourth for good measure.

Then, I grin.

That was *funny*.

"Thank you for that insightful description, Boylston. Wouldn't have gotten there without you."

"Glad to be of service. Time to put the attitude away for five minutes so we can both go home."

"I'd spend the money on construction to make the avenue more accessible for people with disabilities. After splitting the prize evenly with my employees, I'd take home five thousand dollars. That's barely enough to put a dent in the plans I'd like to propose, but it's a damn good start."

"Okay." Her fingers dance across the keyboard, a waltz of clicks and a tango of letters. "Could you elaborate a bit? Accessible how?"

"I'd like to provide individual ramps to each business so people who rely on wheelchairs or other mobility devices like canes and walkers can get into their store without risking a fall. I want to add more handicap parking spaces. Do you know there are only seven on this mile-long stretch of road? I'd level out the curb in areas besides major intersections. At crosswalks, I'd like to see the timing between light cycles extended."

That's the abridged list I'm rushing through so I don't bore her to death. I could ramble for hours about the pages of measurements and drawings I have tucked away in my desk, sketched with a pencil late in the night as the wheels in my brain turn too rapidly for me to sleep. I keep the city codes and blueprint designs for a slight street expansion to accommodate my proposed changes in my back pocket in case anyone ever asks. I don't want to overwhelm her with the knowledge that I look at the renderings at least three times a day, so I keep it short. Sweet. Just enough information so she doesn't ask for more.

"You've thought about this extensively," Bridget whispers.

I nod. "Yeah. I have. You're also the first person I've ever told, so thanks for not shutting it down."

"Shut it down? Theo, I think it's brilliant. I have a ramp in our storage closet and bring it out when someone needs it."

"You do?"

"Yeah. If it creates a comfortable environment, why wouldn't I provide it for them?"

Jesus Christ.

Is this woman some Christmas angel sent from above? How does she always know the right things to say? And why do I suddenly care? I've never given a fuck about what people think of me. I don't seek their approval or need their validation to get through life. Hearing Bridget call my plan *brilliant* flips a switch in my masculine brain. I want to beat my chest. Grin like a smug bastard. Light a cigar and smoke it, because her compliments mean more than I ever thought they could.

A fuck ton, apparently.

"Well." My hand runs over the counter, wiping a patch of rogue crumbs away. "That's admirable of you."

"Doing the bare minimum shouldn't be considered admirable."

"What would you spend the money on?"

"Literary resources to people in lower-income areas. Have you heard of Little Free Libraries?"

"No, I haven't."

"They're boxes where people can leave books they've finished reading and take a new one home with them. I'd love to get a dozen set up in neighborhoods where physical libraries aren't as accessible. I'd also like to create a Book Bus and drive around to locations and do pop-up events. I try to host some here, but it's difficult for kids to attend when their parents work late."

Why?

Why couldn't she give me some bullshit answer about vibes, aesthetics, or other words I'm unfamiliar with? Why couldn't she talk about catering to the individuals who will keep her store profitable?

Nope.

Here she is, laying out another altruistic act. Heart full of gold. A smile that could bring peace to the most hurting souls. Ideas that can change the world. And she's talking to *me.*

"What if the Book Bus were a regular school bus?" I ask. "It could pick kids up during the holidays and summer break from designated meeting spots and bring them here. It eliminates the need for relying on parents for transportation. It gets them to the store. You could do a rewards program, too. Come to five readings and earn a free book."

I'm overstepping, I know. I shouldn't be proposing any changes to her idea. There's this incessant urge, though, to throw piles and piles of cash and books at Bridget's feet, asking her what else she needs to be successful.

To be happy.

She spins on her stool. Her knee knocks against mine. The touch is a jolt straight up my spine, and I don't bother to pull away. I've learned over the years pain makes me feel alive.

And I haven't felt this invigorated in ages.

"Did you come up with that right now?" she asks.

"Yeah."

Bridget's hand moves from the keyboard to my forearm. Her fingers press into my muscles. She grins. Teeth. Pink cheeks. Joy. Admiration. "That's incredible, Theo. You just gave me so many good ideas."

I think my location and time of death might be here and now. Quiet Riot playing, leather material under my ass, words like *brilliant* and *incredible* ringing in my ears, and her touch, the final nail in the coffin. The surrounding space feels warm, far too pleasant of a sensation for an evening in a bookstore.

"Thanks for sticking around for a bit," she continues. I haven't found my voice yet, too preoccupied by the unintentional drag of her fingernails over the stem of a sunflower—Mac's favorite—on my arm, below my elbow. Sharp. Biting. Not hard enough. "I was wondering if you wanted to get everyone together on Monday and talk about logistics. It would put us right under six weeks out from the deadline. We could do introductions and stuff."

"Yeah," I finally say. "I'll let them know. Do you want to meet here?"

"Sure. I can grab pizza for us. I had a theme idea for the contest. It's kind of cheesy, but it might work. Home for the Holidays. I thought maybe everyone between the two stores could share a tradition that's important to them. Does your family do anything fun for the holiday you celebrate?"

Do I tell her about the car accident? The one that left my mom in a wheelchair, unable to reach the mugs at the top of the counter because standing is impossible, so we just... stopped?

Do I mention we do the bare minimum these days, an artificial tree a feeble attempt at Yuletide cheer? I take a minute to find my words. How much do I want to share? How much do I want her to see? What happens when she learns these parts of me?

There's a pause in the music, the room becoming quiet as I say, "hot chocolate with marshmallows on top. In mugs with our names on them. That... that was our tradition."

Her smile is secretive and beautiful as she moves her hand back to the keyboard, resuming her typing. "That sounds lovely."

I jump off the stool and slink to the exit, recognizing the natural end in our conversation. I pull the door open, fresh air filling my lungs. Pausing in the threshold, I'm compelled to share one more thing, to let her know what's been on my mind since I walked inside sometime ago. "I think I could get used to being around you, Bridget Boylston."

She tosses her hair over her shoulder, brown waves floating down her back. She meets my gaze, eyes dancing in the dim glow of the room. "I've been used to you for a while now, Theo Gardner, but take your time catching up. I want you to be sure. Once you start, there's no going back."

On the walk to my truck, hands shoved deep in my pockets and a smile lingering on my lips, I replay those words.

I'm stupidly certain I don't want to go back. I want to keep going forward.

I think I want her there, too.

TEN

BRIDGET

"PEPPERONI AND CHEESE pizzas are set up on the counter. Beer is in the cooler on the left. Soft drinks and water are in the one on the right. There's a plate of cookies at the far end, too. Help yourself to whatever you like."

A frenzy of hands and elbows answers me. I scoot out of the way, almost knocked over by the mad dash to the food. The noise in the bookstore fills to an electrifying volume, drowning out the holiday tunes I queued up earlier in the afternoon.

"You like to take care of people, huh?" Lucas asks, hanging back with me.

I've seen him in passing dozens of times as I go in and out of the store, always offering a wave and a smile as I hurry to other tasks. But I don't know anything about him. In just the last five minutes, as he unloaded the steaming pizza boxes from my hands, I learned he loves mushrooms, lives alone, and is Ziggy's new best friend, if dog slobber pooling in the cuff of his jeans is any indication.

"Guilty," I admit, sheepishly.

"That's not a bad thing. We all need someone to take care of us. Some people are just too proud to admit it."

For not knowing me well, he certainly hit the nail on the head. The desire to make sure everyone in my life is comfortable and happy is at the core of my being. The trait is high on the list of characteristics past partners have found undesirable.

Also included?

Dropping everything to help someone in need and getting too emotional about too many parts of my life. I have big, messy feelings, and for a long time, I assumed that was a bad thing, because I hadn't been told otherwise. I laugh loudly and I cry. I love people fiercely and wildly, even if they might not deserve it and the affection isn't reciprocated. I've been criticized for expressing those emotions outwardly instead of keeping them inside, but I can't help it. Like taking care of people, the emotions are a part of me, regularly displayed, and a significant portion of my chaotic livelihood. And I know, deep down, there's nothing wrong with me.

I just haven't found my other half who understands how I operate, selfless acts done not for recognition or attention, but because I can't function otherwise.

It's a terrible curse.

"I think I'm a fixer," I admit to Lucas as I blow out a breath, surprised by how easy it is to talk to a man I've known for eight seconds. "If I'm not helping, I feel inadequate."

His laugh is low and he nudges his shoulder with mine, a friendly gesture. "We should start a support group. It's the worst, isn't it?"

"Yeah." I grin. "The worst."

"This was a great idea, Bridget. What if we included a gift exchange, too? Something small, like a token of appreciation for getting through the madness that's probably going to ensue over the next month and a half."

"I like that. Fifteen dollar spending limit. Silly and fun. No stress."

"Bingo."

"Is Theo coming?" I ask curiously. He didn't arrive with the rest of the hardware store group. I've tried my best to pretend I don't notice his absence, like it's no big deal he's missing. Except...

It's so obvious he's not here.

The room feels different. Almost whole. Almost complete. But not quite. A small sliver of *something* is missing.

Have I gotten used to his scowls after only a few interactions stretching longer than credit card payments for coffee? Do I miss his scoffs and his grunts, noises that used to sound caustic now a beautiful medley? Am I actively looking for his leather boots and chestnut hair from across the store?

When I turn to Lucas, he's grinning. "Soon," he says. "I left him grumbling in his office. I told him he had twenty minutes to get over here or I was going to drag him out by his hair." A check of his watch, followed by a nod. "Should be any minute now."

The door to the shop swings open. Theo (scowling, of course) pauses in the entryway while he assesses his surroundings. The scowl escalates to nerves, I think, the assuredness evaporating in the blink of an eye. His shoulders cave in. He scratches his forearm and retreats backward, losing his bravado. His face pales and I can see him swallow, hands curling into fists of worry.

"Lucas," I hiss. "Is he okay?"

His friend sighs. "Yeah, he is. If you're going to be working with him, you should know he doesn't like large groups. Mingling with people he doesn't know never goes over well. But"–he squints, then nods again–"he hasn't turned around and fled yet, so that's an encouraging sign."

"I didn't know. Shoot. We could–"

"Bridget." Lucas is kind yet firm as he interrupts me. "If he's here, it's because he wants to be here. Trust me."

Wants to be here.

It's what Theo said the other night when he stopped by, staying later than he should have because he chose to be here then too, with me. Poignant, important words, sealed with a rock song on the radio. Shared dreams and ambitions. Long-kept secret ideas. His knee against mine, warm, firm, solid.

My heart flutters at the memory.

"He kind of looks like he's going in for a root canal," I observe.

"You should see him when he gets really pissed. It's a treat. C'mon. Let's get this shindig started."

AFTER THE PIZZA has been distributed, the plate of cookies replenished, soda cans and beer bottles popped open, everyone forms an oddly shaped semi-circle in the center of the room. I'm sandwiched between Theo on my left and Jordan, one of his employees, on my right. I clear my throat and offer an awkward wave.

"Hi," I begin. "Should we do the unoriginal name and fun fact about ourselves? I know icebreakers suck, so I'm open to other ideas."

"We'll be done in six seconds," Chandler points out.

"True. What about two fun facts and your Last Supper meal?"

"What's a Last Supper meal?" Lucas asks.

"It's the appetizer, entree and dessert you'd want to eat if it were your last night on earth," I say. "Who wants to start us off?"

Theo, to my surprise, is the first to stand. He sets his paper plate down and rises to his feet. Large palms run over his denim-clad thighs, and he faces the group. "I'm Theo. I'm left-handed and I hate cilantro. My last meal would be chips and queso, chicken pot pie with a side of mashed potatoes, and a warm blueberry muffin for dessert."

He returns to his seat, and his boot lightly kicks my Converse, suggesting it's my turn next.

"I'm Bridget. I'm afraid of heights and I've never seen snow. My meal would be mozzarella sticks, a cheeseburger with French fries, and an ice cream sandwich for dessert."

We learn about each other as we make our way around the room. Lucas is practically a carpentry master. Chandler wants to go skydiving. Brooke listens to horror books on audio while she does yoga. Felicity from the hardware store has never been on an airplane. Malik, another of Theo's employees, is fluent in Mandarin. When we get back to the beginning of the circle, I pull out my notebook and click open my pen.

"We all know there's a big prize on the line for winning this competition. It's going to be a team effort, y'all. I don't want anyone to feel like they aren't being included or someone is holding too much power. I came up with a possible idea for a theme we could do, but I want to hear what other ideas you might have."

"We didn't think up a theme," Felicity says. "We entered and didn't think we'd be allowed to participate, so we're here with no plan. What's your idea, Bridget?"

"Home for the Holidays. We all come from different backgrounds and upbringings. How cool would it be to showcase our special traditions? Although we celebrate in unique ways, the underlying message is the same: the holidays are better with the ones you love. Whether it's a tree, a menorah, or acts of service, when you combine all those special moments, they create something wonderful. That beauty deserves to be showcased."

ELEVEN

BRIDGET

THE IDEA ISN'T ALL that great. It was born on a whim two days ago when I listened to a pair of customers discuss their impending holidays plans. One was going on a cruise with her wife, forgoing any "normal" celebrations to spend a week away together. Unplugged, childless, just themselves. The other woman was debating where to put the twelve-foot Christmas tree her family was purchasing that weekend. For the last eight years, she said, it had been in the foyer. This year, though, she was considering moving it to the living room.

Their conversation made me pause. I realized, through their individual holiday interpretations, the definition of home is fluid. It could mean a literal house with four walls and a door. It could be Christmas dinner on a cruise ship. A tree tied to the roof of a car. An intimate celebration between husband and wife, exchanging their first gifts as a married couple. If you asked a million people what home meant to them, you'd get a million answers, each as equally important as the last.

"It's a great idea, Bridget," Jordan says. "It shows the holiday season isn't just one way of believing. If it's important to you, it's worth celebrating."

"I'm Jewish," Felicity pipes up. "I know Christmas is probably the predominantly celebrated holiday in the group. It would be cool to see a menorah lit, though, since the dates for Hanukkah overlap this year."

"Menorah." I scribble and nod in agreement. "Absolutely. Some Hanukkah food would be amazing, too. Do you have any suggestions?"

"Jelly donuts are a popular dessert. Potato latkes and brisket for dinner. They're all pretty easy to make."

"Those sound delicious. Maybe we could do a little cooking class together and put out a spread for the judges."

"No one's ever asked for specific Hanukkah ideas. I'd love to collaborate with you, Bridget."

"That's because everyone else sucks," Chandler supplies. She drops an arm around Felicity's shoulder and gives her a squeeze, like they've been friends for years. "I can't cook for shit, but I want to join in."

There's a murmur of agreement, others voicing Chandler's sentiments. Felicity's eyes grow misty as she wipes a tear away, but her smile is far from upset. It's proud and thankful. Her delight, that feeling of being *seen* and *valued* is why a theme like this is important.

"What about photos from past holidays?" Jordan suggests. "We could hang pictures from our childhood on the walls and across the store on a clothesline or something."

"Didn't y'all use those big, clunky cameras back in the day?" asks Bradley, Theo's youngest employee. "The ones that sat on your shoulder and you could record stuff?"

"Christ," Lucas grumbles. "You make it sound like it's from *Jurassic Park*. It's called a camcorder, Bradley, and it was only twenty years ago."

"I could probably convert the old tapes to DVD form, then

make a movie," Bradley continues. "We could project them on the wall."

"What about actual decorations?" Brooke interjects. "With student loans, I really can't spend much."

I doodle on my paper and consider her question. "We could use strands of lights we all already own on both exteriors. Christmas trees here. Woodworking pieces in the hardware store. Maybe some reindeer? A sleigh? A couple trees we can paint? Lucas, do you think that's possible?" A nod in confirmation, and I jot down another note. My paper is beginning to fill with ideas. "We could create a timeline of our holiday snapshots, weaving through both shops. That shouldn't be too expensive. It doesn't need to be fancy. Just enough to give off that cheer, you know?"

"It's perfect," says Theo. "Great job, Bridget."

The praise works its way from my toes to my neck. Color invades my skin, swathing me in hues of red and deep pink. Theo's focus fractures, dropping to the top of my v-neck shirt, the spot unobstructed by fabric. The effect of his words is visible for all to see, but he's the only one staring. Three seconds, maybe more, is how long he lingers. When his eyes drag back to my face, the brown has shifted. Darker now, a starless night sky.

The edge of his mouth curls up, understanding. It's not cruel or mocking, but pleased. Proud. After two more beats–*god, I wish it were more*–he looks away, severing our contact and leaving an ache, an anguished need, behind.

I'm close to launching myself at him. He's attractive. Absurdly, so. This is the first time I've had a physical reaction to him, a drift to a sensation more desperate than plain attraction. He's a black hole and I'm being pulled into his orbit, the catalyst for losing my train of thought and all meaningful dialogue.

All that's left behind is him.

"Right," I say. I cough and clear my throat, doing my best to regain focus on the group and not the man sitting to my left. He's closer than he was five minutes ago, his calf near mine and the side of his boot pressing into the leg of my chair. I swear a burst of heat radiates from him. "What works best for everyone? Email? Text?"

"Snapchat?" Bradley asks.

"Is that the one with pictures?" Theo asks.

"Yeah, boss, it's this awesome app. You send a private photo to someone and it disappears after the other person opens it. It's perfect for–"

"Do not finish that sentence," Chandler warns. "No one wants to hear about your junk. Are you even old enough to drink?"

"I'm 22," Bradley answers, then throws a wink her way.

"Texting it is!" I rip out a sheet from my notebook and hand it to Jordan. "Put down your name and phone number. I'll get a group chat going. Now that we've gotten the hard part out of the way, what about a group activity once a week? It'll take our minds off the competition, which will be nice. I like y'all. It would be fun to hang out when we're not yelling about where garland should hang."

"What about ice skating?" Lucas proposes. "It's festive and it gives us a break from the Florida weather. I know the rink is decked out in cool lights and they have good food. Maybe it'll feel more like the holidays and less like a never-ending heat wave."

"All in favor of ice skating?"

Fifteen arms lift in the air, and Lucas pumps his fist victoriously.

"Done," I say. "Does Friday at seven work for everyone?"

I tilt my head in Theo's direction, hoping he can sense my silent question.

Does that work with your schedule and Mac?

"Friday at seven sounds good," he confirms.

"I'll call and make reservations. Oh! One last thing. Lucas suggested a gift exchange. Fifteen dollar max limit for spending, and we can draw random names. If everyone is okay with the idea, we can do that on Friday after we skate. Okay, that's all I got. Y'all can stay and hang out if you want!"

I expect everyone to head out relatively quickly. We've been here for a while, and I imagine people have lives they want to get back to. Instead, hushed side conversations begin. Bradley pulls out his phone and starts a livestream on a social media app. Brooke and Chandler drop their heads together, talking animatedly. Malik shows Molly, one of my employees, a video saved on his camera roll. They both laugh, and she scoots her chair closer to his.

I smile, excited giddiness building like a spring. It feels *good* to have so many people here, enjoying each other. A camaraderie is forming. Alliances are being made. Friendships are starting.

I... like it.

I like the sound of chattering voices and phone numbers being exchanged. Of high-fives and another round of beer bottles cracking open.

A swell of emotions hit me. This is how it always starts; a rising tide. A gradual build. Those goddamn feelings filter to the surface and I curse under my breath. My lip trembles and I do my best to keep a neutral face as I stand, collecting the remaining plates and soda cans and bringing them to the large trash can and recycling bucket by the café.

"Hey."

Theo's voice, low and recognizable, sounds behind me. I drop my chin to my shoulder and give him a feeble smile.

"Hey," I say.

His eyes sweep over my face. A frown sits on his lips and he steps toward me, boots moving across the floor in two large strides. "Are you okay? You look upset."

"I'm not upset. I'm a stupidly emotional person, and it's so wonderful to see everyone having a good time together. And I know that makes me seem like an idiot, because who the hell would cry over a damn pizza box and Christmas trees? Yet here I am, needing a pack of tissues because I'm so happy. I won't blame you for turning around and walking away. I must look ridiculous."

Theo's elbow rests on the counter, his right hand digging in his front pocket. He extracts a clean napkin, slightly crumpled into a ball of paper, and hands it to me.

"Will this work?" he asks with uncertainty. "I can track down a tissue for you, but this is the best I have right now."

I emit a watery laugh. "This is perfect. Thanks. I don't know why I'm making this a big deal. I think it's because I know the other stores are just going to throw a design together separately. They don't care about anything other than the prize. They're not going to go ice skating or send text messages. Yeah, I want to win, but what happens after the contest is over? After we've spent all this time together? I just go back to not talking to any of your employees? You go back to not offering me a napkin when I'm crying over little things? I like that everyone seems to want a friendship. I'm a people-pleaser, and I like that people seem pleased. I don't know. Like I said. I'm an idiot."

"Would you..." Theo trails off. Scuffs his boot against the floor, drags his eyes to mine. "Do you want a hug?" he finishes softly.

He does that, sometimes. When he voices something he's not sure he's allowed to say. He becomes quiet and timid, like he never should have asked in the first place. I like the soft Theo. The one not many people get to see.

"Yeah," I whisper back, a chuckle caught in the words. "I do."

He stands up straight and opens his arms. I walk toward him, a magnetic pull. We've never hugged before, but it's instinctive and automatic, our bodies knowing exactly where to connect. My head finds his shoulder, and I rest it there. In the crook of his neck, nose tipping up the column of his throat. His chin drops to the top of my hair. A weight leaves my body as I exhale, relaxing into him. His arms envelop me, sheathing me in a cloak of warmth. A blanket on a cold night, a cocoon of quiet. A net of safety.

Theo sighs, the hot puff of air gliding over my forehead. His palm splays over the small of my back, rubbing up from the base of my spine then down before pulling me even nearer.

I think I could stay like this forever.

"I haven't hugged anyone besides my kid in a while," he admits into my hair.

"Good news. You're not terrible at it." My voice is muffled by the collar of his shirt, and his answering chuckle rumbles his chest.

"A compliment I'll hold dear. Bridget, I hope you know you're not an idiot. You're allowed to express your emotions however you see fit. If that's crying, yelling, or laughing, they're all allowed."

"I know," I whisper. A tear clings to his shirt. "I just don't want to look silly."

"Trust me, you don't look silly. Thanks for taking charge at the meeting. I'm normally more assertive, but new folks kind of make me want to close off."

"I'm just glad you're here. This might be the best hug I've ever had."

It's the right amount of pressure, and our difference in height matches up well. I can fit against him without contorting my body. Easy and natural, controlled and spontaneous. No one has hugged me like this before. My limbs become pliant, knowing they're safe here. With him.

With a squeeze, he pulls back. His arms unwind from my waist. My cheek leaves the hollow of his chest. I raise my chin to look at him, and his smile tips up. Every time he does that–glows bright like a damn Christmas tree–I think it's the best thing I've ever seen. Each one of his grins is my new favorite sight.

"I'm glad I'm here, too," he says.

"You can bring Mac on Friday if you want. Not that I'm trying to tell you how to parent or anything," I backtrack. "Just. You know. It's an option."

"Still not over being flustered when you talk about her, huh?"

"You're an ass." I reach out to flick his ear.

He lets out a full belly laugh while he attempts to dodge my attack. It's the first time I've heard it, loudly and wholly, and it's better than all of the small chuckles in the world.

A cheerful sound, filling the room. It reaches every corner, every nook and cranny. The noise, as rare and elusive as it is, is my doing. *I'm* the one causing his shoulders to shake, his eyes to close, his nose to scrunch, wrinkles and laugh lines forming on his skin.

His gaze moves to my cheek. "You have pizza on your face. How does that happen?"

"Who knows, Theo? Probably from the napkin you gave me. Do you have another? I can–"

I can't finish my sentence because soon he's licking the pad of his thumb. He's moving into my space, close enough where I can smell the spice and pine of his cologne. The clean fabric of his shirt and the mint from his toothpaste. His finger swipes the sauce away, lingering on my skin, far too long to be considered cordial or friendly. I hold my breath, terrified to exhale. I'm afraid if I do, I'll blow him away and he'll disappear forever.

I see a small, white scar above the top of his lip. A jagged, faded line I've never noticed before. There's less ice behind his eyes, too. They're thawing. Shards of pain, a haunted past, and an abundance of hurt melting away. I stare at my reflection in his glasses and wonder if he sees me like I see him.

Hopeful, a little bit flawed, and a plethora of dreams. Doing the best he can alone in the world. I guess we're kind of similar in that way, two souls trying to figure it all out, no one to guide us or help us along.

"Better?" I ask. My voice wavers at the reverence he's demonstrating. The gentle touch, the careful consideration.

"Perfect." His hand falls to my hair, and he tucks a rogue piece behind my ear.

I've stopped breathing.

I've stopped thinking.

All I can focus on is his skin on mine.

Purposely, continuously, tenderly.

His fingertips trace along the curve of my jaw, leaving sparks in their wake.

"I think this has the potential to be the best Christmas I've had in a while," he murmurs. "Maybe ever. The jury is still out, but we'll see."

The moment between us snaps, and he steps back, our beaker of bliss breaking. I miss his touch already.

"Yeah. I guess we will."

TWELVE
BRIDGET

"BRIDGET! Time to put the tinsel down. We have dicks to talk about!"

Chandler's crude statement comes as I hang the final garland strand on a bookshelf, stepping back to admire the curtain of green.

"Coming!" I answer, making my way to the front of the store.

It's been two days since our group meeting, and phase one of the initial decorating is underway. We rearranged the store to accommodate the trees I'm buying soon. The interior walls are now covered in flickering lights, a task I conquered yesterday afternoon during a lull in foot traffic. Chandler's holiday drinks were added to the menu–sugar cookie, cinnamon babka, spiced hot chocolate, and sticky toffee pudding rounding out the flavors. I put out the first batch of chocolate-peppermint brownies and snowflake cookies this morning, and they were gone within a few hours. Brooke bought a box of mistletoe and keeps sneakily trying to dangle the plant from doors when my back is turned.

The hardware store also looks great. I popped in yesterday to deliver a basket of fresh pastries and found stockings with every employee's name tacked behind the register. Even Theo has one, complete with a Santa hat drawn on with felt paint. Lights are up over there, too, hanging from the ceiling and looking like falling icicles.

We're prepping the individual stores first before moving on to the joint effort of painting, building, and arranging. With how quickly we're moving, we should start phase two at the beginning of next week.

The phallic objects Chandler raucously mentioned have nothing to do with our Christmas plans and everything to do with the book club we recently started. Curated as a safe space for women of all backgrounds to gather, we talk about our favorite novels that might not be appropriate for the dinner table.

Classic literature like *Pride and Prejudice* and *Wuthering Heights* will always be adored, the lyrical prose woven through descriptive imagery. We wipe our eyes at the prolific love declarations cemented as must-read stories, wondering where our own haughty Mr. Darcy is.

At the same time, we also enjoy reading less traditional romance novels. The ones bordering on *filthy* and *taboo*. The kind of material that strays far away from the words of Jane Austen or the Brontë sisters. We indulge in books where sex is plentiful. No woman goes unsatisfied, and the language is far from tame or Shakespearian.

The Fictional Dicks and Fizzy Drinks book club came into existence one morning after Chandler and I had exceptionally bad dates. My mishap was a dude who'd rubbed my boob three times in his car, seat warmers on full blast despite the sweltering temperature outside, and asked if I finished. Chandler had a man whose fingers wandered to the wrong hole, claiming he "thought they were the same." She said it wasn't so much the direction he went, but that he assumed he was *right*. She was appalled, and spent the next thirty minutes with her legs spread, educating him on proper techniques while he took *actual* notes. She claimed she was doing a favor to the rest of womankind.

We lamented about the disastrous occurrences over banana bread, conversation shifting away from men who *think* they have the magic touch to books where they *know* how to deliver and the various kinks we enjoy.

Me: hair pulling, sex toys and praise.

Her: degradation and spanking.

After forty-five minutes of deliberation we decided to create a club where we could talk about these topics freely, with other like-minded women.

Plus, it gave us an excuse to read more smutty romance novels.

A post about our first meeting circulated on social media. It was shared between a couple of friends and ended up in some local book groups. Then, it exploded on Instagram, garnering 10,000 likes, hundreds of comments, and folks *begging* us to live stream the event so they could watch.

Which leads us here. Almost sixty people in attendance, a wide range of ages chatting with each other, a book tucked under their arm. I grin as I make my way through the group mingling about the shop.

A tripod sits in the corner of the room, camera already streaming to social media. We haven't even started yet, and the number of viewers is rapidly climbing into the high hundreds. I pluck a flute of champagne off the counter and take a swig to calm my nerves. Doing my best to smile and wave to the group while juggling my book and booze, I take a spot at the front of the store.

"Hi, y'all. Welcome to the first official meeting of the Fictional Dicks and Fizzy Drinks book club."

A cheer goes through the crowd. They lift their glasses my

way, smiling eagerly. I grin back and indulge in another sip. The bubbles pop on my tongue, easing the tension at the base of my neck.

"We're so excited to have you here," I continue. "This group was formed so we could have a place to get together and talk about sex, books, and sex *in* books. Anything that gets shared here tonight doesn't leave these walls. Your faces won't be on the video, and I'll be deleting it right after, but please don't feel obligated to participate. You don't need to share if you aren't comfortable. This space is yours. Talk, don't talk. Read, don't read. It's up to you. The only thing I ask is for everyone to be respectful. Are we cool with the rules?"

Head nods and verbal confirmations answer me. I peer out to the crowd and spot my three best friends; Lucy, Skylar and Polly. They wave, encouraging me along.

"Since this is our first meeting, we asked y'all to bring a book you enjoyed because it took you out of your comfort zone. I can't wait to hear what you picked. At the end of the night we'll decide on next month's choice together."

I take a seat and let others dictate the direction of our conversation. We talk about *everything*; honest, candid discussion with no judgment, only questions. We share the books buried deep in the trenches of our Kindle libraries. There's frantic note-taking. Blushing cheeks and energetic laughter, too. Acceptance and reassurance blossom in the room. Many discover for the first time other women who like the same things they do.

Sex shouldn't be a divisive topic. We shouldn't be ashamed of the books we read, the positions we like, or the names we want to be called in bed. We're allowed to be loyal partners and attentive mothers, hard-working business owners, teachers or lawyers *and* be vocal about what satisfies us. You don't have to pick and choose.

"Bridget! You're up!" Lucy calls from across the room, tossing her red hair over her shoulder.

I clamber to my feet. "Hi, I'm Bridget. Through reading I've discovered I really enjoy being told what to do in the bedroom, and then praised when I do it correctly. I think it's because I'm so used to being in control during my day-to-day life, and it's refreshing to just let go and give the control to someone else. The book I brought has public touching, a grand gesture and sweet, tender moments. I reached out to the author on social media, and she sent me a few signed copies. They'll be at the register if anyone wants to purchase one. Alright, Chan. You're up."

"Hell, yeah," she exclaims and jumps to her feet. "I can't wait to talk about how I think I'd like to call someone dad–"

"Evening ladies."

My jaw nearly drops to the floor when I spot the man walking through the front door. "Jamie?" I sputter.

"Hey, Bridget." The deputy mayor shifts to his right, revealing a very pissed off Theo.

"Crap," I mutter. "I'm in trouble."

THIRTEEN

BRIDGET

I STOP at Chandler's chair on my way to be scolded.

"Can you turn the video off and keep everyone occupied?"

"While you take your punishment?" She winks. "I just did. It's a shame. The comments were gold. We should have kept it rolling."

"What do you mean?"

"They asked who the 'tall, hot guy without a tie who barged through the door' is. Talking about Theo, obviously. What else? Oh! 'He looks like a daddy.' 'He's definitely an ass guy.' 'Those tattoos would look great around my neck.' 'Big dick energy.' Just a sampling."

My chest tightens and my pulse slows as I listen to the flirty messages aimed at Theo read aloud, broadcast to the world for all to hear. Protectiveness, I imagine, clouds my vision, turning everything hazy and blurry. It's like... I don't want the world to see him and I only want to keep him for myself. Which is preposterous, I know, because there's no claim on him. He's not *mine* to defend. There's still a surge of something... possessive as I approach the man with a murderous glint in his eye.

"You're being too loud," Theo says in lieu of a greeting.

"Loud?" I ask. "What are you talking about? We're hardly shouting."

"I can hear you through the walls. Can't you save this for a Saturday night at your house? Not somewhere I'll be subjected to it?"

"Let me get this straight. You heard us talking about sex toys at a slightly raised volume, and you decided to call in reinforcements?"

"If I have to hear one more word about a damn vibrator, I'm going to lose my mind."

"Sounds like someone needs more than a vibrator to relax," I say under my breath.

His eyes flash at my joke, warning me to tread carefully. I kind of like prodding him, though. I wonder how far he'd let me go.

"I'm trying to do accounting work and I have a massive headache you're contributing to," he says.

"You're doing work this late? Don't you have someone who can help handle that kind of stuff?"

"No. I get to handle all the stuff. It's due tomorrow, and I've been distracted for two hours."

I'm about to apologize. Already, the letters of *I'm sorry* are forming on my lips. It's unavoidable the longer I look at him. He's dead on his feet. Dark circles underline his eyes, stark against the paleness of his cheeks. Stubble lines his jaw, brown mixed with a hint of light gray, and his shoulders curve inward defeatedly.

The ambiguous statement, the part about him handling everything by himself, snares my attention. It's another untold story of his. One I want to know. One I want to ask about. Theo's a complex riddle made up of many pieces, and this is one I can't crack.

"Theo. Bridget. If I may." Jamie bravely interposes himself, playing referee. "The curfew just now went into effect. Technically, Bridget hasn't done anything wrong. There's no reason to give her a citation for a noise complaint."

"Thank you," I say to Jamie.

"For fuck's sake," Theo grunts. "Are you two going to keep flirting or fix the problem at hand? I thought you were smart, Bridget. Surely you can come up with a solution."

The cruel and sarcastic words sting, pricking my skin like sharp needles. They were designed to hurt, and land like a savage assault on my emotions. My lip wobbles and I bite the sadness–and fury–away, breaking our eye contact. The apology from before is long forgotten as I plaster on a fake smile.

"Jamie," I say, purposely ignoring the other man, "thank you for letting us know. We'll clear out of here soon, and I promise it won't happen again. I'm sorry."

"I appreciate it, Bridget. All a simple misunderstanding! Theo, should we leave them alone to wrap up in peace?" Jamie asks.

"I'll be there in a minute," Theo says.

"Are you sure? We–"

"Leave us alone. *Please*," Theo says, more forcefully this time.

Jamie nods, knowing better than to argue, and hurries to the door.

When we're alone, I level Theo with an uninterested look. "I have nothing to say to you, you gigantic asshole."

He pauses before answering, caught off guard by my bluntness. Genuine concern replaces the previous occupant of annoyance, and he expels a ragged breath. "Fuck." It's a stifled curse, the vowel dragging out longer than necessary. "I made you mad."

A thread in me snaps, patience finally, *finally* running out. My voice shakes with anger as I continue on.

"Of course you made me mad. I don't care that you interrupted. Walk in during a dildo discussion whenever you'd like. What I think is really lame is how you didn't talk to me first, deciding to storm in here like a bat out of hell. I would have listened if you had come to me directly, like an adult, and let me know how you were feeling. I'm not giving into whatever game you're trying to play. Instead of getting me in trouble, next time speak to me like an adult, so we can solve our problems without getting other people involved. We're not in kindergarten, Theo. We don't need a mediator to talk about things."

I stunned him into silence. He huffs, a hand running through his hair and mussing up the pieces. Another huff. A clearing of his throat, and a rock on his feet.

"There's no game. Next time you're here late, can you at least give me a heads up?"

"Do you want me to send you a text with a PDF attached to let you know all of my plans?"

Theo unfolds his arms. Puts down his invisible weapons, and takes a step toward me. Another. And another. I don't stop him. I don't retreat. I don't give him an inch. He rubs his temples, still grappling with what to say.

I hate that I'm not angrier, the sudden burst of rage gone.

I hate that I want him to pull me into his embrace–again–and nestle into his arms. Hand on my back, between my shoulder blades. Breath on my forehead. Gentle words in my ear.

I hate that I'm waiting for what he was to say.

I hate that I don't hate it at all.

"Bridget." His voice takes a smoky turn. The sharpness fades to regret. "I'm sorry. I hate large groups of people. I have since..." The sentence stops, and I hear the twinge of pain behind the unfinished words. "Joey walked in like he owned the place, turning a small complaint into a big deal. I promise that wasn't my intention."

"Are you calling him the wrong name on purpose to be a dick?"

"Come on, Boylston," he murmurs, mouth tipping up. "You know that comes naturally."

Damn him.

Damn him for owning up to his mistakes. For having a heart of gold somewhere under there.

And damn me for caring so much.

"I didn't realize how loud we were being," I admit. "It's our first meeting, and now I know for next time how thin the walls are and how our voices carry. I'm sorry."

"It's not your fault. It's mine. I also didn't mean to imply anything about your intelligence level. That was really shitty of me. And very untrue. You're incredibly smart. I'm really, really sorry."

"Wow. I think I like when you compliment me. And all your groveling is a nice touch, too. Are you going to get on your knees next?" I joke.

The look he gives me is serious, borderline sinister. He's never looked at me like this before. He hums, a low, deep melody I feel in my belly and beyond. He inclines his head, a kiss of feverish warmth tickling my neck, just below the shell of my ear.

"I wouldn't be opposed to getting on my knees for you, Boylston, if that's where you want me. But it wouldn't just be to ask for forgiveness."

I suck in a breath and look away, because how the hell am I supposed to respond?

Yes, please?

No, don't, let me get on mine instead?

Go fuck yourself?

A combination of all three but primarily the first and second because this man is both confusing as hell and turning me on more than anyone has in years with just his words?

"Bridget!"

Chandler's voice yanks us out of the moment, out of the fantasy beginning to form in my head. Of Theo, looking up at me, hands on my hips and skirt bunched at my waist. The drag of his teeth on my skin, whispering "forgive me?" into the apex of my thighs followed by an apologetic kiss, and another, and another.

He blinks and steps back. The air becomes colder the further away he moves. I let out an exhale and my lungs scream in relief. I give my friend a wave and hold up a finger, letting her know I need another minute.

"What else would you do on your knees?" I ask, striking a match and deciding to play with fire.

An arsonist, I should call myself, toeing this dangerous line. A spill of gasoline. A flame ready to engulf every surrounding inch.

"Your meeting tonight has given me lots of new ideas."

"Guess you didn't completely hate it."

"Guess not."

Two beats of silence. My skin, burning. His eyes, roaming. A twitch of his hand like he's about to reach out and pull me to him. Another exhale, another moment of *maybe*, and I return to reality.

"Why don't I give you a heads up next month when we're planning on meeting? Is that a good compromise?" I ask.

A neutral topic, not the salacious thoughts currently running through my head.

What would the press of his thumb on the back of my neck feel like?

What would his smile look like when he's satisfied and pleased?

Is he a talker, or would he communicate through grunts and groans?

"I accept your terms." He digs in his pocket and pulls out his phone. "Here. Put your number in."

"You don't have it from the group chat? There have been close to a hundred messages."

"Your belief in my ability to distinguish who is who in a group chat I haven't looked at is appreciated."

I laugh and hold out my hand. Theo drops the device, fingers brushing over mine, featherlight, a gentle glide. When he touches me, whether accidentally or on purpose, he leaves behind an invisible mark, a reminder he's been there. My skin singes long after he's gone.

A quick tap on the screen, I type in my name and number, passing the phone back over. "There you go."

"I'll let you get back to this."

"You barge in and you don't want to stay? Are you sure? Maybe you could learn a few things," I say.

It happens in slow motion. Theo's eyes rake down my body. My hair. My shirt. The skirt that suddenly feels far too short. My thighs. My feet. Then *up, up, up, up*. When he reaches my face again, he licks his top lip and smiles.

"Trust me, Bridget. It may have been a few years, but I don't need to learn anything."

I'm grateful he's walking toward the exit.

I'm grateful he's about to stroll outside, far, far away from here.

That was...

Hot.

Electrifying. For a second, nothing existed but him and me, the only two left on earth. No other sounds. No other sights.

Just...

Us.

"All good with the asshole?" Chandler asks, appearing by my side.

"Yeah. Just a... a misunderstanding. He apologized for being a dick."

"The never ending cycle." She laughs. "It's interesting, though."

"What's interesting?"

"The way Theo looked at you. Like you were a bite of food and he was a man starved."

I gape at her as she walks away with a wink.

I wouldn't be opposed to getting on my knees for you.

The declaration rings in my ears. It's magnified, repetitive. I grab another flute of champagne and chug the contents, using the alcohol to try and soothe the ache he left behind.

"I CANNOT BELIEVE I'm doing this." I drop to an empty bench. The ice skates in my hands hit the rubber floor, bouncing and rolling precariously close to my toes.

"You aren't excited?" Bridget asks.

She sits next to me, working expertly to lace up and tie two perfect knots with far more finesse than someone living in Florida should have. She adjusts the hem of her pants and stands, giving me a quizzical look.

"I don't know how to skate, given I've lived in this godforsaken state for four decades."

"I knew you were over forty! Damn, we should have made a betting pool."

"Forty-one," I grumble. "And I feel it every damn day." I kick off my work boots and slide into the death traps. "Good thing I already have a will signed." The skate is warm around my foot, and moisture clings to the interior. Dampness seeps into my socks and I grimace, revolted. "For the record, this is disgusting."

Bridget giggles and moves in front of me. She crouches between my parted thighs and looks up at me through a fan of eyelashes. *Hell*, that is *not* a position I need to see her in while

I'm surrounded by small children and families. "Do you need me to hold your hand, Theo?"

Yes.

Maybe.

"I'm going to throttle Lucas for suggesting this in the first place. The fucker played hockey growing up, so he's a pro on the ice. Selfish bastard."

"Did he?"

"Yeah. For twelve years. He was offensive wing or whatever the fuck they call it."

"Ah. Whatever the fuck is my favorite sports position."

"Smartass," I mumble.

"This is going to be so much fun." Still positioned between my legs, Bridget bats my hand away. She takes the laces in her fingers, finishing the job I'm taking too long to accomplish. A couple of quick loops later, she gives the side of my foot a pat.

Tonight she's wearing tight, black, flared pants paired with a green top that barely covers her stomach. The shade almost matches her eyes, dancing with mischief. She looks pretty. The light behind her, tendrils of brown framing her face, falling free from her ponytail. The loose pieces don't seem to bother her, and she bats them away.

I remember the feel of those locks tickling my nose the other night when I hugged her. When I held her close. When I didn't really want to let her go, but I did anyway. If I hadn't I might have kept her there forever.

She's infiltrated my mind in a way no one has in years. Physically, I'm attracted to her. That's obvious. How could I not be? She's a beautiful woman, bright and kind. A nice smile, a figure with curves. But, more scary than the physical attraction, is how I want to get to know her. I *never* want to get to know people and yet, I want to learn things about her.

All the goddamn things.

Every guy in the building stared at her when she strolled inside. I can't blame them. She's like a supernova, an explosion of color and light. A beauty you can't look away from. It holds you captive and you're *thankful*, eager to enjoy every second you get to be in her presence.

The woman has too much power.

"Have you skated before?" I ask, searching for a topic–any topic–to break myself free from her spell.

"I took skating lessons for a couple of years," she says. "Then I switched to rowing. It's where I met my friend Lucy."

I nod and push off the bench, wobbling as I stand. That explains the muscles in her legs. The strength in her back as she strains for the top level of the bookshelf in her store, just out reach. The slight curve of her biceps. "Can I talk to you about something?'

Her chin rises and her head drops back. I want to dance my fingers across her cheek and rest my palm there. "Sure."

In the days since the book club incident, I've felt like a complete asshat. Guilt follows me around, refusing to leave me alone. It's my fault the situation happened in the first place. I'd stayed up late the night before helping Mac finish a science project. I worked on the solar system diorama until five a.m. The paint on Neptune was still wet when she left for the bus.

Work was busy as hell, complete with long lines, dozens of returns, questions about hammer durability and bathroom tile. When I collapsed into my desk chair to finish the paperwork I had put off, I was near my breaking point. Hungry, exhausted, and out of sorts.

The laughter coming through the walls didn't bother me. It was the frequent consistency that did me in. It didn't stop and I could hear every word the women were saying, like I was there in the room with them. Loud, shrill voices, the ache forming across my temples intensified with every giggle.

I walked out the door, ready to politely ask them to keep it down, and ran into Mayor Whatshisface on the sidewalk. He made it a big deal, wanting to swoop in and save the day like Prince Charming. He made me out to be the bad guy, and I knew from the second I opened my mouth and those hurtful words came out, Bridget was pissed. It's a wonder she didn't reach up and slap me straight across my face.

It would've been well deserved.

Sarcastically calling her smart and telling her to stop flirting with a guy I can tell she doesn't like was juvenile. I hate that I made her upset. The change in her demeanor was remarkable. My heart hurt seeing her anything but happy. There was a flash of pain. A hint of suffering. An ember kindling in the ashes of an inferno.

I can't stop thinking about it.

I meant my apology to her. The part about getting on my knees slipped out unintentionally, a private thought that found its way out in the open. I would have gladly kneeled, the bite of the wood floor against my skin worth it for her forgiveness.

I've considered sending her a message and checking in. I've typed and deleted the text a dozen times, too chicken to hit send.

What the hell would I even say?

Hey, sorry I'm such a toolbag.

I've never felt so awful about my choice of words before.

Do you know how pretty you are when you get fired up about something?

Abso-fucking-lutely not.

"I'm sorry again for the other night. Storming into your store like a tyrant was uncalled for. It won't happen again."

The edges of her lips tip up, etchings of a smile forming. There's a twinkle in her eye, a flicker of a secret behind the gold-flecked green. "I know it won't."

My brows wrinkle in confusion. "You do?"

"Yeah." Bridget steps closer, and I notice a million things at once.

The mellow look on her face as she speaks, no resentment to be found. The urge I have to brush the pieces of hair falling into her face away. The smile growing wider and wider. My thumb itches to trace the shape of her mouth, moving over her lips and down the length of her throat. Her skate kicks mine and she reaches out to grip my arm, steadying herself and searing my skin in the process.

"You're a good guy, Theo," she continues. Her tone is reverent. Tender. It makes me feel like I'm the only guy in the room. The only guy in the whole damn world. And fuck it makes me want to be the *best* guy in the world. For her. "Even if you don't see it. Even if others don't see it. I do. And it's a lovely, wonderful thing. Have some fun tonight, okay? You deserve it."

With a wave, Bridget turns, heading toward the entrance of the rink. She gives Felicity a high-five and leans over the wall, waiting her turn to jump onto the ice. She looks back over her shoulder a final time, gaze meeting mine. I think the remaining oxygen leaves my body when she grins. A single dimple pops out. Her smile is bright. It's wide.

It's for me.

FIFTEEN

THEO

"GETTING BETTER, MAN!" Lucas calls out as he speeds by. Shards of ice kicked up from his skates hit my shins and settle into the cuff of my jeans.

I've spent the last hour stumbling around the rink and I've completed two whole laps. I think I'm close to dying. My legs are on fire, calf and quad muscles screaming. My forehead is damp with sweat. My lip is close to bleeding from how hard my teeth are sinking into it.

Needing a minute—or thirty—I stumble off the rink. I collapse onto a bench, grateful to be on solid ground, and wipe a hand over my brow.

"Water?"

A bottle beaded with condensation is thrust my way.

"Didn't think you'd ever be the one to offer me a reprieve," I say. I give Chandler a weary look.

She shrugs and sits next to me. "Consider it a one-time thing."

Her elbows drop to her thighs and she stares out at the circle of people. Some are laughing loudly. Others are wearing Christmas sweaters even though we're still in November. Some grip the edge of the rink like their life depends on it. A few—Bridget, I notice—are doing spins in the middle of the ice, looking like damn Olympians.

"See something you like?" Chandler asks, following my gaze.

Yes.

"I don't know what you're talking about. Is this whole thing miserable for you, too?"

"If I have to hear the chicken dance one more time, I'm out of here."

I snort a sound of agreement. "I think your departure would be justified. The chicken dance is downright horrific."

"Why don't you like being here? I mean, I know you're grumpy and all that shit, but there's gotta be another reason."

My lips roll together, pondering her question. "Too many people."

"Is it because of the accident?"

I crack my neck. Scratch my forearm. "It certainly hasn't helped."

"Bridget doesn't know," Chandler says. It's not accusatory, but matter-of-fact.

"I figured she didn't. 'm surprised you haven't told her."

Chandler looks aghast. "Why would I? It's not my stuff to share."

"It's public knowledge. There was a damn newspaper article."

She sighs. "As someone who's been through shit I don't want others to know, I'm not going to be the one to tell her. You will. When you're ready."

"That's incredibly kind of you to say."

"Yeah, well, don't get used to it."

"Hey," Bridget calls out.

She's gliding over to us. Her hands are on her hips—*those*

hips will be the death of me—and she's shaking her head, huffing in annoyance.

"Not fair," she continues. "You two aren't allowed to sit on the sidelines. This is a team bonding activity and you two aren't bonding."

"That's not true. Maybe Theo and I are best friends now," Chandler points out.

"Yeah, and hell has frozen over." Bridget leans over the barrier, extending her hand toward me. Her fingers wiggle in my direction and I shake my head.

"No," I say. "I'm done. There's a welt in the shape of California on my ass. I've grown gray hair."

"You wouldn't look bad with gray hair," Chandler adds.

"Stop it. You're freaking me out."

"Come on!" Bridget says.

"Nope."

Her mouth forms a pout and her bottom lip juts out. "Please?"

Oh, fuck.

The word threatens to obliterate every grain of intelligence I thought I had. I stare at her and my pulse quickens.

It's not like she's dropping to her knees and staring up at me —again—and asking me to take her or begging for more, more, more. There's nothing special about the six letters. Pieced together with bright eyes, full, pink lips, and half her ponytail coming undone, it's enough to make even the strongest man crumble.

And I'm weak as shit.

"Fine," I relent. I act like it's a chore, a bother to stand when I'm doing my best to not spring to my feet.

I trudge back toward the ice. I expect Bridget to drop her hand and turn away, leaving me to fend for myself while she rejoins a group of friends. She doesn't, though. She waits until

I'm within reach. When I am, her palm slips into mine, soft and smooth, and squeezes once.

"Doing okay?" she asks.

"Yeah," I say. My skate finds the ice again. "I'm good."

"Good. Ready to have a little bit of fun?" Bridget tugs me along, picking up our pace, hand never leaving mine.

Fun is an activity that's become unfamiliar. I purposely avoid anything entertaining in life, bogged down by personal and professional commitments. If I'm not at work, I'm shuttling Mac to and from soccer practice or helping with homework. If I'm not with her, I'm answering emails, counting inventory and making sure our advertisements are running smoothly and efficiently.

I've shunned the things that used to make me smile and laugh, putting everyone first and ignoring what *I* might want to do. What brings *me* joy. Hell, these days I have a hard time even knowing what that joy might be.

Cautiously, I lean into it. I accept my surroundings, letting them pulse through me. I shove away pesky responsibilities and savor the here and now.

The music thumping around me, a combination of a traditional festive song paired with some electric dance soundtrack. The smell of nachos and hot chocolate in the air. Strands of Christmas lights fixed around the edge of the rink, flashing from red to blue to green. Bridget's thumb against the back of my palm. A kind smile.

It's an incredible feeling, one I've forgotten for many years.

Maybe there's hope for me.

"First time out of the house in a while?" she asks as we glide along.

"Yeah," I admit. "My usual socialization is with Mac or my two best friends at a restaurant over beer. This is a whole new ball game."

"And?" Bridget presses. "Thoughts so far?"

"I don't hate it. It's nice."

"Success!" She laughs gleefully and switches sides with me, shifting to my right.

"Why did you ever pick skating as a sport?" I ask her.

"I watched the Olympics one year and it looked fun. So I just kind of did it. I thought the jumps would scare me. Turns out, they don't."

"What does scare you? Besides the height thing."

Bridget is quiet for a moment. Contemplative, gazing out across the ice. Her hand flexes, tightening its grip around mine. I expect her to say something silly, like spiders or snakes.

"Being alone, I think. I love people, but I enjoy my quiet time of solitude after a day full of interacting. There's this fear I'm going to go home to an empty house every night for the rest of my life, though. And I want someone to just be in the quiet with me. The kind of relationship where you don't have to talk all the time. You don't have to ask questions. You can sit side-by-side on the couch in silence and be the happiest person in the world, because you're there together."

I didn't mean for the conversation to take such a serious turn as I process what she said. That's one of my fears, too. It's been years since my last relationship, but I always enjoyed being half of a whole. I liked having someone to share my day with. To send a stupid picture to at three o'clock on a Thursday. Someone next to me in bed, tangled together under the light of the setting moon and rising sun, sleep ignored

as we explored each other until dawn.

"What about you?" asks Bridget. "What scares you?"

I shouldn't go down this road. I shouldn't start to peel back the layers because when she sees what lies beneath, she might not want to stay.

And I think I'd like her to stick around.

"People leaving," I answer. "People always leave. I've gotten used to it. It's why I keep everyone at arm's length. It's easier to pretend things are okay when they inevitably go."

"Ah." She hums in understanding. "Maybe you're only looking for the wrong ones, then. The right ones won't leave. The right ones will stick around."

I scoff at her unwavering optimism. "Not when they know everything about me."

"*Because* they know everything about you. We all have flaws, Theo. Life's about finding the person who welcomes them."

"How do you do that? How do you always find the good parts of life? Does it get exhausting? Do you ever just want to... yell?"

Bridget chuckles. "Sometimes. There's so much you can't control, no matter how hard you try. But then I remember some people are worth being tired for, because they have a lot of good to offer."

"The right ones," I supply.

"Yeah," she agrees, a serene smile in place. "The right ones."

"I'm learning."

"You are." Her palm eases out of mine and splays out over my lower back. With a light push, she ushers me away. "Ready to try skating on your own?"

I stay upright as I make a small stride. "Not so bad," I admit. Another few steps forward and my feet shuffle out from under me. Before I can stop it, I'm toppling to the ground, face first. I land on my stomach, melted ice soaking through my shirt. "Well. Shit. That didn't go like I'd hoped."

Bridget crouches down and offers her hand. "Come on, Collector. We'll try again."

For the next two hours she doesn't leave my side, gently guiding me around and around the rink. She lifts my arm above my head so she can spin underneath. She gets me to smile, helping me forget about the stack of paperwork on my desk or the to-do list I need to accomplish next week.

I'm in the moment.

This moment, with her.

And it's all kinds of perfect.

I have an army of dings and scratches by the end of the night. Red marks and bruises paint my body. My knees hurt and a Band-Aid got slapped on my elbow. As I kick the skates off and slip back into my boots, vowing to never step foot on the ice again, her laughter–louder than the music, brighter than the Christmas lights–eases the pain of all the aches.

SIXTEEN
BRIDGET

THE BAY WINDOW at the front of the store is covered in spray paint, adding a frosty look to the glass. Snowflakes are etched onto the rest of the surface, trickling from the roof to the ground. A wreath made by Chandler sits on the front door, small books overlaid in the branches. Inside the shop, tall candles line the windowsill, fake flames flickering in the waning afternoon sun. It's festive. Merry and bright. You can see the foundation of our theme as the store transforms.

I took a walk yesterday, interested to see what kind of designs the other participants were implementing. People, like I assumed, are going all-in on big ticket items. I found train sets looping around the floor of the flower shop. Outside the men's warehouse store, there was a ten-foot tall inflatable Santa, towering over the roofline. Cove Jewelers' window display had enough glitter and diamonds to rival the shops on New York's 5th Avenue.

All the stores were beautiful. Elaborate and detailed, they caught your eye from a block away. The twinkling lights and flashing signs drew you in, wanting to see more. When I came back through the door of our place, I grinned. I might be biased, but the subtle scent of chocolate and balsam hitting my nose was sweet and savory rather than overpowering.

The Christmas music playing over the speakers was calm, a quiet background noise to tap your foot along to the beat instead of an ear-splitting concert dominating the room. We draped holiday blankets over the backs of the recliners, the slight dip in temperature encouraging shoppers out of the cooler air and into the store.

There's no inflatable man out front greeting patrons and pedestrians, but we have a table for making your own ginger-bread cookies, complete with sprinkles and chocolate candies for toppings. It's been a hit with kids, parents thanking us profusely for giving them an activity to do while Mom and Dad browse the store.

Our space doesn't look like it belongs in the pages of a holiday catalog or magazine. It's more personable than staged or precise, an easy design one might do in their own home. It's a soft hint of festiveness that brings less impressed gasps of surprise and more nostalgic smiles.

It's exactly what we're going for. Maybe it's the wrong direc-tion to take. Maybe we should add a touch more gaudiness to the garland sitting atop the large wall bookshelf. Maybe we also need a choreographed light show synced up with a string quartet one of the owners had said they were hiring for the judg-ing. Our store feels *special*, though, a continuation of ourselves. So we're sticking with it.

My knees crack and creak as I lower myself from the loveseat I've occupied for the last hour to the floor. A string of white lights frame the window pane, making it look like it's snowing, blending with the stenciled flurries.

It's perfect.

"BB!"

Mac is charging through the doorway. A backpack is slung over her shoulder, and she heads toward me at full steam. Since Theo introduced us, she's been in and out of the store five or six times. Whenever she stops by, she asks for new book recommendations, nodding along while I rattle off a list of ideas I think she might enjoy. She'll jump onto a stool at the café counter, eating the piece of brownie I slide her way before hurrying back to the hardware store, wiping incriminating crumbs away from her mouth.

She's a great kid. Smart, funny, and kind, she always offers to help me unbox new arrivals or asks questions about why I pick certain books for the featured displays. Her presence is never cumbersome and always welcomed. I look forward to spending time with her, even if it's small quantities when Theo is running from place to place, his daughter hot on his heels. He's been bringing her around more frequently, and I still can't believe I went for so long without knowing she existed.

"Hey, kiddo. What's up?"

"My dad is on his way over. He said something about a crisis–a delivery arrived ahead of schedule. He's freaking out."

"Uh oh. That doesn't sound promising. Want to hang out with me until he gets here?"

Mac follows me to the café. Plopping onto a stool, she rummages through her backpack and pulls out a folder labeled **MATH**. "Normally I hang out with Grams and Gramps after school. Today Gramps is taking Grams to the doctor, so Dad had to pick me up."

"Is everything okay with your grams?"

"Yeah. She's fine. It's a routine thing."

"Glad to hear it. Are you hungry? Do you want a snack or some hot chocolate?"

"I'm starving," she declares.

"Awesome. Are cookies before dinner allowed?"

"Definitely allowed."

"Should I pretend to feed you hummus or something that's way more nutritious and not tell your dad?"

"Tell me what?"

Theo's voice travels from the door to the counter. He lumbers across the floor. His feet drag as he moves, haggard steps lagging behind their usual tempo. His hair is standing up on its ends. The closer he gets, the more details I can spot. There's a bead of sweat rolling down his cheek, falling into the dip of his neck. One sleeve of his shirt is rolled up above the elbow. The other isn't rolled at all.

"What the hell happened to you?" I ask. My eyes bounce to the smudge of dirt on his forehead. I notice the downward curve of his lips. The exhaustion radiating from him and how long it takes him to reach us at the counter. "Are you okay?"

Theo hangs his head. His hand snakes through his hair, attempting to tame it, and lets out an exasperated sigh. He's admitting defeat, I think, in a battle I'm unfamiliar with. "Besides still feeling the aftermath of ice skating days later? No. Many things are going wrong, and I'm far from okay."

I shuffle toward him. "What can I do to help?"

"I know this is a huge ask, and I hate to even bother you with it, but would you mind watching Mac for a bit? A couple hours, tops? A huge shipment came in and I don't want her in the stockroom when there are nails everywhere. I forgot my parents are busy today and I wasn't planning on spending the rest of my afternoon–"

"It's not a problem," I interrupt. "We can do some homework and decorate the first tree I brought in. It looks pathetic standing there without any lights."

"A tree?" Mac perks up, attention moving away from the worksheet in front of her to the fir sitting in the corner, begging to be adorned. "Dad, can I please stay?"

Theo stares at me, torn on what to do. "Are you sure? I can try and work something else out. Maybe Lucas can help."

"I'm positive. It's totally fine, and we'll be okay. Take all the time you need. We can order some pizza and hang out until you're finished. How does that sound, Mac and Cheese?"

She giggles at the nickname. "Pretty freaking sweet."

"You'll text me if anything happens? If you need something?" Theo asks.

"I promise."

"You'll let me know if you have somewhere to be?"

"My schedule is literally empty, but sure. I will."

"I'll be back the second we're finished."

"No rush. Seriously."

"Okay. If you're sure."

"I am sure. And wait. Before you leave." I grab a pair of tongs. Stuffing two blueberry muffins inside a to-go bag, I hand it over to him. "Take these. You look like a zombie. Those can hold you until you grab some pizza with us later."

The creases of his frown lines soften. I want to drag my finger there, between his scrunched brows, and smooth out the edges. The dark brown of his eyes grows warm and thankful. He shifts from my face to the pastries, then back again. When his gaze meets mine, he stares. I stare back, unafraid. Unyielding. He won't win this fight.

He raps the counter twice with his knuckles. "Thank you, Bridget. This–" He swallows and exhales. "Text me if you need anything."

"Will do. We'll see you later."

He leans down and presses a kiss to the top of Mac's head.

He walks to the door and pauses there, fingers gripping the knob. Tan over brass, he hesitates. Waits. For a minute, I think he's going to turn back around and say something else. He shakes his head once, deciding against the argument in his head, and departs through the exit, leaving Mac and me alone.

"I FORGOT how brutal the school workload is." I groan and rub my temples. We've been tackling Mac's homework for ninety minutes, and my brain is fried. "And you play soccer, too? You're like Wonder Girl."

Mac giggles and shoves her completed worksheets into her backpack. She's smart as hell, answering the questions before I could finish reading the first four words. We knocked out algebra and biology, and I can't take anymore talk about ecosystems or variables.

"I like school," she says. "I'm going to try and do some of the advanced placement classes in high school."

"As you should. You have the brain for it. Any idea about what you want to do when you grow up?"

She shrugs. "No, not really. I like writing. And reading. I like math, too. We'll see. I'm keeping an open mind like my dad says."

"Sometimes, on very, very rare occasions, your dad is right. Ready to get decorating?"

"Yes!"

I lead her over to the boxes I have set up. We pillage through the ornaments and start our work on the seven-foot green canvas waiting for us. While we weave the lights in and out of the branches, Mac tells me about her soccer team. She shares what positions she likes to play. I listen to her debate what gifts she should get her dad for Christmas, and I nix the idea of a suit jacket. We giggle over our chaotic attempt of evenly placed bulbs, the bottom of the tree looking far brighter than the top half. Mac asks me about the significance of some of the hanging ornaments and I talk about the year I spent studying abroad in London. When it comes time to put the star on, she climbs onto my shoulders and laughs so hard, it takes five tries to get it positioned right.

"I don't think we'll be winning any awards with this design." I grin as I set her back on the ground. "But, A for effort."

"We can call it abstract! I kind of like how wonky it looks."

"I'm not sure wonky is a great adjective, kid."

"Okay. What about unique?"

I hum. "We're getting there."

Mac snaps a picture of the finished product on her phone, and her smile dims as she stares at the device. "Hey, BB? Can I ask you something?"

"Sure. If you ask me about quantum physics I might not have the answer, but I'll help you find it."

Her chuckle is stilted and I frown, concerned about what question she might have. "There are some girls at school who have been kind of mean to me lately," she starts. "I thought we were friends, but all they talk about is how they think it's dumb Dad owns a hardware store while their parents work in an office. I—I never know what to say when they start talking about it. It's why I thought about getting him a suit jacket for Christmas. He'd look more professional. More like their dads. Do you think that would be a good idea?"

Embarrassment laces the admission. The toe of her shoe scuffs the floor, and she sniffs, wiping her nose. It took courage to share this with me, and I'm so flattered she thinks I'm a safe person to talk to. Before I can think twice or debate if I'm overstepping, I gather her into my arms and give her a hug. Small hands wrap around my waist and she squeezes me tight.

"Oh, sweetie," I breathe out. "Let's get some hot chocolate. I'll order us some pizza and if you feel like sharing what's going on, I'd love to listen. If not, we can just sit and not talk about anything. How does that sound?"

Mac sniffs again and pulls away, giving me a grateful look. "Perfect."

SEVENTEEN

BRIDGET

TEN MINUTES LATER, we're both holding mugs of steaming hot cocoa; marshmallows for her, none for me. We take a seat in a pair of recliners facing each other and Mac pulls her legs to her chest. Her chin drops to the top of her knees and she sighs.

"First things first. Dinner. What kind of pizza do you like?"

"Pepperoni and green pepper," she answers.

"Get the heck out. Those are my favorites, too. Let me order and text your dad, then I'm all ears."

Bridget: Hi! It's Bridget.

Theo: Is it? Your name at the top of my screen wasn't a dead giveaway.

Theo: What's up?

Bridget: How's everything going? Are you doing okay?

Theo: We're moving faster than I thought. We should be wrapping up soon.

> Bridget: Oh, good! Mac finished her homework. Man, the algebra shit is hard, isn't it?

Theo: It makes me feel woefully inept. Thanks for helping her, by the way.

> Bridget: I'm not sure how much help I was. She can run circles around me.

Theo: Don't worry. She does the same with me.

> Bridget: Phew. I wanted to see if you could pick up pizzas for us if I order them. Maybe on your way back over?

Theo: Yeah. Let me know when and where. I'll grab them.

Theo: And how much too. I'm not letting you pay for them.

> Bridget: Oops! Too late. Thirty minutes from Antonio's up the road.

Theo: It's like you purposely want to piss me off.

Pizza ordered, I toss my phone to the side and give Mac my undivided attention. "Do you want to talk?"

She nods and heaves out a sigh, a heaviness settling in the air. There's a maturity to her emotions, like she's lived far longer than her age dictates.

"I love my dad," she starts. "A lot."

"I know that. *He* knows that," I assure her.

"A girl in my class said Dad must not be very smart if he works around tools all the time. Someone also said he only got the job because of his parents, and he doesn't have to actually work to make money. But I know how much time he spends at the store. He's there a lot. He could give some duties to other people, he just won't. Uncle Lucas talked to him about it once, and my dad blew him off, saying something about personal responsibilities."

"Mac, your dad is very smart. I got my degree in business management, and running a successful company is a helluva lot harder than being an employee at an entry-level position with a large corporation. Making all the important decisions? Paying people so they can afford to put food on their table? Figuring out budgets and insurance all by yourself while you're not making millions of dollars a year? It's really, really difficult.

"Girls your age can be mean. Some outgrow it. Others don't. Maybe they're bitter that your dad comes home for dinner every night, while theirs are distracted by their cell phones. Maybe they are jealous you get to hang out with him whenever you want. Or, maybe, they are brats who will never learn to be kind."

"Yeah." Mac nods. "Maybe."

I know this is an important conversation for us to have, and I want to say the right things. I want to give Mac guidance and not dismiss her. What she's going through is a big deal, and I can tell it's weighing on her.

"Theo loves you so much. I've known you existed for like, two minutes, and I can tell you without any doubt, you are his entire world. What you say means a lot to him. Have you talked to him about how much he works? Or about the people who are being unkind?"

"No." She puffs out another sigh. "Sometimes..." A frown and a shake of her head. "It's too terrible to say."

I shrug and take a sip from my drink. "There's no judgment here. You can also keep it to yourself. Both are good options."

"Sometimes I wish I had someone else to talk to besides him. Like a mom or a sister. Not in place of him," she amends quickly. "Just like, they're there too. Grams is nice, but she's older. I feel like I'm alone with all these stupid changes I'm going through. If I told Dad some of this stuff he'd think it was his fault, like he did something wrong. He'd *flip* if he heard what that girl said." Mac takes a breath after the long-winded revelation. "I love him, and he's the best dad in the world. I know I'm his priority, but what about the other things that make him happy? He can't love work *that* much, can he?"

"How old are you?" I ask her.

"Twelve. I'll be thirteen right before Christmas."

"Your self-awareness is freaking impressive. Sweetie, he'll listen to you. Nothing you can do will ever make him not happy. Trust me. If you think he works too much, you should tell him. And forget those girls. Someone's job doesn't define them as a person."

"Can you talk to him for me?"

"Nice try, squirt. I'm at the bottom of the totem pole of people Theo cares about. I don't have a lot of pull."

Mac considers my statement thoughtfully. "That's not true. He was really nervous to introduce us. He wouldn't shut up on the walk over that afternoon and kept saying the stupidest things. When we left the store after meeting you, he was smiling in the car. He smiles sometimes, but not as much as he used to. And definitely not from letting me meet a stranger."

I take another sip of my scalding beverage to keep my lungs from seizing. "He did?"

"Yeah. When I asked him about it, he told me to mind my business."

I grin. I can picture it now. The roll of his eyes, the denial. The grumble under his breath as he insists she's making things up. All bark and no bite, trying to change the subject from her prying questions.

"Wait." Mac's feet drop to the floor and she sits up straight. "You're smiling, too!"

"Am not! You're seeing things."

"All you adults and your secrets. It's unfair. What should I do about the girls?"

"Kill them with kindness. Invite them to the store. Ignore them. The nicer you are, the more likely they are to drop it. People hate when their words don't have an impact."

"You're not that old, BB, but you're really smart."

"I appreciate your backhanded compliment," I laugh. "Are you feeling better?"

"Yeah, I am. Thanks for talking with me. I appreciate it."

"You can talk to me about anything. I'm happy to listen and give an unbiased opinion. Unless it's something dangerous to yourself or others, my lips are sealed."

"Do you have a boyfriend?"

I blush at the abrupt question. Damn kids and their lack of filter. "No. I don't."

"Why not?"

"For the record, there's nothing wrong with being alone. I guess I've always kind of settled instead of holding out for the love I deserve. Which you should never, ever do, by the way. So now I'm just waiting until something feels right. Owning the store doesn't give me a ton of free time, either, so packing in the dates is difficult."

"You could date my dad. I said the same thing to him about you."

"Okay, matchmaker. I see what's going on here. Theo and I are... we're different kinds of people. Night and day. Hot and cold. Summer and winter. I'm pretty sure I annoy him."

"Anna annoyed Kristoff in the beginning of *Frozen*."

"The next Disney movie featuring your father, scowls and all, will really sell tickets," I laugh. "He needs someone who can ground him, I think. Reserved. Relaxed. I'm not really any of those things."

"Or maybe," Mac counters, smug and mighty, "he needs someone who's *not* like him. Look where it's gotten him. He's old and alone, spending his Sunday afternoons waiting for me to finish a manicure. I bet the night gets lonely sometimes, wishing for some sunshine. Different isn't always bad."

"That's true, but–"

"I think," she continues, "he's waiting for someone who can put up with him long enough to throw a glass of water in his face."

"Wow. Is that all it takes to pass your matchmaking test?"

"You haven't done that, have you?"

"No, but I've been scarily close."

"See," she says. "You called him out the first time I met you. No one else, well, maybe besides Uncle Lucas and Uncle Baxter, could ever do that and live to tell the tale."

"I think that's enough meddling for one night, kid. Maybe you can try again tomorrow. Do you want to help me take a couple photos for the store's social media page? I'm trying to show some behind-the-scenes content from the contest. I bet they'd love to see the final product of our dreadful decorating endeavor."

We head back to the tree, posing for photo after photo. My thumb clicks away, filling my storage with pictures of me and Mac. She jumps on my back and flings her arms out. I stick out my tongue and she throws up a peace sign. We lie on the ground and take a shot from above, faces bathed in white lights as we make pretend snow angels.

When a pair of work boots bracket my hips, I jump.

"Holy crap," I say. I look up to find Theo standing above me, steaming pizza boxes in his hand and a smirk on his face.

"Am I interrupting something?"

"Dad!" Mac springs up and gives him a hug. "Look at the tree we decorated."

"It looks great. Can you take these to the counter, sweetheart? We'll be over in a minute." Theo passes the boxes to Mac, who marches away with purpose.

"Hey," I say.

"Hey. Did she behave? No rebelling? Any secret tattoos I should know about? Is she part of the Bowie clan now, too?"

"She was a perfect angel. We finished her homework. Decorated. Took some photos. It's how I ended up on the floor. Guess I need to get up now, huh?"

"You could stay down there if you want."

"View isn't too bad." I smile at him.

He tilts his head to the side, studying me, and I get a smile in return. "Not bad from up here, either. Do you want some help?"

"That'd be great."

He crouches down and extends a hand my way. Our palms connect, thumbs locking against each other. He doesn't yank me up, not right away. He stares at the bob of my throat, the dip of my shirt.

His fingers run over the back of my palm. Down to my wrist, up to my fingertips, charting unexplored territories. My eyelashes flutter closed, the faint touch almost enough to undo me. I savor the smell of blueberries, of pine and paint clinging to his clothes. I inhale, reveling in the familiarity.

Another hand finds my left arm. His palm makes its way back to the spot he's been before. The spot that missed his presence, calloused, warm. Gentle, yet firm.

I smile again. It still feels as nice as the first time.

"Going to lift you now, okay?" he asks. Gruff, full of steel. Notching its way down my vertebrae.

"Okay."

He pulls me to my feet and his hands keep me stable until I'm back on two feet. His breath is scorching on my forehead, down my neck, and everywhere in between. Long fingers are still locked with mine, no urgency or rush to let go.

"How was the delivery?"

"A shit show, but bearable. You're sure Mac wasn't too much of a pain?"

I look over his shoulder, finding his daughter already digging into the pizza. She rips off a piece of crust and slyly hands it to Ziggy. "You've got a good kid, Gardner. She's smart. Well-spoken. Kind. A bit of a meddler, but still awesome. I hope you know how special she is."

Theo squeezes my palm before he lets go. "Yeah," he says. "I do. I'm glad you get to see it, too."

"Do you like pepperoni pizza?"

"It's my favorite."

"Green peppers?"

"I'm a fan."

"Would you like to eat pizza with us?" I ask.

This time when Theo smiles, it's a full-on grin. His whole body leans into it. Jovial eyes. Relaxed shoulders. It's teeth and lips and puffed out cheeks. A cluster of leftover muffin crumbs. A magnet, a string, a yank and a tug trying to pull me closer.

"Yeah, Bridget," he says. I like how my name sounds coming from him. "I'd love to."

I raise on my toes, knock his shoulder with mine, and head to the counter with him by my side.

It's silly how normal all of this feels. Spending time with his daughter. Throwing quips at him. Pulling apart stringy pizza and going through fifteen napkins. It's like we've done it for years. Easy, effortless, fun. I look at Theo as I open the pastry display case to grab us dessert. There are three hundred colored lights reflecting in his glasses, but I notice he's only looking at me.

It's silly how much I like it.

EIGHTEEN

BRIDGET

Bridget: Hi!

Theo: Hey. What's up?

Bridget: I have a favor to ask.

Theo: Let's hear it.

Bridget: How would you feel about accompanying me to a Christmas tree lot and watching me purchase six trees?

Theo: Six trees? What the hell are you going to do with that many?

Bridget: I have ideas.

Bridget: You could bring Mac!

Theo: She's at a friend's house tonight.

Theo: But sure. I'll go with you.

Bridget: Can we use your car?

Bridget: Before you say no, let me throw in the offer to buy you ice cream after.

Bridget: Really sweetens the deal, huh?

Theo: Stop with the puns.

Theo: They're really melting your delivery.

Bridget: Oh my god. Was that a joke? Do you have a concussion? Are you sick?

Theo: Send me your address. You close early on Saturdays, right?

Bridget: Yeah. We close at 4:30.

Theo: I'll pick you up at six.

Bridget: Can't wait! I'm going to sprinkle in some Christmas cheer!

Theo: If I knew how to put my phone on Do Not Disturb, I would. The puns are getting worse.

Theo: Good bye, Bridget.

Bridget: Bye, Theo! I cone hardly wait.

Bridget: Okay that one was stupid. Please don't block me. I really need your car. It's bigger than mine.

Bridget: Bye!

"NO ICE CREAM JOKES ALLOWED," Theo warns me through the passenger side window of his black truck. I pull the door handle and find it locked. He slants a serious stare my way, and I can tell he's not kidding. "No entry until you agree."

"Okay, you Grinch. I swear I won't make any more ice cream jokes." The door unlocks and I jump inside. "Thank you."

"Hey, Boylston. How was your Saturday? Busy day at work?"

I wiggle my butt back, finding a comfortable position. The seat heater is on the lowest setting, the cloth fabric warm against the back of my bare thighs. The windows are rolled down and the wind kicks up my hair as Theo shifts the car to drive, setting off down the road. I exhale a sigh, feeling weightless and content. There's something refreshing about being outside and chasing the last remaining light of day. My arm out the window, fingers gliding through the wind. In front of us, the sun begins to set, dipping below the horizon line and casting the world in orange and yellow.

"It was good. We're closed on Sundays, so Saturday afternoons can be mayhem. It's a good mayhem, though. It makes the time go by fast. I baked. I did a fun read along with some kids. I blinked, and the afternoon was over."

"What book did you read?" he asks, flipping on his blinker. He leans forward, checking the side mirror as he merges lanes.

He's ditched his usual flannel tonight, opting for a plain white tee. The thin piece of cotton stretches over his chest, hugging his bare biceps. Strong, defined muscles peep out under the hem of his sleeves, veins running along the length of his arms down to his palms. His beautiful body art is on display, a kaleidoscope of color catching in the sunset, etchings glowing bright.

I want to trace the outline of the markings, learning all the shapes they make and the hidden stories and meanings behind each one. Which is his favorite? Were any done impulsively, inked one night in a drunken stupor?

"*Where The Wild Things Are,*" I answer. "It's my favorite."

"I haven't heard of that one."

I shift my body to face him, pulling my leg onto the seat. My left shoulder leans against the headrest. I like looking at him from the side; he's got a nice profile. Chiseled jaw. A slight raise of his lips. Eyes darting to me then back to the road.

"It's a classic. Did you ever read to Mac when she was growing up? Do you have a favorite story?"

Theo is pensive for a moment, eyes turning a wistful shade of brown as he slips into a memory. He rubs the back of his neck with his right hand before resting his arm on the center console. His fingers drum the leather gear shift, tapping to the beat of the tune on the radio, notes crooning softly through the car.

"I don't have a favorite story. I read to her some when she was younger, but singing was the more regular occurrence. She loved it," he says.

"Please tell me you serenaded her with classic rock. Is there a video of a young Mac singing along to the Sex Pistols somewhere?"

He chuckles. "I'd make up all these stupid songs. If there was a tree, I'd start singing about leaves and branches. If there was a yellow car, I'd try to find a word to rhyme with taxi. She was too young to understand what I was saying, but she would grin at me whenever I started a tune. This toothless, bright smile. Guess I wasn't too terrible."

"It sounds like you missed your calling to be a musician."

"Hardly. You've met my daughter; the kid smiles at anything. I could've said the word 'dog' nineteen times in a row and she would've laughed. It was nice, though, those quiet moments we got to spend together."

I sit back, relaxing. A Bowie song begins on the radio. "Heroes." I smile at the tune, one of my favorites. Theo's fingers shift to the steering wheel and drum over the stitching, the beat memorized. His lips mouth along to the lyrics, like he's sung it a hundred times before.

This is the first time we've been alone together outside the stores. When I texted him earlier and proposed the plan, I didn't expect him to agree. He probably had a dozen other things he could have done tonight instead of picking out trees with me.

But here we are. Side by side. His arm inches away from mine. The breeze kicking up those brown locks and whipping them across his forehead in an unruly manner. The hint of a smile on his face as the music switches to Led Zeppelin.

I can't help but think this is the most handsome he's ever looked. The most laid back, too. Maybe the two go together, getting to witness a man letting loose on a very rare occasion in his busy life is wildly attractive. There's a tingle zipping through me with all of these observations. A throb between my legs as I wonder how the scruff of his cheek would feel against my inner thighs. How would his hand look in mine? What would those tattoos look like under the light of the moon, wrapped in bed sheets of silk?

I'm not sure what's different. I'm not sure what's changed. Perhaps it's the warmth radiating from him and raising my body temperature like a burning furnace. Maybe it's the realization of knowing I don't *have* to talk to him, but I can if I want. The simple understanding we're both content to just *be*, the road in front of us and the peaceful, easy enjoyment of the person by our side.

Whatever the explanation, whatever the cause, I like it. I like the shift from cordial strangers to feeling like I know him, deeply, in some way. I like this relaxed version of him. A smile, a slide of his glasses, the brush of his shirt against mine. Street lamps above illuminating his eyes. There's a glitter of a twinkle, just barely, but enough to know he's happy to be here.

So am I.

"Thanks for coming with me tonight," I say, the first to break the silence. "I really appreciate it."

"What's the idea behind six trees? You and Mac already decorated one, so it'll be seven total?"

"My thought process was 'why not'? Why not have seven trees and line them up in a little tree trail? Each person in the store is going to decorate one. That's four trees. I also wanted customers to be able to participate while they browse the shop. I cut out little book shaped ornaments so they can write their favorite titles out and attach it to the branches."

"That's a cool idea. Okay, that's five. What are you going to do with the last one?"

"It's open-ended for now."

"But you already decided to buy it?"

"Yeah. It's hard to describe without sounding silly. When I was falling asleep and counting them, my brain kept saying: *no. You need six, not five.* Somewhere down the road, I'm going to find a place for that tree. I don't know why. I don't know how. But I will."

Theo glances at me from across the truck. "That's not silly."

"It's not?"

"No. You have this unique way of finding a purpose for things, Bridget. This whole contest you've shifted away from the mindset of beating the other stores to getting the chance to show off things we find special. And that's really cool."

A short drive later, we pull up to a tree lot on the edge of Park Cove. It's a little cooler out here, away from the city center. It's quieter and darker, too, the sounds of nature more noticeable than the clank of a car puttering over the brick road through downtown. I jump out of the truck and inhale, welcomed by scents of pine and wood shavings. Theo follows behind me as we approach the first of many tents, ready to begin our search.

"I'll admit I was expecting an offering of a dozen trees,

maybe, not hundreds. What am I looking for? What's the criteria? Do you have a rubric?"

"Nope. No rubric. I liked the one Mac and I put together. It leaned a little to the left. It was a little wobbly. It wasn't perfect, but it still looked good."

"Left learners," he confirms with a nod, like I've given him the most vital piece of information. "We might be here all night."

TWO HOURS and six trees later, we've successfully wrangled all of my purchases into the trunk of Theo's truck.

We're panting from exertion. With as much stealth as I can muster, I tell Theo I'll be right back, making up a flimsy excuse about needing to grab one last thing from the lot. I take in Theo's shirt as I retreat, stained and ripped at the collar. My own arms are covered in sap and pine needles. I have red scratches on my legs, below the cuff of my denim shorts, after insisting I could lift a fifty-pound tree by myself. Theo had stood back and let me try, arms crossed and head shaking. After I gritted out his name and a few *goddammit*s and *mother fucker*s, he finally intervened. Lifting the object with ease, he proclaimed through *tut*s and *tsk*s that he wasn't the only stubborn one.

The marks on our limbs and stains on our clothes only serve as evidence of how much fun we've had. We strolled down a candy cane pathway lining the rows of trees. Families came and went; some in matching sweaters, some arguing. A few groups sipped hot chocolate, pausing for a photo in front of a reindeer display. Jubilant laughter rang through the air like bells. Theo and I had a solid ten-minute argument about the most underrated Christmas song. He was willing to die on a hill for "Merry Christmas Everybody" by Slade. I proclaimed "I Wish it Could be Christmas Everyday" by

Wizzard is the real dark horse of the season. He stared at me, flabbergasted, and shook his head in disappointment. Bickering aside, it was the first time this year I truly felt the holiday season upon us.

There were twinkling lights and some humming along to "Jingle Bell Rock." Fake snow falling on our heads and a large wooden sleigh I forced Theo to sit in as I took his photo. When I tried to shove a Santa hat on his head, he plucked the article of clothing from my hand and threw it in the trash, grumbling under his breath.

The best part of the night wasn't the festiveness. Wasn't the holiday tunes or the free wreath the cashier added to my purchase after I spent so much money.

It was Theo.

A totally out-of-his-element, living-in-the-moment, *fun* Theo.

I'd thought he would drag his feet after the first few minutes, conveying boredom or annoyance I was taking too long. I'd prepared myself for eye rolls and huffs of irritation. None came. He stood thoughtfully in front of each selection, nodding his head in approval or shaking his head if he thought it should be a pass. We debated options, him passionately declaring the tree in his hand was a hint more green than the one I was holding and would look better in the store.

Halfway through the evening, I scared him by popping out from behind an arrangement of plastic Santas. The bombardment of four letter words I was awarded definitely would have gotten us in trouble if anyone had been around to hear. I wish I had captured the terror on his face on my phone.

Later, we stopped for a beverage to keep our spirits up. He retaliated by purposely handing me a cup of black coffee instead of hot chocolate. When I spit the beverage out in disgust, he keeled over, clutching his sides and howling with a loud burst of laughter. I couldn't bring myself to be mad. The sound was so pure, so genuine, so carefree my own laugh was uncontainable. It had been rich, overflowing with glee and delight, the most boisterous I'd ever heard him.

So now, as he stomps back onto the lot and finds me attempting to hide for the second time, he mumbles under his breath about how he knows what I'm doing. He tells me I suck at being sneaky and tosses me over his shoulder like a light sack of feathers, not an adult woman weighing 150 pounds as he walks us back to his truck.

It's hot as hell. The grip on the back of my thighs is tight, possessive, and hard enough to leave a mark. His fingers toy with the hem of my shorts, playing with the strands of frayed denim that have come loose. As he walks us back to his truck, his touch dances across my bare skin methodically, lazily. My laughter dies in my throat when I realize I want him to inch higher. To keep skating up, up, up, under my shorts to the underwear he's *so close* to slipping inside. I want–I *need*–him to pull the zipper down with his teeth, eyes on me as he finds out how turned on I am.

In his arms, I watch the corded muscles of his back stretch and strain. I see the faintest traces of gray beginning to pepper his brunette hair. I can rest my hand in the valley of his shoulder blades, daringly rubbing once, the material of his shirt soft against my palm. The ragged exhale he expels is magnified in the stillness of the empty tent, and he holds his breath when my fingers drift up to the nape of his neck, using the tufts of his hair to steady myself.

Far too soon he's setting me back on the ground. I chance a glance at him, finding his cheeks painted a bright candy cane red. He turns away from me so quickly, I think I might have done something wrong. As he walks around the front of his car, I catch him adjusting the front of his jeans. He flexes his hand and gazes at the sky, muttering under his breath.

I think he might have liked having me in his arms.

I liked it, too.

"How do you feel about food?" asks Theo.

"I'm generally a fan. I'm so hungry, I could eat anything. I can still taste that coffee, too, and I want to gag."

"Don't play the game if you can't accept the consequences, Boylston." We're moving slowly off the lot as we head for the exit, precious cargo bumping and sliding unsteadily in the trunk. "Pick what we're having."

"Burgers."

"Burgers it is."

He's grinning as we drive to dinner. I reach over and turn the volume up on the radio, a Queen song blaring through the car. His seat is positioned far too close to the steering wheel to accommodate the trees, but he remains unbothered, belting out the lyrics along with me. A water bottle gets tossed my way after I complain, again, about the coffee residue. His eyes roll, but they lack any actual irritation.

This is the moment—the horrifyingly, spectacular, *incredible* moment—I realize I have a crush on Theo Gardner.

NINETEEN
THEO

WE COMMANDEER a secluded picnic table off to the side of the burger shack. I sit on the bench, plastic creaking under my weight. Bridget takes the space to my right rather than across from me, thigh pressing into mine. I don't bother arguing, because I like her there. I take a bite of my burger, staring at the woods in front of us. A breeze, light and chilled, billows through the trees above, a scatter of leaves fluttering to the asphalt.

With only two weeks until Thanksgiving, the month of November is flying by faster than I'd like. I realize the competition has been a distraction, a reprieve allowing me to focus on other parts of life besides the usual conflicting feelings that dredge up during the holiday season.

This year is different. The only things raising my damn blood pressure lately are the bruises and welts on my ass from the night of ice skating, faded purple and yellow marks still covering my skin.

Well, and when Bridget was slung over my shoulder an hour ago. I got *hard* when she wiggled and laughed, ass practically in my face as she grinded against me. Her skin was smooth under my palm. I could feel her heart thumping against my shoulder.

She parted her thighs, barely a millimeter, and I had to set her down before I did something stupid, like tug her behind a tree and kiss her senseless.

Or sink to my knees and go down on her.

"So," Bridget says. "I have a question."

She's considerate in her dialogue, I've noticed, never diving straight to the point. It's always a twisty, roundabout way of talking to make sure the person is comfortable with proceeding.

"Ask away."

"You don't have to answer if you don't want to."

"You've been around me long enough to know I wouldn't answer otherwise."

"Seriously, I won't be offended."

My hand twitches, quelling the urge to reach over and clamp down on her bouncing thigh. I pick up a greasy fry instead. "Any day now would be great."

Bridget pauses. I shift my hips so I can look at her straight on. The tip of her tongue is caught between her teeth. She taps her cheek in rapid succession, causing the dangling snowman earrings she's wearing to shake and shimmer under the fluorescent lamp from above. There's a debate waging in her head, the conviction in her desire to finally talk is obvious. Her shoulders straighten, she takes a deep breath. Then, she speaks.

"What happened to Mac's mom?"

I knew this conversation would come up eventually. The inquisition dives deep into the category of Personal Shit I Keep Close to my Heart. It's intimate, not information I grant many people access to. So, naturally, I'm surprised it took Bridget this long to ask. It's usually one of the first questions out of someone's mouth when they find out I'm raising a kid on my own.

"Are you divorced?"

"Do you have sole custody?"

"Is she alive?"

Bridget, I'm finding, is not like other people. There's the urge to be honest and forthcoming. To sit down and tell her everything she wants to know. I don't want to share parts of myself with the world, but I want to share parts of myself with her. I take a breath and slide my glasses up my nose. My neck rolls from the right to the left. And I begin.

"Mac was born on December 23rd. We took her home on Christmas Day. She was a big surprise. Not planned at all. Stephanie–her mom–and I had been dating for three years. I was planning on buying a ring at the start of the new year. We weren't sure if children were a part of our future plans, and we were always careful when we were together. But accidents happen." I frown at my poor word choice. "I'm not calling Mac an accident or mistake."

"I didn't take it that way," Bridget assures me. She scoots an inch closer. "I promise."

"We spent that Christmas with our families, bouncing back and forth to let them meet the new addition. At the end of the day, we went to our place and put Mac to bed, taking turns watching her sleep. We didn't want to leave her alone for longer than a second. She was such a beautiful baby, and we couldn't stop staring at her."

"Theo. You don't–"

"I woke up late the next morning. I was exhausted from all the excitement. When I rolled over, the bed was empty. Mac was wailing from down the hall. Her diaper was dirty and she was hungry. Stephanie was gone. There wasn't a note. No voicemail. Not a damn text message. I thought something had happened to her, then I saw her dresser drawers were cleaned out. The suitcase I bought her for her birthday was gone. Her purse wasn't on the kitchen table like it was the night before. Two days stretched to five, which stretched to a week, then three. On Mac's one month birthday, she had the audacity to call. She said she would be back soon. 'Just another week or two' she told me. She needed *time*. Then she had a field day pointing out everything wrong with me. She told me I was too difficult to be around. I was selfish. I never made her happy and we weren't compatible. A baby wasn't what she wanted. Things she had never, ever voiced before."

"The fucking nerve," Bridget hisses.

"I researched postpartum depression. Mental health statistics in new moms. I was trying to figure out what the hell was going on. That's when I realized she wasn't coming back. It wasn't a temporary thing. It was permanent. And I took it hard. People told me to get over it. They said to move on. Clearly *I* was the issue if a new mother wanted to leave her baby so soon. They pitied her and I got the blame. When she left, everything became convoluted. It was like this expansive void of darkness and sorrow. I became a shell of a man, not knowing who I was anymore. Hollow. Broken. Her words stung. I know I'm not the easiest to be around sometimes, but hearing that from someone who claimed to love you? Who you talked about *forever* with? It's brutal. I internalized all those thoughts and feelings until one day I got off my ass, sat down in a therapist's office, spilled my guts, and here we are."

"Oh, Theo," she whispers. The quiet words cascade over my shoulders. Down my arms. It's a hug without any physical touch. A stroke against my heart, an alleviation of some of the pain. She *sees* me, and I'm letting her.

"So, there you go. Mac's the love of my life, and I'm so lucky to have her. As much as that period of time hurt really fucking bad, it also brought me her. And I can't imagine not having her around."

"Did you ever track down her mom?"

"No. A mutual friend told me she found someone better in Pennsylvania. It's where she ended up. She hasn't written, hasn't sent a birthday card or a Christmas gift. Most days I forget she exists."

"Better than you?" Bridget asks. Her question is sharp, serrated with anger.

My gaze trips from the piece of mulch I've made my focal point up to her face. There's a ferocity there. Protectiveness, almost. "What do you mean?"

"I'm just..." She huffs and shakes her head, brown hair spiraling everywhere. "You're smart. Hardworking. Successful and kind. Funny when you want to be, which is rare, but your jokes aren't terrible. You're good looking. A fantastic father, successful business owner. How the hell do you get better than that? Does the dude have two dicks or something?"

A laugh bursts out of me. "Wow. That was a long list of compliments. Are you flirting with me, Boylston?"

She rolls her eyes and kicks my shin. "You'd know if I was flirting with you. I'm abysmal at it. It'd probably be done through a joke. Have you dated anyone since?"

"Here and there. A couple flings. Some lasted two or three dates. Some were purely physical. Nothing's stuck. Women have told me I don't give them enough attention. They might be right. I guess I'd rather learn to braid Mac's hair than sit in a stuffy restaurant wearing a tie and a real shirt."

"Yeah," Bridget agrees. "You'd look positively ghastly in a button-up."

"Your sarcasm is far from endearing."

"Must not be too terrible, because you're still here, aren't you?"

I smile at the quip. I *am* still here, sitting on a bench that's poking my ass in the back of a nearly deserted parking lot. A lukewarm burger in my hand and an almost empty cup of fries between us. I'm not eyeing my truck, searching for an escape. My phone buzzed in my pocket ten minutes ago, and I haven't bothered to retrieve it, too focused on the woman next to me, the Christmas sweater–and her–taking up all of my attention.

"Guess you have a point."

"Is that why you're afraid of people leaving? Because she did?"

"Yeah. I'm not still in love with her nor do I harbor these emotions toward her, and if I saw her today, I'm not sure I'd feel anything, really. It wasn't the disappointment of *her* leaving me, but rather someone I'd spent all this time with. I shared memories and years with this person, and she easily walked away. Like it had no effect on her, and there I was, sifting through a million questions I didn't have the answer to. I *still* don't have the answer to them. Am I the problem? What will the next person think? A couple of my close friends also stopped hanging out with me after Mac was born, saying I wasn't as much fun as I used to be. Well, no shit. I have a kid I'm in charge of. I can't close down the bar when I'm busy warming up baby bottles. At this point in life, I don't expect anyone to stick around."

"She wasn't meant for you, Theo. You probably know that by now. The person you're supposed to be with will see these parts of you, the parts that others might not have liked, and embrace them. They'll welcome them with open arms. She called you selfish, but that's so far from the truth. Would a selfish person try to be home for dinner every night? Would a selfish person let Felicity off work early last week for a Bar Mitzvah and cover the rest of her shift? Offer to watch the register for six minutes while Chandler runs to the pharmacy and refills her prescription? It's sad you spent three years with that woman, and she has no clue who you really are. I know you were hurt by her, but how freaking lucky are you that now you have the chance to find someone who will stay, and be glad to do so?"

It's a good perspective. Lucas often tells me similar things, but coming from her, coming from a woman, coming from someone who has started to see these bits and pieces of me, it makes everything feel more... hopeful. Like it could maybe, *maybe* happen.

"I'm not sure where I'm supposed to find this mysterious woman. In the doorknob aisle?"

"Oh my god, what if you did? Think of all the knock-knock jokes you could tell!"

I groan. "I thought we were past all the jokes."

"Sorry, pal, they're not ending anytime soon. Can I ask you another question?"

"This is the most I've talked to someone who isn't my therapist, my best friend or my kid in years, so we might as well keep the ball rolling."

She takes a bite of her burger. Ketchup drips onto the pavement and a drop runs down her hand. I want to use my tongue to lick it up and bite the inside of her wrist.

"What's your proudest moment in life?"

"Being Mac's dad," I say automatically. "I swear I do more things in life than parent her, but it's the truth. I was scared shitless in the beginning, afraid to mess up. And, fuck, I messed up a lot. I thought I'd get bored over time. Waking up and making lunches every day? Helping with homework? It had to get monotonous at some point, right? I figured after the first few years I'd start to resent the tasks associated with fatherhood, burnt out from doing things alone. I didn't, though. I love them more and more each day. Every morning I wake up, fucking *stoked* to slather peanut butter and jelly on bread, watch her do her homework, and buy her nail polish. I'm so... I'm so fucking excited to be her dad. And the coolest part is I'm not just a dad. I'm a *girl dad*, and it's the best fucking role in the entire world. How lucky am I?"

Bridget is listening rapturously. With a sniff of her nose and a wipe of her eyelashes, she dips her chin, attempting to hide her emotions. I reach out, tentative and unsure, placing my palm on her cheek. My thumb catches a falling tear, and I wipe it away. She leans into the gesture and nestles into my hold.

"God," she whispers. She puffs out a breath, warmth tickling my hand. "I wish you'd let other people see you how I see you."

"How do you see me?" I whisper back. My voice shakes and I'm afraid to hear the answer.

"You have so much depth, Theo," she starts. My name is sweet like honey, each syllable dripping in decadence and something akin to *care*. "I understand why you try to keep people out, but you have so much to offer. I'm so sorry anyone's ever told you otherwise. You're not difficult. You're not hostile or unpleasant. You're a little prickly, but that's okay. Even roses have thorns. You're loyal. Passionate. You have so much love in your heart to give and nowhere to share it because you think, and rightfully so, someone's going to snatch it and never return. You're... you. And it's a really, really wonderful you."

Wonderful is not a word I've been called before. It's not an adjective I'd associate with myself, far brighter and cheerier than my personality allows. From Bridget, who's sunshine incarnate and lightyears beyond *wonderful* herself, it's the best compliment I could ever receive. It makes me want to be better. To smile more. To loosen the reins of rigidity and allow myself to welcome the description, trying it out for size.

"You need to stop saying nice things to me," I murmur. My hand moves from her cheek to her shoulder, pressing her side fully into mine. Bodies aligned, her hair tickles my neck, and a drop of mustard falls onto my jeans, a splatter of yellow staining the denim. "I'm not sure I deserve the praise."

"That's where you're wrong," Bridget says. It's firm and certain, not an opinion she's going to debate. Her finger, painted red with little green wreaths on the nail, presses into my chest, directly above my racing heart. I think she bruises and brands the organ in the process, creating a new tattoo on my body. "You *do* deserve it. You *are* worthy. And I like seeing this... this soft side of you. It makes me feel special."

You are special, hangs on the tip of my tongue. "Can I ask you a question?" gets said instead.

"Theo." It's still as sweet as the dozens of other times she's said it before. Sweet like the warm blueberry muffins she hands me across the laminate counter. Sweet like the extra cinnamon she sprinkles on top of my drinks. "This isn't a give and take sort of thing. You can ask me anything."

"What would make you happy in life? Tell me what would light up your world."

She hums. "I want a house with lots of dogs. Lots of acres and plenty of space for them to run around. I want to curl up on the couch and have a man on the other end, smiling at me. I want to watch lightning bugs in a field. I want game nights and movie nights with friends. I want to make love on a blanket in tall grass, nothing but nature around us. I want to fuck in the back of a truck, rough and dirty as the windows fog up. I want to run in a rainstorm, soaked to the bone and frozen to the core, dancing under the drops. I want a white Christmas with snow everywhere and a cozy fireplace. I want to make snow angels and a snowman until my hands are numb from the cold. I want to laugh and scream and cry and... and just feel alive. I want to be wild and free, settled and stable. God, I want so much. Too much, I think. I'll never be able to have it all. I dream too big, but it doesn't change how *badly* I crave those silly, joyful things."

Her soliloquy wounds me. It's a shot straight through my body, a bloody arrow coming out the other side. It punctures every organ along the way. My brain turns to liquid mush. There's a rushing sound in my ears, waves crashing around me. The only thing I can process is the need... the urge... the strangling desire to give her everything, *everything* she asked for. And more.

How many dogs? Eight? You got it, angel.

Running in the rain? I'll hand you a towel at the finish line and shelter you from the storm.

Making love on a blanket in the grass? I'll pick you a bouquet of flowers after, daffodils and dandelions tucked behind your ear.

I scoot away from her. Drag my ass across the plastic, farther and farther away. I rub my pectoral muscles, trying to soothe the lingering lonely ache that's been persistent for years–decades– slowly crumbling away with more and more of her words.

"Theo? Are you okay?"

Her voice is calming. Nurturing. A flower blooming out of an assault of weeds, victoriously prevailing from the dirt and ready to brighten the world.

"Those... those aren't too big of dreams," I say. My voice cracks and I clear my throat. "You deserve that. The rainstorms. The dogs. All of it. And more."

"Glad to know I'm not reaching for the stars. Now it's your turn. Tell me what would make *you* happy."

"This," I say earnestly. "This makes me happy, Bridget."

Bridget laughs, light and gentle, slicing through the quiet of the night. "This makes me happy too, Theo. Really stinking happy."

As she stands from the bench and offers me a hand, salt from the French fries sticking to my palm, and a smile on her face, I think this might be one of the best nights of my life.

TWENTY

BRIDGET

UNTANGLING CHRISTMAS LIGHTS is not how I thought I'd be spending my afternoon.

My back hurts from uncoiling the strands welded together from a year of sitting unused in my attic. Colored lights. White lights. A few bags of blue, too, my dad bought for me as a joke. They've taken up residency across the coffee counter, an array of bulbs stretching from end to end. I let out a groan as I roll my head from side to side.

We're doing another group event tonight—a holiday movie in the park put on by the city. This time of year, they set up a large screen and roll the free films for anyone who wants some merry cinematic cheer. When Bradley asked what *National Lampoon's Christmas Vacation* was, Malik declared our next get-together would be a night of festive cultural appreciation for one of the best holiday movies ever produced.

Business has been slow today. We're inching toward Thanksgiving, and family is taking precedence out of strolling down the avenue or shopping. The stillness of the room is a nice break from having a line out the door of folks waiting for lattes and cookies. I love being busy and find time passes quickly when I'm slinging cups and plates as humanly possible and giving book recommendations as I restock the depleted shelves. Between the contest, decorating, work, spending time with the hardware store employees, sleeping and *Theo*, though, I'm feeling like I can't catch my breath.

"Goddammit."

The curse causes me to look up. Theo's standing in the threshold of the shop like I manifested him, angling his head to avoid a shower of green pine needles landing in his hair. A large Christmas tree is on one hand. There's dirt on his forehead. A scowl on his face. A tear in his shirt.

Despite his disheveled appearance, I grin. I haven't seen him since the Christmas tree lot, the hours we spent together ingrained in my memory. Him, asking what makes me happy and the words that spilled out, as if he could be the one to make them happen. Me, nestling into his palm as he wiped away a pesky tear that escaped from his honest admission of being Mac's dad.

It's like that every time with him, I've learned. My heart trips, stumbling and fumbling with every touch. My smile grows when I see him, and stretches wider when I see *him* happy, eager to hear what he has to say. When his breath grazes my skin, my brain short circuits and goosebumps erupt in its wake. Everything is magnified, senses and emotions heightened when he's near.

I haven't been able to get him out of my head.

Last night when I was in bed, I let my hand drift up my thigh. It dipped under my sleep shorts and teased over my underwear. My back arched as I thought about being over his shoulder, the heat in his eyes and the drag of his fingers. The warmth of his palm. How I was so close to him, I could have kissed him if I wanted to. In his car, behind the row of trees, on the plastic bench with a burger in my hand. Hell, I *really* wanted to. I wanted his lips on mine, devouring me, possessing me, controlling me.

He wasn't even trying to get me worked up, and I was almost panting with need. How destructive would he be if he gave an ounce of effort?

He'd probably be my ultimate ruin, one I'd gladly welcome.

"Where do you want this behemoth? It didn't feel the heavy when we loaded it into the truck on Saturday."

Theo's question pulls me away from the daydream of sheets pooled around his waist. My leg hooked over his. Sunrise sneaking through the windows as he looks at me from above, a reverent, lustful gleam in his eyes. Still waking up, still a little delirious, but already knowing how badly he wants me, hands tickling my waist as he buries his face in my chest.

I blink and shake my head, gesturing to the open spot I created earlier in the day.

"Let's put it over here. Do you need any help?"

"I walked with it for five minutes by myself. I think I can survive ten more seconds." He lifts the tree by the stump, heading toward the pre-positioned stand and setting it inside. "Is it straight?"

"No. It needs to go to your right. No. The other right, Theo. Okay, there."

"Kind hard to move it when I have sap in my eyes and can't see," he grumbles.

I hold back my chuckle, knowing laughing at his misery would probably spook the hell out of him. I walk over and grip the interior of the tree. "Are you coming to the movie tonight?"

When he doesn't answer, I look down to find him on all fours, head hidden by branches as he works. Through his white shirt—no flannel again today—his muscles are visible, contorting and flexing with physical exertion. His body is probably in prime condition from hours of working with his hands.

His arms, constructing and building, and his chest, chiseled and toned. His stomach, sharp lines and masculine definition. I exhale a breath, flares of heat scorching me from the inside out.

"Yeah," he finally responds with a muffled voice. "I am. I'm also bringing Mac."

"You are?"

I must sound surprised, because he leans back on his shins and stares up at me. The late afternoon sun hangs low in the sky, threatening to slip beyond the horizon. Gold hour casts shades of red and yellow and orange through the front window like stained glass prisms, covering the room and Theo in an unearthly glow.

"Yeah. I think it's time I accept the fact I can't hide her forever. I need to get over myself and let her live her life how she wants. When I told her where I was going tonight, she practically begged me to come. I apologize in advance if she talks your ear off."

I chuckle, easing my grip on the tree. It stays steady, no wobble bowing the trunk. "You don't need to apologize. I'm excited to see her again."

"Good. She really likes you, Bridget." Taking a glance around, Theo's eyebrows raise. "Shit, this place looks incredible."

I turn my chin, wondering how the space appears through his eyes. There are lights everywhere. A machine we hooked up that creates fake snow whenever someone opens the door sits in the corner by the entrance. Small gingerbread villages take up half the card table near the coffee counter. The first of Lucas's creations, a wooden Christmas tree coming up to my shoulder, is propped against the door to the back hallway, waiting for its first coat of paint.

"Do you think so? Or are you just trying to not hurt my feelings?"

Theo scoffs. "I'm being honest. I'm seriously impressed."

"It's going to look even better with all the other real trees. We'll have a whole forest!"

"Speaking of, do you mind if I bring the rest by tomorrow? I want to shower before the movie, and I also need to grab Mac from my parents' house."

"Of course. I really appreciate all your help. This wouldn't be possible without you."

I extend my arm toward him. He smiles wryly as his rough fingers wrap around mine, accepting the offering. I lean back and pull, bringing him back to his feet. When he's upright, taller than me and tilting his chin so I'm in his line of sight, his hand pulses in mine. We savor the touch for another beat before he lets go, our palms falling to our sides and away from each other's grip.

"Happy to do it. I'll see you tonight."

"Looking forward to it. I'll save you a seat."

TWENTY-ONE

BRIDGET

THE SMELL OF FRESH, buttery popcorn wafts through the air. The city set up a machine for moviegoers to munch on during the film, alongside a hot chocolate station. I fill up a bag of kernels and trek across the park, waving to Chandler.

"Hey." I take the spot next to her. She's arranged a large purple blanket across the grass. A handful of pillows are tossed on the polyester. "Are the girls on their way?"

"Yeah, they're parking." She rubs behind Ziggy's ears and his tail wags. "Did you bring any treats?"

"Of course I did." I rifle through my satchel, finding the plate of pastries I made in preparation for tonight. "I have to keep the people happy. Cheesecake bars and shortbread cookies. Oh, and blueberry muffins."

"You're the reason why I gain ten pounds every holiday season," Chandler says. She doesn't wait for me to set the plate down, unwrapping the aluminum foil while it's still in my hands. "I love your cheesecake bars."

"From the woman who ate the eleven-layer carrot cake at Ocean Prime—the best dessert I've ever had in my life—and called it *okay*, hearing your love for the cheesecake bars is great for my self-esteem."

"That's why you keep me around. It's why I keep you around, too. For the damn cheesecake bars."

"A mutually beneficial relationship."

Chandler licks cream cheese frosting off her fingers and narrows her eyes in concentration. "Is that Theo over there? Who's he with? His sister?"

I turn and find him standing on the far side of the lawn. He's cleaned up, wearing a fresh pair jeans, a blue flannel, and those paint drip boots. His hand rakes through his hair and his eyes dart through the crowd. When he spots me, his lips raise and he offers me a sheepish wave. Mac's next to him, talking animatedly and gesturing to a group of people.

Through a flurry of uncoordinated hand movements, I ask if I can come over. With a jerk of his head, he agrees.

"It is," I say. "I'll be back."

I make my way over to them, covering the distance quickly.

"Hey BB," Mac calls out.

"Mac and Cheese! I'm so glad you're here."

"I only had to ask Dad fifteen times before he finally gave in."

"Fifteen? That's it? Sounds like you're turning into a pushover, Gardner," I say.

It's a feeble attempt to help ease some of his tension. I see the way his focus pingpongs around, the gathering size swelling to crowded as more and more people fill the park. How he shifts on the balls of his feet back to his heels, a nervous rock. The deep breath he takes, holding the inhale for three seconds before releasing it through tense shoulders.

The joke works, and his eye roll is paired with another smile. Less stiff, more authentic. We're making progress.

"It was late, and I was tired from lifting an entire Christmas tree farm. And a human, too," Theo answers.

"Dad told me about your idea for the stores, BB. It sounds awesome. Seven trees!"

"You'll have to come by and see it! Were you two planning on sitting alone or...?"

I let the open-ended question hang there. The invitation for them to join us, if he wants.

Theo clears his throat. Rubs the back of his neck. Swallows and nods. "If there's space, we'd love to join you."

"I was hoping you'd say that. We have plenty of room, including pillows. I also brought some treats. Come on, Mac. I'll introduce you to the gang."

I lead us over to our group, Mac by my side and Theo trailing behind. In my absence, my three other best friends have occupied the blanket with Chandler. They're gabbing away, laughing loudly, and I clear my throat to interrupt them.

"Y'all."

Four heads swivel and look up at me. Chandler's mouth is covered in crumbs. Lucy's hand pauses, halfway into the bag of cookies. Polly is poised like always, spine straight and legs tucked under her. Skyler, who is constantly on her phone for work, halts the lengthy paragraph she's texting to give me her attention.

"I'd like you to meet Mac." I glance over my shoulder, asking for silent permission, and Theo gives me a single nod. "She's Theo's daughter."

It was shitty of me to not give them a heads up before dropping that information so casually. I should've sent a message in our group chat with a quick FYI, because I don't want to make Theo or Mac uncomfortable or put them on the spot to share personal details.

My friends all blink, processing the news. Skylar cranes her neck, looking at Mac, then back at Theo. Lucy's hand falls to her lap. Polly grins and waves, unfazed, and Chandler looks like she's seen a ghost.

"Hey, Mac!" Polly, pragmatic and predictable, is the first to speak. "I'm Polly. This is Lucy, Skylar, and Chandler."

"Chandler works at the store with me. She makes awesome drinks," I say. "Is it cool if she and Theo hang out with us? The rest of the hardware store folks will be here soon."

"Yeah." Chandler breaks her silence. "Of course they can. Come try one of Bridget's cookies, Mac. They're incredible."

Mac smiles and finds a seat on the blanket. Lucy hands her the plate to pick a treat, and Polly starts asking her a question. I shuffle back to Theo. He's quiet and stoic, a little on edge.

"Hey." I nudge his shoulder. The line of my arm rests against his, and I keep it there, hoping to convey a sense of compassion and empathy about how anxious he must be right now. "You'll let me know if I'm doing something wrong, right? She's your kid."

"You're not overstepping," he says. "Working on recognizing the learning curve associated with her being out in the world is a goal of mine. It's not easy. I know she's going to meet people. They're going to find out about this part of me. It's an adjustment, but Mac is a big part of my life. Keeping her away doesn't bring me any relief. It doesn't benefit anyone. So, here we are. Taking it step by step."

"I'm proud of you," I say honestly. I press into him a little further, the warmth of his body fighting off the chill in the air. "Is this crowd level okay? I tried to find a more secluded spot."

"It's great. Thanks for thinking of me."

I've been thinking about you a lot lately, Theo.

"No sweat off my back. I have something that might make you a little less tense. Some positive reinforcement, as my therapist would say."

His head turns slightly to his right, dropping his chin to look at me. "You're in therapy?"

"Yeah." I shrug, unashamed. "Lots of people are."

"I mentioned it briefly the other night, but I'm... I'm also in therapy. Still. I'll probably go for the rest of my life. It's made me a better father."

"It's a beautiful thing, isn't it? Certainly helps with the pesky intrusive thoughts that pop up from time to time. Look at us. Tattoo twins. Therapy twins. Keep it up, Gardner, and I'm going to start to think..."

I'm going to start to think you're who I've been waiting for.

The reason no one else has made sense.

"Start to think what?" he prods, raising an eyebrow.

I wonder if the desire to know him emotionally and physically is written on my face. I wonder if he can tell I want to grab him by the collar and press my lips against his, right here in front of everyone. I wonder if maybe, possibly, *hopefully*, he feels the same way.

"You're copying me," I finish. It's a terrible lie, but it works, earning a low chuckle of approval.

"What's the positive reinforcement?"

"Blueberry muffins."

"My damn weakness. You like blueberry muffins, too? Now who's copying who?"

"No. I hate them. Chocolate muffins are my favorite."

"Then why the hell do you make so many blueberry muffins?"

"Because *you* like them, Theo. They're your favorite. I remember the first time you came into the store and asked for one. I watched your eyes light up when you saw I had a whole tray. They had been in the case for two days, and not one person had ordered one. I was about to toss them in the trash and then you were there, acting like they were the rarest jewel. A prized possession. You were so *happy*, over such a small thing, and god, it was so beautiful. I didn't know if I'd ever see you again. I didn't even know your name. But I put blueberry muffins out again the next week, hoping you'd come back. And you did. You've kept coming back. I know you have a busy life. You don't do a lot of things for yourself, and I know how much you love those damn muffins. I bake them for *you*, Theo. Because we all deserve someone who looks after us every now and then."

"Bridget."

He's said my name before. It's been more frequent the last few weeks, but this one is different. It sounds like he's afraid he'll never get the chance to speak the word again. Embedded with awe, a touch of nerves, an ounce of hope.

"Yes?"

"You are..." He blows out a breath, shakes his head. Rubs his jaw and smiles. "Extraordinary."

I smile back as the compliment nestles near my heart. It works its way inside, curling beside the other important things he's told me. The other parts of him I've seen, honest. Raw. Unfiltered. Each as equally important as the last.

"I'm not extraordinary," I answer. "That's too high of—"

"You are." It's emphatic, not up for debating. "You really, really are."

"Thanks." I whisper it, because every time I interact with this man, it's like we take another step toward something new. Something outside the realm of *randomly assigned competition partners*. It scares me a little. But it's a good kind of scared.

"I'm not sure if I deserve that kind of attention. People don't usually focus on my muffin preferences. They like to ask why I'm not at more meetings or why our sales numbers are lower than six years ago."

"They're missing out, then. Remember what I told you? Some people are worth being exhausted for. That includes you,

Theo. Come on. The rest of the gang is here, and the opening credits have the best song."

OUR GROUP STRETCHES ACROSS four blankets. Snacks get passed around. Drinks are consumed. Someone—Bradley, if I had to guess—brought a case of beer. He distributed the cans, knocking the aluminum in a round of cheers. Malik and I quote the movie under our breaths, high-fiving when we nail the lines perfectly. Theo sits next to me and grins the whole time. A chuckle shakes his shoulders during every scene.

It's dark by the time the movie ends. Mac is talking to Chandler about her soccer team, excitedly sharing how she's switching positions from defense to offense. I'm undoing Lucy's hairstyle from earlier, French-braiding the auburn locks into two pigtails, when I feel someone staring at me. I look up, and Theo is watching us. He mouths "thank you," a grateful expression punctuating the words. I answer it with a smile.

"We should get going," Theo says. "The kid has school tomorrow."

"It was great to meet you, Mac," Chandler says. "You'll have to come by the store one day when I'm there."

"That would be so fun. Thanks for doing my hair, BB. I'm glad I got to see you."

"It's not great, but probably looks better than what your dad can do."

"You'd be surprised," he draws out. "I know how to French braid, too."

I stand, pulling Mac to her feet. She gives me a hug and I return the gesture. "See you soon, kiddo."

"I'll come by tomorrow and set up the rest of the trees," Theo says.

He waves to the group. Even Chandler offers him an incline of her head and a small smile. As he and Mac turn to leave, his hand brushes against mine, thumb rubbing over the ridge of my knuckles.

It's the faintest of touches, the lightest of grazes, but I feel it the rest of the night.

MY HEAD IS KILLING ME.

A pulsing sensation radiates across my temples, extending to the nape of my neck and down my spine. It's unceasing, the pain continuing to plague me late into the afternoon. It's not a hangover or a headache I'm nursing after a wild night out, reliving my younger years. It's more of a general discomfort, my exhaustion level waning–more drastically than usual–after stretching myself thin the last couple of days.

Decorating for the contest is in full effect, and so is socializing and group events. After work yesterday, I spent two hours helping Bridget arrange the five remaining Christmas trees she purchased in their stands. I dragged the firs across the floor, patiently waiting as she shook her head and asked me to move them six inches to the right. Then to the left. Then forward, closer to the door. Back and forth we went, sweat rolling down my cheek, her apologizing profusely, me grunting in return. It was a cycle that went on and on until she threw her hands in the air exasperatedly and yelled "fuck it!" Through a huff of annoyance, she said to put them anywhere.

I could tell she was frustrated. Frazzled and mentally

drained after fielding nonstop questions about plans from my excited employees with a polite look on her face. I was close to walking out and leaving the placement as it was, but I saw her keep sneaking glances at the trees, a long there. Like she didn't *want* it to be perfect, but anything else wasn't good enough. When she stepped into the storage room to grab a fresh sleeve of paper cups, I moved the army of firs back to their original location; the setup where she smiled the brightest, tired eyes fading away to elation. Watching her push through the swinging door and light up, surprised jubilation on her face, was well worth the extra twenty minutes of work. She was so *happy*, and I was proud to be the one who delivered that happiness to her, a present with a bow on top.

I'm paying for the effort today, thankful for the lack of customers filing into the store. No foot-traffic is horrible for sales, but fantastic for my battered state. It's been pouring all afternoon, inclement weather forecasted to last late into the evening. I let my employees clock out early, holding down the shop alone for the remaining work hours. They aren't needed. No one is daring to brave this monsoon. I can barely see through the front windows, heavy drops of water pelting the glass. The avenue outside is empty, a ghost town. A car hasn't driven past in the last thirty-five minutes and the clothing store across the street closed up early, everyone heading home.

With the world painted in shades of gray and dreary blue, a flash of color catches my eye. It contrasts the monotone palette, barely discernible through sheets of rain.

I turn, expecting to hear a roar of thunder, the rumble shaking the earth.

No sound comes.

I step toward the window and blink, making sure I'm not losing my mind.

It's not a lightning strike I saw.

It's Bridget, standing on a tall, rickety ladder that stretches far too high in the air. In one hand is a strand of Christmas lights and a staple gun. The other arm is reaching out, attempting to plug in an extension cord to an outlet that's severely out of her range.

What the *hell* is she thinking?

She's going to fall off that contraption in seven seconds or end up electrocuted. Neither scenario sounds particularly entertaining. I look away, trying to find a task to busy myself with. Something to distract my mind, because what she does isn't my business. If she wants to stand on a metal object in the middle of an electrical force field, more power to her. I don't care.

Except I can't stop watching her. Worry, sheer fucking panic, pumps through me.

"Dammit."

I can't let her stay out there. Every two seconds I'm craning my neck, checking to see if she's finally started to use the common sense I know she has. My heart is racing, like I've been sprinting for miles. After a particularly loud roll of thunder, I give up. I can't take it anymore. I hustle to the door, using my shoulder to push it open. A strong gust of wind greets me, nearly knocking me backward. Down the sidewalk, my boots stomp in large puddles, drenching my feet through the leather.

"What are you doing?" I bark out when I get to the ladder. I'm close to yelling so she can hear me over the din of water hitting the pavement. The sound of wind whipping through the branches of towering oak trees, their limbs swaying dangerously, threatening to fall.

"Hey, Theo!" Bridget says. Amidst the dark clouds and the fury raging around her, she's a ray of sunshine. The only source of light in this desolate world. Her hair sticks to her face like cooked noodles. The dress she's wearing clings to her body, accentuating the curve of her ass. The jut of her hips. The swell of her breasts. "I figured I'd get this hung while the shop is slow. What better time than–"

"Get off the ladder."

She blinks, trickles of rain drops falling from her eyelashes. "Pardon?" she challenges, pushing back.

"I said, get off the ladder." More forceful this time, through gritted teeth, my heart thumping harder than before.

"I'm fine."

My fingers tighten into fists. A deep breath, trying to settle the storm brewing inside me. "Every time I look out the window, I see you. I'm checking to make sure you haven't slipped or crashed to the ground. Not happening on my watch. If you're so hell-bent on hanging those lights, you can do it after I leave for the day. Preferably not in the middle of a fucking thunderstorm. Get off the goddamn ladder now, Bridget. You're scaring the ever-loving fuck out of me." I swallow and add an additional word to lessen the blow. "Please."

My voice snags on the ask, cracking. A tremor nearly racks my body as another bolt of light flashes through the sky. I'm four seconds away from either dropping to my knees and begging her to climb down or ascending the rungs myself, hauling her over my shoulder, and guiding her to safety.

The fiery, fighting flicker in her eyes dims. Her lips form an "O" shape and her face softens. She nods. "Okay. Yeah. I'm sorry. Could you help me?"

I grunt in agreement. The ladder must extend twelve feet in the air, and while she's not at the top, she's close. Too fucking close for comfort. I shift my position to either side of the frame, holding the metal steady. Her foot moves down the first rung, the start of the treacherous descent. I don't think I'm breathing.

"Shit," she curses and my arms go up instinctively, poised to catch her.

"What's wrong? What's going on?" I ask.

"This is my first time looking down and it didn't feel this high when I climbed up an hour ago."

Fuck. Her fear of heights. How did I forget? Why the hell did she go up there in the first place?

She's stopped moving. Her chin is raised toward the sky and her hands grip the rails of the ladder. I can tell she's petrified. Her muscles are rigid, her spine is straight. I think she's shaking, too.

Fucking fuck.

"I don't think I can do it," Bridget continues. Still, she hasn't budged, and my panic is creeping toward hysteria.

"Bridget. I want you to listen to me. I'm here. I'm not far. You can hear me, right?"

"Y-yes."

"Seven steps and I'll be able to grab you. Let's take them one at a time. I want you to look directly in front of you, not down. You don't need to look for me. I'm not going anywhere."

"Do you promise?"

"I promise. I've got you. You're going to be safe."

"Okay."

"I'll tell you where you need to put your foot. Do you think you can do that?"

"I-I'll try."

"Turn your body so you're pushing against the–yes. Perfect. Just like that. Okay, right foot first. Take your time, princess. I'm here."

The term of endearment slips out. It's a gentle roll off my tongue, a wave on a beach during low tide. Soft, precious, it's unintentional. Except... as she makes the step down, I see her shoulders relax. Marginally, but enough to know she liked it.

"There we go. One down. Six to go. Left foot now."

The whole thing takes ten minutes. She moves slowly, with precision, and I do my best to keep my voice neutral, not spiked with concern as the rain intensifies and the rumbles grow closer.

Soon, she's close enough to touch. I reach out, my shaky palm hovering above her lower back. My fingers float across the soaked fabric bunching near the base of her spine. I grab it, hard, to have a grip on her.

"I'm going to touch you now."

"Touch away." She's breathless, from exertion? Fear? Something... darker?

I kick my foot up on the bottom step and grasp her hips, just below her waist. My fingers dig into her skin, hard. She's three rungs away from the ground now. My thumb rubs up her vertebrae, an apologetic gesture for my berating earlier.

"Good girl, Bridget. You're doing great. Almost there."

I barely make out the soft gasp, I almost miss the way her shoulders roll back, inching closer to me. The tilt of her head, neck exposed.

Fuck me, she likes to be praised.

The night of the book club, over the laughter and chatter, I heard her sharing the book she enjoyed. She liked when the fictional man took control in the bedroom, encouraging and praising his girl along the way. I didn't think the fascination would translate to tasks outside closed doors, to a simple command. Here I am, noticing her body's reaction, and trying to find a way to say it again.

At the final step I yank her away from the death trap. My arms wind around her, palm splayed out across her stomach. Her back is flush against my chest and she's shaking. Freezing cold, drenched and miserable. Instinctively, my arms tighten, giving her body warmth. Heat. Whatever she needs. Ten seconds on the ground and she hasn't pulled away, staying in my hold. Tucked into my body, protected from the world. Her head drops to my shoulder and she shifts, backside pressing into front of my jeans.

I swallow, trying to find my voice and not let out a moan. "Bridget." My other hand runs up her arm, from her fingers to her shoulders and back again, traversing over a forest of goosebumps.

She spins in my hold, a graceful maneuver. Retreating under the awning to hide from the downpour, she leans against the exterior of the shop. Her shoulder blades press into the brick, and... *goddammit*, this position isn't any better. I can see the rise and fall of her chest, working in overdrive. The pointed peaks of her nipples, hard and visible through the thin material of her dress. Her eyes widen, the hazel darkening the longer she stares at me with a parted mouth.

Holy hell.

I want to kiss her.

Not just kiss, but *possess*.

Consume and care for.

With a hungry, aching need. A pulsing desire. A yearning to touch more and more. I want to cover every inch of her body and learn my way as I go. I'd draw a map so I never get lost, high-lighting my favorite parts and revisiting them again and again.

I lick my lips greedily. Her eyes dart to my mouth, fixating on my tongue and aware of my every move. Feeling bold and reck-less, drunk off her and in no rush to sober up, I take a step closer. My hands land on either side of her face, bracketing her head and caging her in.

Tell me to run, Bridget.

Tell me to get out of your space.

Tell me where to kiss you first.

The column of your throat? The shell of your ear? The spot above your chest that's a constellation of freckles?

Tell me this makes you happy.

"Theo," she whispers. My name sounds like a ragged pant. A shaky plea. An arduous ask.

It's an offering. A dare. A challenge. One I almost, *almost*, accept.

"Bridget," I repeat. I cup her slick cheek, palm fusing to her skin. I allow myself two seconds to pretend. Two seconds of believing I'm going to pull her close, put my lips on hers, and drown under the storm clouds, forever fused to her body and soul.

Another shiver racks her body. Her teeth chatter, and I crash down to reality. The pink is rapidly fading from her cheeks, replaced with pale alabaster that makes her look fragile. Breakable. So far from the badass, world-avenging woman I know.

"You're going to get sick standing out here."

"I'm f-fine," she says.

I should shut this down. Tossing her a towel and walking away is an option. The *safe* option.

I've never been fond of being safe, I guess, because I utter the five dumbest words in the history of the universe.

"You're coming to my house."

WAVES OF WATER cascade down her cheek, then her neck, disappearing under the hem of her dress like shooting stars.

"What does that mean?" she asks.

"You can use my shower while I dry your clothes. It's less than a ten minute walk up the road."

And I'll do my best not to think about you naked, I want to add, *and probably fail miserably.*

"I can run home and grab something. Or turn the heat on in the store."

"Have you ever turned the heat on?"

Her lip quirks up and she shakes her head. "No. I just don't want to impose or anything. It sounded like the better answer."

"Impose on what, exactly? All the things I do in my house midday?"

"Your private residence. Whatever you might keep in your secret hideaway. Maybe you're Batman. I wouldn't want to ruin the role of hardware store owner you play really well."

I chuckle. "It wouldn't be imposing. You're freezing, Bridget. The rain isn't stopping any time soon. And I'm not Batman, so no worries there. A Batmobile would be pretty cool, though."

She gnaws on her lip, considering. I'd never force her down the sidewalk, even if the sight of her shivering makes the muscle in my jaw tick. I wouldn't expect her to do something she's not completely comfortable with, even if I want to peel her wet dress off with my teeth. Patiently, I wait while she decides. After a moment of thought, she dips her chin, wordlessly accepting my offer.

My hands drop from the wall and I step back, giving her space. "Do you need to grab Ziggy?"

"No. He's at daycare today. It's just me. I told Brooke to not bother coming in. Give me a second, I need to grab my phone and lock up."

She heads inside and I decide to be a useful member of society. I move the ladder out of the way, collapsing it down and resting it against the entryway. I unplug the unfinished lights and wrap them into a tight coil. Bridget reemerges and locks the shop door, giving another nod indicating she's ready to go.

We start the walk toward my house, a craftsman a few blocks up, off the main drag. I'm kicking myself for not bringing an umbrella. For not popping back into my office and digging out the raincoat I know is buried somewhere in there. It's painful to watch her out of the corner of my eye and know I can't do anything to help her yet.

It makes me mad all over again.

A car speeds down the road, a spray of water dousing the sidewalk. I slow my steps so I can switch sides with Bridget, nudging her toward the buildings and away from the street.

"Do you live alone?" she asks, dodging a puddle.

"Yeah. Lucas and I used to live together. Then he got married, Mac was born, and I bought this place by myself."

"Lucas was *married*?"

I chuckle. "Yeah. He's been divorced for three years."

"Holy crap. Have you ever been married?

"God, no. I told you I was planning on buying Mac's mom a ring and, well, thank fuck I didn't. Put the savings toward a house instead. What about you?"

"No." She shakes her head, flecks of water from the strands of her hair landing on my cheek. "One day, maybe. My sister got married earlier this year and shit, what a spectacle."

"Does it make me a bad person if I use my kid to get out of social obligations I don't want to go to? 'Sorry, I can't make your wedding even though we haven't talked since college. My kid has a dance recital.'"

Bridget laughs, and we turn onto my street. "Honestly, it kind of makes you a genius. Do you walk to work every day?"

"I try to. Healthy living and all that. We'll drive back later, though. No more walking in the rain. What about you?"

"Yeah. It's a twenty minute walk. When it's excruciatingly warm outside I'll drive. But I definitely prefer walking. I like the fresh air."

"Same. It's a nice break from being in the store all day."

I gesture to my house and we climb the stairs to the porch. My hands fumble with the keys, cold and stressed. When I finally push the door open, Bridget files in behind me. She stands in the foyer, staring at me, waiting for instructions. Water runs down her legs and pools at her feet, covering the rustic hardwood.

"Clothes off. Now."

My voice is strained and I spin, focusing my attention on the couch. On the wall. On the television mounted to the wall. Anything except the woman getting naked behind me. I hear an article of clothing hit the floor, followed by a smaller sound.

"Okay," she whispers.

I clear my throat. "Bathroom is down the hall on the left."

Light footsteps pad away, and when I hear the shower turn on, I finally relax.

She's safe.

I grab her discarded clothes, heading for the laundry room. My pulse quickens when I close my eyes and imagine her up on that ladder. The fear in her voice, trembling and nervous. The terror in her eyes, wide and scared. If it had been anyone —*anyone*—else outside, I wouldn't have confronted them. I wouldn't have gripped their hips like my life depended on it. I wouldn't have brought them here to use my hot water or dry their clothes.

Yet here are.

I toss her clothes in the machine and stalk toward my bedroom, sorting through my dresser to find her something to wear. A pair of shorts. A T-shirt I haven't worn in five years. Subtle, non-incriminating attire that will make her look like she's getting ready for the gym and not obliterate my brain cells. I knock on the bathroom door, waiting for Bridget to answer.

"Yeah?" she calls out.

"I have some clothes for you."

"You can come in!"

I push open the door, grateful for the steam engulfing me. My glasses fog and I can't see, vision obstructed by condensation. It's a good thing, really, the water cycle. The less I see, the less I'll imagine. The less I'll picture myself in the shower with her. Falling to my knees as my hands run up her thighs. Water in my hair. Her hands on my shoulders. A moan, long and low, *satisfied*, in the air.

"Yours should be done soon."

"Thanks, Theo."

I nod, even though she can't see me through the shower curtain—thank *fuck* for a shower curtain—and head toward the safe haven of my kitchen. I open the fridge, find the crockpot leftovers of the white bean chili I made last night and pour a heaping serving into a bowl. Popping it in the microwave, I set a timer and lean against the granite island in the center of the room. I scroll through my phone while I wait.

A message from Lucas on his day off, asking if everything was okay at the store. A text from Mac, letting me know she's going to a friend's house for dinner and she'll call me later.

"Whatcha making?"

My neck jerks up at the sound filling the room. Bridget is standing on the opposite side of the island. Her hair is still wet, clinging to her neck and shoulders. Her face, though, looks bright. More full, the color returning to her cheeks. She's smiling, a wide grin stretching over her lips. I deflate at the sight. My eyes move down, away from her face, and I have to hold the edge of the counter to keep from toppling over.

I knew I handed her my clothes to wear, but seeing them on her body is pure fucking torture. A combination of both a heaven and a hell I never knew imaginable.

The black shirt is long, faded, and hanging well past her waist. The shorts she has on are baggy, a pair from my days as an athlete, hitting above her knees. Most of her skin is covered, fabric hiding her shape. Hell, I can see less of her body now than when she was wearing that soaked dress, the wet material almost sheer.

It's difficult to breathe again. I'm staring at this woman, gawking at her like she's a mirage. An image I've constructed in my head.

Seeing my store's name—*my fucking name*—across her chest is debilitating. I think I've been knocked out with a concrete block. It's as if the lightning outside struck me, electrocuting my nerve endings.

I blink, realizing she's waiting for me to answer the question she asked more than a minute ago, and I run a hand through my hair. "Soup. Or, chili, more specifically. I thought, uh, it might help warm you up. Are you hungry?"

"Yeah." Her smile widens. "I could eat."

"Okay. Cool."

Monosyllabic sentences are my best bet right now, afraid of turning into a blubbering idiot who's never spoken before. The timer on the microwave dings, saving me from humiliating myself any further. I dive for the appliance, grabbing the scalding porcelain bowl and nearly dropping it to the floor.

"Fuck," I groan, setting the dish on the counter. "That hurt." Small welts form on my fingertips.

"No shit. It came out of the microwave, you numpty."

Bridget saunters over to me with a sinister swish of her hips. She bumps me out of the way. Then, she pulls me toward the sink.

"What are you doing?" I ask.

"As someone who's frequently burning their hands on glass dishes from the oven, a few seconds under cool water will stop any blistering."

She rolls up my sleeve and turns on the faucet. Her fingers curl around my wrist, gently guiding me to the water. When she leans over, I inhale, her scents cloaking me.

She smells like all the wonderful, nice things in life.

Cake. Vanilla. Coffee. Summer nights. Fall days. Piles of leaves. Three scoops of chocolate chip ice cream. Laughing in the rain. Sunbathing. Open fields. Bonfires. Flowers. All things I've ever enjoyed, summed up in human form.

"Where's Mac?" she asks.

"At a friend's house. Normally she's with my parents after school until I finish work or at soccer practice."

"That's nice you have help." Bridget grabs a dish towel and hands it to me.

"I wouldn't be able to do this otherwise. My mom insists she sleep over twice a week so I can have some time to myself."

"What do you like to do in your free time?" she asks.

"Watch sports. Read. I do chores and run errands. Sometimes I sit quietly and stare at the wall."

"Have you read that book I gave you?"

"I did, actually, and I enjoyed it. Good recommendation." I reach into the utensil drawer, pulling out two spoons. I hand her one and slide the bowl her way.

She dips into the chili and brings it to her lips. "Holy crap, Theo. This is delicious."

"Oh." I shrug. "I also cook."

"What can't you do?"

"Drive a stick shift, believe it or not. What about you? What do you do in your free time? Besides baking enough pastries to end world hunger."

"I read a lot."

"A shit ton?" I ask.

A grin and a twinkle in her eye at the joke. "A fuck ton, actually. Romance novels are my poison. I hang out with my friends. I'm meeting them tonight for dinner. I love theme parks. I also love sports. Basketball is my favorite."

"Really? My buddy is a coach."

"In the NBA?"

"Yeah. Third assistant, but it still counts."

"That's awesome! Skylar is a commentator."

"No shit. I thought she looked familiar. Good for her. I wonder if they've ever crossed paths."

"Maybe. She avoids anyone in the league like the plague and keeps business and pleasure very separate," Bridget says.

"Makes sense. Where are y'all going to dinner?"

"Pannullo's on the avenue. It's kind of our weekly thing."

"That's fun. They seemed like a nice bunch. I appreciated how welcoming they were to Mac."

Her tongue licks up the drop of liquid hanging on the corner of her mouth. *God*, that shouldn't be a sexy sight. "They're good people. I expect an interrogation from them tonight, but I won't tell them the whole story."

I shrug. "You can tell them whatever you want. I know what you say won't be malicious. You don't need to lie to them."

"I kind of like having a secret," Bridget answers. Her eyes wander around the room. "Your house is really nice."

"Thanks. Perk of working at a hardware store is getting shit for cheap. This place looked totally different when I originally moved in."

"And no Christmas tree up, I see."

"No." I shake my head. "Not until after Thanksgiving."

"Okay. At least it's part of the plan. I need an idea for our next group outing. We have the holiday hayride the week after Thanksgiving. But I don't have any other plans."

"Caroling?" I suggest. "We could do the scenic boat tour and carol around the lake? Or down the avenue? Anything except getting back on an ice skating rink. I refuse."

"That's a great idea! I love the scenic boat tour. There aren't many places on this side of the world where you can jump on a boat and do a lap around a lake in December."

"Beats the hell out of shoveling snow."

"Yeah, maybe. But I think it would be fun to have a white Christmas. Like, to wake up in the morning to a fresh blanket of snow. To go skiing and drink hot chocolate around a fireplace."

She makes a good point. The contest is amplifying the holiday cheer this year, but wearing flip-flops on Christmas Eve just feels wrong, sometimes. Mac hasn't seen snow, and it's been years since I've been skiing. I'd like to take her one day.

The dryer buzzes from the laundry room and I frown, checking the time. Has forty-five minutes already passed? It feels like we just got here.

"I guess I should..." Bridget juts her chin toward the bathroom.

"Yeah. I'll grab your clothes and drive us back. No more getting drenched today."

"Thank you, Theo. I'm sorry I scared you."

"I'm sorry for being an ass."

"I forgive you." She smiles softly, putting the empty bowl in the sink.

"Come on, Boylston. Back to work."

TWENTY-FOUR
BRIDGET

"HI! I'm so sorry I'm late." I apologize to my four friends who are already at a booth inside the restaurant. I slide into the last empty spot next to Polly, ducking my head to avoid hitting the light fixture above the table.

"Where were you?" Skylar asks. "I passed the shop to see if you wanted a ride, but the lights were off. Did you close early?"

"Oh. Yeah. I was... um, at Theo's house?"

It comes out rushed, words bleeding together and barely making sense. The girls blink at me, confused.

"Theo Gardner?" Chandler clarifies, having the comedic decency to act like we know another Theo.

"Yup. That's the one." My voice is pinched, an octave too high. A touch too strained, like I've done something wrong. Fumbling for the water glass in front of me, I take a long sip, grateful for the liquid to help cool me off.

"Like, hanging out?" asks Polly.

"I mean, I guess? In a way?"

"We're going to need the full story," says Lucy. The other three nod aggressively in agreement.

"It started with a ladder."

I launch into the tale, mindfully leaving out key details like how he called me princess, the endearment causing my heart to flutter like a butterfly. The way I shamelessly rolled into his hips, reveling in the firmness of his body and the ache the light graze satisfied. I don't share that when Theo's voice caught on the word *please*, pure terror behind those amber eyes, I thought my soul cracked in two. I omit his use of *"good girl,"* and how I nearly combusted, years of pent-up desperation clawing to the surface. I don't tell the them there was a part of me that had hoped Theo would pull back the shower curtain, searching my face for an invitation to climb inside and join me.

I would have let him.

He was forceful in his demand for me to get down the ladder, yes. But he was patient and considerate while I descended, encouraging me along and never making me feel rushed or alarmed. In a time of crisis, I've never had a man ask how he can help or what he can do.

Theo did.

Every other word out of his mouth was a question, inquiring how I was feeling. If I needed anything. How he could help make the process easier and that he was *proud* of me.

His hands were warm and soft on my body, coaxing me closer and closer to him. I accepted the closeness, trying to prolong the time I was in his embrace. Near his chest. In his bubble, my space becoming his.

Nothing about the encounter felt weird.

It felt right.

When I finish, the girls are looking at me with mixed expressions. Polly is grinning. Skylar's brows are furrowed, confused and pondering. Lucy's smile is smaller, more coy, like she knows something no one else does. Chandler appears on the verge of a heart attack.

"So this man stood outside in the middle of a thunderstorm,

begged you to get off the ladder because you were scaring him, helped you to the ground, took you to his house and… while your clothes were drying, he fed you. Did I miss anything?" Skylar clarifies.

"The shower," Polly adds. "You forgot about the shower."

"Right. You were naked in his house."

"I was *showering*, not parading around in the nude."

"I think it's cute," Polly says. "He was worried about you and offered a solution. Normally, men only like to hear themselves speak, but Theo did something about it."

"He didn't give her much choice, did he?" Skylar counters, tapping her chin. "What else was she going to do?"

"I'm still trying to process the fact this man has some sort of kindness in his heart," Chandler muses.

"Are we forgetting he has a daughter, too?" Lucy asks. "He's hot, *a dad*, and obviously cares about Bridget."

"Okay, he doesn't care about me," I interject. "I was distracting him."

"I'm sure your dress sticking to your body was the worst thing he'd ever seen," Skylar draws out.

It doesn't compare to how he looked at me when I walked into his kitchen wearing his clothes. The material was soft, warm, and well-loved. Traces of fabric softener and wood, maybe, hung on the sleeves. I inhaled deeply, savoring the scent of *Theo*. When his gaze roamed my body–he didn't bother hiding the perusal–he was pleased. Proud, possessive. He licked his lips after, satisfied with the findings. When I went to hand the shirt back to him after I'd slipped back into my dry dress, he turned his back and muttered a rough "*keep it.*"

So I did, the gray article now tucked in my purse next to my cell phone and wallet like it's belonged there forever. Maybe I'll sleep in it tonight, savoring the scents of Theo clinging to the material.

"How old is Mac? She's cute," Lucy says.

"Almost thirteen. The bastard sprung her on me one day at work. I also watched her at the store for a little when he was busy one afternoon."

"Do we know what happened to her mom? Is it an awkward custody situation?"

I know Theo said it was okay to tell the story, but it feels wrong to share all the details. It's a deeply personal portion of his life. Even with his permission, I appreciated hearing the story from *him*, not from someone else. Instead of divulging the truth, I shrug.

"No. She's not in the picture. That's it. I still can't believe I didn't know he had a kid. Ms. Greta never mentioned it. I've never heard any whispers about her. You'd think that would be a piece of gossip she would go feral over."

"Speaking from experience," Chandler interjects, "Ms. Greta never talks about shit that personal. Kids are off-limits and people who are... well, anything involving a police report or someone's health are also out of her self-proclaimed jurisdiction. Some stuff we want to keep to ourselves, you know? She could've... but she didn't. And I respect that."

I give Chandler a sad smile, fully understanding what she means. "I respect it, too. Mac's important to him, and I'm glad he's able to tell people how *he* wants, not how others want."

"Can we expect Theo to be around more?" Polly asks.

"Oh, god, no. I mean, I highly doubt it. This wasn't a prince-saving-a-damsel-in-distress ordeal. It was more like an angry man pissed off by a stupid girl. I don't know what I was thinking, standing up on that ladder during the storm."

"I'm glad you're safe. I know you're committed to the contest, Bridge, but come on." Lucy is the motherly figure out of all of us. She spends her days teaching high schoolers art history and doubles down on academia by coaching the crew team. It's where we became friends almost twenty years ago.

"It won't happen again," I promise.

"Speaking of, how is the contest going? Some of the shops I passed last night looked outrageous. It was like Christmas threw up on them." Polly wrinkles her nose.

Practical and professional, she's a theme park engineer whose love language is calculus. She's the first female head engineer in theme park history. Regularly engaged in disagreements with her arch nemesis Chase, from the rival theme park up the highway, she's grown into a fast-thinking, quick-talking spitfire. Her idea of decorations involves an artificial tree and a single stocking over her fake fireplace. Minimalistic and straight to the point.

"It's awesome so far. The hardware store employees are really enthusiastic, constantly asking what else they can do to help."

"Probably because they need a break from the tyrant that is Theo." Chandler scoffs.

"Wow," Skylar says. "She really needs to get laid. I like her better when she's getting some action. She's always a little nicer."

An avid basketball fan and sports broadcaster for the Orlando Wizards, the professional team in town, Skylar is constantly calling out internet trolls, fielding dating requests from crazed fans, and breaking barriers and glass ceilings in the male-dominated industry. Preferring sneakers over heels, Sky could school almost anyone on the court. She went viral last year after challenging a guy to a game of HORSE after he claimed she was hired because of her looks rather than her basketball IQ.

She kicked his ass.

"Nope. I'm content with dying alone, an old maid

surrounded by dogs. Men can fuck off." Chandler takes a sip of her wine. After two *disastrous* relationships, she's in no hurry to stumble into another serious arrangement. Friends with benefits, sure, but she adamantly refuses to ever give a man anything more than a night of fun. No emotions. No commitment. No strings. No heartbreak.

"I'm still not over the fact that Theo is kind of a DILF," Lucy says. "After getting hit on by far too many creepy men at open houses, I prefer a dude my age. Theo though... he's clearly raised a good kid. He works hard. And those tattoos are hot."

"Wouldn't hate them on my body," Polly giggles. "I wonder if he has more besides the ones on his arms. Bridget, care to weigh in?"

I roll my eyes. "Sorry to disappoint, but I haven't seen anything except his arms. He's not that bad. His kid is great. His house is far from a dark cave or something like a spooky lair. And he fed me leftovers when he could've–and probably should've–left me out in the rain."

"Yeah. I'm officially on the Theo Gardner train," Skylar says.

"There's no train! We're done talking about him. If we say his name again he might show up, and I really don't want to explain the DILF comment."

"Fine." Chandler accepts the motion to move on. "Are we all good with the traditional gift exchange again this year? Twenty dollar limit per person?"

"I'm in!" Lucy claps her hands together. "No sex toys allowed. I still have the last two you gave me, Chan. I can't add a third."

"They aren't still in the box, are they?" Chandler sounds offended that the multi-use, double-sided toys she purchased for each of us last year might not be sitting on someone's coffee table, proudly on display for all to see. "What a waste."

"No sex toys," I agree. "Something practical. And no clothes."

My friends all nod and we dig into our meals. Lucy catches

us up on the team's spring schedule. It's a building year for them, she says, and she's implementing the Ted Lasso method of positivity to survive a calendar full of inevitable last place finishes. Skylar talks about the changes the Wizards are undergoing, mentioning the head coach might be out of a job soon if their losing record is any indication. Polly shares about the new roller coaster idea she had, inspired by her trip to China for a work conference.

Owning a business doesn't afford me a lot of time to spend with my friends, and these weekly meetings help me feel like we're still a strong presence in each other's lives. Our friendship has withstood years of cross-country visits, different colleges, relationships that developed quickly then fizzled out, and enough crappy jobs to weather a lifetime–and we're only in our early thirties.

Life's just beginning.

"Anything else to share?" I ask, using my napkin to clear away the remnants of the pesto dish I devoured.

"No, but if Theo yanks you down a ladder again I better get a text message," Lucy says. "Except don't get on a ladder during a storm again."

"Yes, Mom." My eyes roll, but my hand finds hers across the table, giving her a squeeze of appreciation.

"One day when we're old and the idea of sex disgusts us, 'yanking you down a ladder' is going to be a euphemism for something else," Skylar adds.

"If you think I'm going to say no to sex at any point in my life, you don't know me at all."

"And that, Chandler Armstrong, is why I love you."

"WHAT ARE YOU DOING FOR THANKSGIVING?" I ask Bridget.

She looks up from the latkes recipe she's been studying for the past ten minutes. A grater is in one of her hands, a half-peeled potato in the other. A couple of people from our group—Bridget, Felicity, Chandler, Lucas, and Bradley, surprisingly—are doing a test run of the meal they're going to prepare the night of the judging. With Felicity's guidance, they decided on a traditional Hanukkah spread: Brisket, potato latkes, and jelly donuts.

I came over to help supervise and eat the finished products, but I think I was looking for an excuse to spend time with Bridget. I brought Mac with me, too. She's lounging on the loveseat, working on her homework, with Ziggy resting near her feet.

I've taken a spot on one of the stools toward the left end of the bar, where Bridget is working, making sure to stay out of the way. The grater she's wielding looks dangerous, and she already almost took her finger off a few minutes ago.

"I can't believe it's in two days. This month is flying by, isn't it? Normally my family all gets together, but this year is a little different. My parents left for a cruise yesterday. My brother is doing a road trip with his friends for a football game. My sister and her husband are spending it with his family. So I'll be at my house."

"Alone?"

"Yeah."

She resumes her grating and I frown. The thought of Bridget —or anyone—alone on a holiday doesn't sit right with me. A pressure forms in my chest, below my ribs. I've been that person by themselves before. It's lonely. Isolating. Too quiet, even for me. You think about what everyone else might be doing while you're there by yourself, loathing the silence.

"What about you?" Bridget asks as she turns the page of the recipe. "What are y'all doing?"

"Mac, my parents and I have lunch in the early afternoon then spend the evening driving around looking at houses decorated for Christmas. We've done it for years now."

Her chin raises and a piece of potato skin is stuck on her cheek. She nudges it away with her shoulder and gives me a smile. "That sounds really nice. I'm glad you get to spend time together."

"Yeah." I nod. "Me too. Do you... maybe you could–"

"Alright, y'all," Felicity calls out, interrupting me. "Looking good. We've got ten minutes left on the brisket, and then it'll sit for twenty minutes. Once we get those potatoes finished, we're going to wring out the moisture with the cheese cloth I provided. Then we'll combine them with the eggs and corn-starch and throw them in the pans!"

"I'm definitely going to fuck this up," Bridget mutters. Her tongue is caught between her teeth, and her brows are furrowed. It's her concentrated face, I've learned. When she's focusing hard, determined to finish a task.

"No way. Your potatoes look awesome. You're doing great."

Bridget perks up. "You think so?"

I nod. "Definitely."

"How's it going, Bridge?" Lucas calls out from his station.

"Not bad! How are the donuts coming along?"

"We should've switched jobs," he laughs. "Theo, you want to help?"

"Nope. The sidelines are just fine."

"How long have you and Lucas been friends?" Bridget asks.

"Thirty years. Maybe more? Long enough where he knows all of my deepest, darkest secrets."

"Such as?" She transfers the freshly grated potatoes to the cheese cloth Felicity laid out. Her hands press the material together, liquid draining from the vegetables. I know she's only half-listening to me, but I like talking to her. She's easy to talk to.

"Hm." I hum and try to think of something to share. "I crashed my parents' car when I was fourteen. Lucas and I snuck out to go to Blockbuster. When I was turning back into the neighborhood, a squirrel darted in front of the car and I smashed into a tree. We were only going twenty miles an hour, but it was enough to do some damage."

Bridget bursts out laughing. She drops the potatoes into a mixing bowl, using her hands to coat them in the necessary ingredients. I appreciate that she isn't afraid to get dirty as cornstarch sticks between her fingers. "How much trouble did you get in?"

"A fuck ton. Thanks for teaching me that measurement, by the way. It's perfect for this story. I didn't even have a cell phone to call them. Lucas ran the mile to my house and my dad was *furious*."

Her laughter grows and her shoulders shake. She has to pause her cooking, unable to keep a straight face. "Please tell me the movie was worth it?"

I groan. "It was *Matilda*. And we loved it."

"Theo Gardner. You are something else. You watched it for Miss. Trunchbull, didn't you?"

"Guilty."

The smile on her face hangs around as she transfers the coated product to the hot frying pan on the stove behind her. I hear her hiss in pain, retreating backward.

"Ow. Shit."

"Are you okay?" I ask. I'm off the seat, leaning over the counter to see if she needs help or if she's hurt.

"I'm fine. The oil is hot."

"Careful, Brownie. I'm a big fan of potatoes. I can't have you hurting yourself before they're finished."

"Keeping me around for the muffins and potatoes, huh?" she says, back turned toward me. She's taking her time, making sure each mixture gets placed in the pan carefully and correctly. I hear the sizzle of the oil. The smell begins to permeate the air, a combination of pepper and onions. It smells *good*.

"One of the reasons."

"Care to share what else?"

Your ass. Your smile. How quick-witted you are.

"Ziggy is nice, too." I look over at Mac. Her nose is behind a book, her hand on the dog's head, gently petting his fur.

"Food and dogs. Easy man to please."

"You have no idea," I mumble, low enough so she can't hear.

"I'm going to check in with Felicity and grab a plate. If these start to burn, you're in charge," Bridget says and I nod in understanding.

"You got it, boss."

I watch her walk away. The sway of her hips, her skirt hitting the top of her thigh. Those long, long legs. Distracting, wonderful, obnoxious things.

"Your tongue is hanging out of your mouth," Lucas says. He drops his elbows on the counter, blocking my view.

"Fuck off."

"Okay, jokes aside, this is fun. Don't tell me you aren't having a good time."

I sigh and roll my eyes. "Fine. I'm having a good time."

"That's what I like to hear."

"I actually had a question for you. A favor, of sorts."

"You want me to watch Mac after this so you can bang a certain book-loving brunette on the counter?"

"Jesus fuck," I hiss. "Would you keep your voice down? No, that's not what I was going to ask. I don't want to bang anyone on the counter."

"You sure about that?" he asks, raising an eyebrow.

I flip him off. "It is about Bridget, though. She's my secret gift exchange person. I already have the gift to give her the night of the judging at the present swap. But I wanted to get her something else."

Lucas stands up, intrigued. "Go on."

I gesture to the far wall. "She told me Chandler sits on her shoulders to put books on the top shelf. I might have mentioned I could make a rolling ladder for her. She got really excited, and then I decided I *have* to make the rolling ladder for her. This competition has been fun. Bridget has played a big role in that and I'd like to do something nice for her. And, you know, I'm terrible at carpentry, so I would love some help, if you're willing. It'd be nicer than a five-dollar souvenir from a mall kiosk. She deserves it."

He stares at me, and I expect another joke to be lobbed my way. "That's..."

"Stupid," I finish for him. "Over the top. I never should've–"

"Shut up, Theo. I was going to say it's incredibly thoughtful. Of course I'll help you."

"I'll pay you for your time and the materials, obviously."

"Hell, no, you won't. This is awesome. I haven't made

anything that rolls before, but it shouldn't be too hard. Let me do some research and sketch out a couple things. Then we can get to work." He pauses. "I know I was kidding around before, but you don't build ladders for people."

"I know I don't."

"You're going to build one for her."

"Yeah, I am."

"Do you want to talk about it?"

I check to make sure Bridget's not nearby. "No. I don't know what I'm feeling toward her. I like being around her. I like spending time with her. She's the only reason I came over here this afternoon. I like seeing her happy. When she's happy, I'm happy."

Lucas nods and pats my shoulder. "That's good, Theo. If you ever want to commiserate over feelings, you know where to find me."

"Thanks, man. I appreciate you." I sniff the air. "Is something burning?"

"SHIT." Bridget barrels over to the stove, smoke rising from the pan. Lucas gets shoved away and I stifle my laughter as he stumbles back. "I burnt the latkes!" She turns the appliance off, using a potholder to fan away the smog.

"Fuck, I was supposed to be watching them." I jump off my stool and duck under the counter, hurrying to stand beside her. Charred, burnt lumps of what *used* to be potato stare back at me. "Sorry, Bridget. That's totally my fault."

"No, it's not. I got distracted and… Dammit." She sighs and squeezes her eyes shut. "Felicity spent so much time on the brisket and I ruined the meal."

"Hey." I drape my arm around her shoulder. "You didn't ruin anything. Look, this one is still salvageable. This one, too." With my free hand, I use a spatula to slide three of the latkes out of the pan, placing them on a paper towel to cool.

"We'll never win if I serve lumps of coal to people who have eaten food from around the world."

I chuckle. "They've probably eaten crickets and fermented sharks. Still think a burnt piece of potato will do them in?"

"That sounds disgusting."

"My point exactly."

"I just don't want us to lose out on $100,000 because I messed up."

"That's why y'all are doing a practice run, right? To learn how to do this better the next time. You've never made these before. In fact... Hey. Felicity. Can you come here real quick?"

"What's up?" she asks as she approaches.

"We had a slight mishap," I start. Bridget keeps her face tucked into my shoulder, embarrassed. "Have you ever burnt your latkes before?"

Felicity grins. "My first time making them, I actually started a fire. There was smoke everywhere. The fire department came. I ruined the first night of Hanukkah. My dad was so pissed, but my mom thought it was hysterical."

Bridget perks up. "Really?"

"Yeah. It's a running joke to this day. If something smells like it might be burning, you can hear my mom hollering through the house, 'Felicity! Did you leave the latkes on too long again?'"

"I burnt three of them. They cook way faster than I thought."

"Three? That's not bad at all. And... Jeez, Bridge. These other ones look perfect."

Bridget pulls away from my hold. "Really?"

"Really," Felicity says, giving her an encouraging smile. "The brisket is done, so let's give all of this a try."

Felicity hands out pieces of brisket. We pass the latkes around, each taking a half. Lucas proudly displays his donuts on a little wooden tree he made for the occasion. Chandler and

Bradley provide the applesauce and sour cream. Mac bounds over with Ziggy, eager to grab a few bites for herself.

It's nice being with these people. Half are standing, half are sitting. The chatter is bearable, and we drift between conversations, jumping in and out in between bites. Each component of the plate tastes better than the last, the food a delicious representation of teamwork. The meat is tender and the crunch of the potato is perfect. The jelly-to-donut ratio is spot on. It's easily one of the best meals I've ever eaten, made in the small kitchen of a bookstore, by a bunch of folks who barely know each other.

Kind of fucking cool, if you ask me.

"This was awesome, y'all," says Felicity. "Was it perfect? No. I definitely over seasoned the meat. But everything tasted so freaking good. It's the thought that counts. I doubt anyone else will serve the judges a plate with both brisket and gingerbread cookies on it. So thank you, for letting me share part of my tradition with you. I can't wait to do this again in a month."

There's a round of applause and Bradley whistles. Chandler takes another donut and Lucas starts to gather up the dirty pans, dropping them in the sink.

I nudge Bridget with my elbow. "See."

She sighs and folds her arms over her chest. "You were right."

"Say that again," I tease.

"Hush." Her foot kicks my shin, and I smile at the playful gesture.

"Do you want to come to Thanksgiving at my house?"

Her lips part at the switch in topics, and no words come out. She stares at me, eyes uncertain about my ask, but I see a tentative excitement sprouting in the green. "Is this an invitation or an open-ended question you want my opinion on?"

I chuckle and shift on the stool so my leg presses against hers. My hand drops to her knee, touching the bare skin there.

"Let me try again. Spend Thanksgiving with me, Bridget. With us. You shouldn't be alone. Bring Ziggy. There will be plenty of food. I'd like you there with us."

"Are you sure?"

"I've never been more sure about anything."

"Okay." Her nervous smile transforms, the happy grin I've seen so many times taking its place. "I'll come to Thanksgiving. What should I bring? What time should I get there?"

"How about pumpkin pie and eleven a.m.? We'll handle the rest."

"Okay," she repeats, nodding her head. "Pumpkin pie. Eleven a.m. I'll be there."

My hand lingers, giving her a squeeze, then dropping away. "I can't wait."

TWENTY-SIX

THEO

I'M the epitome of a nervous wreck.

Look up the term in the dictionary and you'll find a photo of me checking my watch every ten seconds and pacing the foyer of my parents' home.

Mac is sitting on the couch in the living room, swinging her legs back and forth as she relaxes on the cushions. She looks up from her phone every two minutes to give me a shit-eating grin. My dad is in the kitchen, grumbling under his breath about the inconsistency of meat thermometers. My mom looks like she wants to ask me five hundred questions but decides to get the potatoes ready for peeling instead, holding off on the interrogation I know she's planning in her head.

A car door slams and I look out the front window. Bridget's walking up the brick path to the front door, holding Ziggy's leash and a glass pan. A bottle of wine is tucked under one arm, and a bouquet of flowers is under the other.

She knocks and I count to five before I open the door, doing my best to not pull the wood off the hinges.

"Hey," I say casually.

"Happy Thanksgiving," she answers, beaming at me.

"Happy Thanksgiving to you, too, Boylston. You look great."

She's wearing a corduroy dress and it might be the most problematic article clothing I've ever seen her in. It's a deep shade of purple paired with a black turtleneck, I can already tell how well the material shows off her curves. Doc Martens are on her feet and black tights cover her legs.

Yeah, she looks fucking stunning.

"So do you, Gardner. New shirt?" She gestures to the plain white tee I'm wearing with a smirk on her face. "Haven't seen it before."

I roll my eyes and wave her inside. "Your jokes are falling flat. Come on in."

"Wow," she breathes out, surveying the high ceilings of the foyer. "This house is stunning."

"My grandfather built it for my grandmother," I say, shutting the door behind her. "Impressive, huh?"

"Very, very impressive. Is it okay if I let Ziggy off his leash? I don't want him to break a vase."

"Totally fine."

Bridget unhooks her dog, and he bounds over to the couch.

"Hey, BB!" Mac says, giving a wave. She presses a kiss to Ziggy's nose. "Hi, Zig."

"Mac and Cheese! Happy Thanksgiving."

"Want me to take something for you?" I ask.

"That'd be great. Here, take the pie."

I grab the glass pan from her hands and lead her down the hallway. "My parents are in the kitchen."

"Can I help with anything?"

"You'll probably get put on potato duty. Think you'll be okay with that after the latke fiasco?"

"Jerk." She chuckles and we step into the kitchen.

"Mom, this is Bridget."

My mom looks up from her usual spot at the table and

smiles brightly. We pull a dining chair away to accommodate her wheelchair, giving her ample space to move around.

"Bridget," she says. She pushes back from the wood and wheels herself over. "It's so great to meet you."

"It's so great to meet you too, Mrs. Gardner." Bridget answers with a sincere smile of her own.

Bridget's attention, I notice, isn't on the jagged scar running down her neck, raised and pink above her skin. She doesn't blink at the brace on Mom's left leg or the brief wince of pain she exhibits as she puts the brakes up on her chair.

Her focus is on Mom's face, keeping eye contact with her the entire time. She squats down, kneeling on the tile floor of my parents' kitchen, and hands over the bouquet of flowers.

"Thank you so much for having me over to celebrate Thanksgiving with you," Bridget continues.

"Aren't you a sweetheart," Mom gushes. "Theo, there's a vase under the sink. Can you fill it with some water for these?"

"Of course." I make myself useful, listening to her instruction. Successfully filled with water, I head back to the women, taking the flowers and plopping them in the container. "I'll put them in the window, yeah?"

It's my mom's favorite spot. The pane is low enough for her to look out to the front lawn and enjoy the sun streaming in.

"Perfect." She pats my cheek. "Thank you, sweetheart. Bridget, would you mind helping me with the peeling? It'll go twice as fast."

"Of course," Bridget agrees.

The pair make their way over toward the dilapidated table in the center of the room. They stop briefly at the oven so she can meet my dad, who nods hello and shakes her hand.

I lean against the door jamb, vase still in hand, and watch the women. Bridget smiles and nods along to the story my mom is sharing with her as she uses a peeler. Instantly, the room feels brighter, in a way it hasn't in years. Everything is warmer. A bit more serene. The air is lighter. My shoulders are less heavy, a sense of peace circling through the space.

"Dad. You're staring."

I jump. My gaze cuts away to find Mac smirking at me.

"Sorry. I'm hungry and doing a time check for when to start the stuffing."

"Hungry for food? Or for Bridget?"

"Mackenzie Ruth," I hiss. "Watch your mouth."

"It's not my fault you're drooling."

"I am not." I subtly run my thumb over my mouth to make sure she's pulling my leg. "Don't you have a job to do?"

"You mean topping the green bean casserole with the crispy onions that took me six seconds? Done. It's not rocket science."

"Wow. Is this attitude a temporary thing or should I expect it to stick around after your birthday, too?"

She giggles. "Be glad I haven't broken my curfew or snuck out to meet someone."

"Christ," I groan. "I'm going to have a heart attack when you go to high school. Did you set the table?"

"Plates and silverware are out."

"How about filling the glasses with water?"

"Dad. I did everything you asked. It's more fun to watch you act like an idiot."

"I am *not* acting like an idiot," I sputter. Heat floods my cheeks and I fiddle with my glasses, pushing them up the bridge of my nose.

"You kind of are," Mac whispers. She pokes my ribs and walks over to the table, leaving me alone.

The kid is way too observant for her own good. I grumble under my breath and head for the stove, turning on a burner for the potatoes. Footsteps approach me from behind. The familiar scents of cinnamon and vanilla tickle my nose. Hips graze mine, fitting beside me in the small nook of space perfectly.

"Hey," Bridget says. Her eyes sparkle in the light, a melody of color. "Potatoes are ready."

"That was quick."

"Double the hands. Makes it a little easier."

"Can you drop them in for me?"

She tips the cutting board toward the pot, chopped pieces falling into the water. "What else can I help with?"

"Nothing. My dad finished the turkey. The potatoes are going. I'm starting the stuffing now and it should be done soon. We're close."

She spins, back resting against the counter so she can look around the kitchen. "How long have your parents lived here?"

"It was a wedding present from my dad's parents. They moved down the road so Mom and Dad could start their life here."

"And you're an only child?"

"Yeah. What about you? A brother and sister, right?"

"I'm the middle child. My sister is three years older. She's a doctor and lives thirty minutes away with her husband. My brother is a year younger than me and is a teacher. He just moved back into town. God, he and Lucy always butt heads. It's kind of fun to watch. She's part of our family at this point, we've known each other for so long. Chandler, too."

"And your parents?"

"Not far from here. I'm born and raised in Park Cove. Left for college, and then I came back. Our city has a charm. I know I complain about the weather and the never-ending cycle of heat, then hurricanes, then more heat, but I'm not sure I'd want to live anywhere else."

"I know what you mean. I'm the same way. This is home. I like that the town is small, and there's still plenty of stuff to do."

"If you could live anywhere else, where would it be?" Bridget asks.

"Probably in the mountains somewhere. A cabin in the woods, miles away from civilization. I'd be happy there."

"That sounds right up my alley. If that ever happens, I'll be looking for my invite."

I smile and nudge her shoulder. "You'd definitely be welcome. No invite needed."

"BRIDGET, you'll have to indulge us for a minute. Every year on Thanksgiving we go around and say what we're thankful for," says my mom before we dig into the food. "You're more than welcome to join, but please don't feel obligated."

"Oh, I love this idea," Bridget says, smiling brightly. "I'd love to join in."

"Wonderful! This year I'm grateful for advancements in medicine and the wonderful staff at Park Cove Hospital," Mom starts.

"I'm thankful for digital meat thermometers," Dad says. "They're far more accurate than the other kind."

"I'm thankful for..." Mac trails off, thinking hard. "I'm thankful for Bridget. Thank you for being someone I can talk to."

"Jeez, Mac Attack. You're going to make me cry," Bridget chuckles. "My turn? I'm thankful for..." She taps her cheek and her eyes meet mine from across the table. "Traditions. New and old. And strangers who turn into... not strangers."

"I'm thankful for holiday competitions," I say. My voice feels scratchy, throat coarse like sandpaper. "And randomly generated computer pairings."

Bridget grins. Under the table, her foot finds mine, tapping against my boot.

"Wonderful! Thank you, everyone, for sharing. Bridget, how is the holiday competition going? Theo's been sparse on details." My mom smiles as she hands over the bowl of potatoes to Mac.

"It's been incredible. Lucas is making us these life-size figures we're going to set up. All the exterior and interior lights are hung. We're also adding some Christmas photos from years past. If you have any baby pictures of Theo in a stocking I'd love to steal them."

"I have some of him from the pictures we did with a mall Santa when he was... Gosh, he must have been about three or four years old. He screamed bloody murder, and everyone in line looked at me like I was torturing my child."

"I think they're in the shoebox upstairs," my dad adds. "I'll track them down after we eat."

I groan. "Do we really need to show off memories of me being tormented?"

"Grams, BB and I decorated a tree and it looks *so* good," Mac says.

"Did you? I'll have to come by and visit. I bet it looks great. What's it like owning a bookstore, Bridget?"

I mouth out a "sorry" to Bridget. Mom loves meeting new people, and it doesn't happen as frequently anymore. With no mobility in her lower body, she relies on Dad to get in and out of the wheelchair. Physical therapy four times a week is the majority of her social interaction. There's a chance—a very, very, *very* slim chance—she might walk again. It's less than one percent. It's less than a tenth of a percent, but Mom's determined.

"Incredible," says Bridget, unfazed. "It's always been my dream. I wanted to translate my passion for books to an occupation. I opened the store with a friend and I can't imagine doing anything else."

"And you're next door to the hardware store, right?" Mom asks. She throws a wink my way. "Interesting."

The rest of the meal passes with good conversation, delicious food, and lots of laughs. Mac regales us with her friends' holiday plans, and the most-wanted item on her Christmas wish list. Bridget blends into the dialogue easily, nodding along, answering questions and never seeming bored or out of place.

"Does anyone need more food?" Dad asks when our plates are clean.

"I'm stuffed," I say. "Bridget made pumpkin pie, so I need to save some room for dessert."

"I can start the dishes," Bridget says.

"I'll help!" Mac announces, standing and gathering the empty plates.

My dad retreats to the living room, getting the television cued up for football.

"She's very beautiful, Theo," Mom says, keeping her voice low. "Incredibly sweet, too."

I shrug, feigning disinterest. Like I'm not watching her out of the corner of my eye, rolling her sleeves up and dipping her arms into soapy water. Like I'm not listening to her laugh traveling over the room. Like I don't notice how much colder the air around me feels without her nearby. "Don't get any ideas. I invited her so she wouldn't be home alone today."

My mom nods and reaches over, patting my hand. "Of course you did, son. Of course you did."

MY DAD IS PASSED out in his recliner, the football game broadcast on the television. My mom, Bridget, and Mac are doing a puzzle in the living room, keeping their voices low. Ziggy found his way onto the couch and is taking a nap on a stack of pillows.

I step out to the porch for some fresh air. I yawn, taking a seat on the top step and stretching out my legs. My parents live at the end of a cul-de-sac, and it's always quiet out here. You can hear the birds chirping, the wind blowing. It's peaceful, calm. To my left is the wheelchair ramp Dad and I constructed five years ago, cutting down the hedges to accommodate the incline from the driveway.

It brings back the bad memories, yeah, but it'd also been the first time since the crash I heard my dad laugh. It was four months after the accident. We were working outside, trying to set the foundation for the ramp. I nailed my shirt to the wood, so distracted I wasn't looking where my hammer was aimed. I lost my shit when I noticed, trying to rip myself free for ten minutes. Dad was no help, cackling so hard he could barely breathe. When I saw him laughing, I'd started too. We stood out there, cracking up for half an hour. Sometimes, in the dark days, you'll take any kind of relief you can find. Even if it includes moronically nailing your brand new shirt to a homemade wheelchair ramp.

I hear the front door snick open then closed. A glance over my shoulder shows Bridget standing on the porch.

"Hey," I say.

"Mind if I join you?"

"Not at all."

Her boots appear by my side and she drops to the ledge, left leg pressing against my right.

"Lunch was delicious. Thank you again for inviting me."

"Thanks for coming. Hopefully it beats sitting at home alone."

"By a long shot."

"I should offer you an apology."

Bridget shifts, turning her hips to look at me. "For what?"

"I didn't tell you about my mom."

Her brows furrow and she frowns. "What is there to tell me?"

I sigh. "The holidays aren't my favorite time of year. I... I really dislike them, actually. That's why I was pissed about the contest and didn't want to enter. Five years ago, my family and I were coming back from a party on Christmas Eve. It's the same party we go to every year at a friend's house. The same route we've driven hundreds of times. We were three minutes away from pulling back into the driveway."

I stare out onto the street, focusing on the pavement. Her hand laces through mine, rubbing the top of my palm in soothing, comforting circles. Across the street, I see a Christmas tree twinkling in the window of the Millers' living room.

Even though I *want* to share with her, it doesn't make it any easier. I still hear the sound of metal on metal. I still see the bright lights and the street lamp glowing above. I still feel the pain across my chest from time to time, where the airbag deployed, bruising my upper body.

"It was a Friday. I remember it being chilly. My dad joked about the backseat not having heated seats. I was driving. I pulled up to the stop sign. I waited. I checked both ways. When I began to accelerate, right when we were in the middle of the intersection, someone came blazing through their stop sign and slammed into our car. They were going sixty five in a twenty."

"Holy hell," Bridget whispers. Her fingers dance over the scar on my thumb from a hammer accident ten years ago. Over the knuckles that have become weathered with years of age and work. Her path is a gentle, guided meditation.

"It was a college kid who hit us. He fled the scene and was tracked down a couple of miles away. He blew twice over the legal limit. It hurt like hell to hear the sentencing he received and the felony going on his record since he was so young. Life has consequences, though, and unfortunately for him, his mistake was a big one."

"Were you injured?"

"I needed stitches. I have a gnarly scar on my chest from a piece of glass, but nothing too bad. Mac had a concussion. Dad broke his leg. But Mom bore the brunt of it. She was on the side in the backseat where the driver hit. It was... I've never heard someone scream like that before. It still haunts me, sometimes. I was disoriented and couldn't get the door open. Dad was yelling at me to get out. Mac was crying. Everything was so loud."

"Is that why..." Bridget pauses.

"You can ask."

"You don't like lots of people. Loud noises. Is it because of the accident?"

"Yeah. I get jittery, almost, around them. Large groups of people make me think someone's going to come up and start talking about everything freely, like I owe them details of the story. Between Mac's mom leaving and the accident, it's been hard for me to find any joy during the holidays."

"That's all valid, you know. You don't have to justify yourself to anyone," Bridget says softly. Her head drops to my shoulder, hair tickling my neck. It's a nice weight, a reminder she's still there. She's still listening. "Is your mom the reason why you'd spend your money on the avenue?"

"Yup."

"It all makes sense. You're a good man, Theo Gardner."

"It was a spinal cord injury and she can't walk. My dad helps her around everywhere. In and out of the wheelchair. He drives her places, takes her to physical therapy. There was no way they were going to be able to keep running the store after the accident, so it got handed down to me. I harbor a lot of guilt. I got emails from guys in the driver's fraternity for years after. They said maybe it was my fault for not looking again before I drove through the intersection. They claimed there's no way I could've missed a car flying at me. Maybe they're right. Maybe if I hadn't stopped to use the bathroom before we left the party, we would have made it home in one piece. Maybe if I hadn't lingered at the stop sign for a second too long, answering Mac's question, we would have missed being hit. I've played this *What If?* game so many times."

"Oh, Theo. Thinking about other possibilities doesn't change the outcome. You'll never be able to alter the past but you *can* focus on the here and now. You're alive. Your parents are alive. Mac is alive and holy hell is she wonderful. Not one person inside this house holds you accountable. I'm not telling you to forget it happened. You have so much of your life left to live. And you deserve to be happy during it."

"How do you do that?" I mumble. My cheek rests against her hair. "How do you always know the right thing to say? How do you know how to make me feel... so fucking good? Sometimes with you I think..." *I think I'm on top of the goddamn world. I think I'm invincible.* "Thank you, Bridget. For your kind words. For being here today. Just"–I pause and swallow over the lump lodged in my throat–"thank you."

"Do you want me to head home?"

"Before we eat the pie you made?"

She laughs. It's a warm hug on a cool, December night. One that keeps you free from harm and whatever nightmares might plague you. It's comforting. Encouraging. The best sound I've ever heard.

Bridget climbs to her feet and pulls me up with her. I reach out and tuck a piece of hair behind her ear. The tips of my fingers ghost over her cheek.

"The pie might be shit," she says.

"Doubtful. If it is, we can just have a food fight or something. I know there's a bottle of chocolate syrup in the fridge."

"Don't tempt me with a good time. Between Mac and me, we could kick your ass."

"In your dreams. You're taking the first bite, by the way. If you die, I'll know it was poisoned."

"Maybe I've brought up my tolerance, becoming immune to the toxins. Maybe this has been my plan all along, just so I can watch you suffer at the kitchen table and get you to admit your deep, dark secrets. The ones more scandalous than a Blockbuster rendezvous."

"I'd sleep with one eye open if I were you."

"Game on." With a flick to my cheek, she turns on her heel and marches back into my parents' house. I hear her jovially call out Mac's name.

It's kind of like her constant presence in my life these days. She's determined. Ambitious. And arrived just in the nick of fucking time.

TWENTY-EIGHT

BRIDGET

"HEY," I say, looking up from the whipped cream I'm piping onto a drink. "I wanted to talk to you about something."

Theo's eyes shift from his laptop to me. He's been working at the end of the bar all morning without saying much, brows knitted and scrunched. His focus has hardly wavered. The only sign of emotion from him was when I set down a cappuccino and blueberry muffin an hour ago. He gave me a bright smile and dug into the pastry.

"What's up?"

"Remember the book club you invaded last month?"

"Did I do that?" he asks. "I don't recall."

"Very funny. I wanted to let you know our next meeting is tomorrow night."

He sits up straighter. "Thanks for the heads up. What book is on the agenda this time?"

"You really want to know?"

"Of course. Since I got an in-depth listen last time, I'd hate to be left out this go round."

"Oh." I run my palms over the front of my apron. I nudge the piping can away and grab a handful of napkins, replenishing the depleted stack in the middle of the counter. My skin is turning pink at his question. I know I could easily ignore it, brush it aside and get back to work. It feels like a *challenge*, though, like he doesn't think I'll tell him. I level my eyes with his. "It's about... um... this... it's about a married couple who realize they're both in love with his best friend. They, uh, ask him to watch them. Then join in."

Holy hell, that was nearly impossible to get out. My cheeks are flaming and my shirt is sticking to my skin, growing damp with sweat.

"What's the title?" Theo asks.

"Um. It's called *More*."

"Cool." He clicks on his computer, tapping away on the keys. "Just ordered it."

"You did *what*?" I blurt out.

"I thoroughly enjoyed your discussion last time, so I want to see what all the fuss is about with the next one. It'll give me something to do when I'm home tomorrow night, not interrupting you."

"B-but you... Men don't..."

"Why don't you finish that sentence? Men don't what, Bridget?"

My name sounds filthy, dirty. Borderline obscene as he dares me to tell him what's on my mind. Theo's studying me, *learning* me, and *god*, it's a wicked burst of sin.

"They don't read romance novels," I whisper. My voice quakes and I swallow, arousal and desire creeping up my spine. Envisioning Theo sprawled out on his bed, one hand holding the paperback, the other buried in his boxers, lazily stroking, eyes half closed. A sated, pleased smile on his face while he asks me which parts are my favorite and which moves I'd like to try. *Fuck*. "They don't... take notes or want to learn new things."

"Sounds like you've only been with boys, then. What a

shame. Real men don't give a fuck about how they learn, as long as their girl gets off. Books. Videos. Live demonstrations. They all sound good to me."

It's embarrassing I have to stifle the moan catching in my throat. "Are you implying if a girl you were seeing wanted to film you in the bedroom, you'd be game? You'd... go watch other couples to learn what you might like?"

Theo's eyes blaze, shadows of embers hidden behind his irises. "Yes, Bridget. Whatever she wanted, she would get."

He resumes his typing and I'm left gaping at him, moisture pooling in my underwear and nipples pebbling under my shirt. Are we going to pretend this conversation never happened? Am I supposed to look him in the eye and carry on like he didn't imply he knows *exactly what to do* to satisfy a woman? And if he doesn't, he's willing to try whatever it takes to get better?

My eyes squeeze closed. This has to be a dream. This cannot be *real*.

I wonder if...

I wonder if he'll think of me when he reads.

Gulping down a breath, I slowly open my eyes. Theo's still there. Still clicking away on his keyboard, unaffected by the exchange. I grab the drink I was working on before I got distracted by... him.

God, now he's all I can think about.

"Try this."

I set the overflowing beverage on the counter. Theo's nose wrinkles in disgust, and he pushes the cup away.

"I'm all set, thanks."

"Come on. I've been working on this for weeks! It's December 1st. We have the interview tomorrow and the holiday hayride on Friday. We're meeting up with everyone to decorate tonight. It'll put you in the holiday spirit."

"Why are you making drinks?"

"I wanted to try something new."

"What the hell is it?" he asks.

"It's a holiday blend. Think of a mix between sugar cookies, cinnamon, butterscotch, and hot chocolate."

"Are you trying to poison me?"

"First the pie on Thanksgiving, now the drink. Is it a fetish? Has someone tried to poison you in the past? Is that why you think I'm going to *Romeo and Juliet* you?"

"How can I be so sure? You wielded a hammer at my head yesterday."

I roll my eyes, exasperated. "That was to demonstrate my knowledge of tools."

"I think you were secretly hoping it would fly out of your grip and peg me right in the skull." Theo sighs heavily. I see the moment he admits defeat. "Give me a straw."

I squeal with glee and drop two straws into the glass. The whipped cream, piled high, hides them from view. I duck out from behind the counter and take the stool beside him. Our knees knock together. He doesn't pull away. Neither do I.

"I want your honest opinion, which I know isn't difficult for you. When you inevitably hate it because it's filled with sunshine and rainbows instead of the usual doom and gloom you enjoy, please give me *thoughtful* feedback on what you didn't like."

"Deal. Cheers."

Theo dips his chin and takes a long sip of the drink. I mimic him, my shoulder brushing against his as I swallow down a gulp.

"Well?" I wipe my mouth with the back of my hand. He ignores me, staring at the glass. "Theo?"

"Hush."

"I know it's terrible. Could you at least–"

"You don't listen very well, do you, Bridget?" Theo asks. He picks the glass off the counter and drinks the rest of it down in four quick gulps. "I like it."

"Pardon?" I sputter.

"See? Not a good listener. Have I rendered you speechless?"

"No. I just... I saw this going a dozen different ways, and you liking the drink was near the bottom of possibilities."

He hums and leans forward. Getting closer, his thumb glides over my my bottom lip, cleaning away the remnants of whipped topping left behind. My mouth parts instinctively, desperately, and Theo grins.

"Do you want to taste, Bridget?"

"Yes," I whimper. I don't know what he's offering me a taste of; the drink. The whipped cream. *Him.* I just know I want it, more than I've wanted anything else in my life. "Please."

"That goddamn word is going to be the death of me," he rasps as his thumb dips inside my mouth, hooking under my lip.

My teeth drag over the pad of his finger. My tongue licks up the length of the digit, and I hear a low groan rumble from him. It's like thunder in the distance; soft at first, then building and building, a mighty storm brewing.

His knees nudge my legs wider to accommodate his frame. I don't care if I'm wearing a skirt. I don't care if I don't have on tights today. I don't care if it's 2 p.m. on a Tuesday and anyone walking down the sidewalk could see us or walk in. I feel the *need* I have for him. The desire for his hand to drop to my thigh, to work its way up my skirt.

"Maybe you do listen," he whispers. His thumb drags out of my mouth. I'm weak, truly pathetic, when I lean forward, not ready to give him up yet. "Look at you. That wasn't enough, was it? You want more."

My eyes flutter open. I find Theo's cheeks flushed, a shade between pink and red. His jeans show the outline of a bulge, straining against the denim. There's heat in his eyes. Murderous, scorching heat. His gaze drops to my legs and he sucks in a breath. His hand twitches, his fingers flex.

My own hand falls to my thigh. I open my legs wider. He makes a strangled sound, a mix of a groan and a grunt. "What if I do?" I ask softly, daringly. "What if I do want more?"

Theo is like a statue. Only his eyes move and they dart everywhere. My lips, my neck. My chest, my thighs. His mouth parts, and he's about to say something else.

Tell me you want more too, Theo.

Tell me what to do next.

The door to the shop opens, a rush of cold air snuffing out the electric charge in the room. The bells jingle, announcing the entrance of a patron. My legs snap closed. Theo scoots back on his stool, nearly tumbling off the leather. He turns away from me, scrubbing a hand over his face.

"Fuck," he mumbles.

"Bridget. Theo." Lucas joins us at the counter and grins. "I'm not interrupting anything, am I?"

"No," we answer in unison.

I jump up, dashing behind the counter. I adjust the hem of my skirt and grab a mug, attempting to busy myself so I don't turn around and show the blush creeping up my skin.

"Doesn't look like it." Lucas smirks.

"Shut up," Theo says. "What are you doing here?"

"Uh, I'm here to decorate like we've been planning for weeks. You're the one who sent out the email. What are *you* doing here?"

"I made him a drink," I supply.

"Really? Is that what the kids are calling it these days?" Lucas asks. "Where's the rest of the gang?"

"You're early. By ten minutes," I answer.

"Shame. Wonder what would have happened if I wasn't."

Theo glances up from his laptop. His eyes snare mine.

Keeping his gaze steady, he licks his thumb–the same finger he had in my mouth moments ago. He chuckles and I can *feel* the rumble of his laughter from over here.

"Yeah," Theo says. His lips tip up and he shakes his head, like he's regretfully pushing a thought away. "Shame. Maybe next time."

Next time, I think. My belly swoops low. A new blush covers me. I nod, then dip my head.

"Guess we'll find out," I answer.

TWENTY-NINE
THEO

"THIS IS STUPID," I say under my breath. "Really fucking stupid."

"Will you stop fidgeting?" Lucas asks. Irritation is evident in his tone as he adjusts my collar, hands working out the creases in the starchy, stiff fabric. The button-up I'm wearing is far more constricting than my normal cotton shirts and flannels. My arms feel confined under full sleeves.

The interview and photoshoot with *Travel Living* have been a dreaded event from the second we agreed to join the competition. In early November, it seemed a lot further away. Something I could procrastinate worrying about, a date in the distant future that would be a problem for later.

Later, unfortunately, has finally caught up with me, and here we are. Kicking off the month of December with an interrogation and flashes of cameras, my scowl and pinched eyebrows splashed across the pages of a magazine for all of America to see.

"I'm still confused why people care. You're telling me someone in bumfuck Michigan is going to be interested in a bookstore and hardware store in the middle of Florida? They couldn't find Park Cove on a map if they tried."

"Ah." My friend chuckles and pats my cheek affectionately. "There's the cynical man I know and love. Theo, have you ever looked at Bridget's social media? Her store has hundreds of thousands of followers. Do you know how she got there? Someone posted about the shop online. Followers mean sales, man. It's a *big* deal to be featured. This magazine is read by a lot of people. Our online store sees minimal traffic. This article and exposure could—and should—bump up our revenue."

"Why order from us when they could go to a big-name chain? And get it in half the time?"

"People always like supporting small businesses, especially during the holidays. It's my job to look at the numbers, man. This can only be a good thing for us. So why don't you tuck that frown away, smile like you love wearing a shirt buttoned to your chin, and have a good time?"

Lucas is right. Our revenue is fairly substantial; we're the best business in the surrounding zip codes. People drive forty-five minutes from three towns over to visit our store because they know they're not just getting a product thrown at them. They're getting information and knowledge, questions answered. We take the time to explain things to each customer, not letting them feel like an idiot when they don't know the differences between gas and electric lawnmowers.

Every year we pull in millions of dollars, but it's not all income and cash flow. A portion goes to charity. We pay ten employees' salaries, including healthcare and 401k contributions. Products have to be purchased for the store. Electricity, gas, and water need to be factored into the cost of running the store.

If he calculated the numbers and says this interview is a good idea, I believe him. At the end of the day, this article isn't about *me*. It's about the store, and the potential to give my staff a larger bonus. To hire an additional body to lighten everyone's work load. It would be in my best interest to quit my complaining and plaster the fakest smile on my face, ready to share my feigned excitement for the holidays.

"Okay. Fine. You win. For the good of the store," I relent. "I'm heading over. Wish me luck."

With a clasp of my shoulder and a reassuring smile, Lucas nods. "You're going to be fine, man. Take a deep breath."

I offer him a terse nod and walk a few short paces to A Likely Story. At the glass I pause, peering through the snowflake covered window to assess the battlefield I'm about to walk into. There are large lights on stands, stretched toward the ceiling. White backdrops lean against shelves. A small group of people are pointing and gesturing to certain areas of the room.

The door to the shop swings open, and Bridget leans against the entryway.

She's wearing a black long sleeve shirt. Dark skinny jeans. On her feet are her black Converse. Her hair spills down her shoulders and on her lips is a bright smile.

Beautiful. The thought catches in my chest. A rumble. A shake. A shove away.

"Hey, Collector," she says

Instantly, I feel better. The patches of dread and apprehension are still there, yeah. But somehow, with those two words and the sound of her voice, I'm more relaxed. I believe that maybe, possibly, I can tackle this.

"Hey, Brownie."

"Are you okay?"

"I'm nervous. You know I'm not great at talking to people. I despise being the center of attention. Now we're combining the two and I'm a little anxious."

I scuff my shoe against the concrete. I hear her walk over to me, and her palm lands on my forearm. It's an action that's becoming a regular occurrence. Like always, her touch grounds me. Reminds me to take a deep breath, then another, then another.

"Would it make you feel better to know I'm freaking out, too?" she says softly, and I bring my chin up.

"You are?" I scan her face, searching for any sign of uncertainty.

There.

Her smile is strained. Pinched in the left corner. Her dimple is hidden away, and her eyes are less bright. She looks tired. Pale.

"Yeah." She gives me a squeeze and her arms return to her side. "We can get through this together."

"Okay," I agree. "Together."

Bridget's chin juts toward the door and I nod. Her arm laces through mine, guiding us to the leather couch positioned in the middle of the room. We sit down and her knee presses into mine, a comforting gesture.

"You with me?" she asks. Low, quiet, so only I can hear.

"Yeah. I'm with you."

"Good. I'm not leaving your side, okay?"

"Okay."

"Hello you two! My, my, aren't they cute. You, especially." A wink from the blonde woman standing over us gets tossed in my direction.

"Hi," Bridget says. "I'm Bridget. This is Theo. We're ready for the interview. I know we received an itinerary to stick to. We both have business to run, and we'd like to get started so we can get back to work as quickly as possible."

Thank fuck for her.

"Of course." The interviewer smiles at us and takes the seat opposite the sofa. "We are so excited to sit down with you. My name is Lindsey, and I'm one of the chief editors at *Travel Living*. The goal of today is to let the readers get to know you a little better. Sure, they might see the social media posts or pop into your stores from time to time. But who really are Bridget and Theo?" Her eyes bounce between us before turning to the woman beside me. She offers a smile that doesn't seem authentic. "Bridget. Why don't we start with you? Tell me about why you started a bookstore."

I tune their conversation out, nodding at the appropriate moments. I hear chunks of Bridget's story. Some of it I know. Some of it I don't. Some of it I'd like to learn more of. Her voice is strong, easily answering the questions lobbed her way. There's an unmitigated joy to her words when she talks about certain parts of her life; her friends, the books, joining the competition. It's love of the small things in life. Finding beauty in the mundane. Christmas magic and cheer, and pure thankfulness for the opportunity to be sitting on this couch, sharing her story.

I'm lucky to be beside her, to listen to her passion and soak up her sunshine. Bridget's special, and the more time I spend with her, the more her thigh presses into mine, reassuring me and keeping me calm, the more I think I want her to stick around.

"Theo! It's your turn now."

"Great," I say.

"Everyone was surprised by your agreement to sit down for the interview. From what I've heard from folks around town, you're typically someone who keeps to himself. You send proxies to town hall meetings. Can you give us any insight into your reclusiveness?"

My spine stiffens and I pull at the collar of my shirt. "As CEO of Gardner's Hardware, I have a lot of tasks I need to accomplish each day. It doesn't afford me a lot of time to sit around and be social. I handle business behind the scenes, while Lucas, our CFO, often takes my place at the town events."

"Interesting. Now, Theo, everyone knows about the accident of course."

My jaw flexes. My hands run up my thighs, turning into fists. This was not a line of questioning I anticipated being asked.

"That night really proved to be a turning point for the company," the woman continues. "Why don't you tell us about the store being in your family for years and the aftermath of such a life-changing event?"

"My family has owned the store for generations. My great-grandfather started Gardner's Hardware before Cove Avenue rose in popularity. It was smaller back then, about half the size of the shop now. His motto was "people over profit." He wanted to make money, yeah, but he cared about the community more. When my parents took over, they found additional ways to get involved with other local organizations. They're well-loved by so many members of our city. The accident was unfortunate and unpreventable. Mom and Dad didn't want to sell, so that left me to step in."

"Do you think you're qualified to sit in the CEO seat despite having no prior management experience? Your sales numbers this year are slightly lower than years past. Nicknames have been tossed around about you, mentioning words such as *abrasive*. How do your parents feel about all this negativity?" the interviewer asks, staring at me inquisitively.

She's baiting me, trying to get me to reveal some revolutionary information that's going to sell copies of the magazine. I'm about to open my mouth and respond in a way that's certainly going to paint me as an asshole, living up to the adjective of abrasive, but Bridget speaks first, intervening on my behalf.

"Lisa," she says.

"It's Lindsey."

"I'm so sorry. My mistake," Bridget apologizes. "It's been a crazy month. Surely you understand."

I know Bridget's apology isn't sincere. Her smile has faltered. Her grip on the armrest of the couch has become a smidge tighter. She's sitting up straighter, back rigid and alert.

My lips twitch at the hidden venom behind her words.

"If you aren't going to ask us questions about the competition, like how many lights we're using, what our theme is, or the best way to make hot chocolate, perhaps we should reschedule the remainder of this interview with someone who *is* interested in doing the job correctly," Bridget says.

Lisa—shit, Lindsey—clears her throat. Her cheeks are pink and she looks mortified by the chastising. "My apologies. What a wonderful question. Theo, how do you prefer your hot chocolate?"

I look over at Bridget and smile. "Always made with milk, not water. Topped with marshmallows. Bridget here hates them."

"Because they are disgusting," she emphasizes.

The interviewer jots a few notes down. "And Theo, how do you feel about the theme your teams are doing? Home for the Holidays, correct?"

"That's right. I'm excited," I answer honestly. "It gives all of our staff members a chance to be involved, and they've also all loved adding personal touches to the decorations. I was hesitant about the contest as a whole in the beginning, but Bridget's plans have been easily manageable and fun to contribute to."

"This question is for both of you. What's been your favorite Christmas gift you've ever received?"

"A Barbie Jeep when I was a kid," Bridget says. "I loved that thing."

"My favorite material item would be a bike I got when I was ten. It had flames on the side. My favorite non-material item would be taking on a new title and role I never expected, and feeling immensely grateful for every step along the journey."

"Lovely. Why don't we move to the photo portion of the day?"

"What kind of photos are y'all planning on taking?" Bridget asks.

"We figured we'd do two sets. One here, then another in the hardware store. The photos over there will have the employees in it, too."

"Sounds easy enough. What are the photos going to be of?" I ask.

"We're going to have you two making brownies."

"I am not making brownies," I chuckle. An apron hits my face at the end of the sentence. I pull the fabric away to find the front is covered with dogs wearing sunglasses.

"Nice try, Gardner. Come on." Bridget inclines her head to the counter set up with an assembly line of bowls and ingredients.

I heave a sigh and reel in the comment I want to make, because I know I'm going to stand up. I know I'm going to follow her to the counter. I know I'm going to tie this damn apron around my waist, and I know I'm going to make brownies by her side, doing my best to not care about how much she lights up at the sight of damn chocolate chips.

THIRTY

BRIDGET

"YOU'RE MAKING A MESS," Theo observes from my left. He's working diligently, whisking the eggs. His attention is laser-focused on the mixing bowl and the rhythmic circles he's drawing in the batter.

He's not wrong. Melted butter covers the countertop. A dusting of salt has accumulated on the floor, looking like freshly fallen snow. Sugar lines the metal farmhouse sink, granulated grains sticking to the lip of the basin. It's a disaster zone I can't wait to clean up.

"Shh," I answer. The shared space seems smaller with his body compared to Chandler's frame I'm used to dancing around, and my hip accidentally bumps his. We've migrated closer as we follow the recipe I picked out for us, doing our best to ignore the dozen cameras clicking away. They're taking photos, directing us when to move on to the next step, how to angle our chins so we fit in the frame. It's a bunch of professional lingo I'm clueless about, and I nod when they ask us to hold a position for several seconds, lens shutters filling the lulls in conversation.

"They could've used statues instead of us," he whispers. "Probably would have been more effective."

I snort, bumping his hip again. This time, it's intentional. "Are you ready to add the chocolate?"

"Bridget, I'm flying by the seat of my pants. I thought we were supposed to add the chocolate six ingredients ago."

A laugh tumbles out of me. I went with a foolproof recipe, one that's impossible to mess up. As he tied his apron in a secure double knot, Theo admitted he's never baked cookies, and certainly not brownies.

Pop-Tarts are the closest he's gotten to being a pastry chef.

I steal a look at him, wanting to make sure he's not overwhelmed. I grin at what I find. There's baking soda on his face, sticking to his cheekbones. Flour, somehow, has also made its way to his forehead. He's staring at the mixing bowl, determined to get every single detail correct.

He's an all-in kind of guy, I've learned. When Theo commits to something, he commits fully. It's with vigor, doing whatever it takes to complete the task at hand to the best of his ability. The sight of him now, a little unhinged, borderline not-put-together, out of his element, is sexy as hell.

"Chocolate it is," I say. I reach past him to grab the cocoa powder. As I stretch, my chest grazes his arm. His grip on the whisk wavers. The metal object clanks loudly against the bowl, jarring and magnified.

My cheeks warm at our position. I jut my chin up and stare into Theo's eyes. A scalding shade of brown that wasn't present seconds ago stares back, unblinking. I suck in a sharp breath and lean in closer.

Closer.

Closer.

"Bridget," he whispers. Soft, hushed, only I can hear the word. It mimics a caress down my skin, fingers teasing their way from my slightly-tangled hair to my hips, dancing across my curves.

It's a lover's touch. Cradling my cheek. Staring devotedly into my eyes, like I'm the only one in the world. A tender embrace hugging me tight, similar to the intimacy between two individuals who know each other wholly. Completely. Deeply.

It's unlike anything I've ever heard from him. A beautiful melody of hope, of passion, of pain.

Pain of not being able to do exactly what he wants.

Further, still, I lean. Even closer, drawn by an invisible force. The tug of a string. The push of a gentle breeze, guiding me and alighting me. *Beckoning* me. His right arm moves, palm landing directly on the counter. I'm caged in, body virtually fused to his. Heat crackles from his muscles, the resistance of staying put. I *feel* the blaze burning me, marking me on its devastating path.

"Theo," I answer.

A verbal blockade prevents me from speaking further. I don't need to. Our actions speak volumes, emotions and sensations conveying what mere dialogue cannot. Words wouldn't be sufficient. Only touch and taste and smell and kisses and intertwined limbs, breaths mingling as one would work.

It's only him and me. Gazes locked. Heartbeats synchronized. Pulse racing. Not another soul in the world. His eyes flick over my face. They move from my colored cheeks to the curve of my mouth. The freckles over my nose. They drag down to the column of my throat, the space beneath my ear. He licks his lips.

Everything around us dissolves, fading away into mist and whittling away to nothing. Theo and the searing, white-hot intensity passing through my veins are the only things that remain.

I want to kiss him.

I want him to kiss me.

The realization, the desire, the frantic, desperate urge barrels into me. My insides explode like dynamite. Yesterday was sensual. His thumb. My tongue. Parted thighs.

This is different. This is tender. Exploratory. His neck tilts down, the slightest, most indistinguishable inclination. All I can think about is his mouth meeting mine. His hands fisting my hair, dark brown waves tangled within the grasp of beautifully inked skin. Our hips pressing together, Theo possessing me... *Claiming* me... as if I were his and he were mine.

I push up on my toes. Is this the moment? The kiss that sweeps me off my feet, surrounded by books of other poetic gestures? The moment in our story I'll point to and say, "that's it. That's when I knew"? His fingers reach out and drag up my cheek, finding their way to my hair.

A flash goes off, a bright, blinding light. Stars form in my vision and I blink, clearing away the spots.

"What a perfect shot!"

The voice hurdles me out of the fantasy, out of pretend, and back to earth.

"Shit," I curse, trying to step away. As I move, I knock into Theo's arm, locking me in place. He withdraws immediately, accommodating my escape with a flex of his jaw, the twitch of his hand, and the bob of his throat.

He grabs the whisk, returning to his task. A red color creeps up his skin, settling on the nape of his neck, below the tufts of his hair. I turn my back to the cameras so I can wash my hands.

It's an unnecessary act, one designed to give me an opportunity to level out my breathing. Quiet my sprinting heart. Avoid thinking about the moisture pooling in my underwear, images of strong, deft fingers gripping my hips tightly as I'm lifted onto the counter eradicated from my memory.

"I think we've got everything we need here. We'll take fifteen minutes then head over to the hardware store for the next batch of photos," a photographer says. The group watching us begins to pack up their materials, folding up lights and turning off their cameras. They talk amongst themselves, ignoring us and our incomplete baking.

Theo adds chocolate chips to the bowl. "We might as well finish this, right?"

"Right. You can pour it into the pan now." My voice is rocky, outlined with longing and lust. I speak as if the moment before was a dream. A single action–an infinitesimal touch–has sent me into a downward spiral, on a collision course for devastation.

Theo's forearms flex, sculpted muscles hardening as he scoops the batter into the greased, glass pan.

Strong. Masculine. Controlled. Thorough. All adjectives to describe his tenacity and focus. The careful attention to detail, prevalent in the way he rotates the bowl ninety degrees to get every ounce of chocolate into the pan. He slides the dish into the oven in a fluid motion. Upon completion, his eyes meet mine for a second time.

His fingers dip into the bowl, salaciously coating the digits in leftover batter. Theo steps closer, reforging our contact. The tip of his boots nudge the tip of my sneakers.

"All done," he says. Husky, low, an undertone to the observation. "But I think we're missing something."

I mentally run through the recipe, one I've done a hundred times, ensuring we checked off each step. "I don't think so. I made sure–what the *hell*?" I squeal.

The chocolate on his finger is now on my cheek, a line running from my forehead to my chin. He emits a laugh. Lazy, amused, his breath kisses the bridge of my nose. The sound swirls in my stomach, a tide pool in the ocean. The chuckle is defined. Intentional. It's for *me*.

My eyes narrow and I reach past him to grab a swipe of residual chocolate, the last of the batch, and palm his face. A drop of chocolate rolls down his neck, catching in the hollow of his throat, staining the collar of his crisp, white shirt. He dips his chin, processing the attack. His movements pause. His tongue darts out, licking up the blob of batter lingering near his nose.

Then, he grins.

THIRTY-ONE
BRIDGET

THE SMILE IS BRIGHT, like the sun at high noon. A rainbow after a storm. Composed of every ounce of his being, it's an exploding stick of dynamite.

Devastating.

Perfect.

"Bad move, princess," Theo murmurs in warning.

I've never liked pet names, cringing at how pretentious and juvenile they can sound. But *princess*...

Princess I can get behind.

The word slithers down my body. It takes residence between my breasts, above my heart. It's not the first time he's said it, but it feels like the first time he's *meant* it. I smile at his threat, wondering how he's going to retaliate. There's two seconds of questioning before I have my answer.

Flour.

The bag of flour, tossed in my face and sticking to my cheek.

"Don't start what you can't finish," he adds.

"I always know how to finish," I volley back. I grab the bag of chocolate chips and tilt it over his head. I pause, giving him a look.

His hand circles my wrist. His thumb runs over my pulse point once, then twice. Up and down. A metronome, finding a pattern and leaving me with a shaky exhale.

"I'd think very, very carefully about your next move, Boylston."

His remark lacks malice and vexation. He's not upset but rather curious, I think, to see what I'll do next. I assess the threat and decide to be a little reckless.

"Catch me if you can, Gardner. Be careful, I'd hate for you to fall and break a hip. I hear recovery time is longer for those approaching fifty."

I pull out of his hold, dumping the remaining chips into his hair. The brown morsels cling to his locks, scattered within the lighter shade. I take off, darting out from behind the counter and running toward one of the bookshelves, searching for a safe haven.

His clunky footsteps, the ones I have memorized, follow me. When I peer over my shoulder, the laughter that flits out of me can't be stopped.

A splatter of batter over the right lens of his glasses. Chocolate on his cheek, continuing to infiltrate his neck. Hair sticking up, discombobulated.

The man is a complete mess.

But...

His *smile*.

It's still present. Vibrant, wider now. I shuffle to the middle of the store and he meets me. His elbows drop to the wood, a barrier between us.

"What am I going to do with you, Bridget?"

"What do you want to do with me, Theo?"

He licks his lips again and I follow the movement of his tongue, marking each inch it covers. "I'm starting to think there might be a list. A rather exhaustive list, because every time I'm around you, I become more and more confused."

"Confused about what?"

Darkened eyes grow an even deeper hue of brown. "How when I'm with you, everything is better. You make life fun. How I keep wondering what you–"

"Aren't you two a hoot?" Lindsay says. She interrupts us, hand folding onto Theo's shoulder. I want to peel her fingers away. "Why don't you get cleaned up so we can keep our day moving along? Your employees are ready for us next door."

We nod in unison, and Theo is the first to step away. He accepts a towel from one of the cameramen, tousling his hair to expel rogue chocolate chips. His smile vacillates, indifference replacing child-like joy.

I move back toward the group waiting to resume the session. From across the room his eyes find mine. A tantalizing glance, paying no attention to anyone except me. His gaze roams freely down my body. My hair. My chest. My legs. Back up. When he turns away, his mouth tilts again.

There's a question behind the raised lip. A promise buried there, too.

He tosses a wink my way, concluding our showdown with a game-winning shot that makes me weak in the knees, happy to lose.

We're not done with our conversation, the look says.

Good, I think. *I want to hear more.*

WHEN WE REUNITE with the gang for the rest of our pictures it's pandemonium. No one can keep a straight face. Someone sneezes. Malik's phone beeps. Paint cans topple to the floor and Lucas throws confetti in the air. Professionalism goes out the window when Santa hats get put on everyone's head. Everyone except Theo, who glares at Chandler when she covertly tries to sneak it over his hair.

We walk the photographers through our theme and design ideas, pointing out the half completed homemade figures. The lights lining the wall, making it appear like it's snowing. We show off the yarn clothesline that will hang pictures of holidays from the past. The two menorahs Felicity brought in, ready to be lit in two weeks. Bradley shares the slideshow he's putting together. After another forty-five minutes, last minute questions, and a few more photos, the magazine staff calls it a day and clears out.

"I made cookies!" I announce, placing the basket of treats on the counter. "We have less than three weeks until judging, y'all. Everything looks great so far. We'll tweak the remaining decorations leading into the final days, including the fake snow and the cool light stuff Malik has been working on. Friday we're doing the holiday hayride out at the DeLand farms. It's going to be cold so bring a sweatshirt! We can organize carpooling in the group chat. Thanks for all your hard work."

A flurry of movement answers me. Someone turns on the speakers, music playing. Hands grab for food. A flash of a cell phone camera goes off.

"No cookies for you?" Theo asks. He leans against a metal shelving unit and crosses his arms over his chest.

"I got my fill with the brownie batter earlier."

"I think there's still some flour on your face."

"No thanks to you. Can't wait to see how that shows up in a magazine. The editing they'll have to do to me."

"What are you talking about?"

"It's stupid."

He turns, facing me, and his brows furrow. "It's not stupid. What's going on?"

"My hair's been frizzy all day. There's dark circles under my eyes. My jeans are too tight. I don't know. I normally love taking photos but a big camera in your face is invasive. I'm sure my flaws will broadcast for all to see. And in ten countries, too!"

"You're not serious."

Now it's my turn to face him. "Serious about what?"

"This... this *flaws* nonsense."

"I'm partially kidding. I'm sure they'll photoshop the shit out of it and I'll look as good as new."

"Bridget. Those aren't flaws. Your hair isn't frizzy, but if you think it is it's only because we live in an actual hellhole and you spend six hours a day bending over a hot oven. You have dark circles under your eyes because you bust your butt, frequently and excessively. And then you go out of your way to help others, too, because you're that kind of person. Your jeans make your legs look like they stretch on for miles and..." He rubs his lips together. "They look great. I think you look great. All the time."

"Y-you do?"

"Yeah. I do. So if you think you're flawed, I guess I'm flawed too, because I like those parts of you. And if being someone who likes your flaws is wrong, then screw being right."

"Oh," I whisper. My lip wobbles, the tell-tale sign of a swell of emotions about to overtake me. I look away and bite my lip, the bubble of knowledge that no one has ever accepted those less-than-perfect parts of me rising in my chest. "Thank you."

"C'mere."

Theo's arms open and I shuffle into the embrace I've been longing for. The arms I've missed, blissfully content as I bury my face in his shirt, tears staining the fabric that's rough against my skin.

"Theo?"

"Yeah?"

"This shirt is awful. I hate it."

He laughs, shoulders shaking and jostling my cheek. "It's fucking terrible, isn't it? I'm burning it when I get home."

"Good. The flannels are better."

"Glad you agree." He squeezes my upper arms twice. "Doing okay?"

"Yeah." I nod and pull away, not wanting to overstay my welcome. Half of my brain is screaming at me to remain put, to enjoy him a little while longer. The other is telling me to leave, to not get too greedy.

It's a game of tug of war where no one wins.

I wipe my eyes and look across the room. I smile when I see Lucas talking Chandler's ear off. She's nodding along, pretending to look unenthused and bored. I can see the way she holds back a laugh, though. She subtly adjusts her position, a fraction of an inch, to get a little closer to him.

"Lucas is a nice guy," I say.

Theo follows my gaze and hums. "He's the best. After the accident, he really helped me out at the store and at home. It was such a big change and he's always been there. I'd trust him with my life. Does Chandler like nice guys?"

"No. She avoids them like the plague, unfortunately, and somehow always falls for the bad apples. She deserves one, though. A knight in shining armor. The guy that would hurt anyone that harms her."

"Lucas could be that guy."

"I'm sure he could be. I'm sure he is. Chandler doesn't want a relationship, and Lucas doesn't strike me as the guy who does anything casual."

"Sometimes people change," Theo says.

"Yeah. Sometimes they do."

"I need to run. Mac has soccer practice tonight."

"I love that she's an athlete. Does she want to play in high school? Did you play?"

"I won't force her or pressure her to pick up a sport. If she wants to play, I'll support her. And yeah, I did play. All through high school."

"Huh," I say. "I never would have pegged you for a soccer guy. Football or rugby, maybe. Something violent with a lot of grunting and anger."

"Your kindness knows no bounds."

"Speaking of kindness, I should tell you there's still a chocolate chip in your hair."

"I'm saving it for later. Thank you for today. For calming me down. For being patient with me. For the food fight and... all of it, really. Thanks for being you."

I smile. "I wouldn't want anyone else to throw a bag of flour in my face."

Theo nods and I nod back. Soon we're two people surrounded by tape measures and yardsticks, nodding at each other like we're idiots. Traces of brownie still on our faces but totally happy, and I wouldn't have it any other way.

He huffs and taps my hand in farewell, fingers drumming over the back of my palm. He glides away, leaving me alone, missing him every second he's gone.

THIRTY-TWO
THEO

IT'S 10:30 in the morning and I haven't been to my office. By now, I'm normally knee deep in paperwork, sorting through shipment tracking and counting inventory.

Not today.

I've yet to step foot inside my building, running hours behind schedule. Lucas sent me a dozen messages asking if I was alive.

I'm not sure I am.

My eyes are so bloodshot, it's a miracle no one's administered a sobriety test. I didn't have time to shave and coarse stubble pricks my palm every time I run my hand over my jaw. Three cups of coffee are doing little to keep me upright and I feel dead on my feet.

Instead of heading for our stockroom, I make a hard left, stopping outside A Likely Story. I pause before walking in. There's a question I need to ask, and I really don't want to. Gathering a slice of courage, I push the door open and walk toward the counter. Chandler's there, finishing the topping for a drink. She slides it to the far side of the coffee area for someone to pick it up.

"What the hell are you doing here?" Chandler asks.

"Uh." I rub the back of my neck. "Is Bridget in?"

She blinks. Stopping by close to lunchtime isn't something I've ever done before. Eyeing me suspiciously she crosses her arms over her chest. "She's grabbing something from the back."

"You're here well past your usual time," Greta comments from a stool on the opposite end of the bar. She doesn't bother to look up from the magazine she's flipping through, wrinkled hands turning the glossy pages.

"Late start," I grunt.

I'm not about to tell these women Mac woke me up in the middle of the night, panicking because she got her first period. I drove around for an hour, looking for a 24-hour pharmacy before finally finding what she needed. I snoozed my alarm, she missed the bus, and now my routine is *all* fucked up.

Mac didn't want to talk about what happened. She hid her face in her hands while I awkwardly shared articles I found from the internet, feeling woefully unprepared for the conversation. When I dropped her off at school and asked if she was okay, the car door slammed in my face. My texts have been ignored, and I think I've fucked up.

I slide onto the leather stool at the end of the bar. The seat has grown familiar to me since I first sat in it a handful of weeks ago, the morning Bridget offered me that egg sandwich. I've found myself on the leather more frequently as of late, and this is the first time I've felt a prickle of dread as I adjust my ass and lean my elbows on the counter, waiting.

The door to the hallway swings open and there she is.

Automatically, the room brightens at Bridget's arrival. Plants grow. Flowers bloom. Sunlight streams through the window. How the *hell* did I go years without ever realizing her effect on her surroundings?

"Theo Gardner. To what do I owe the pleasure?" she asks.

Her hair is up in a messy bun, pieces falling out of the elastic and framing her face. She's wearing a purple shirt paired with a jean skirt that barely hits the top of her thighs. Yellow ankle-high Vans. And a smile on her face, looking at me like I'm a prize.

"There was a small crisis in the Gardner household, hence my late arrival."

"Is Mac okay?"

"She's fine. I'm stopping by because I have a question for you."

"Yeah?" Her voice is breathier, lighter. "What's up?"

"You can say no. Don't feel obligated to agree."

Her smile shifts to timid and shy. Nervous, maybe. "I can't agree to anything if you don't ask me."

My hand runs through my hair and I notice Chandler and Greta watching us. It would have been nice to have this conversation somewhere without an audience present.

"I was wondering if you could watch Mac tonight for me. I kind of... I have a date."

The admission feels bitter on my tongue. Acidic, sour, a terrible taste left behind. As soon as I say it, I wish I could take it back.

Bridget's smile cracks and crumbles. Her face dims and she casts her eyes down. The air whooshes out of the room, a rush of oxygen leaving as her nose scrunches up. Her chin drops to her chest and she grabs a dish rag.

"A date?" she repeats.

"Yeah. I forgot about it. We planned it a month ago after I ran my shopping cart into hers. I thought she wouldn't text but she did and I—"

"And you said yes," she finishes for me.

"I did."

When I finally went to bed sometime in the early hours this

morning, I barely slept. I tossed and turned, debating on what I should do. Should I cancel? Does Bridget deserve to know? We're not technically *together*, even if we've exchanged a handful of moments I can't get out of my head.

I can't stop thinking about her. I can't stop finding ways to touch her. Subtle grazes, accidental brushes of my hips against hers, intentionally slipping my arm around her shoulders. I can't stop fantasizing about how I'd kiss her for the first time. I don't know if this... this desire to be with her is because it's *her*, Bridget Boylston, or because she's the first woman I've let get somewhat close to me in years.

So I agreed to the date like a goddamn moron and I'm kicking myself for agreeing. Because seeing the... the *hurt* painted on Bridget's face makes me want to stand this other woman up and drag Bridget home with me.

But I need to be sure. I can't upend my life for a maybe, no matter how right I think I might be.

"Wow. Uh. What time should I be there?" She turns her attention to the counter, furiously scrubbing a spot on the laminate I can't see.

"Whenever. Mac's fine by herself for a little while, so just after 6 is fine. You can bring Ziggy, too."

"Cool."

"Are you okay?"

It's a stupid question, the answer very evident on her face. Bridget raises her gaze, eyes hazy and unfocused. Her lips form a straight line and she shrugs, draping the dirty cloth over her shoulder. "I'm fine."

She doesn't *sound* fine, but before I can question her further, she turns and barges through the swinging door, leaving me alone.

"You're an idiot," Chandler announces. It's a good thing looks can't kill, because this woman would have murdered me seven seconds ago.

"Pardon?"

"I said: you're an idiot. I should probably throw a fucking in there, too. Yeah. Let me amend my previous statement. You're a fucking idiot."

"Yes," Greta agrees. She nods vigorously to punctuate her point. "You truly are."

"Men," Chandler grumbles. "They never get it, do they? We have to spell everything out, yet *we're* the problem."

"Maybe if someone told me what the hell is going on," I grit out. My voice raises and I take a deep breath. "Did I upset her?"

"No one is going to tell you anything. You can figure it out yourself." Greta's scolding is an insult to injury.

I glance at Chandler and she shakes her head. "Nope. You're on your own."

I curse under my breath, using every colorful expletive in the book. I peel myself off the stool and stalk toward the door. "Fine. Thanks for nothing."

"Maybe instead of searching for something," Greta calls over her shoulder, "you should open your eyes and see what's in front of you. What's *been* in front of you for a long damn time."

THIRTY-THREE

BRIDGET

"LET ME GET THIS STRAIGHT," Mac says as we drag an artificial tree across the living room floor. Ziggy dodges the skinny cardboard box, jumping onto the couch and safely out of the way. "My dad is out on a date with someone and you're stuck here watching me?"

"I'm not stuck doing anything," I answer. "I'm here because I want to be here. I'm helping him out."

"Oh my god," she groans. "Dad is such an idiot."

"How in the world is he an idiot?"

"He should be out with *you*."

I wrestle with a rogue piece of the fake fir. "Mac, he's allowed to go on dates with whoever he wants. He and I aren't... We're not together."

"Why *aren't* you together? He likes you. You like him. It can't be that difficult, can it?"

I forget how blunt kids can be. They don't understand the broad scope of actions and life outside their small bubble of reality. To Mac, her dad and I are two adults relatively close to the same age, both without anyone else in the picture. Why *wouldn't* we be dating?

"Feelings aren't always black and white, kiddo. Maybe he really, really likes the woman he's out with tonight. Maybe the two of them had a great connection and he's interested to see where it goes." I shrug. "He's not doing anything wrong by being out with someone else. I'm okay, I promise. I'm not mad at him."

Confused would be the appropriate adjective. I guess I interpreted our moments together differently than Theo did. It's no one's fault I'm disappointed he's out with someone, because we never had a specific conversation about it. I didn't realize how much I cared for him until I heard the word *date* come out of his mouth and knew he wasn't asking me.

I wasn't going to tell him no, either. We haven't been intimate. We haven't had an explicit conversation about *us*. Do I daydream about him pushing me against a wall and *finally* kissing me instead of playing games that raise my blood pressure and soak my underwear?

Repeatedly.

Factually, however, we're merely platonic companions with no romantic ties to each other.

Mac huffs and crosses her arms. "If he dates someone else will you still be around?"

"Sweetie," I laugh. "We're getting way ahead of ourselves. Take a deep breath. Besides, those are questions you need to ask him. If he finds someone who makes him happy, then I'm happy for him. But I won't jeopardize his relationship to hang out with y'all."

"Fine," she draws out. "I'm glad he's getting back out there. I've never seen him with a girl before. Ever. Like, never ever."

"Really? It's been that long?"

"Yeah," Mac says. "Not even anything where he's snuck around and hidden it from me. So, good for him for going to dinner, but I'm not as stoked about this as I should be. I wish you and Dad were together. I love him. You're great. It would be perfect."

"Put it on your Christmas list," I joke. "Maybe Santa will bring it for you. We're not putting the tree up without him here, are we? He'd be bummed to miss out on the decorating."

"No. He always complains about climbing into the attic, so now it's done and he has no excuse for not decorating with me this weekend!"

"Smart girl. Am I going to be in trouble for letting you on the ladder yourself?"

Mac shrugs, an evil glint to her eye. "Maybe."

I groan and grab a throw pillow, chucking it at her. "Not cool, kid. I just got on his good side."

Together we pull the eight-foot fake tree out of the box, adjusting the branches and height. Mac climbs back up the ladder to the attic again, pulling down the box of ornaments.

"Where are the lights?" I ask, setting the plastic box to the tree.

"Dad keeps them somewhere. He'll grab them when we decorate." She winces and squats to the ground, laying out the tree skirt.

"Whoa. What's wrong?"

"Nothing, I'm fine."

"You're holding your stomach like you're in pain. Oh, hell, is it your appendix? Do we need to go to the hospital? Shit, Theo is going to kill me."

"No. No hospital. It's embarrassing."

"Tattoo gone wrong?" I ask.

"I wish. I... I started my period last night."

"Ah, shot."

"For the first time."

"Double shot. Does your dad know?"

"Unfortunately," Mac groans. "He was all weird about it. He

got me what I needed but he tried to show me websites and stuff and it was *so* uncomfortable."

I burst out laughing, burying my head in my hands. "I'm sorry. I'm not laughing at you. I'm picturing Theo trying to talk to you about all of this and looking awkward as hell. Poor guy. Okay. Here's what we're going to do. We're going to order some pizza. We're going to eat the crap out of a tub of ice cream. We're going to put on a good movie. Are you allowed to watch PG-13?"

"I've seen *Titanic.* Dad pretends to not like it, but he always cries at the end."

I don't know why the admission causes my heart to swell. I envision Mac and Theo sitting on the couch a few feet away from me. A bowl of popcorn between them. A discreet wipe of his eyes when he thinks no one is watching.

My mind stupidly inserts myself into the vision, on the opposite end of the couch, with Ziggy at our feet. I rub my chest at the thought and how *nice* it sounds.

Now I know why he looked so tired this morning. I wonder if every time he's come into the shop a little dead on his feet, stubble on his cheeks, eyes barely open, he was up late, doing something for Mac. Helping with a school project. Offering her his best advice on heartbreaks. Nodding along with what outfits would look best for school picture day.

I think of Theo—handsome, kind Theo—then I remember he has this whole other part of his life I didn't know existed for so long. Of all the sides of him I've learned about, I think the title of *Dad* might be my favorite.

It's the time in his life when he's the most vulnerable and selfless. The time he relinquishes all control, handing it over to the five-foot-five girl next to me, not a single care in the world except her wellbeing.

I'm going to have to shake these feelings, locking them away as he possibly gets back out in the dating world with other women. I can't hold onto the knowledge of him carrying a stack of pads and tampons to his car in the dead of night. I can't imagine myself picking out a Christmas tree with him next year, debating the best options. I have to throw those memories away, into the wind, and not look at them again.

If Theo wanted to date me, he would date me.

And he's not.

"Okay. We're going to stuff our faces. We're going to find the best romcom movie on TV. We'll cry our eyes out then mend our hearts. How does all of that sound?"

Mac grins. "It sounds perfect."

"ANY QUESTIONS about what I showed you?" I ask Mac, scooping out a large portion of ice cream and dropping it into a bowl.

"No. Thank god for you, BB. I cannot imagine Dad looking me in the eye and talking about all of this."

"When I was in elementary school—maybe it was middle school, I forget—we had a week-long class on all of this body stuff. It was severely traumatizing. Be glad the internet exists these days."

Mac's nose wrinkles and she takes her helping of dessert. "Ew. That's gross."

"Disgusting," I agree. "Ready for a movie?"

"Yeah, but this TV sucks. The one in Dad's room is better."

"Are we allowed to go in there?"

"He won't care." Mac waves me off, trotting down the hall. I sigh and drop the tub of ice cream back in the freezer. I grab my bowl and follow behind, pushing open the door to his room.

It's so *Theo* in here. Clean. Organized. His shoes are lined up against the far wall, a mix of boots and sneakers. A rainbow of flannels hangs on the hook inside the closet door that's half-closed. The scents of pine and wood linger in the air, on the rug, near his bathroom door. I swallow around the lump in my throat.

"BB? Are you okay?" Mac asks.

"Yeah," I answer, joining her on the bed. A plaid comforter covers the mattress. On his bedside table is the book I recommended for him weeks ago, next to an extra pair of glasses. So many tiny pieces of him I might have to let go. I force a smile on my face and grab the remote. "Christmas movie or regular love story?"

THIRTY-FOUR

THEO

THE DATE WAS, admittedly, not great.

It might have been my fault. I was distracted at dinner, offering half-hearted answers to questions. Shrugging when she asked me personal details about myself. Smiling slightly when she shared all her ambitions, but not talking about what I'm looking for in a partner.

On paper, the woman was damn near perfect. Sitting across from her though, something didn't click.

I'm a little out of the game, but I distinctly remember there being an excitement.

A thrill.

A spark at the possibility of *maybe* and *more*.

There was none of that tonight.

I'm too old and too tired to settle for *almost*. If it's not a "home-run at the bottom of the ninth with the bases loaded" kind of perfect, I don't need it. I don't want it.

While I sat there and listened to her yoga routine, her wine preferences, and what she does for work, my mind kept drifting elsewhere. It wasn't on the woman three feet away from me. It was six miles away, in a craftsman house, with a dog, a young girl, and a pretty brunette, wondering what sort of trouble they were getting into. If they were having fun, and if they missed me like I think I missed them.

I cut the evening short after ice cream, politely turning down the offer for a drink at her condo. As I park in the driveway and unbuckle my seatbelt, I take a deep breath.

Climbing out of my car, I amble up the front steps, turning the key in the lock as quietly as possible. The lights are all off when I push the door ajar, darkness throughout the living room and kitchen greeting me.

"Bridget?" I call out. I shut the door behind me and walk inside, frowning.

I flip on a switch, finding nothing amiss or out of place. Scanning the room, I head for the hallway. I peek inside Mac's room, and it's empty. The bathroom and behind the shower curtain are too.

I'm about to head back to the kitchen and give Bridget a call when my attention catches on my bedroom door. It's cracked, and through the small sliver of space I can make out a couple of shapes. I approach it slowly, pushing the barrier fully open.

I stop in my tracks at the sight. My heart catches in my throat, working its way up from my chest. My feet can't move another step.

Bridget and Mac are on my bed, under the covers. The television on the wall flickers silent images. My daughter's head rests on Bridget's shoulder, curled on her side. They're breathing in unison, synchronized chests rising and falling. Ziggy is at the foot of the mattress, not bothering to open his eyes at my arrival.

A single, lonesome word repeats itself in my head loudly, persistently, as I stare. An unrelenting bastard that doesn't give up.

Happiness.

This is exponentially more soul-crushing than the kiss on the cheek I got from—*fuck*. What was her name again?

It doesn't matter. I'll never need to remember it.

I'm torn between wanting to take a photo, desperate to preserve this memory forever or down eight shots so I never have to remember this happened. Because it. Fucking. *Hurts*.

So goddamn bad.

I tread closer. The antiquated hardwood floorboards creak under my feet. The sound is magnified in the silent space and Bridget's eyes flutter open, blinking sleepily at her surroundings. I freeze again, trying to avoid startling or alarming her while she gets her bearings. A few moments, stretching for longer than I've been alive, is what it takes to break the fog of slumber. She sits up, more aware, adjusting her position on the pillows to not disturb Mac.

"Hey," she rasps.

I hold up a finger and hustle to the kitchen. A cup, filled with water, marched down the hall and thrust into her hand. She takes a sip and I sit on the edge of the bed.

"Hey," I answer quietly.

"Do I have drool all over my face?"

My eyes drop to her mouth—*that mouth*—and I smile. "Everywhere. You heathen."

"How was your night? What time is it?"

"Past 10. How'd Mac do?"

A thoughtful smile and a tender look down at the sleeping girl. "Great. We ate pizza. Made ice cream sundaes and watched a movie. We talked about why you were late to the bookstore this morning."

"She's upset with me, isn't she?"

"Upset with you?" Bridget asks. She adjusts her position on the pillows and—*shit*. She's wearing one of my shirts. An old soccer jersey, tattered and torn from years of wash. She has no right to look so damn good in a faded white scrap of clothing.

I clear my throat. "Yeah. I think I botched things up last night. I didn't know what to do or say. I wasn't... I forget that's something she'll have to experience and there's not..." I squeeze my eyes shut. "There's no woman in her life to talk about these things. I know my daughter. She would never ask my mom. She barely told me. I heard her crying in the bathroom at midnight and asked what was going on."

"Theo," Bridget says softly. "She's not upset with you. She's embarrassed and confused. Having to learn this part of life is overwhelming. It means she's not a kid anymore. Being a woman sucks, like, 83% of the time. Between periods, birth control, having to wear a bra, underwear that goes up your ass, catcalls and taunts from men who don't understand what *no* means, and having your heart broken when you least expect it, some days are bleak as hell. I told her it only gets easier from here, because being a woman is also totally badass."

"You said all that stuff to her? And she listened?"

"Yeah, she did. She's a great kid, Theo. You've done really well."

It's the highest compliment a parent can receive. I've heard it before from Mac's teachers, the parents on the soccer team. From Bridget, it's a different caliber. It's authentic and honest. Candid and pure, tired eyes blinking open and closed while her focus fluctuates between me and the nap I pulled her from.

"Thank you," I murmur. "That means a lot."

"Sorry we came into your room. She said the TV in here is way nicer and it's true. I got a heating pad hooked up for her, too."

"Make all the jokes you want about my age, but the heating pad is a game changer. I'm going to put her to bed. Meet me in the kitchen?"

"Sure," she agrees.

I walk to the opposite side of the bed and scoop Mac into my arms. She's gotten older, but she still feels like the baby I held almost thirteen years ago. I smile as I carry her to her room and pull the covers up to her chin. Ziggy jumps onto the bed, circling up and taking a spot at Mac's feet. A quick kiss on her forehead and I pull the door half-closed, making my way back to the kitchen.

"I hope she wasn't too clingy," I say. "Also, your dog loves her."

"She's Ziggy's new best friend," Bridget smiles.

Neither of us says anything else. It's eerily silent in the space between us. I'm not ushering her out the door. She's making no effort to leave. With her here, I'd be content with the quiet forever, I think.

"I, um, also stole another one of your outfits. My shirt had paint on it and my jeans weren't conducive to getting comfortable and watching a movie. Sorry. I can—"

"Turn around," I say. My voice sounds unfamiliar, a rough demand instead of a gentle ask.

Bridget swallows and I follow the bob of her throat. I watch her chest rise and fall twice before she nods. A slow spin awards me a view of her back, my name written across her shoulder blades. Like she's *mine*. She looks at me over her shoulder, lip stuck between her teeth.

Possessiveness like never before consumes me.

I grin greedily at the sight.

I can keep my hands to myself.

I know how to look and not touch.

But not this time.

This time, I know what I want, and I'm going to get it.

I want *her*.

Fuck it.

I stalk toward her and her eyes widen, surprised. Excited. There's a hint of a smug *finally, you asshole* look on her face, too.

I twirl her, chest grazing against mine. Gripping her cheek, I tilt her chin to meet my gaze.

"Took you long enough," she breathes out, an exhale of a laugh I feel against my neck. "Guess I need to walk around in your shirt more often to get your attention."

"This smart mouth." My thumb traces her lips. "Will you stay for a little? Have a drink with me?"

"Yeah." She nods. Her hands trail down my back, stopping at the base of my spine before falling away. "I will."

"Let's go out back. We won't have to whisper."

A nod, a smile. Her cheek turns, soft lips ghosting over my palm. I shudder at the contact and she hums in delight. "See you soon."

"BEER?" Theo asks. He holds a bottle out to me.

"Sure." I accept the drink, knocking the glass against his. "Cheers."

We both take a deep pull and I savor the carbonation on my tongue. I take a seat on the edge of the pool, my feet dangling in the warm water.

"So," I start. "How was your date?"

He shrugs and walks around the concrete, winding up directly across from me. "It was fine."

The light of the moon reflects off the ripples of waves, bright enough for me to see him clear as day. It's quiet out here, no sound except the water lapping against our shins and the chirp of a cricket. A chill is in the air but my body is feverish, heated, electrified, like something important is about to happen.

"Fine?" I press. "Your description for a night out with a woman is *fine*? You're allowed to tell me. We're friends, Theo."

Theo sips his drink, lips wrapping around the top of the bottle. He's so handsome. Sharp jaw. Long neck. His eyes never leave mine as he swallows and sets the glass on the deck. "I guess we are friends. I'm not seeing her again."

"Why not?"

"Because she isn't you, Bridget."

I nearly tumble into the water at his admission. A pressure forms behind my ribs. I think the world is spinning, flying by at rapid speed, flashes of colors and words. "Wh-what?" I stammer.

"Come here," he says roughly. "Please."

I stand, walking down the steps into the water, submerging myself to my chest. Theo watches my every move, eyes tracking each step. The soaked shirt clings to my body, fabric heavy as I make my way toward him.

His thighs open and I stop in front of him. My hand reaches out to grasp his calf, using his muscles to stabilize myself. His palm cups my cheek, thumb tracing over my lips for the second time tonight. It's like he's committing the shape, the feel, the size to memory.

"I hate that I went out with someone else, but I needed to do it. I've thought about kissing you for goddamn days, and I can't get you out of my head. I think about you when I go to sleep and when I wake up in the morning. I needed to know my feelings toward you weren't just because I haven't been with anyone in a while. I had to figure out if this was deeper than surface-level attraction or because you're a beautiful woman. And it is. The date was only *fine* because I knew within two seconds I wasn't interested. She didn't make me laugh like you do. She didn't smile at me like you do. When I got home and found you in my bed, hair sprawled out over my pillow, with an arm around my daughter I realized no one else will *ever* be you. That date solidified it would be the last I go on with someone who isn't you, Bridget."

There's conviction and purpose behind the words. His hand drops to my neck, fingers splaying wide over the column of my throat. His thumb presses into my windpipe and I reach up to fist his shirt.

"I was so jealous," I whisper. "I didn't think I had a reason to be because we're not... I haven't—"

"I know. I was so stupid. I'm sorry you were jealous. I'm sorry I was shitty. I hate that I made you feel like you were only a babysitter to me and not something more. I'll take you on a date, angel, and it'll be more than fine."

"I don't think friends go on dates. I don't think friends kiss each other, either."

"Then fuck being your friend," Theo growls. It's low and throaty, hot as hell.

He shimmies my shoulders back and slides into the water, clothes and jeans still on. Drops speckle his glasses and he wipes them away. I watch his eyes bounce to every part of my body he can find. The curve of my jaw, the line of my neck. The space below my ear and the freckles across my nose.

"Seeing you like this makes me want to die," he whispers into the still of the night. Special words meant for me and me alone.

"Like what?" I whisper back.

"Under the stars. In the light of the moon. Wearing my clothes and paint on your face. A smile, a beautiful fucking smile." He huffs and shakes his head. Reverence, I think, in his next words. "It makes me feel like I'm the luckiest guy in the world. I *am* the luckiest guy in the world."

Finally, *finally*, his hand reaches out, finding mine. He tugs me closer. Muscles, firm and defined under his wet shirt greet me. The outline of hardness in his jeans–thick and long–presses against my thigh. His palms run down my arms, dancing across my skin, until they stop at the hem of my shirt.

"This goes well past the point of friendship," he says. In warning? In anticipation? In hope?

"Fuck being your friend," I say, using his words back on him. "I want you more."

The confirmation snaps whatever restraint Theo might be holding onto. His fingers tug my shirt upward, pausing as the material rises over my stomach, a silent question. I nod, the bite of the cool air nipping at my exposed bare skin. His hands are back on me in a flash, peeling the clothing off and dropping it into the water. I watch it sink to the bottom.

Theo's palms rub across my stomach. Up my back. Between my shoulder blades, eyes never leaving mine.

"You okay?" he asks. It's strained, with a touch of care, too.

"I'm fine."

He huffs a laugh and gathers me in his arms. Lifting me, my legs circle his waist, heels settling against his lower back. We're on the same level now, chest to chest. Eye to eye. His right hand finds my hair, twisting damp strands around his wrist. His left hand goes to the swell of my breast, thumb swiping back and forth across the underside, marking a trail no one has traveled in years.

My lips are a hair's breadth away from his. A centimeter, maybe less. He swallows and brushes his nose against mine. Chuckles, as if to wordlessly say he can't believe this is happening, *finally happening*. Then, his lips press against mine, a kiss I feel all the way to my toes.

It's cataclysmic. World-ending.

Hotter, sweeter, and more passionate than anything I've ever experienced before. There's an urge to jump into the destructive waters of Theo Gardner and never come up for air.

He's greedy. Ravishing and unceasing. His tongue asks for permission and I grant it, welcoming him in. His grip tightens, hand moving from my breast up to my cheek. He's clutching me like I'll vanish at any moment, disappearing into thin air. My hips roll into his body, up the hardness beneath me.

"Bridget," he whispers. He pulls back, eyes glassy and bright. He looks drunk, a hazy blur of lust and need.

"What's wrong?" My hand cradles his face and he presses a kiss to the center of my palm.

"I haven't been... it's been years since I've done anything physical with a woman," he admits. "And this–" he says, gesturing between us, giving my nipple a surprise pinch. My back arches in response. "–is close to making me finish. So, please, don't... don't judge me based on this one time."

"It's been a year for me," I whisper. My lips find his throat and I kiss down his neck. He groans loudly, unabashedly, as his head drops back. "And I've thought about this. What it would be like with you." I shift my position in his arms, enough to drag myself down the length of his thigh. I can feel every ridge of his body through the flimsy shorts I'm wearing. Every muscle and every piece of the hard, *aroused* man. "This could be enough for me, too."

"Yeah?"

"Yeah."

He nods once, hand closing around my neck. "Then take what you need to feel good, princess, because you moving up and down like that is going to do it for me. You're so fucking sexy."

I turn frantic, then, at the direction and permission. The endearment, the way Theo looks beautiful in the colors of silver and white under the moon. I rock and grind against him, *using him* to find the perfect rhythm. His hand falls to my breast, pinching my nipple. A twist, a pull. Teeth graze my throat. In my ear, he murmurs words of encouragement until I'm close, *so close* to becoming undone.

"Theo," I beg. His hand disappears in the water and a beat passes before I feel his thumb press against my center, through my shorts and underwear, finding the exact, perfect spot on the first try. A circle over the fabric, and I'm trembling.

"That's my girl," he grunts, placing a kiss below the shell of my ear. It's my downfall. My salvation. I light up, exploding like a million stars under the night sky.

My forehead drops to his shoulder, biting the collar of his shirt to stay quiet as he works me to the finish line. I fumble my hands, palming him through his jeans, fingers curling over the outline of his length and giving a light squeeze. A sob racks my body and I hear him let out a soft, long moan of his own, thrusting into my hand a half-dozen times before he stills.

I inhale, trying to level my breathing. His arms wrap around me and he rubs my back. A kiss is pressed to my hair. My forehead. My cheek. I think I'm dreaming, floating above the water in a fit of ecstasy, an out-of-body experience.

"Angel," he whispers. It's strangled, a croak of a word. "I think you killed me."

I half-laugh, half-cry, and nod in agreement. "Same."

"Last time I came in my pants I was twelve years old. Almost thirty years in between? It was a good run."

I bite my lip to keep from giggling. "Is it weird I find that hot? Because I do."

He untangles our limbs and peels his chest away from mine, searching my face. "Doing okay?

"Yeah." I wipe my eyes and nod. "Incredible."

"Stay with me?" Theo kisses my forehead. "I don't want... I mean, I do want to be with you. Badly. But I mean that in a, let's shower and sleep for a few hours kind of way."

"What about Mac?"

"I'll sneak you out in the morning before she wakes up. Not because I'm embarrassed or anything. It's just... I'm not ready for that conversation yet."

"I understand." I lean forward, my lips meeting his. He sighs, a content hum against my mouth. "She's pissed at you, though."

"For what?"

"Going out with someone other than me."

Theo smiles, forehead resting against mine. "It won't happen again. I promise."

THIRTY-SIX

BRIDGET

THEO DIVES to the bottom of the pool to retrieve the shirt he yanked off me.

"I prefer you without it," he says. "But just in case."

We slip back inside, walking silently down the hall. His hand is laced through mine and we're careful not to make any noise. When we reach Theo's bedroom, he closes the door and locks it. I follow him to the bathroom and shiver, drenched clothes weighing me down every step.

"Shower or bath?"

"Holy cow," I exhale. "Your bathroom is huge. Did you do all of this yourself? A soaker tub *and* a walk-in shower? You're a serial killer, aren't you?"

He rolls his eyes and folds his arms over his chest. I can see the outline of abdominal muscles through his drenched, navy-blue shirt. "Pick, Boylston, or I'll pick for you."

"Shower," I say. "Definitely shower."

Theo nods and turns the knob on, steam forming and fogging up his glasses and the mirrors over the double-sink vanity. His arm stretches out, testing the water. Satisfied with the temperature, he pulls his shirt off and throws it onto the hamper sitting in the corner.

I'm left with an exquisitely bare upper body.

My throat dries. Theo is... beautiful.

He's toned, tan. An athletic shape without being overly muscular or broad. His tattoos extend up his shoulder and across his pectoral muscles, covering the skin all the way to his heart. Hair dusts his chest and down his stomach, disappearing under the waistband of his jeans.

"Where's your Bowie tattoo?" I ask. His lips quirk and he turns slightly, tapping the space above his bicep.

"Tattoo twins," he muses.

My eyes dip and I see a long scar, from his right hip up over his abdominal. A white, jagged line. It's faded slightly, almost translucent, but still there. Still a memory. I walk toward him.

"Can I?" I say.

His head jerks in acceptance and I don't think he's breathing.

My fingers run along the shape of the damage. I trace it from end to end. It's smooth, slightly raised, warm to the touch. I crouch down, pressing a kiss to the top of the mark. Another kiss, and another. Theo's body shakes with restraint. With release. With finally letting go of a hidden burden he's kept to himself. I work up his stomach, over his chest, across his clavicle. My lips brand every inch of skin I can find until I'm on my tiptoes, kissing his neck, then his cheek.

"You're beautiful," I whisper, lips against his. "Perfect. Thank you for letting me see this part of you."

"There's not a part of me I wouldn't show you. That's what's been happening all these weeks, why I can't get you out of my head. I want you to see this side. I want you to *have* this side no one else does. Thank you for making it so easy to let you in," he whispers in return.

He pulls my shirt off again, chuckling as the material gets stuck in the ends of my hair. He presses his chest against mine and kisses me. It's more gentle than the pool. It's learning, patient. Making mental notes of what I like, what I don't care for. Theo picks up on my cues quickly, and when his hand plays with the drawstring of my—his—shorts, he pauses to look at me.

"Yes." I nod. "Please."

He licks his lips and his eyes blaze. "You sure?"

"Positive."

Dropping to his knees, his fingers loosen the material around my waist. It's a process that happens in slow motion, when all I want is for him to rip them off. He slides the shorts down my thighs, helping me step out and shove the clothing away. His hand runs up my bare leg, gripping my hips.

"Remember what I told you, Bridget? I'd gladly get on my knees for you." Hooking his thumbs around the waistband of my underwear, he yanks the material down with force until I'm naked before him.

I shift on my feet, hands awkwardly dangling at my sides until Theo presses a kiss to the inside of both wrists. The affection releases any embarrassment or nerves, further abated as he raises my calf and sets my foot on his shoulder.

A puff of air escapes his mouth. He grips my waist, pads of his fingers sinking into my skin hard enough to bruise. With a lean forward, he bites the juncture of my hip and pelvis, and I moan in response.

"Angel," he warns. His voice turns stern, less forgiving. "You have to be quiet. Can you do that?"

I whimper and nod, grasping his hair, his shoulders, his neck for support. Anything I can reach to stay upright. "Yes," I finally breathe out.

He hums, fingers moving up across my belly before trailing lower, lower, lower. "Good girl."

It's a rumble of thunder against my skin and my eyes flutter closed. I try to focus, to keep my lips sealed together in silence. I try, and I try, until the tip of his finger slides inside, just barely, just enough to flip my world upside down.

My back arches. My chest pushes out, nipples pebbled and pointed. My grip in his hair—or is it on his arm?—falters.

"That okay?" he mumbles against my skin, words almost slurred with need. I nod, incapable of voicing anything except quiet pleas of *God, yes* and *more, Theo, please.* I feel his chuckle of pride, knowing he's doing the right thing. The circle of his thumb and the low moan of approval when he's greeted with wetness. The hesitation of his finger as he teases along my entrance.

"Theo," I beg. "I need..."

"What do you need, Bridget?"

"You. I need you."

He exhales, and I hear his own nerves in the sigh. He pushes inside me, taking his time, and I welcome him. I claw at his hair. I roll my hips against his finger. The delirious, mind-boggling stretch is almost at the point of *too much* but dangerously close to not *enough.*

"This pussy would turn sinners into saints, finally having something to worship." His words are sharper, hungrier. Filthy and dirty, exactly the way I like it. As if he's reading my mind and finding the fine line between sweet and wicked. Caring and rough. Considerate and consuming. "For *weeks* I've wondered what's under those clothes of yours. Your dress on Thanksgiving. The pants you wore ice skating. Now that I can see it..." He adds a second finger, plunging deeper than before. I let out a cry of pleasure. "Now that I can taste it..." His tongue gives me a taunting swipe. "I'm a ruined man and I don't ever want to be put back together. I'm going to be distracted for the rest of my goddamn life."

His thumb circles—four times is all it takes—and I free-fall for the second time tonight. Quickly, willingly, straight into his waiting arms.

It's too good. Too powerful. It's unlike anything I've ever experienced before. I think I tell him as much, through some convoluted mess of dialect. He lifts me, scooping me into his arms. Cradled against his chest, he steps us into the shower, warm water staving off the chill of my skin.

I bury my face in the crook of his neck. I inhale and press a kiss above the mole there, to the right of his windpipe.

"Jesus," I whisper.

"I'll accept the name change," Theo jokes. "I'm going to set you down, okay?"

He lowers me onto my own two feet. I lean against the wall, getting my bearings and calming my heart rate.

"Shower in your clothes often?" I ask, gesturing to the jeans still plastered on his body. "Also, I like how you look without glasses."

His hair is wet and shaggy, and he brushes the locks away from his face. "I don't want you to feel obligated to return the favor."

"What if I want to return the favor?"

"Then get on your knees, princess, and open that pretty mouth of yours."

I oblige immediately, the tile floor pressing into my skin. I look up at him and blink, beads of water running down my face. His fingers undo the button of his jeans, and he guides the zipper down.

"I have a confession to make," he murmurs. He takes his time to step out of the wet denim, foot pushing it to the side.

"What kind of confession?"

"The book I bought the other day isn't the first one from your book club I purchased."

"W-what?"

"The first night, I heard you talking about the book *you* liked. I almost jerked off in my office listening to you describe everything in great detail. The praise. The dominating guy. I was intrigued, so I went and read it myself. I took thorough notes." Theo peels off his underwear and I lick my lips. Thick, long, hard. His hand grips the length and he gives himself a tug. "Turns out, I like what you like."

My eyes snap to him. I've never had this conversation with a man before. What I enjoy in bed has never been broached as a topic of discussion. I've been content to keep those desires and fantasies to myself, never fully indulging in how *bad* I want them.

But here's Theo, talking openly and laying it all out there for me as I rock back on my knees, close to crawling the distance to him.

"That's... that's good," I say.

"I'd say so." He takes two steps toward me, the water from the shower running down his back, over his shoulders. Across his chiseled chest and stomach. My pulse spikes, a flurry of heartbeats I can hear in my ears. He brushes his head against my lips and I open greedily.

I lick his shaft, from base to tip, grinning against the skin as I feel a tremor course through him. I hear him moan, and I let him wrap my hair around his wrist and pull. Hard. My head tilts back to accommodate his size, hollowing out my cheeks until he hits the back of my throat. Tears spring to my eyes, and Theo reaches out, thumb wiping them away.

"So pretty," he murmurs. "You on your knees might be my favorite sight." Another tug to my hair stretches my neck back further. "Watching my good girl take me all the way down is a fucking treat. Look at me, Bridget, so I can see you swallow every drop I give you."

I hear the two words I love the most.

The two words I could combust from alone.

Good girl.

But I hear the word before it, louder.

My.

His.

It spurs me on. I look up, staring into his eyes. I don't blink. I don't gag. I don't falter as I bring my hand to join my mouth, moving in tandem. It's not perfect. It's sloppy and out of practice. Saliva slides down my chin, catching in the hollow of my throat. Tears stain my cheeks. But I've never felt more beautiful. More *powerful.* Theo watches me like I hung the moon, lust and longing, tenderness and promises behind the look.

I work him to the brink through twists of my hand, light grazes of my teeth, laps of my tongue, wanting to make him feel as good as he made me feel. He pulls my hair in warning and I ignore it, guiding him to the back of my throat. I taste the saltiness seconds later, coating my throat. I swallow the remnants down, not spilling a drop. And when I pop him out of my mouth and wipe my lips, Theo hauls me to my feet.

His kiss is bruising, claiming. Marking me as *his.* We stay intertwined for hours, days, maybe, until his hands find my cheeks and he eases away, nose brushing against mine.

"I think," he starts through a breathless pant. It's low and husky. Pleased. "I think you might be an actual angel."

"I think you might be out of your mind. First blowjob in years will probably do that to you."

He tips his head back and laughs, magical and light. The groans and grunts of pleasure are nice, but *that.* That right there will forever be my favorite sound. "Let's get cleaned up and head to bed. I don't have another round in me, but I want—"

"Yeah," I interrupt. He doesn't need to finish the sentence, because I know. "I want, too."

Theo's smile is drowsy. Lust-ridden. Happy and exhausted. For *me,* because of *me.* And I think, in this moment—in all the moments—he's never been more perfect.

THIRTY-SEVEN

BRIDGET

"ARE we keeping our hands to ourselves tonight?" Theo asks from the driver's seat. His palm is on my thigh, thumb rubbing small circles over the thigh-high stockings I'm wearing, half-distracted from the road. I nudge his side when he stares at me for too long.

We're driving out to the farm where the holiday hayride is, forty-five minutes away. Through some serious finagling and messages with Lucas where Theo offered to do his laundry, we ended up in a car alone together.

"Eyes on the road, pal," I say. "It would probably be for the best, unless you're ready for an interrogation."

"You're right. Mouths shut."

"Until we get home," I amend.

Theo groans and he pinches the top of my knee. "Not helping, Boylston."

When we park the car, we keep a foot of distance between us as we approach the group. With a quick tap to my lower back and a brush of his shoulder against mine, Theo and I go our separate ways. I join Chandler and Brooke for hot chocolate. He and some of the guys play a game of touch football while we wait our turn. I sneak a glance at him from across the field, and find him looking at me, too. I giggle and take a sip of my drink, brushing off Chandler's question about what's so funny.

The sun has set by the time they call our name. It's cooler now, and I shiver as we walk toward the tractor parked out in a field. Christmas lights bejewel the orange groves along the way. Plastic snowmen and reindeer are set up in various scenes and displays.

The driver gives us instructions on how to sit on the attached platform, talking about weight and balance. He advises us to fill the front first, before moving toward the back. I slow my steps and Theo falls in time with me, away from the rest of the pack.

"It looks so pretty out here," I say wistfully. "With the stars and the lights and the fresh air. I can pretend we live somewhere other than a flat, warm state where it'll be seventy-five degrees on Christmas morning. It makes me believe the holidays are almost here. Minus the snow, of course."

"No snow in the forecast," he says. "And only two weeks until Christmas. Have you gotten your shopping done?"

"God, no. I'm behind this year. I'm having fun with the competition, but it's also making the days fly by much quicker than in years past."

"I know what you mean. I'm not counting down the seconds until January, which is a rarity for me. I'm anxious for Christmas Day and to see Mac's reactions when she opens up her gifts."

"What are you getting her?"

"Books, obviously. She also wants a cheap laptop for writing. Some soccer stuff."

"She's so freaking cool," I say.

When we get to the tractor, I stop in my tracks. Bales of hay sit in rows on the trailer bed attached to the back of the vehicle. It's high off the ground, probably close to seven feet. I gulp and take a step back.

"Oh, shit," Theo mutters. His hand glides against mine, then he leaves it there, our palms just barely touching. "Do you want to wait for everyone back at the lodge? You don't have to get up there, Bridget."

"No." I shake my head. "I can do this."

"I'll be here with you. You say the word and we'll find a way off, okay?

"Promise?" I ask.

Theo chuckles and his knuckles run up my arm then back down again. "I promise."

"I jump, you jump?" He raises his eyebrows in surprise. "Mac might have spilled the beans that you like *Titanic*," I confess.

"That little shit," he grumbles. "Yes, Bridget. You jump, I jump."

His assurance gives me courage, and I climb the rungs of the ladder, keeping my attention on the tractor, and not the ground. I can sense Theo beneath me, though, waiting in case I ask for help.

I sigh in relief when my feet reach the top.

"Are you okay, Bridge?" asks Chandler. She knows about my fear and she gives me a worried look.

"I'm good." I smile and walk to the last remaining bale of hay in the last row and plop down.

The straw is covered with a blanket, keeping my legs free from scratches. Theo climbs up the ladder with ease, eyes finding mine as he trots down the aisle.

"How're we doing?" he asks. The tractor rumbles to life, loud and clanky, and drowns out his words. The wheels jut forward, beginning to move down the dark dirt road. I pluck a spare blanket off the planked floor and drape it over my legs.

"Better now," I answer. We're the only people in the back and I scoot closer to him. His hand drops to my thigh hidden by the cover. His fingers squeeze my leg.

"Good. I had an idea to help distract you," Theo whispers. His nose runs along my cheek and his lips press a kiss to my ear.

"What kind of idea?" I ask.

The tips of his fingers drag over my stocking, stopping where the wool gives way to bare skin.

"Are you trying to kill me, Bridget?" he asks. The question comes out like a tortured groan as he toys with the lace hem.

"I didn't think I'd have your hands between my legs when I got dressed this evening." My eyes close, shuttering out the twinkle of Christmas lights and the gleam of the stars in the cloudless night sky. My head lolls to his shoulder, nestling in the crook of his neck and finding the spot where I feel like I belong. "Handsy hayride wasn't on the agenda."

His thumb traces the curve of my jaw, following the path to my chin. "And now that it is?"

The answer to the obvious question is my thighs parting. My back arching and leaning further into his embrace. "Distract me," I say softly. "Please."

"I hate when you say that word." A kiss is pressed to my forehead, then my cheek. "It makes me want to lose control."

"Grumpy business owner brought down by the girl next door." I chuckle, a breathless laugh amidst the eager anticipation of what comes next. My hand covers the large one resting on my leg, guiding his palm to my underwear. "Who would've thought?"

His fingers brush over the cotton and he grins against the column of my throat at the dampness greeting him. "Can the girl next door stay quiet while the grumpy business owner fingers her on the back of a tractor?"

I swallow my whimper and nod aggressively. I position my body so my back leans against his left arm, propped up. "Yes. She can."

"Then be a good girl and spread your legs for me. There you

go. That's perfect," Theo says, and I cling to the praise. I hold it tight. My thighs open and my skirt bunches at my waist. His fingers hook in my underwear, dragging the material down to my feet.

He runs his hand up the length of my leg from my calf to my hip. It's teasing. Taunting. Seeing how far he can get before I break and ask for more.

"Theo," I whisper. It's an acknowledgement that I recognize the consequences and repercussions, and I don't care. He kisses my neck. The top of my chest. Everywhere and anywhere he can reach.

"Ask me," he grunts.

"Please. I need you to... I need you."

"Try again."

I almost sob at the tortuous feeling. The light dance of his fingers, featherlight, over my belly. The trust I feel for him, recognizing no matter how much he plays, I know he's going to let me win.

"Please touch me. Please let me come. I don't care how, but I—"

His mouth covers mine at the perfect moment. His fingers sink inside me and I melt. I wiggle and buck my hips against his hand. I writhe and grind. Incoherent, indecipherable words tumble from my throat, mumbled prayers that go unanswered. I don't know what I'm saying. All I can focus on is Theo, already knowing *exactly* what I like. Whispers in my ear of *"open your eyes, Bridget"* and *"look how you take me"* and *"good. So good, angel."*

Every time I'm close to the precipice of release, the edge of ecstasy, he pulls his finger away, slick sounds almost deafening out in the empty fields. He brings them to my mouth, offering me a taste.

My tongue accepts the gift hungrily, one finger turning into two. It's the single most erotic thing I've ever done. Exhibitionism hasn't been on my list of things to try, but I'm so turned on, so *desperate,* I don't care who sees. When the driver turns around to gesture to a clump of trees, I clench around Theo so tightly, he grins, victoriously.

"Maybe not an angel after all." He chuckles wickedly in my ear. "This pussy wants to be seen, doesn't it? It wants the world to know how much it likes to be taken care of, out here where anyone could watch."

"Yes. It does," I whisper, voicing the truth. My sweater has fallen off my shoulder. My hair is a tangled mess of knots, coming out of the ponytail I started the evening with. The blanket almost falls off my thighs, baring myself to the world. "But it's yours."

His attack ceases. His precision wavers and he slows. Dirty, rough movements become gentler. Lazy circles. A deep kiss I feel in the depths of my stomach, growing stronger and stronger.

"Mine," he repeats, strangled and hoarse.

"Theo. Please."

His lips quirk up. He looks pleased and proud. Silently adding a third digit, he brushes the hair off my face. "Want to see you when you come," he mutters. His fingers curl inside me, finding the spot I rarely hit on my own.

His gaze never leaves mine, looking down at me with his lip caught between his teeth, a flame of desire behind his eyes, and his heart nearly tumbling out of his chest.

A match strikes, working its way down my spine, across my stomach and settling between my legs. He anticipates the moment, knows it's close. His lips find mine in a searing kiss as I unravel, wave after wave of pleasure working through me. I ride the sensation all the way to shore, chest heaving with exertion and exhaustion.

My limbs are heavy as I come down from my high. My

muscles are pliant. I think I've transcended Earth. Theo nudges my cheek. He fixes my sweater and does his best to brush out my hair with his clean fingers.

The others he licks until they no longer glisten, free from the effects of his distraction techniques.

"That was something else." My throat is scratchy and I see the lodge coming into view.

"Alright, folks, welcome back," the driver says. The tractor shifts to park. "Be careful on the way down. We've got cookies, cider, and hot cocoa set up in the barn. Feel free to take a look around, and thanks for coming by."

"I could go for another hot chocolate," I say, stretching my arms above my head.

"I'll grab you some when we get down," Theo says.

"Thank you. No ma—"

"Marshmallows," he finishes for me. "I know."

"You said that during the interview, too. How do you know how I like my drinks?"

A quick kiss to my hand before he stands, kicking loose pieces of hay off his boots.

"I think I've been picking up small clues about you for a while now, Bridget. Take your time with the ladder. I'll be waiting for you at the bottom."

A dip of his chin and a twinkle in his eye as he bids me a temporary goodbye lassos around my heart and tugs, hard.

I grin like an idiot, hustling to my feet to chase after him, already missing his body against mine.

THIRTY-EIGHT

THEO

I SMILE down at the photo of Mac when she was four. It's her on the bike she got for Christmas that year. Her first one, bright blue, complete with tassels streaming from the handlebars. Training wheels are anchored to the back and a pink helmet sits on her head. She's wearing Barbie pajamas and missing the front two teeth of her smile. I'm crouching next to her, wearing a hideous Christmas sweater and a Santa hat. I'm smiling too, bright and wide as I squint toward the camera hidden by the sun.

I rub my chest at the memory. All these years later, and I still remember the day vividly. We went to my parents' house for lunch then took the bike to the path around the lake. We watched the *Peanuts* movie and Mac fell asleep with her head on my shoulder, a candy cane in one hand and her empty stocking in the other.

I think of the presents I have hidden in my closet to give her this year. She's long outgrown new bikes, preferring a soccer ball or cleats. I know we all get old. It's a part of life. I'm aware of myself aging. My parents, too, with their graying hair and slower-moving bodies. It doesn't feel *real*, though, until I look across the store and see my little girl hanging photos and laughing with Lucas. That's when it hits me how big she's gotten. How much she's matured and how damn wonderful she is.

Last night in bed, between texting Bridget and watching my buddy's basketball game on the TV, I kept adding more and more items to my online shopping cart for Mac. Maybe it's the guilt of how prickly and harsh I've been in years past, or how difficult I am to be around at times, but, I want this to be the best Christmas ever. For the first time in half a decade, I'm excited. I'm excited when I see the decorations in the store. I'm giddy to watch Felicity prep the menorah we'll be lighting any day now. I feel so fucking *happy*, like I'm on top of the world, and I know the brunette next door is the leading cause of that glee.

It's been a week since our first night together, and Bridget is incredible. Every time we talk, Mac is the first topic of conversation. She asks about how her practice is going and how the new position is working out. She asks me about my day, too, and if I need help with anything.

We haven't put a label on this yet. We haven't had sex. I haven't even taken her on a date yet, too busy with work and painting noses on the reindeer Lucas creates. I'm too busy grabbing her hand behind the back of our building, kissing her quick and sweet. I'm too busy accepting the fresh blueberry muffins she shoves my way.

Whatever is going on between us is special. I can tell. I don't want to rush into anything and miss all those little moments. Like how Bridget is ticklish under her left rib cage and her eyes are more brown than green late at night, under the star-lined sky.

"Dad," Mac calls out. "Lucas and I are leaving."

"Do you have your bag?" I ask. I tuck the picture into my wallet and slide it away in my pocket.

"Yup."

"Homework?"

"Yes!"

"Phone and charger?"

"Dad," she whines. "I'm thirteen in like, two weeks."

"You're right." I look at Lucas. "I'll see you at dinner after?"

He winks, looking smug and all-knowing. "Yup. Take your time closing up."

I roll my eyes at the implication, but he's not wrong. I haven't seen Bridget yet today and I've been looking for an excuse to sneak over and say hi. I didn't think pathetically asking my best friend to take my kid to my parents' house would be the level I'd stoop to, yet here we are.

"Love you, Dad," Mac says. She throws her arm around my waist and I kiss the top of her head.

"Love you too, kiddo. I'll grab you later tonight, okay?"

"Okay."

She waves goodbye and drags Lucas out the door. I give them a head start, watching his truck peel out of the parking space in front of the shop, driving down the road.

When they are out of sight, I shut the lights off and lock up, heading for the bookstore. It's dark at A Likely Story, too, and I'm surprised to find the door unlocked.

"Bridget?" I call out. The hallway door swings open, and she walks out.

"Theo? What are you doing here?"

I shuffle toward the counter, cursing as my toe stubs the edge of one of the bookshelves.

"I wanted to come by and say hi."

"Hey," she answers with a smile. She ducks under the counter and heads my way. "How's Mac? How was your day?"

"Not bad. Busy. Lucas finished the last figure for the contest.

The pictures got hung, too. You can check those off your list. How was your day?"

"I baked five dozen cupcakes for a kid's birthday party. I got berated for selling books that depict sex on page. A college guy hit on me, thinking I was 22."

"Wow. Busy day. A college guy, huh?"

She shrugs and toys with the ends of her hair. "He's a little young for my taste. Besides, I've kind of been seeing this older guy who's pretty wonderful."

I huff and thread my arm around her shoulders. "Do you want to see multiple people? He probably has better stamina than me."

Her cheek finds my chest, resting there, above my heart. A spot I hope she never leaves. She sighs, content. "No. I want to spend time with you. Just you, Theo."

"I want to spend time with just you, too, Bridget."

Her chin lifts. She presses a kiss to my throat. Then my chin, my cheek. My eyes flutter closed and it's my turn for a contented sigh, one hand splayed out over her lower back, the other wrapped in her hair.

"What are you doing tonight?" she asks. Her finger grazes down my shirt, and I shudder.

"Supposed to go to dinner with my buddies. Fuck them, though."

Her chuckle is warm and light. "I don't want you to miss out spending time with your friends, but maybe you can stay? For a little?"

"Yeah," I mumble into her hair. "As long as you want."

I'm learning this woman is the single person on Earth besides my kid I would alter my entire schedule for. I've been doing it slowly over the last few weeks. Driving to a Christmas tree lot with her by my side. Popping in twice during the day. Staying late so I can walk her to her car. Listening as she tells a joke that's horribly *not* funny, but I laugh anyway because it gets her to smile.

And *fuck*, I love her smiles.

Small seconds, many minutes, dozens of hours. It feels kind of insane, really, to feel so connected to another person. To let myself open up and let her see every part of me. But I am, and I do, and the best part is she's letting me see her in return.

She's staying.

"I missed you," Bridget whispers. Her lips brush over mine, a ghost of a kiss. My arms circle around her waist, like we're slow dancing in the store without an audience.

"I missed you too," I say. I kiss her back fully, leaving no question about the accuracy of the statement. She melts into me, molding to my form.

"Theo."

"Yeah, princess?" My lips trail down her throat, marking the small spot below her ear I know causes her to shiver.

"I want you."

"You have me."

"No. I *want* you," she clarifies with emphasis, right leg hooking around my thigh.

My movements stall. My breathing stops. "Here? In the bookstore? I haven't even bought you dinner yet."

She laughs, soft in the quiet space. "If you don't want to, we can—"

"Shh." I silence her with another kiss. "This isn't about wanting." I bring her palm to the front of my jeans. They're tight, strained. "Does *this* feel like I don't want you?"

Bridget's thumb runs up the seam of my zipper and back down. I let out a string of illogical words.

"What I mean," I continue through a pant and a groan, "is I'm not prepared. Believe it or not, I don't carry condoms in my pocket."

She reaches into the pocket I didn't occupy, producing a foil packet. "I am."

"Jesus, woman. It's like you're begging me for it."

Her palm cups me, intentional hand movements causing my hips to jerk.

"Maybe I am. Please, Theo. I've been thinking about you all day."

That *word*. Every time she says it, I want to give her anything she asks.

"Okay."

It's an easy agreement. She hustles to lock the front door, turning the sign in the window to 'closed.' When she comes back, I kiss her tenderly, fingers undoing her ponytail. Brown cascades down her shoulders. I back us up until we reach the counter. Her hands fist my shirt and grab the hem, tugging it over my head. My glasses knock to the side.

"Can you see without these?" she asks, adjusting the frames on my face.

"Sort of. I can see up close. I can see you." I pull her shirt off. A black bra is underneath. It's nothing fancy or racy, just simple cotton, but beautiful nonetheless. It's enough to make my head spin. I kiss her bare shoulder, the patch of freckles there. My fingers trace the marks and I smile.

I wonder if she can feel the tremor in my hands as I cup her cheek. I wonder if she notices how fast my heart is beating under her palm.

"I want this to feel good for you," I mumble. "Tell me what you like, okay?"

"Everything you've done so far has been... it's been so *good*."

The affirmation shakes my nerves. Releases the tension in my shoulders, years of inactivity forgotten. I spin her around, her back to me and chest toward the counter.

"Hands here," I instruct, guiding her palms to the laminate.

She obliges, fingers curling over the edge to steady herself. My foot nudges her feet apart. I step back, admiring the view.

Her skirt is bunched around her waist, ass unobstructed. Round, smooth. An offering to me. I drop to my knees, a man ready to make a prayer, and she whines.

Her hand reaches behind her, finds my hair. Fingers curl around my locks, a tug on my scalp.

"I like you on your knees," she whispers.

"Good, because I want to spend all of my life down here."

Head between her legs. Hands bracketing the back of her thighs, rubbing the patch of skin below her backside. Tongue relishing in her delicious taste. It'd be a good way to go.

I hook my fingers over the hem of her underwear, pushing them aside. My thumb parts her, dipping into the sweet wetness I know is waiting for me.

"T-that feels good," she exhales. It's shaky, but sure. I hear the sigh that follows. The breathy moan. The pleased hum. I move my thumb away, exchanging it for my pointer and middle fingers next, finding a steady rhythm.

Bold and empowered, encouraged by the rock of her hips, the dampness of my fingers, I drop a kiss to her ass, teeth gently sinking into her skin.

"Okay?" I ask, the hardwood floor bruising my knees. I don't even mind the sting.

"Fine," she answers.

"Being a smartass will get you in trouble."

"I told you I like trouble," she whines.

I give her no warning, my tongue replacing my fingers, savoring the sweet, delicious taste of Bridget Boylston. I lick every inch I can find, without shame or abandon and it's still not enough.

"Theo."

My name, her lips. My own personal heaven. And my own

personal hell, because every depraved thought known to man flies through my head wanting and wanting and wanting *more*.

Her on the counter on all fours, ass in the air.

Her arms wrapped in pretty Christmas lights, begging me to make the knots tighter.

My fingers pump her and my tongue flicks her clit. It's a place I know she prefers, one of her favorite spots, and she clenches around me. That book of hers gave me a million different ideas, and knowing how much she's going to love the next words out of my mouth makes me want to roar with greed.

"Are you going to be the good girl I know you are and come on my fingers, princess?"

She squeezes around me, *holy fuck she's so tight*, a loud, *loud* moan tumbling from her mouth as she ascends above. I work her down slowly. I cover her skin with kisses as I rise to my feet. Her ass again. The inside of her thigh. The small of her back. Between her shoulder blades. The nape of her neck. When her breathing begins to still, I withdraw out of her slowly, reaching around her waist.

"Open up," I say. I outline her lips with the fingers coated in her release. She listens, eyes opening as her tongue darts out, licking its way down both fingers at the same time. "So beautiful. So perfect," I whisper, brushing her hair out of her face. She whimpers, teeth nipping the pads of my finger. It's my turn to groan and I fumble for the condom on the counter.

"I want you so bad," she says as I rip the foil pack open. Her lips are back on mine and I unbutton my jeans at lightning speed. I shove them down my thighs, denim gathering at my feet.

"Want you too," I grit out roughly. I pull my briefs off and roll the latex over my length. I tease along her entrance, inhaling deep. With as much restraint as I can muster, I push inside her, barely an inch, giving us a second to adjust.

"Jesus," I groan. My head drops to her shoulder, beads of sweat covering the freckles there. "You're so tight."

Another nudge forward, and I'm halfway inside her. I take my time, rocking back and forth, her panting intensifying.

"There we go." I exhale, one thrust away from being fully seated inside her. "You take me so well, angel."

"Theo," she gasps. Her eyes shutter closed. Her nose scrunches in a beautiful anguished scene of desperation and need. "It's too much."

I pause, stopping before the finish line. "You want me to stop?" I whisper, kissing her ear. "You say the words, Bridget."

"No. God no. Don't stop. Don't ever stop."

"I've got you," I assure her. "I promise."

A moan first, then, "I've got you, too."

With a final jolt, the final inch toward nirvana, our bodies fuse together completely. She collapses onto the counter, chest against laminate, hair covering her face.

"Heaven," I grunt. "Just like I thought. Just like every other part of you. I never want to leave."

"So don't. Ruin me for anyone else."

She's a smart woman, and I'd be wise to listen to her.

So, I do.

I do ruin her.

I ruin her in the way I become rough. Unhinged. My left hand gripping her backside, my right cupping her neck, tattoos juxtaposed against her fair skin. My hips rolling, my lips whispering in her ear. Every word of praise, every adjective to describe her beauty, falls from my mouth. And a bit of filth, too.

"I liked your come on my fingers, Bridget, but I'm going to like it even more when it's on my cock."

She groans, long and low, and I feel her flutter. I feel her convulse and squeeze. I hear her whimpers and pleas. A prolonged hum tells me she finishes and I kiss the top of her head, not finished with her yet.

"Good." A thrust. "Fucking." Another thrust. "Girl." A third.

My forearm loops under her, keeping her upright as I bury myself inside her, again and again. I'm close, and the rock of her hips, the press of her ass, the murmured words of "So good, Theo" bring me to the edge. The base of my spine tightens, the sensation radiating across my stomach and I tip over, body stilling as I find my release.

We're silent, our panting the only noise in the dark, deserted store. My fingers traverse from her hip up her back, kneading her muscles. They ripple under my touch and her spine arches.

"You okay?" I ask.

Bridget nods and sniffs. Gently, I slip out of her and wince at the loss of contact. She spins and looks up at me, sated and satisfied. A smile is on her face.

"Okay," she says. Her voice is low and raspy. "Besides Mac being born, because I know she takes the top spot... where does this fall on your list of best Christmases?"

The flickering lights from the multiple trees behind us give her skin a pretty glow. Her hair is a mess and there's a tear hanging on the end of her nose.

My palm cradles her face, thumb brushing over her cheek, down to her jaw. "It's the best one. By a long shot."

THIRTY-NINE

BRIDGET

SUNDAY IS my favorite day of the week.

I make pancakes for lunch, savoring the sweetness of the syrup I bought at the local farmer's market. I pull a new romance novel off my shelf and wrap a blanket around myself. I prop my feet up on the couch, Ziggy curled up beside me, content to spend the rest of my day turning pages of a new favorite book.

With only ten days until Christmas, everyone is starting to become frantic. Traffic on the avenue comes to a standstill multiple times a day. Parking spaces are limited, the sidewalk is overcrowded, and we can't get any decorating done because of the frequency of patrons filing in and out of the store.

It's been chaotic.

I'm glad to be away from the hustle and bustle today, a steaming cup of hot chocolate waiting for me on the end table in my living. The tree I set up weeks ago twinkles in the overcast light. Presents for friends and family members sit on the skirt embellished with candy canes and snowmen. A candle is burning on my entertainment center, a festive scent of balsam and vanilla.

I settle back onto the cushions of the couch, draping a crocheted blanket over my legs. I tuck my feet under me, opening my book to the first page.

Barely two lines in, my phone buzzes next to me. I pluck the device off the leather arm beside me, frowning when I see Theo's name.

"Theo?" I answer. "What's wrong?"

"Wrong?" His voice is deep and confused on the other side. "What would be wrong?"

"I don't know, you tell me. You're the one calling."

"That's generally what people do when they want to communicate with someone, Bridget."

"Yeah, maybe if they're in their eighties or something. A text isn't sufficient?"

"I'm driving right now. Safety first. I wanted to see if you were busy."

"I just sat down to read, but I'm not busy, no. Why? What's up?"

"I'm taking Mac to the mall so she can do some shopping. She asked if you could come. Then she berated me and said you aren't allowed to babysit her when I go out with another woman again. Anyway, I don't want to take up your day off or anything, but I—"

"I'd love to join," I say with a smile. "When are you going?"

"We can grab you in an hour.

"Sounds good. I'll be ready."

"BB! I'm so glad you could join us." Mac greets me as I take the front seat in the truck an hour later.

"Hey, kiddo. Thanks for inviting me." I look over at Theo. His eyes are on the road as he shifts the car to drive, but he's wearing a smile. A *real* smile.

"Hey," he says.

It's a neutral and innocent timbre, unassuming to anyone besides me. I hear the secret affection behind the greeting, though. The same affectionate tone I heard when we were alone in his house last night. My head on his chest, his fingers tracing up my arm, talking about the constellation of stars on my shoulder.

"Hey, Collector," I answer, smiling back.

"Why do you call him that?" Mac asks, looking up from her phone in the backseat.

"Have you seen his arms? They're like an art gallery."

"He has a lot," she agrees. "It's unfair. He told me I can't get any until college."

"Because I'm not sure your homeroom teacher would be fond of me if you showed up Monday with a sleeve," Theo points out, glancing at her in the rearview mirror.

"Oh, Ms. Martin is fond of you. She asks about you every day."

I lean over the center console and elbow Theo's side. "Are you starting fights at PTA meetings?"

He rolls his eyes. "I'm not scowling enough, apparently."

"You really need to step it up," I say. "Mac and Cheese, what kind of Christmas gifts are we looking for today?"

"Something for Dad," she says. "Can you help me?"

"I'll do my best. I have a feeling he's nearly impossible to shop for," I muse. "Maybe we'll buy him a closet full of dress shirts. You'll have to help me find something for my secret gift person, too."

Mac giggles, returning her attention to her phone. "I'm glad you're here, BB."

Theo reaches over, fingers dancing over my palm in the

quickest of gestures before returning to the steering wheel, smile firmly in place.

"Me too," I say. I'm only staring at him.

"I'LL MEET you two back here in an hour. Bridget, you'll text me if you need anything?" Theo asks.

"Of course." I drape my arm over Mac's shoulder and wave goodbye. "Come on, kid. Let's go spend some of your dad's money."

"I also want to pick out a birthday outfit," she says as we walk away.

"Your birthday is so soon! Are you doing anything fun? Turning thirteen is a big deal."

"We're having a family dinner on the 23rd. The party with my friends is on the 27th. Oh! Can you come to dinner?"

"Maybe. We can ask your dad. I don't want to intrude."

"Yeah, but it's my birthday and I want you there. It wouldn't be intruding! Grams likes you, and she keeps asking Dad when you're coming back. He just grumbles under his breath and doesn't answer."

"Your father is nothing but predictable," I laugh. "Hey, I have a question for you. Speaking of Theo, he's my secret gift exchange person. He told me y'all used to have some fun Christmas traditions."

"Yeah," Mac says. "After the accident, things kind of changed. It was like Dad stopped living."

"He said you'd get personalized mugs every year. I was thinking of buying him one. If you think it might be too hard for him to see, or bring up too many bad memories, tell me. I'll pick something else."

We walk in silence, stopping in front of a store. Mac looks at the mannequins in the window and inclines her head. "I think he'd really like that. The accident already happened. We can't change the past, so we might as well do something that brings us joy. He would get so excited by those mugs, wondering what the colors were going to be. What the font was going to look like. And..." Her lip trembles and she wipes her eyes. "I miss seeing Dad happy."

"Oh, sweetie." I give her a hug, chin dropping to the top of her head. "He is happy. He's happy when he's with you."

"He's happy with you, too," she answers. The words are significant coming from her, purposeful. I catch them with a net, not letting them fly away. "Do the mugs, Bridget. It would mean a lot."

"I'm glad you said that. I already bought them."

She grins up at me. "I like you, BB. You do what you want and ask for permission after."

"Easier to ask for forgiveness than permission. Come on. Let's find you a birthday outfit."

WE MEET Theo at the food court an hour later. Our hands are full and our cheeks are red from the two laps we did around the concourse, making sure we didn't miss a store.

He looks up from a table in front of the Chinese takeout restaurant, eyebrows raised. "I see my credit card was used sufficiently," he says.

"There's not *that* much stuff," I justify. "Only a couple of things."

"Dad, Bridget helped me pick out the coolest outfit for my party. Speaking of, can she come to my dinner?"

"It's okay if not," I add. "We can talk about it later."

"Nothing to talk about." Theo shrugs. "We'd love for you to be there."

"Yes!" Mac cheers. "Best birthday ever!"

"Speaking of birthdays and presents, I had an idea about a Christmas present for your mom."

"Let's hear it," he says. "She's difficult to shop for. I'll take all the suggestions."

"Okay. Um. Well, you know how she gave me that photo of you with the mall Santa for the store?"

Theo rolls his eyes and crosses his arms over his chest. "Unfortunately."

"What if you and Mac recreated it? I mean, obviously you're not sitting on his lap, and you won't be screaming like a possessed demon, but... she loves that photo of you."

He studies me for a minute. His arms fall to his sides. His face is pensive, contemplating. He nods, a smile starting to form. Right side first, then left.

God. I like this man a lot.

"I could get on board with the idea," he says.

"Yeah?"

"Taking a picture with a mall Santa at the age of forty-one and reliving a traumatic childhood experience is not something I ever thought I'd do. I'm learning, however, this year is full of things I never thought I'd do. So, screw it. Let's take a photo with jolly old Saint Nicholas."

I gape at him, surprised. "Seriously? Is it that easy? I had a whole rebuttal planned for when you inevitably shot me down!"

"Save it for when you're trying to get a Santa hat on me again. That's the one thing absolutely not happening."

I grin at him and his smile grows. "Deal."

We take the escalator down, following the crowd of people looped around a fake igloo. We're the oldest ones by a landslide, the only group without a child under seven. Theo is undeterred.

Mac entertains us while we wait, pulling out the clothes she purchased and showing them off. After a fashion show, she stuffs the items back into the bags and turns her attention to her phone.

"I hope the outfits are okay. I kept the receipts so you can return anything you don't like," I say to Theo.

He shakes his head. "Unnecessary. They're all great. Thanks for doing that with her. I'm sure she appreciated someone who gave her actual feedback on clothing rather than her dad who shrugs and doesn't know the difference between short lengths."

"Ah. That's why you keep me around. I'm a clothing expert."

His hand touches my elbow, at the crook of my arm. His thumb presses into my skin. "I'd like to keep you around, Bridget. Not only for the shorts advice, though it is a perk. But because you make me happy. You make Mac happy, too. Maybe we can slowly ease you into being around her more. In a... not-so-friendly way. If you... if that's something you'd want. It's something I want."

I blink away tears and nudge the tip of my shoe against his. "Yeah. I want that, too."

"Good."

"Dad! We're next," Mac announces. She pockets her phone. "What pose are we going to do?"

"Pose? I'm not posing. I'm going to smile. We're going to take a picture. And that'll be that."

She rolls her eyes. "Boring. So boring. BB, any ideas?"

"A piggyback ride, maybe?" I suggest. "Then you won't look like the creepy guy standing for a photo with Santa by himself."

"I'm always going to look like the creepy guy standing for a photo by himself. But fine. I'll agree to a piggyback ride."

Mac cheers and Theo pulls out his wallet, paying the man—the elf—at the entrance to the North Pole. He bends down and mutters something in the guy's ear, who nods and gives a thumbs up.

"Here. I'll hold your bags." I take the clothes from Mac and she frowns.

"You aren't going to be in it?"

"This is for you and your dad, sweetie. You're recreating the memories. I'll be right over there."

I shuffle to the side, letting Mac and Theo walk up to Santa. I laugh as the old man stays in character, asking Mac what she wants for Christmas and telling her a dog is definitely in her future. She climbs on Theo's back, long legs and laughing, and they pose for a couple snaps of the camera.

"Bridget."

Theo says my name in that special, precious way of his. It's a cross between reverence, joy and adoration. I could listen to it on repeat forever, the emphasis on each letter. The swoop of each syllable. How he looks positively *delighted* to talk to me, even in front of three hundred waiting families and an actor ready to clock out for his lunch break.

People say my name every day, but hearing him utter the word is my favorite thing in the whole world.

"What's up?"

"Come be in a photo with us."

"No, this is your—"

"It's not. Please?"

It's different from the "please" on the day of the ladder and the rain. This one is deeper, insinuating if I walk over there, it makes *us* real. It makes *this* real. His eyes stay on mine, brown, warm and bright. He's patient, letting me decide for myself what I want to do.

"Okay," I finally whisper.

I drop the bags to the floor, making my way over to the pair.

Some of the women in line place their hands over their hearts. Mac is grinning broadly. And Theo...

Theo is looking at me like a man starved and I'm his only chance of salvation.

Maybe Chandler was right all those weeks ago. Maybe he's been looking at me like this for a while.

I slide into the open spot on his right. Mac jumps off his back, taking the spot on his left. His hand snakes around my waist, giving my hip two squeezes.

"Big smiles, folks!" The elf behind the camera snaps a couple more photos. My heart thumps in my chest, powerful. Loud. Decided.

I want to live life with this man by my side.

"I was right," Theo murmurs, lips ghosting over my ear. "Best Christmas ever."

Mac grabs our photos and the cheesy mall Santa looks over at us.

"Happy Holidays," he says. There's a twinkle in his eyes. An understanding there. "I'd ask what you want for Christmas, but it looks like you might already have it."

"Yeah," Theo says. "I think we might. Took a few years, but it's about damn time."

As we walk to the car, Mac leading the way, Theo hooks his pinky with mine. A smile on his handsome face, looking at me like he's decided, too.

FORTY

BRIDGET

"ALRIGHT FOLKS."

My hands clap together twice. The conversations around me come to a halt. It's Sunday afternoon and both groups of employees are gathered in the bookstore. Standing shoulder to shoulder, they're listening intently to what I have to say.

"This is our final time together before judging in a week. I split us into groups to tackle our tasks. Some of you are painting the last of the wooden figures. Some of you are working with Malik on the lights. Some of you are cleaning, making sure the floors are swept and glass is wiped down. Our other two groups will be moving the completed projects to their final spots. We'll do a walk through at the end of the day, then head out for the boat tour and caroling."

Everyone springs to life. Decked out in ugly holiday sweaters, Santa hats, light-up necklaces and Lucas in a reindeer onesie, they break into their groups, eager to work.

"Doing okay?" Theo asks, nudging my side.

"Yeah," I answer. "Just nervous."

"What can I do to help?"

"You've done plenty. More than enough."

I spent last night at his house while Mac was with his parents. Tucked in his bed under the warm, clean sheets, his arm draped around my waist and fingers splayed out over my stomach, I couldn't sleep. I tried. I tossed and turned, huffing out sigh after sigh of annoyance.

I peeled the covers back, ready to take my pillow to the couch so I wouldn't disturb him anymore, when Theo turned on the lamp. It was hours before sunrise, the world dark and still outside his window, and he asked me what was wrong. For the next forty-five minutes, he listened to me ramble about figure placements, the order of photos, and how many trays of cookies I should put out for the judges. His eyes, half-closed and with sleep caught in the corner, stayed on me through my wild gesturing and animated soliloquy. He rubbed the space between my shoulder blades, small circles over the valley to my back, mouth shut and refusing to interrupt. When I finished, throat sore and thoroughly spent, he kissed me softly. He pulled me tight into his chest. He held me close until I finally drifted off to sleep.

When I'm with him, I think I can conquer anything.

"Your concentrated face is one of my favorites," he adds. "It's cute."

"I don't have a concentrated face."

"You definitely do."

"Oh yeah? What does it look like?"

"You stick out your tongue, like you were doing a few seconds ago. If you're not using your hands, you tap your cheek with your pointer finger—the Bowie finger. If you *are* using your hands, your shoulders hunch up to your ears. Your eyes narrow and you get tunnel vision. You huff, but it's always very quiet. I think you're afraid of people noticing, because you're trying to find a way to make things perfect so everyone is happy."

I stare at him, processing his vivid description. All the little details he picked out, like he's known me for years. "You pay attention to me," I whisper.

"Yeah." Theo nods. "I do. I have for a while now. Unintentionally at first, but then on purpose. Now I can't fucking stop."

"I've never felt like someone has seen me before."

"I do." His voice is quiet, almost a whisper. "And I don't plan to stop anytime soon." He drops a quick kiss to my head, so fast you wouldn't know he was ever there. "I'm going to help Lucas. You'll let me know if you need anything?"

"Yeah." I nod. There's the threat of emotion, threatening to spill out. I clamp down on it, shove it away, and smile up at him.

"Miss you already, Brownie," he says, walking out the door to the hardware store.

I watch him leave, missing him already, too.

"So how much longer are you going to pretend you two aren't together?" Chandler asks, sliding to my side. "Are we waiting until after Christmas or...?"

I rub my temples, pain spider webbing across my forehead and to the base of my neck. I sigh, knowing there's no point of lying, so I don't bother. "We're enjoying each other."

She grabs my arm and drags me over to the paint station I assigned us. A brush gets shoved in my hands. "Spill," she says.

I dip the brush into the palette. "It started the night I was babysitting Mac. But I think it's been building for a while now. We've been seeing each other for a couple weeks. I don't know, Chan. He's a great guy. Sometimes I wonder why he hides these wonderful parts of himself, but then I remember he's afraid to let anyone get too close. I've broken through the barrier, I think."

"Could you see something with him long-term?"

"Yes," I answer automatically. "I could."

"Even with a kid? That's a big role to take on. It's not just one person in the relationship, it's two."

"Mac's great. I know very little about being a parent, obviously, but I could see myself with them many years down the road. Definitely."

"You're in love with him," Chandler says. She dips her paintbrush into the swirl of brown and swipes a coat on the finished piece Lucas lugged over an hour ago.

"What? I am not."

"You are," she answers. She doesn't sound mad. She sounds excited, almost. "You'll see."

I consider her words. I haven't been in love in *years*. I haven't actively searched for it, either. It's been so long, I think I've forgotten what it's like. It should be grand gestures, right? Loud, emphatic declarations or obvious signs of attraction. Not handing over pastries or throwing chocolate chips at each other.

Except...

Every time I look at him, I want to smile. I *do* smile. Even when he's irritated. Even when he's tired. Even when he's asleep and I wake up before him, studying him in the early morning light. I've been smiling for weeks.

Every time I look at him, I want to find an excuse to keep talking. I want to ask him a question or two, or three, and wait for his answer.

Every time he touches me, it's like the first time all over again. Fireworks in the night sky. An earthquake, the ground shaking beneath me. Pleasure and bliss, delight and awe. Every spot he touches is magic.

"That would be crazy though, right? Isn't it a bit fast? A bit too aggressive? Feelings like this... they don't exist in real life, do they?"

"Trust me, Bridge. Love doesn't care who the person is. It doesn't care how long you've known them. It doesn't care if they treat you like a queen or barely know your name. When it wants to find a way, it will. There's no playbook, unfortunately, telling us what's right or wrong. No cheat code or answer sheet to figuring this shit out. It's something you feel inside of you. Love is a blessing, but it's also a goddamn curse."

My hand hovers in the air as I process her words. A drop of paint falls off the tip of the brush I'm holding, landing on the floor. I watch it splatter across the hardwood.

Black paint.

Just like the drop on Theo's boot.

Theo.

It's like his name is lit up in flashing lights.

I always thought the fairy tale ending when you found *the one* would be pretty and follow a straight line.

It doesn't, though. It isn't always perfect. It has roadblocks and mistakes. A prickly man who is afraid to let anyone in and the woman who never give up on him.

It's two people falling in love slowly, lazily, haltingly with the messy, imperfect, flawed parts of another soul waiting patiently for its ideal companion.

It's finding the other half to your whole. The one who will light up your world brighter than the Florida summer sun.

Fairy tales take time.

Minutes for the lucky ones, an instant connection forged at first sight.

Weeks for the middle of the road folks, engaging in diligent research and an array of samples to draw a thorough conclusion.

For others, it takes years.

Years of stone walls around your heart, protecting yourself and your loved ones fiercely.

Years of being next-door neighbors.

Years of blueberry muffins and extra dashes of cinnamon.

Years of Polaroid pictures with a mall Santa and laughing while ice skating.

Years of letting go of the past.

Years of *maybe* and *what if?*

When all those years finally meet in one place, a culmination of joy and suffering, happiness and despair, it's the most perfect moment in the world.

Everything makes sense.

Everything is clear.

Nothing else matters except thick-framed glasses, paint drip boots, flannel shirts and Bowie tattoos. Midnight kisses and rides in trucks with an army of Christmas trees.

And how lucky am I to have found such a beautiful thing?

The paintbrush clatters to the table. My lungs feel like they're closing in, breathing nearly impossible. I grip the edge of the wood, keeping myself upright.

"Oh, shit," I whisper.

"There it is," Chandler sings. "If you're happy, then fuck a timeline. Fuck how long it's been."

"From the woman who has sworn off relationships and ever loving again? That's a sincere stamp of approval."

"People like you deserve to be loved, Bridget. You give so much to others. I'm glad to see you finally accepting it, too."

"Well." I wipe my eyes with the back of my sleeves. I sniff and clear my throat. "Let's paint some reindeer and pretend this conversation never happened because I swear everything around me is spinning."

"Sorry, friend. Now that you've realized it, it's going to be impossible to ignore."

FORTY-ONE
BRIDGET

"I CAN'T WAIT to see how everything looks," Lucas says. He rocks on his feet excitedly, grinning at the buildings in front of us.

The sun has set, giving us a chance to see the full splendor of our design. Exterior lights hang from the roofline and awning of both shops. We went with colored lights outside, a rainbow of blues and greens and reds blinking under the night sky. Snowflakes cover the glass of the windows, an impending blizzard on the horizon.

"Okay." I take a deep breath. "Ready for the tour, y'all?"

"Lead the way, Bridget," Theo says, tapping my elbow and dragging his fingers down my forearm.

I march to the door and push it open. I freeze in the entryway, words stuck in my throat, unable to speak.

It's beautiful. To the right, there's a line of candy canes leading to the coffee counter. To the left is the Christmas tree trail. No two look the same. Brooke's has blue lights. Chandler went with white. Molly branched out and did red and green. Michaela, my last employee, did icicles. The tree that customers have been decorating over the last six weeks is covered in ornaments, must-read books written on the small scraps of paper.

I step inside, investigating further.

Each tree has ornaments special to the decorator. Souvenirs from memorable trips. An art project from the early 90s. A gag gift given to them years ago, now a staple adornment. A wishlist sits on the tree skirt under every fir. Favorite toys and movies are shared on the handwritten notes, complete with a plate of cookies and milk.

Malik rigged the music playing through the speakers to coordinate with the lights on the trees, a dancing symphony of sights and sounds.

"Holy shit," Chandler says. "This is incredible."

A menorah sits on a table, ready to be lit at the start of Hanukkah. Additional lights run along the perimeter of the interior walls, the space as bright as noon on a sunny day.

"I can't wait to see what next door looks like!" Felicity says.

We head to the hardware store next. In here, nine reindeer stand, dispersed through different aisles. Toward the back of the store is a large sleigh, a stuffed Santa sitting behind the reins. Above our head runs a clothesline from the door to the rear exit. Polaroids and printed photos dangle from clothespins. I see Jordan with her little sister on skis. Bradley and his mom on a couch in matching pajamas. A little Lucas holding a baseball bat with a bow, grinning at the camera. Young Theo and the mall Santa that terrorized him. Me sitting in a stocking as a baby. Chandler wearing a Christmas tree dress, a candy cane headband on her head.

A collection of years past, proudly showcased for all to see. Some have popular gifts from the 80s in the background, Speak & Spells and Walkmans. Some were taken with cell phones. Vastly different but still so similar, a common bond uniting all the images.

"What does home mean to you?" I ask Chandler, surveying all the snapshots.

She taps the photo, smiling at the memory. "Mom's dresses. She sewed one for my sister and me every year. They were always over the top. Total diva outfits. She was always so excited to snap picture after picture, so we wore them without complaints."

"Playing baseball with my dad was what I looked forward to the most growing up," Lucas adds next. "I'd get off the school bus and he'd be there in the front yard, an old bat in his hand and a ball in the other. The Christmas in the photo was the first year he got me a bat of my own. Home to me is the stitches of a ball running against my knuckles. Dad standing at our pinecone first base, ready to knock the shit out of a pitch I lobbed his way."

"With my family around a menorah. This is the shamash," Felicity says. She gestures to a photo of her with two girls around a table, a lit menorah in front of them. "It's the helper candle used to light the rest of the candles on the menorah. The picture I picked was the year I got to light it for the first time, signifying the start of the holiday. I was terrified, thinking I might drop it or light things in the wrong order. I didn't, and it was a huge honor to have that role."

"Besides the mall Santa incident, this is home to me," Theo starts. I spot a photo of him laughing, a bow on his shirt. "My parents' living room. Mac and I opened presents, wrapping paper everywhere. It's the last time I enjoyed the holidays. Until now. This year knocks the socks off of years past."

"What's home to you, Bridge?" Chandler asks.

I pause and look around the room. "When we entered this competition, I hoped it would be a friendly arrangement. Getting along and having a few laughs. But y'all... you make me happy. And when I think about a place where I'd want to be, it's here." My eyes find Theo's. He tips his lips. Smiles. And taps his heart twice. "You are all my home."

"COME ON, THEO."

"No."

"Please?"

"That might work in the bedroom, Bridget, but it's not working here."

"It's a Santa hat. I'm not asking you to swallow a radioactive pill."

"I'm not putting it on my head. I'll look stupid."

"We *all* look stupid," I press.

Chandler was right. Now that I've realized how deep my feelings are for Theo, I can't stop noticing them.

I noticed the way he offered his hand and guided me up the small steps onto the boat a few minutes ago. I noticed the way he took off his jacket and draped it over my shoulders, claiming he wasn't cold. I saw him shiver when he turned away. I noticed the way his eyes always search for mine, lighting up when he finds me.

Except now, he's pissing me off.

"You're going to stand out in the photo without one," I add.

"I'll take the photo," he counters.

"Fine." I throw my hands up in defeat and plop myself into a seat.

We're onboard a thirty-person pontoon boat that's decked out with lights, speakers and thermoses of hot chocolate. The guy who runs the company is a friend of Theo and Lucas, offering to take us out for an hour free of charge. The goal? To sing Christmas carols at the top of our lungs as we pass through the Park Cove canals, bouncing between the four small city lakes, serenading anyone who might be out on their back porch.

And laughing our asses off while doing so.

Bradley decided to spearhead this outing, and he stands at the stern of the ship, distributing sheet music.

The captain slowly lurches the boat off the dock, propellers kicking on as we glide across the still, quiet water, picking up speed.

"Peace offering?" Theo asks. He drops to the seat beside me, handing over a thermos.

I unscrew the top, investigating the contents. "Any marshmallows in here?"

"Nope. I asked for the marshmallow-free version."

"Why? You like marshmallows with your hot chocolate."

"Yeah." He shrugs. "But I like you more."

I smile as I fill two Styrofoam cups with the scalding beverage. Steam rises into the air, warming my nose and fogging Theo's glasses.

"Cheers," I say.

"I think we're ready for the judging. The stores look fantastic, Bridget. You've worked so hard."

"We've worked so hard," I correct him. "Everyone has been amazing. It's too late to change anything, but I'm feeling good about what we have. It feels special, you know?"

"I'm so proud of you."

He kisses my cheek then, and I don't care that we're around our employees. I don't care that strands of my hair get caught in my mouth and cover my eyes as we hug the shoreline of Lake Vifrgina, a rousing round of "We Wish You a Merry Christmas" ringing out for all to hear. I don't care that Theo isn't wearing a Santa hat.

When I join in, singing off key at the top of my lungs, nose red from the cold and cheeks flushed with happiness, I don't care about that, either.

Because I'm falling in love with someone who brings me the kind of hot chocolate I like. A man who tells me he's proud of me and acknowledges my efforts. A man who pulls out his cell phone, shyly asks if he can take a photo with me, and blushes when I say yes. We grin from ear to ear, a chocolate mustache coating Theo's top lip.

A man who sees me, *all* of me, and still leans close, squeezes my knee twice and whispers, "*Stay the night with me?*"

Yeah.

I'm head over heels for this man.

FORTY-TWO
THEO

THE DOORBELL RINGS and I check the time, a string of curses falling from my mouth.

I'm cooking dinner for Bridget tonight, and I'm behind schedule. The food that should be ready hasn't been put in the oven yet. The dessert I bought is sitting on the counter, not in the fridge where it belongs. I'm still wearing my work clothes even though I've been home for two hours.

And I'm nervous as hell.

We're going a little backward here. Yeah, we've spent over a dozen nights together. I keep asking my parents to watch Mac, finding excuses for why I need to be alone. She thinks she's getting a shit ton of Christmas presents with how many times I've mentioned wrapping gifts. For all the mornings I've woken up beside Bridget in bed, tangled hair in my face and her leg over my thigh, I haven't taken her on a date. I haven't made her a meal or bought her flowers. The last thing I want her to think is this is a strictly physical thing. The pull I have toward her is magnetic and indisputable. She's been on my mind nonstop. As much as I'd love to spend our night together in bed, her wrists above her head and a smirk on her face as I kiss the inside of her thigh, I also want to get to know her when no one else is around.

I throw the chicken and pasta dish in the oven, setting a timer. I wipe my hands clean and head for the front door. When I open it, I find Bridget leaning against the wall.

"Hey," she says. Her chin tips up and her lips quirk.

"Hey," I answer. My voice cracks and I clear my throat. "You look really pretty."

She does. A navy blue dress that hits above the knee. White Converse on her feet. A jean jacket over her shoulders.

Exquisite, really.

Her smile stretches to a grin and she spins. The material fans out, giving me an unobstructed view of the long legs I can't wait to wrap around my waist.

"Thanks. You have sawdust in your hair. Intentional, or have you not showered yet?"

"Unintentional, I'm afraid." I motion her inside and close the door behind us. My mouth presses against hers in a welcoming kiss. "I've been running around like a madman trying to get things right for tonight. I've barely had a minute to breathe."

"You know you don't have to impress me right?" Her arms loop around my neck. "Sitting in your kitchen with a bowl of leftover chili is plenty sufficient."

"I know." I kiss her neck. The line of her throat. The spot just at the top of her dress, where the material meets bare skin. "I wanted things to be nice. It's the first night we're spending time together."

"That's not true. The Christmas tree lot. In the pool. When you fucked me in the store. Every morning I've woken up with you hard between my legs... should I keep going?"

"I meant the first time together without being physical. Like a date."

She brightens at the word. "What do you have planned?"

"Dinner. Dessert. A Christmas movie. Thoughts?"

"Depends. What's the movie?"

"I was tempted to pick *Die Hard* but, uh, I went with something a little more cheesy. Is *The Holiday* okay?"

"You want to watch *The Holiday* with me?" Bridget asks slowly.

"Yeah. I mean, unless you don't like it. People said it's a good romantic, festive movie. Bradley, actually, was the one to tell me that. I know you love romance novels and I figured I'd suggest it."

"I'd love to watch *The Holiday* with you," she says softly.

"Good. Mind if I shower real quick?"

"Not at all. I brought a book with me."

"A book? Do I bore you?"

She laughs, and the sound echoes in my chest. "I bring a book with me everywhere. You never know when you might need it. You never know when someone will take a shower and not invite you."

I groan and adjust the front of my jeans. "When you say that, I want to drag you in there with me."

Bridget shrugs and turns for the couch, tossing her hair over her shoulder. She pulls a paperback out of her purse. "Wouldn't get any complaints from me."

I grind my teeth together. "I'm trying to be good here, and you're tempting me."

"Go shower, Theo. Then we'll eat. Watch a movie. And have our sleepover."

"Fine. You win. Only if I can eat you out, too."

She grins, hiding her face behind the pages, a color of red flushing her cheeks. "That can be arranged."

I'VE NEVER SHOWERED SO QUICKLY in my life. There's still shampoo in my hair, and I miss washing the left side of my body entirely. I don't care.

Pulling on an old T-shirt and a pair of joggers, I make my way back to the living room. Checking the timer on the oven, I see we still have twenty minutes before the food will be ready.

Bridget hasn't noticed me yet, back settled against the cushions and absorbed in her reading. I walk over and bend down to read over her shoulder.

I hold my arms out, pressing them together. He looks at me with a wicked glint in his eyes and grabs the strand of Christmas lights off the coffee table.
"Is there something you want to ask me?"
I lower my gaze to the floor. "I-I want you to tie my hands. Please."
"What my good girl wants, my good girl gets."

"Taking notes?" I ask, husky and low near Bridget's ear.

She jumps and the book goes flying. "Holy *shit*, Theo, don't ever scare me like that again."

"Hard to hear me walk up when you're so immersed in your reading. And such thrilling material, too."

Bridget spins on the couch, rising onto her knees. Her cheeks are red, and I watch her swallow.

"Someone didn't let me shower with them, so I had to take matters into my own hands."

"Hands tied," I say carefully. "We haven't tried that yet. It was also mentioned in your second book club pick. Something you've done before?"

"Once." She pauses, hesitating to share the next part. "I liked it."

I hum. "Give me two minutes. Get on your knees, princess."

Her eyes get glassy in the way they do every time I use the

endearment. I stride to my room and reach under my bed. Mac and I decorated the fake tree a week ago, but we didn't use all the lights. I grab the handle of an old shopping bag, bringing it with me to the living room.

When I turn the corner, I find Bridget on her knees, just like I asked.

"Look at you waiting for me." I walk to the rug and cup her chin with my fingers. Tilting her head back, I hold up the strand. "Interested?" I ask.

Her nod is staccato and vigorous, quick jerks conveying an enthusiastic answer. "Very," she says.

Even though it's a fantasy of mine, I've never tied someone up. The swagger and bravado I had as I marched down the hall evaporates as I stare down at Bridget.

It's because it's *her*, I realize. I don't want to hurt her. I don't want to do anything that might mess up the foundation of what we've started to build.

"Theo," she whispers. Her eyes stare into mine, aroused. Excited. Infatuated. "I trust you. I know you'll keep me safe. I jump, you jump, remember?"

I huff out a laugh and run my hand through my hair. My fingers tighten around the cord. Reassured and turned on as hell, I rub the bulbs of the lights against her cheek. "Stand up and take your dress off."

Bridget rises from the ground, like a goddess from water. Her hands toy with the fabric of her dress straps, inching it down painstakingly slow. I don't think I've ever been this hard in my life, watching and waiting for her to get rid of the damn thing.

The left shoulder first, then the right. With both straps free, she holds the material against her chest. Before I can tell her to drop it, she spins around. Looking at me over her shoulder, lip caught in her teeth, she lets the dress fall to the floor. It pools at her waist and she nudges the clothing to the side with her toes.

My eyes travel down her back, along the route I've touched and kissed numerous times before. Braless, the ridges of her shoulder blades stand out. I follow her spine, dipping further until I see a red pair of underwear, barely covering her ass, a little bow on top of the lace.

"Come here," I say. I don't bother to mask how badly I want her, the need prevalent in my tone.

Another spin and she's facing me again, hair spilling down her shoulders and covering her breasts. She walks to me, arms outstretched and waiting. I plug the lights into the outlet on the wall and wrap the strand around her, pausing as I wait for a nod to continue. Bridget kisses my cheek and I forge on. Over, then under. Back and forth in a figure-eight pattern until the colors dance up her arms, painted in reds and blues and greens. I'm careful to not let the lights touch her, keeping the warming bulbs away from the skin.

"There we go," I breathe out when I'm finished.

"How do I look?"

"Beautiful. Perfect. Like the best Christmas gift. But you'd look even better on your knees."

Immediately, she sinks back to the floor, mouth already parting, tongue running over her top lip.

"I had a whole night planned for us," I say, loosening the drawstring of my pants. "I wasn't going to do anything but kiss you. I wasn't going to tie your hands up so you'd be at my mercy. I wasn't going to run my cock over your lips and paint your stomach with my cum before I sank into you."

"Plans can change," Bridget pants.

I step out of my joggers and kick them to the side. I didn't bother with underwear; I knew the second I left her on the couch I wouldn't need them. "Yeah, they can. Now open your mouth, princess, and suck my cock like the good girl you are."

She moans. Scooting forward on the rug, her lips wrap

around my head. The lights don't afford her any room to use her hands. Pausing briefly, she adjusts her angle. Her thighs widen. She sinks closer to the floor. Her neck tilts to accommodate more of my length.

She's got me halfway down now, and I wrap my fingers into her hair. "You can go deeper, can't you, Bridget?"

Her cheeks hollow out as she nods. I slide in another half inch, nearing the back of her throat. Tears catch in the corner of her eyes and a drop of saliva hangs from her bottom lip. I use my thumb to wipe it away.

Her teeth graze up my length and she looks up at me through a fan of eyelashes, the picture of innocence until she slides all the way to the base of my shaft. I let out a groan, long and loud. I'll be shocked if the neighbors can't hear me. I watch in awe as her head bobs up and down, bringing me closer and closer to the edge.

"Jesus, Bridget." I stop her movements, pulling out of her mouth. "Couch. Now."

She jumps to her feet obediently and practically launches herself at the furniture. I toss the pillows aside and wait for her to get on her back. My knees bracket her hips, and I move her arms above her head, Christmas lights shining on her beautiful face.

"Theo," she says. She licks her lips and squeezes her legs around my waist.

"Yeah, sweetheart?"

"No condom. I'm clean and on birth control. I want to feel you. *Just* you."

I kiss the top of her knee and rip, literally rip, her underwear away. "You want it raw and rough? The second I slide inside you with nothing between us, that's game fucking over, Bridget. No other man will ever get to feel your sweet, tight, pussy again, because you're mine. I'm yours. And I don't fucking share." I press the head against her entrance, damp arousal coating the tip. "One more inch and you're never going to get me to leave."

"Please," she begs. Her thighs quake. Her eyes squeeze closed. "Only you, Theo. Take me. I'm yours."

"Open your eyes," I murmur. "I want to see you. All of you."

She blinks, smiling as her focus returns to me. I swallow and grip her calf, rocking forward half a degree, sliding inside.

Every inch of her is heaven; warm, wet, tight. Every thrust is another reminder of how perfect she is. Every moan is music to my ears; a beautiful orchestra. A melodic symphony.

They bounce through the room. She's loud, *so fucking loud*, and keeps saying things like, *thank you* and *right there* and *yours, forever*, over and over again.

She's close.

My hand moves to her neck, applying pressure to her windpipe. Her eyes widen.

"You with me, angel?"

"I'm with you," she answers, eyes hazy and smile wide. "Forget jewelry. The only thing I need around my neck are your hands. Harder, Theo. You know you want to. And I want it, too."

It's the last piece of composure I have and I watch it crash to the floor. My fingers push, *harder*. I thrust, *harder*. I bend down and kiss her, *harder*. Ruining and ruining and ruining until I hear the shift in her breathing.

"Thatta girl," I whisper in her ear. My thumb snakes over her body, pressing her clit. "Once you finish around my cock, angel, I'm going to fill you with my come, feed you dinner, then fill you up again."

That does her in. She lets out a sob. A moan. Her hands grip the armrest of the couch as she tightens around me, convulsing as she comes down from her high.

"Yours, Theo," she whispers. Her heels push into my lower back, bringing me closer to her body. It's like we're one person now. When she looks me in the eye and I see the satisfaction there, I trip over the edge too, following her down.

"That was..." Bridget starts. She licks her lips. Rolls her hips into mine. "Incredible."

I untangle the lights from her arms. My fingers run over the marks left behind, kissing each spot as I pull the strand away.

"Dinner time. Then round two. Forget the earlier plans."

FORTY-THREE
THEO

"YOU'RE good at a lot of things," Bridget says. "But you're exceptional at cooking."

I scoop another portion of pasta onto her plate. "High praise from the woman who has a line of people out the door of her shop, waiting for baked goods."

"Baking is different," she explains. "Cooking involves timing and balancing eight different parts of the meal. You can't go socialize with someone and expect things to be in the same place when you get back. Look at the latkes! I couldn't even do that."

"You also had a sous chef who was socializing and not paying attention," I add. "I can change things as I go with cooking. With baking, it's a lot of guesswork and estimation. You don't know how they turn out until the end. I couldn't make muffins to save my life, and you do them perfectly."

"I'll make the muffins, you make the chicken," she proposes.

I stick out my hand and she shakes it, holding onto my palm for an extra second. "Deal. Where's Ziggy tonight? You could have brought him."

"He's with Chandler. She offered to watch him for me."

"That was nice of her."

"Yeah, until she told me how weird it is to have a dog stare at you while you have sex. I don't want to know *how* she has experience with it, but I took her advice."

I grimace. "That's not a visual I need to see."

"You're telling me," Bridget giggles. She stands, bringing her dirty dish to the sink.

"You can leave the dishes. I'll get them later."

"You cooked. I can clean."

"Yeah, you can, but you're also wearing my shirt and when you turn around and reach up, I can see your ass. And I really want to touch it."

She sets the plate down and walks to me, climbing into my lap and resting her head on my shoulder. "This has been a good first date," she says softly.

"I'm weeks behind schedule." I kiss the top of her head. "I wanted to talk to you about something."

"You'll let me use the Christmas lights on you?"

"I wouldn't be opposed. No, this is about what I said at the mall the other day. About you being around Mac more. I'd love for you to be here for dinner and on Sunday afternoons. I'm not asking you to step into a parent role, but I want Mac to get accustomed to seeing us together."

Bridget is beautiful when she looks at me. Bright eyes and a wide grin. Care and adoration in the kiss she presses to my cheek. The trail of her hand down my chest, resting over my heart.

"I'd like that, too," she whispers. Powerful words magnified in the quiet room. They notch their way inside me, breaking down all the walls I've ever put up. Crumbling the facade I've worked so hard to keep firmly in place. Now that I have a woman who sees me and understands me, now that I have *her*, I don't want anything standing in the way.

"Okay. Maybe we can go grab her from her sleepover together tomorrow morning."

"You're in charge. I'll follow whatever lead you want to take."

I kiss her then, tenderly, thankfully, utterly confused how a person as wonderful as Bridget Boylston ever found their way into my life. She answers me in return, vigor and fervor behind the grip on my shirt. The shift of her hips to straddle my lap. The fingers tugging the tufts of hair at the nape of my neck, causing me to moan and close my eyes.

"Want you," I mumble, standing up. I lift her with ease, calves wrapping around my middle like a pesky vine. I drop her on the counter and spread her legs, letting out a puff of air at the sight.

Every time I see Bridget like this—a hickey on her neck, hair tousled and askew, a lazy smile on her face and damp, parted thighs—I think I die and go to heaven.

"Want you so bad," I add. "Here." I touch low beneath her belly and she hums, satisfied. "And here, too." I touch her heart, palm splayed out over the old, tattered shirt starting a renewed life on her body.

"You have both," she answers earnestly. "You have for a while."

Her legs drive me closer. Nearer. This isn't the frenzied passion I expected. It's a consideration. Patient. *Loving.* Two people who care for each other deeply. Nails drag up my bicep, marking me with a temporary tattoo I'd gladly make permanent. My tongue swipes down her neck, a sheen of sweat on her throat. Her breath is warm against my ear. I shift forward, ready to take her again, the second of many, many times. Forever, maybe.

"What is it with you and counters?" she murmurs. I chuckle, a kiss dropped to her chest.

"You're irresistible, I guess."

"You resisted me for years," she counters.

"I resisted *everyone* for years," I correct her. "You're the only one I've ever wanted to let in."

There's something else hanging on the tip of my tongue, something else close to slipping out, but I don't have the chance. Bridget scoots toward me, back flat on the granite. Legs wide, my heart in her hands. Her heels press into the small of my back, encouraging me along. I huff and nod, sliding straight inside.

Our groans are synchronized. Our movements are coordinated. Her hand, in my hair. Mine, on her neck. Her fingers, clawing my back. Mine, rubbing where she's wet, *so wet*, and sensitive. Her gasps, my grunts. The building rhythm, the rise of pleasure.

"More," she whispers. "I want all of you, Theo."

"You have all of me," I get out, between thrusts and pants. Between kisses and pleas. "Feel good?"

"Perfect. It's perfect."

Her shirt—*my shirt*—is up near her neck. Bunched up, material wrinkled, chest on display. Her hair is a tangle of beautiful brown. I run my fingers through the strands and give a tug to her scalp.

"Theo," she whispers. Her hand taps my shoulder. "Theo." Her voice becomes sharper and I freeze, scanning her face and down her body.

"What? What's wrong? Are you okay? Did I hurt you?"

"N-no. Your phone. It won't stop buzzing."

"Shit," I curse, pulling out of her. My immediate thought is something happened with Mom. She tried to stand on her own and toppled over, hurting herself. I fumble for my phone, hidden under Bridget's dress and purse. I see Mac's name on the screen, showing five missed calls.

I hit her name to call her back, and waiting for her to answer is excruciating.

"Dad?"

"Mac? What's going on?"

"I-I'm on the way to the hospital."

"The *hospital?* Are you hurt?"

I hear Bridget jump off the counter. She stands beside me, hand pressing between my shoulders. She kisses my cheek, letting me know she's here if I need her.

"I was jumping on the bed with some of my friends. It was a dare to do a somersault off the mattress and I landed wrong. I think my arm might be broken. It hurts so bad. Julie's mom is— we're parking at the ER now."

"Which hospital?"

"Park Cove."

"I'll be there as soon as I can."

I hang up and pull my joggers up my thighs, tying the drawstring tight.

"What's going on?" Bridget asks.

"Mac fell off the bed. She thinks she broke her arm."

"Oh, shit. Okay. Do you want me to go with you? How can I help?"

"No," I say sharply. "No. What the fuck am I thinking? This is all my fault."

My voice becomes panicked as I search for my wallet and keys, overturning a fruit bowl and shoving dish towels to the ground.

"It's not your fault, Theo," Bridget says gently, sidestepping out of my way. "You couldn't have prevented this."

"You wouldn't understand," I snarl. "I put myself first for once in my goddamn life and look what happens. My kid ends up in the hospital."

"Sweetheart." It's the first time Bridget's ever used a term like that on me, and I feel myself melt at the affection. "It was an accident. Accidents happen."

"You're not a parent. You wouldn't get it. You'll never fucking get it." I wince at the harsh words, pinching the bridge of my nose. "I didn't mean... *Fuck*, that was uncalled for. I'm so sorry."

"You're right," she says softly. There's no anger or disappointment in the words. No desire to launch a plate at my head for the insensitive and horrible comment. It's calm and patient. Understanding. "I'm not a parent. Mac's not my kid, and I can't imagine how scared you are right now. I know you're trying to blame yourself and I know you're about to sprint to the hospital to be by her side. It's not your fault, Theo," she repeats firmly.

"I have responsibilities in life that don't include fucking someone on the counter." The heels of my palms press into my eyes. "I'm sorry. I'm so sorry. I'm not thinking straight. I don't mean it. You're not just someone. You're–"

"You do have responsibilities," Bridget agrees, interrupting me. "And you handle them all effortlessly."

"I need to go," I whisper. "I can't—I should—"

"I know." She kisses my cheek. "Will you let me know how she's doing? And if you need anything?"

I nod, giving her hand a squeeze. "I'm not... I'm not trying to run away from you. I need to... There's a balance here. I'm just not sure what it is, or how you factor into it."

"Take your time, Theo Gardner. You're worth the wait, and I'm not leaving. I'm staying, for a long, long time."

I'm immobile as she exchanges my shirt for her dress. As she slides her purse over her shoulder and drops my keys and wallet into the palm of my hand. As she stands on her tiptoes to kiss my forehead, quietly slipping out of the front door.

I rush to my car, fingers nervously tapping the steering wheel with every mile I drive. I pass houses with fake snow covering their lawns. Christmas trees standing proud in windows, twinkling with lights. The closer I get to the hospital the more conflicted I feel.

Can I really split my time between my kid and another permanent person in my life? It's not anything I've had to do before, and I feel useless on how to navigate it. I don't know what to do.

I care for Bridget. A lot. Is it a coincidence that the night I let go *just a little bit*, something bad happened? I groan, frustrated, tossing my keys to the emergency room valet and hustling to the desk. I need to figure my shit out, but other things take priority right now.

Mac. She's the most important thing in my life. Everything else has to wait.

MAC LOOKS SO small in the hospital bed, gown slipping off her shoulders. She's propped up against four pillows, a sling over her right arm. I stand in the doorway and grip the doorknob, fingers curling around the metal as I stare at her.

Fuck, it hurts to see her hurt. I'd carry the burden for her if I could, freeing her from the mattress and healing her wounds with a quick flick of my wrist. This is the first time she's ever been seriously injured. We've never been in an emergency room before, and I hope to God this is the last time we have to step foot inside one. It's too sterile in here, too cold. Too drab and too dim. It could use some color, a little bit of light.

Like Bridget, my mind traitorously whispers.

"Hey, sweetie," I say softly. "How are you feeling?"

"Hey, Dad." She shrugs and takes a sip of water on the tray in front of her. "Fine. My arm itches. But no pain."

"That'll be the drugs. Don't get any ideas, kid." I step inside the room, closing the door behind me. "Can I bring you anything? Are you hungry?"

"No. I'm okay for right now. We stuffed our faces with pizza and cake at Julie's house."

"Sounds like a fun night. I talked to Julie's mom and thanked her for bringing you in. The doctor said they'll be putting a cast on you soon."

"Great. No soccer for over a month." She sighs and plays with the ratty blanket covering her legs. It looks like it's been eaten by moths, the polyester riddled with holes. "Sorry I ruined your night."

"You didn't ruin my night. I was wrapping presents." I take a seat on the bed beside her, legs dangling off the mattress.

Mac arches an eyebrow. "For the tenth time?"

"You're getting a lot of gifts."

"Oh, stop lying, Dad. You've been weird all month. It's different, but a good different."

I rub my temples and pinch the bridge of my nose. I shove my glasses up and sigh. "It's Bridget."

"I *knew* it!"

"You knew nothing."

"Yeah? Is that why I notice how you smile every time you're near her? I haven't seen you smile like that in years. I also know she's been at our house when I'm not there. There's a book on your bedside table that's definitely *not* yours."

"Okay. Fine. Yes, I smile every time I'm near her. But I'm not sure where we go from here."

Mac frowns. Her unbroken arm folds under the sling and she glares at me. "Why?"

"Why?" I repeat.

"Yeah, why? Why wouldn't you be with someone who makes you happy?"

"Because I was acting like an idiot when my own kid got hurt. I missed your calls, Mac. What if it had been worse. What if you had *died* and I didn't get to say goodbye? Because I was being selfish?"

Hot tears leak onto my cheeks. I bat them away hurriedly,

not wanting Mac to see this side of me. The raw, broken side who can't stop thinking about the woman I was kissing an hour ago. It's difficult to speak, but I do my best to power on.

"I was acting like I didn't have a worry in the world. Like I don't have someone who relies on me for things. If something worse had happened to you, I never would have forgiven myself. Hell, I'm so upset *right now* and it's a broken arm. I can't... I don't want to imagine how bad this could have been."

"Daddy," Mac whispers.

God.

She hasn't called me that in years. It stopped when she got to fifth grade, wanting to shorten the word. Her face softens and she scoots closer to me, head resting on my shoulder.

"Sorry," I exhale. "I don't need to unload all my problems and inner turmoil onto you."

My arm falls to her shoulder. Even with the sling, even with the stiffness of the cheap mattress under my ass, even with the arctic air conditioning casting a frigid temperature in the room, I hold her close. I breathe a sigh of relief and relax marginally.

"It was an accident, Dad," she starts. "It could have happened anywhere. It could have happened at our house while you were at work, or during a soccer game. Accidents are going to happen, whether you're dating someone or not. I'm growing up. I'm going to high school soon, then college probably. You won't always be around to take care of me."

"No, but I'm here *now*. I can be around *now*."

"What are you going to do when I'm 3,000 miles away? What are you going to do when I meet a guy or girl and move in with them? Are you going to buy the house next door?"

I tuck away the use of both guy *and* girl, knowing we'll need to come back to that later.

"I'm going to have kids one day, too," she continues. "I don't want you sitting around, alone, for the rest of your life. Bridget is amazing. I know that. *You* know that. Someone else will scoop her up in a heartbeat. I want you to be *happy*, Daddy, and you are with her. I don't want to go through life thinking you're only halfway content because you've allocated all of your time and love to me."

"Jesus," I mumble. "When the hell did you get so smart? Allocated? Are you already preparing for the SAT?" I kiss her head. "Sometimes people have to sacrifice parts of their life for other things and other people. I'm okay with that. I'm okay waking up alone in the morning."

"Are you?" Mac presses. "When you think down the road, and you think about Bridget with someone else, and not *us*, how does that make you feel?"

My lips press together. I imagine someone else making her smile. Someone else kissing her cheek. Someone else wiping away the chocolate that lingers in the corner of her mouth when she eats a cookie. My chest tightens at the thought of her rolling over in bed, sleepy eyes finding a pair that aren't mine.

"Shitty," I admit honestly. "It makes me feel really shitty."

"You're going to have to accept that you won't always get to be there for me. You can't control every part of my life. I'm going to get hurt. I'm going to make mistakes. I'm going to get my heart broken. I'm probably going to break someone else's heart, too. But you can control your happiness. Take me out of the equation, Dad. If you could have only one thing in your life, what would it be?"

Bridget.

Wholly, unequivocally her. In any and every capacity.

She calls me "Collector", and she's right. I do collect things. Her joy, her laughs. Her breathy moans and her yawns in the morning. Her giggles late at night and the smile she gives me —*just* me. The jeans that make her ass look incredible. The ink on her fingers left behind from a day of reading and high-lighting her favorite passages. The way my heart warms whenever she's nearby. The butterflies that flutter in my chest every time I look at her. The contentment I feel with her in my arms.

Those things... they're worth more than any fine painting. They're indefinable, I think, but at the same time alarmingly obvious. They're years of pain abating. Hours of anger soothing. Days of insecurities coming to a screeching halt, all at the hands of the beautiful brunette who makes blueberry muffins for *me*. And captured my heart and soul in the process.

"See," Mac whispers. "I know you love me. I know I'm your world. But you deserve to be loved by someone else, too."

"For the record, I hate how mature and wise you're getting," I grumble. I wipe my eyes again and sigh. "I don't know what to do, half-pint."

"It's simple. Apologizing for being a dick would be a good place to start because I know you probably said something stupid. Then tell her how you feel."

"If Grams hears you talking like that, she'll have me murdered."

"Hear you talking like what?"

I look up and spot Dad wheeling Mom into the room.

"What are you two doing here?"

"Our granddaughter called us and told us she was in the hospital," Mom says. "And apparently an intervention is happening, too."

I groan and climb off the mattress. "You're grounded from now until eternity, young lady."

Mac rolls her eyes and grins. "Fine by me."

I shuffle the chairs in the room so Mom can get closer to the bed. She talks softly with Mac, looking at the sling and asking about what color cast she's going to put on.

Collapsing into the chair off to the side of the room, I rub my temples. Mac spelled it all out for me. It's *okay* to have space for two people in my life. I think, for the first time in a very, very long time, I know I deserve that love, too.

"What's wrong, son?" My dad takes a seat next to me.

"Life shit. It's a woman. I think I might… I think I might love her."

"Ah." He chuckles. "The best kind of headache. Did I ever tell you the time I asked your mother's best friend to the school dance instead of her?"

"No. I haven't heard this one before."

"I liked your mother of course. Knew I was going to marry her the second I laid eyes on her. I didn't want to come off too strong, though, so I asked her best friend to the dance. Your mother was furious. When I got to the statue on campus where I was supposed to meet my date, she wasn't there. Your mom was. She crossed her arms over her chest and said, 'We'll have the rest of our lives for you to act like an idiot, but tonight you're dancing with me.'"

"Holy shit." I grin. "Mom is badass."

"Indeed she is. She wasn't wrong, though. I was an idiot a lot of times in our relationship. I still am, sometimes. But you know what? She loves me because I'm an idiot. Because I make mistakes and mess up. Whoever this woman is—and I have a feeling it's someone who knows how to make damn good pumpkin pie—you have to ask yourself this: Is the thought of life without her better than even the worst days with her there? If it isn't, you need to go and talk to her. And make this right."

The only thing I'm positive about is Bridget. I want her to tease me mercilessly about my age. I want to roll my eyes at her jokes. I want her to make me blueberry muffins and I want to hold her in my arms and kiss her every morning and every night.

If this is how I feel after only a few weeks with her, how much better could my life be in a year? In five years?

I suck in a breath. I know what I need to do. I know what I need to say.

"Do we know when the doctor is coming in?" I ask, standing to peer out the hall.

"Are you in a rush?" Mom asks, frowning.

"No. Yes. Kind of."

"What in the world do you have to do at nine o'clock at night?" she presses.

"He has to go get his girl!" Mac squeals. "For real, this time. He's not going to hide her anymore!"

"Eternally grounded," I interrupt. "Forever. Until you're 65."

"Worth it." Mac sticks her tongue out at me and flops back onto the pillows. "Whatever it takes to get you off your butt. Tell the doctor to hurry up, Dad. We have places to be! People to ask to join our family! Screw the cast!"

FORTY-FIVE

BRIDGET

FOUR DAYS BEFORE CHRISTMAS, and it's raining.

Not just raining. Pouring.

A massive storm is rolling through town and last-minute shoppers have to put their errands on hold until the bleak weather subsides. With gloomy clouds and small puddles of water catching in the divots of the sidewalk, the avenue is forlorn. Empty, save for a lone umbrella-clad patron fighting a losing battle with a gust of wind.

I watch the scene unfold from the loveseat in the window of the shop. My eyes drift from the parasol spectacle to the raindrops rolling down the snowflakes on the glass. The white shapes stand out, bright and bold amidst doom and despair. Not even Greta is rolling by on her scooter, searching for a sniff of gossip. I laugh to myself, the older woman a catalyst for the last six weeks of my life unfolding differently than expected.

I didn't just enter the contest and hang up strands of lights. I fell in love along the way, with a man who's not sure he can give himself to me fully. Attention always a little bit stolen, responsibilities always superseding emotions like *fun* and *relaxed*.

Theo texted me yesterday, letting me know Mac was okay.

The messages were brief, stilted, enough to let me know his guilt had settled, if only temporarily. A photo of the pink cast over her arm was also sent my way, and it made my heart trip and sputter like a car in need of a repair. We didn't have a conversation about *us*, and how I might factor into his—*their*—life completely. I also didn't ask. It's not for me to decide. It's up to him.

I close the book in my lap with a *snap*. I haven't turned the pages in an hour. Standing and stretching, I fluff the pillows bedazzled with polar bears and candy canes, arranging them into a neat line. We're less than twenty-four hours away from the judging, and the next time I walk in here will be for the chance to win *a hundred thousand dollars*. The culmination of blisters, paint-stained floors, scuffed knees and the lingering smell of burnt latkes will soon, *hopefully*, be worth it.

I drape my purse over my shoulder, cursing myself for not bringing an umbrella or rain jacket. I'm going to be drenched when I pick Ziggy up from daycare. Slipping out the front door and locking it behind me, I hustle down the pavement. Parking was a nightmare this morning, and I was forced to find a spot around the corner three blocks up. Four seconds outside, and I'm already soaked.

That's when I hear a noise behind me.

"Bridget!"

Spinning, I squint through the sheets of rain. I find Theo charging toward me, a man on a mission. His hair is plastered to his face. His glasses are halfway down his nose. He's moving with a purpose, resolute footsteps almost echoing through the air.

"What are you doing here?" I have to shout over the din of the storm so he can hear me. "What's wrong? Is Mac okay?"

As he grows closer, I see the worry on his face. The panic in his eyes and the hurried movements. "I need to talk to you. There's something I have to say."

I wrap my arms around myself in a bear hug, rocking on my feet to fight off the cold air. "Okay."

"The last forty-eight hours have been hell, Bridget. With Mac in a cast and the last words I said to you, I've been a damn mess. I'm not good at expressing emotions or telling people how I feel. It's never been my strong suit. I recognize it. I'm working on it."

I reach out, palm resting against his chest. His heart races under my touch, sprinting toward an invisible finish line. "I know you have these parts of your life you need to be present for. I have no idea how to parent or divide my time between things other than work, myself and my dog. I'm sorry I ever made you feel like you had to give up anything to be with me."

"This is *my* fault," he says fiercely. "Not yours. For years I've been determined to make my kid my only priority, fearful of what would happen if I let someone else in. I need to learn how to balance all these parts of myself."

"You shouldn't have to pick."

"I'm not picking. I'm allocating my attention to different enti-ties, according to Mac. I won't love her any less because I want to spend time with you. Life's not going to stop moving if I answer her call on the second ring instead of the first. And, I want that life to include you. You are..." Theo trails off and shakes his head. Flecks of water fly from the ends of the dark strands. "You've given me so much joy and happiness. So much direction. I can only hope I give you the same. I want to jump into pools with my clothes on and I want to dance in the fucking rain. I want to have food fights and important conversations. I want you, Bridget, more than I've ever wanted *anything* in my life."

My eyes prickle with tears, and a sob catches in my throat. The smile on my lips starts deep within my soul, hidden inside before it finds its way to my lips. "Okay," I whisper. "Yeah, let's do it, Theo Gardner. Let's dance and laugh and listen to Bowie in your truck. Let's buy five hundred Christmas trees and decorate each one. We'll get matching tattoos and smile every day. I want your flaws and I want to show you mine, too. I want *you*."

He nudges me carefully, gently, with so much fucking care into the wall adjacent to our building. I gasp as my back meets the brick, rough against my shoulder blades. Theo swallows the sound down, hand threading through my hair. He tilts his neck and kisses me like I've never been kissed before. As if this is our last moment on earth and he wants to go out with his lips against mine, my heart in his hand.

He kisses me like he's been starved, deprived of my existence his whole life. It's teeth and tongue. Laughs and brushes of noses. Even with the wisp of a chilly breeze billowing against my skin, goosebumps creeping up my arm, I feel warm. So *warm*, from the inside out. Because sometimes warmth doesn't come from weather or temperature. It comes for a person, the one who makes you feel totally whole.

Like Theo does for me.

My heart flutters, a hummingbird rhythm, constricting and coiling from every touch of his body against mine. The flex of his thigh, muscular, brawny, nudging its way between my legs. The smell of his cologne, cedar and spice. The gentle words and binding promises he whispers in my ear.

It's an obliteration of my emotions, my feelings. It's overwhelming and shocking, a rip current pulling me out to sea. An electric fence jolting me within an inch of my life. A free-fall from an airplane without a parachute, him on the ground, ready to catch me.

If I jump, he jumps.

It's beautiful and messy, raw and *perfect*.

"Bridge," he whispers. His lips, warm and soft, move from my mouth down my neck. They run along the column of my throat, dipping dangerously close to the collar of my shirt. Each press of his mouth invites my body a little further, an inferno kindling along the way.

"Yes?" I answer. My fingers slip into the belt loop of his Levi's —the frayed favorite pair—and I tug him toward me.

"We need to get out of the rain, angel. It's cold. I don't want you to get sick before Christmas."

Angel.

The simple, soft word sneaks its way into our embrace. I like when he calls me princess when he's being rough and ragged. Sweat rolling down my cheek and his hands on my ass. *Angel*, though, is different. It's heavier. More powerful, full of promise. I want to etch it onto my body like one of his tattoos.

"Okay," I whisper. "Where are we going?"

For him, I'd move mountains.

For him, I'd agree to everything and more.

He detangles our limbs. Adjusts his glasses on the bridge of his nose. Fixes his shirt and takes a breath.

"My house?" he asks. It's weightless, like he gave every ounce of himself to me. Which is good, because I plan to give all of myself to him in return.

"I need to grab Ziggy from daycare. Do you want to come with me?"

"Yeah. I do." His hand finds mine, palm slick in my own and he squeezes twice.

"Then?" I ask.

Theo shrugs, unhurried and unbothered. "We have the rest of our lives to figure it out."

THIS IS my first time in Bridget's house. Like her bookshop, it's warm and homey. There are subtle traces of her in every room. A vase of flowers on her square kitchen table, petals bright and vibrant against the white walls. A stack of books next to her couch, bookmarks shoved into nearly half of them. A dog bed next to the door out to her backyard.

Ziggy is in the living room, curled up and uncaring about his surroundings. Bridget and I are in her bed, showered, fed, and warm. She's propped up against the pillows, staring at me. Her leg hooks around mine, and I smile at the feel of her socks against my bare feet.

A wool pair, with little alligators wearing top hats on them.

"I have a question," she whispers.

I turn on my elbow to face her. Under the glow of the moon, she looks like she's made of ether, a woman from a different world besides Earth. Her hazel eyes blink hesitantly, and my thumb reaches out to rub the scrupulous bend of her eyebrows away. "What's that?"

Bridget blows out a breath and drifts closer. "You said all

those wonderful things earlier, but I have to ask. Is this just a Christmas thing? A declaration in the heat of the moment?"

The question is backed by nerves, and she's afraid to hear the answer. Buried under the need for assurance is a lilt of hopefulness, too. My hand reaches out and I tilt her chin, tracing the line of her jaw.

"No, Bridget. I was thinking more of an everyday thing. A forever thing, if you were okay with it."

Long eyelashes fan out as she blinks, bottom lip wobbling. "Really?"

"You don't deserve one holiday, Bridget. You deserve them all. New Year's. Valentine's Day. St. Patrick's Day, too. A random Tuesday in July when we're both drenched with sweat from the summer sun, wishing for a spot of clouds. Even then, it'll be you and me."

"Every holiday? What about Arbor Day?"

"I'll plant you a forest of trees."

"Way down in the bottom of November?"

"I'll like you then, too. Over and over again, I'll keep choosing you. And then we'll do it year after year."

"I'll keep choosing you, too, Theo," she whispers back.

"I want to show you something," I mumble, peeling away from her.

"Oh, my god. You aren't... this isn't..."

I pause, one foot on the ground, my knee balancing on the mattress. "You think I'm *proposing* to you when I don't know your middle name?"

"I don't know," she sputters. "You got all serious."

"It's not a ring. I promise."

"Is that something that would interest you? Marriage? Hypothetically, of course. Down the road," she says.

"I'm not opposed to marriage, but I'm also not ready to run

down the aisle just yet. I want you, Bridget. If you wanted a wedding, we could have a wedding. If you want more kids, or you're fine with just Mac, I don't care. I've spent so much of my time not living *my* life. And now that I am, I want to do what makes me happy. Turns out, you make me the happiest guy in the fucking world. So whatever you want is fine with me. You're up there with Mac for me, angel. There's no one more important than you two."

"I think you're under Ziggy on my list. We'll reevaluate after the holidays."

"I'll concede to the rightful Bowie heir." I chuckle. "I'll be right back."

I climb off the bed and pluck my wallet from the back pocket of my damp jeans. Opening the leather, I fumble through the sections until I find what I'm looking for.

"Read this," I say, handing her the small scrap of paper and an assortment of photos.

"'Theo, I was out of line with my interview questions. When I saw the pictures from the magazine shoot, I realized you aren't abrasive at all. You're a good guy with a kind heart who's head over heels for a wonderful woman. I thought you might want to keep these.'" Her forehead wrinkles and she looks up at me. "I don't understand."

"Look at the pictures."

Bridget exchanges the handwritten note for the small, glossy images. The first is of me in the bookstore, looking over my shoulder. I'm searching for something off camera. Bridget, I presume. There's a wide smile on my face, and a gleam in my eyes. The second is of the two of us together, side by side at the counter, chocolate batter on our faces. I'm staring down at her, rolling my lips to stop a grin while she laughs. The third is the one of me and Mac on her bike, Christmas morning long ago. The final photo is from the mall. I'm sandwiched between Mac and Bridget, my arms around both of them, grinning from ear to ear.

"No one's gotten me to smile like that in years," I murmur. My chest pinches with the admission, the firm barrier around my heart crumbling to rubble. "People have tried. Some have come close. But fuck *close*. It was you, making brownies, flour on our faces and chocolate chips in my hair, that got me to grin. And laugh. And fucking *live*. It was falling on my ass ice skating and lifting tree after tree into my truck. It was seeing you with my daughter. It was hanging lights and painting reindeer. It was burnt latkes and Thanksgiving dinner. I'm not big on fate, but there's a reason you bought the store next to mine. There's a reason we were paired together for this competition. It brought me to you."

"Theo." Her hands reach out and clutch my cheeks. I'm her lifeline, keeping her afloat. A place of warmth and peace. And she's my anchor; steady. Secure. Withstanding even the roughest seas. "I'm going to do my best to get you to smile like that every day damn, because it's the most beautiful thing I've ever seen."

I love you, I want to say. It's close, *so fucking close*, to spilling out once and for all. Because that's the thing about love, I've learned. It's unexpected, a surprise that greets you one day and alters the trajectory of your life. It happened with Mac. It happened the first day I ever walked into A Likely Story, the waft of sweet blueberries tugging me inside and finding the bubbly brunette smiling at me like I was *important*.

Like even then, she could see what lay beneath the sharp exterior.

There's no going back now, so much of myself woven into the woman next to me, a thread tethering us together. Forever, I hope.

"Want to break the news to Mac?" I ask. "She's going to flip her shit."

"Yes," Bridget says. She's giddy as she rolls off the bed, grabbing the nearest article of clothing—a T-shirt of mine and a sweatshirt—and yanking it over her head. "Bring the tissues. It's going to be waterworks central, buddy. Hope you're prepared to deal with that for a long, long time."

She disappears into the bathroom, hands working to pull her hair into a ponytail.

"Yeah," I say into the empty room. "I am."

I PARK OUTSIDE MY PARENTS' house. Bridget is in the passenger seat and Ziggy is in the back, staring out the window. He whines, and I reach around to pat his head.

"Are we going inside?" Bridget asks, gaze bouncing between me and the porch.

"Nah. It'll be more fun this way." I send a message to Mac, letting her know I'm out front and to take the back seat when she gets to the car.

"She already has one broken arm, Theo. Don't encourage her to break the other."

The front door opens and closes, and I watch my kid skip down the path to the truck. She slides into the back, slamming the door behind her. "Why the heck am I not in the front, Dad? And what's Ziggy doing here?"

"Hey, kiddo." I grin at her through the rearview mirror. "Sorry. I have to demote you to permanent backseat privileges. Someone else has longer legs than you, and she needs the space." I look at Bridget and tilt my head.

"Hey, Mac and Cheese," she says. Her body contorts in the seat, twisting to give Mac a wave.

"FINALLY," the half-pint bellows. Ziggy punctuates the

interjection with a loud bark. "Oh my god. What does this mean?"

"It means Bridget's going to be around more, if that's okay with you."

"Of course it's okay," Mac says quickly.

"I don't mean in a friend capacity, either," I clarify.

"Mac," Bridget interjects. "I'm excited to spend time with you two. I like your dad, and I like you, too. If you're uncomfortable with this, please tell me. You won't hurt my feelings. I want to make sure we're all okay with these new roles going forward."

"What should I call you? Mom? BB?"

Bridget looks at me, panic-stricken, before schooling her features and clearing her throat. "You can call me whatever you want. BB is just fine."

"Okay." Mac nods solemnly. Her glee has faded, and I think she's understanding how big of a step this is. "I don't care what the title is. I'm glad you get to be a part of our lives." Her eyes dart to me. "We're lucky, Dad. You're not allowed to do anything to screw it up."

I chuckle, palm falling to Bridget's knee. "Trust me. I know we are. No screw ups planned this time, punk."

Bridget's shoulders shake with a rumble of laughter. "We'll have a more serious conversation about this soon. Until then, we have a competition to win and a birthday to celebrate!"

FORTY-SEVEN
BRIDGET

"I'M SO FREAKING NERVOUS," I say to Chandler on our walk to Central Park. The sidewalk is bustling with eager shop owners and employees making their way to the judging announcement. A nervous chatter is shared between hopeful participants and my fingers lace together, giving my hands something to do to quell the rising anxious energy.

"I don't know why," she answers bluntly. "Our store looks incredible."

Our store *does* look incredible, but the other stores on the avenue look different. It's a high-quality designer level with their professionally strung lights, each bulb equally spaced out and not flickering ominously like half of ours do. They have matching color schemes and ballerinas waltzing to *The Nutcracker* on the sidewalk. We passed a towering ice sculpture in the shape of a Christmas tree three doors ago, and my jaw is still on the ground because of the intricate carving.

When the judges walked through the stores two days ago, it was hard to tell how they were feeling. They took detailed notes on their clipboards and asked for elaboration. I guided them to the Christmas tree trail. Bradley had the home videos rolling on the projector, a constant loop of sleigh rides and present opening. The judges were impressed with Lucas's woodworking skills and the lit menorah. They took their time, meticulously examining all the small details; the photos on the clothesline, the notes to Santa under the trees, the uneven brush strokes on the hand-painted reindeer.

At the conclusion of the tour, we brought them back into the bookstore. Felicity presented the Hanukkah spread, complete with perfectly seasoned brisket, unburnt potato latkes, and enough jelly donuts to fill a well. We added in some homemade peppermint bark with sides of hot chocolate, eggnog and cider.

The food was delicious. They couldn't offer explicit comments on the flavors or presentation, but I saw two of the judges take a plate with them, hiding it under their jackets.

"We deserve this," Chandler adds. "We've worked so damn hard."

She waves to our group gathered near the front of the stage. There are flowers and a large check set up on the platform. Cameras flank the outside of the park, photographers capturing the socialization. Buffet tables cover the grass, rows of food and drinks offered. My stomach is in knots, a tight spool of worry as we approach everyone. I spot Theo beside Mac and Lucas wearing... a *Santa hat*?

What the hell?

Theo must feel my attention on him, because he pauses his conversation and looks over his shoulder. His eyes find mine from across the grass and he beams, bright and wide. Whenever he does that–looks at me like I'm the only person in the world–I like him... *shit,* I *love* him a little more.

He shuffles around the group, nodding hello to people before finding his way to me.

"Hey," he says.

"Hey," I say back. "You're wearing a Santa hat. I thought that was a no-go for you."

"Yeah. Figured we could use some Christmas luck. And, well–" He pauses, hand rubbing over his jaw. His eyes twinkle and his shoulders lift, a lackadaisical shrug. "I knew it would make you happy. So here we are."

"You are..." I trail off, words mingled with a laugh. I shake my head. "Incredible. Absolutely incredible."

"Come here, angel."

Theo opens his arms and I find my way to them, metal to a magnet, just like I found my way to them every night this week. My palms slide into the back pocket of his jeans. Something sharp pricks my skin and I wince.

"Ow. What the heck?" I pull out a piece of mistletoe.

His smile is sheepish and timid. "You're home to me, too, Bridget. I didn't know I paused on the sidewalk before walking inside your shop until you pointed it out to me. After that, I figured out why. I watch you through the glass. Sliding new pastries into the display case. Dragging boxes of books to the shelves. All with this smile on your face and this love and joy I want to be a part of. I'm glad you put out those blueberry muffins three years ago. I'm glad you didn't toss them in the trash. I'm glad you waited for me to come back, because you're everything I never thought existed. But you do, and I'm the lucky fuck who gets to spend every day with you."

"Holy crap," I whisper. "That was quite the declaration."

"I also realize we like to do things out of order, so I wanted to ask you this officially. Bridget... *fucking hell*. What's your middle name?"

"Camden." I giggle. "What's yours?"

"Phillips. Let's try this again. Bridget Camden Boylston. Maker of blueberry muffins. Keeper of my heart. Dog owner, book lover, woman I adore. Will you be my girlfriend and stay a while?”

I nod, the buttons of his shirt rough against my cheek. “Yeah, Theo Phillips Gardner. I will. It’s going to be more than a while. Decades and decades. It’ll be so long that when you scowl, you won’t have any teeth.”

“Looking forward to it.”

“Is the mistletoe a flower alternative?”

“No. It’s my pathetic excuse to do this.”

He holds the plant above our head. His chin tips down and his lips brush against mine, a kiss that’s not quite a kiss. I grab the collar of his flannel–a deep red tonight–and yank him toward me, crashing my mouth into his. I hear a faint whistle. A cheer and the sound of a scooter horn, blaring in rapid succession. They’re all muted noise. My only focus is Theo’s chuckle, and how it mixes into a low groan from the back of his throat when I jump into his arms.

“If we win–” he murmurs, teeth nipping my bottom lip, “I’m fucking you in my truck after. Checking it off your happy list.”

“Deal.”

“Took you two long enough.”

My attention slides from Theo’s face to the right. Greta’s there on her scooter, smiling at us.

“Wow, okay,” I laugh as I slide down Theo’s body and fold my arms across my chest. “So much for being discreet.”

“A kiss in the middle of a crowded park is not what I would call discreet,” she counters. Her eyes move to Theo. “Glad you finally realized what I meant. No need to search for something that’s been there the whole time.”

“You’re right, Greta. I’ll admit you know everything,” he says, arm around my shoulder. “I’ll listen better next time.”

“You look better with a smile on your face,” says Greta.

"Happy for you two. You're next," she adds, pointing at Chandler.

My best friend bursts out laughing. "Yeah, and hell will freeze over, too."

"Never say never," the older woman says. "I have a feeling you all will have a lot to celebrate tonight." With a wink, she drives off, horn blaring to disperse the crowd in her way.

"Ambiguous as always," I say to Chandler and she rolls her eyes.

"Alright folks!" Jamie walks onto the stage, waving to the crowd. "How's everyone doing? We're so lucky to have Jacqueline Muller, head of *Travel Living* here to announce our competition winners. We had an enormous outpouring of interest from readers and viewers online. Additionally, thanks to your spectacular designs, the prizes have changed slightly. Third place will now receive compensation, a total of $50,000. Second place will win $100,000. Which means first place will win $200,000."

I almost crush Theo's hand with how tight I'm gripping his fingers.

"Without further ado," Jamie says. "Here's Jacqueline."

A hush falls over the crowd. I'm afraid to even take a breath.

"Thank you for inviting us to your lovely town. We've spent a lot of time here the last two weeks, watching you all put together displays and decorations. We are so proud of all your hard work. The magazine and our sponsors felt the hard work should be compensated fairly. This was very, very difficult to judge, but we felt like the top six locations stood out a touch above others. In third place is Sarah's Flowers and Men's Warehouse."

I drop Theo's hand to applaud, grinning as Sarah and Bryson, the two owners, make their way to the stage.

"Shame he's wearing a shirt," Chandler whispers in my ear and I giggle.

"In second place is Pottery House and Lavender Boutique."

Shit. They were the ones with the ballerinas. If that was second place, we don't stand a chance. My hope in our dreams begins to falter, and I swallow.

"There was a lot of conversation surrounding our first place winner. When we walked through all the stores, there was only one that evoked a sense of *home* when we stepped inside. Elaborate decorations are nice, sure, but sometimes we need to take a step back and realize it's not how much we spend, but how we spend it. When I saw the tagline for this particular group of stores, it made me so happy. It made me want to dash back to New York to see my kids and husband. So much so, I canceled my flight tomorrow and I'm taking the last one out tonight," Jacqueline chuckles. "Home for the holidays, wherever it might be and with whoever it might be. Congratulations to A Likely Story and Gardner's Hardware for being our grand prize winners!"

FORTY-EIGHT
BRIDGET

THE WORLD IS NO LONGER MOVING. I pinch the inside of my wrist, trying to make sure this isn't a dream, that this is *really freaking happening*.

And then the noises begin. A rousing round of applause and cheers. Clapping and screaming, hooting and hollering. Music playing and off-key singing.

I'm swept into Theo's arms and he's spinning me around, a jovial glint to his eyes and a wide smile on his mouth.

"You did it, baby," he whispers. "I'm so proud of you."

I shake my head, a sob falling from my mouth and joining the other sounds around us. "I didn't do anything. We did. We all did."

It takes some direction and corralling, a solid ten minutes of gentle pushes and clasps on backs before our group finally files onto the stage. It's all a blur, a mix of handshakes and flowers, laughter and flashes of cameras. A large check gets put in our hands and we pose for photos, smiling brightly and wiping away our tears. Jacqueline gives me a hug, pulling me aside to tell me how moved she was by our design. She also tells me she's going to be the one to interview us in January and said she'd be in touch about a future collaboration featuring indie-bookstores throughout the country.

My hands are shaking too violently to hold onto anything, and I delegate Bradley as the official check holder. He takes his duties seriously; the first thing he does is jump off the stage, crowd surfing with the large piece of cardboard marked with $200,000 over his head.

"What the hell?" Chandler laughs, hugging me tight. "How did this happen? Did we really just win with home photos and painted decorations?!"

"Yeah," I answer, squeezing her tight. "We really did. Thanks for going all in on a silly bookstore with me."

"I'd do it again in a heartbeat. Love you, Bridge."

"Love you too, Chan."

I move to Lucas, who mimics Theo, picking me up and spinning me around. "Guess we'll be seeing more of each other," he says when I'm firmly back on the ground.

"I promise I won't take your best friend away."

"Nah. You're not taking him away. He's finally where he belongs."

It's only after another round of high-fives, pictures and waves to the audience before we finally move off the stage, forming a large circle in the grass.

"Y'all. I am *so* proud of you. Thank you for sharing your photos and traditions. Thank you for all your hard work. Thank you for making this fun and an incredible experience. I wouldn't have wanted to sand and paint nine reindeer, hang thousands of lights, or carol on a boat in the middle of the lake with anyone else."

"We definitely need to celebrate," Lucas interjects. "Does December 26th work for everyone? We can meet at the stores, eat all the leftovers and bask in our winnings."

There's a chorus of agreements, some already planning what they'll be using the money for.

"I feel like opening silly gifts after that announcement is kind of anticlimactic," I admit. "We totally don't have to–"

"Presents!" Bradley yells.

And that settles that.

Lucas got Chandler a sweatshirt from *The Bachelor* after hearing how much she likes the show. Felicity got Malik a compass keychain. Jordan hands Brooke a bird feeder.

"Who's your person?" Theo asks, bumping his hip against mine.

"You, actually." I hand him the present. "I consulted with Mac, but if it's inappropriate, let me know and I'll take it back."

He raises his eyebrows. His fingers slip under the piece of tape holding the wrapping paper in place, taking his time to peel it away. The plaid outer layer falls to the ground and he opens the packaging inside. Styrofoam pieces cling to the porcelain mug, and the look on Theo's face shifts to anguish.

"Shit," I curse. "I didn't mean–"

He cuts me off with a searing kiss. "It's fucking perfect. Thank you so much." His voice is rough, on the verge of tears.

"I bought others, too. For Mac and your parents. I know you said it used to be a tradition of yours, and I thought, maybe, when you're ready, you can start it up again."

Theo shakes his head and drops his forehead against mine. "You are something else," he murmurs.

"A good something else?"

"The best something else. You were my person, too."

"I was?"

"Mhm." He picks a bag up off the ground. "Open the big one first."

"Two presents? You're spoiling me."

I undo the first box and pull out...

"A mug?" I ask. My name is written in loopy letters, stars accentuating the curve of each shape.

"Guess we were on the same wavelength. I want you in those traditions too, Bridget. I want hot chocolate out of matching mugs with you. No marshmallows, of course. Now open the second one."

"Jeez." I wipe my eyes. "It's going to be hard to outdo the first gift." Passing off my new mug to him, I open the smaller box. "A snow globe?"

"Yeah. The first night we all met at the start of the competition, you mentioned never seeing snow. This is close enough to the real thing for the time being."

"I love it so much. Thank you, Theo."

The crowd begins to disperse, everyone eager to join their families for the holiday festivities and celebrate our prize-winning design.

"You'll be over for Christmas dinner tomorrow, right?" Theo asks Lucas, shaking his hand.

"Obviously. Bridge, are you joining us this year?"

"I am," I grin.

"Do I really have to sleep at Grams and Gramps's tonight?" Mac whines, walking up to us.

"Yup," Theo says. "All your presents are there anyway. We'll be there first thing in the morning to open gifts."

"Fine," she huffs. "There better be good stuff for me under the tree."

"One day in, and the teenage attitude has already started," I whisper to Theo. "Good luck."

AN HOUR LATER, after dropping off Mac and Ziggy, we park in my driveway.

"So," I start, speaking over Meatloaf and "Paradise by the Dashboard Light" crooning softly over the radio. "About that comment of yours."

Theo turns the car off and looks over at me as the car plunges into silence. "Which comment?"

"The fucking in the truck part. Does the offer still stand?"

"Fuck, yeah, it does."

I get tangled in the seatbelt, forgetting to unbuckle myself. I lurch forward, laughing as I try to unravel my arm from the polyester. "Damn safety restraints," I curse, finally free. I shift over the center console, legs straddling Theo's lap. His length presses against me, and through his jeans I can feel how hard he is already.

"This isn't going to be sweet, Bridget." He circles my hair around his wrist and with a rough jerk, tugs my neck backward. "I distinctly recall you saying you wanted *rough* and *dirty*. Is that still true?"

"Y-yes," I answer. My eyes close, a groan already forming in my throat. "As rough and dirty as you want."

Theo *tuts*, and a second later he pinches my nipple. "I want your eyes on me, Bridget, when you ask me to fuck you nice and hard."

This man.

The same man who called me his *home* two hours ago is grazing his teeth down my throat. He's dancing his hands across my chest, finding my other nipple and pinching it as hard as the first. My eyes snap open at his ask and I blink until I find his face. There's so much heat behind his eyes, a need and desire to consume me. Adoration, too, mixed with the brown.

And I want to be devoured.

"Fuck me nice and hard, Theo," I whisper. "Give me everything I want."

With lightning fast speed and agility, he surprises me as we tumble into the backseat. He tosses a dog treat to the ground, and a book gets thrown into the trunk. That's our life now, little knickknacks from other important parts of our family leaving their mark on every space.

"Lift your skirt," he says through a kiss on my neck. His fingers work deftly to unfasten his jeans, pushing them down his thighs to the floorboard of the car.

I comply eagerly, shimmying my plaid skirt around my waist. His hand reaches between my legs, pulling my underwear to the side and grinning when he finds how wet I am.

He teases me, a taunting and featherlight touch for a handful of maddening minutes until I'm a panting and withering mess. A car loops around the corner of my street, headlights illuminating the darkened space around us. It's the same moment Theo decides to slip his fingers inside me, *finally*, and I let out a groan of gratitude. His mouth covers mine as I work with him, riding his hand within an inch of my life.

"Feels so good."

"Looks so good, too," he answers. He nips at my chest over my sweater, using his teeth to pull the fabric of my bra away from my skin. Releasing the material, it snaps back, a sting I feel to my toes. "Does this make you happy, angel? Back seat of the car with the windows fogged up? Knowing you're going to come all over my hand when your neighbor could walk outside at any moment, seeing how well my good girl takes what she wants?"

My moan is a guttural noise from deep within my chest. I want to sob. I want to scream. I want to laugh, a mix of so many goddamn feelings, a delirious sensation of ecstasy building low in my belly.

"Don't stop," I whisper. My tempo increases, my legs spread

wider. I look depraved and desperate, frantically searching for a release.

"I'm never going to stop," Theo murmurs in return.

He shoves my legs wider, thumb circling my clit again and again until I explode, body shaking and quaking. Sweat rolls down my cheek and it's difficult to breathe, a stifling heat settling in the air. I can barely process what's happening before Theo's hands are on my cheek, jerking my head to the left.

"Fogged enough for you?" he asks, gesturing to the windows.

It's like we're in our own personal snow globe, a thick layer of condensation covering the glass. I smile at the sight, envisioning us naked together in a winter wonderland.

"No," I answer, yanking his briefs down. "We can do better."

He chuckles, the laughter fading into a moan as I sink onto him, taking every inch in one quick motion. "That's my girl."

I'm ignited, stars and electricity cackling from my fingertips. I kiss him like it's my dying wish, like I'll never have him again, meeting him thrust for thrust. I bite his neck, leaving a mark. His fingers grip my backside, bruising the skin no one else will ever see.

Theo whispers praise and encouragement in my ears. I groan at the depth. The intensity. The angle. The surprise when he lifts me, flipping us so I'm flat on my back, cloth warm against my thighs. He drapes my calf over his shoulder, left hand keeping me safely from the edge of the seat, a manic look in his eyes as he takes, and takes, and *takes*.

His kisses up my shin, pinches my clit, yanks my hair, and I lose it, again, a wordless *thank you* falling from my lips as I spiral down, down, down, chasing the second orgasm in a matter of minutes. Five more thrusts and Theo meets me, movements stilling as I feel him trip over the edge, see the sag in his shoulders, hear the change in his breathing.

"Holy," he pants, "hell. I'm out of practice."

I giggle, reaching up to wipe the thin layer of sweat from the back of his neck. "Guess we need to keep practicing."

"Jesus. I'd say so." He looks up at me. A lazy, tired smile tugs at his lips. "Are you happy, Bridget?"

"Yeah, Theo," I whisper. "Undeniably happy."

FORTY-NINE
THEO

BRIDGET'S BODY is wrapped around mine when I wake up. Her feet press into my shin and her head rests on my chest. She's breathing peacefully, a rhythmic inhale and exhale that tickles my bare chest with every puff of air.

I like seeing the brown waves scattered across the pillow like spilled chocolate. I like seeing her hand on my chest, chipped Christmas trees painted on her red nails. I like the smell of cinnamon lingering on the sheets even though she hasn't been inside the store for close to forty-eight hours.

She's stunning in the morning light with her sleep-mussed hair. Swollen lips from prolonged kissing. A naked body, clothes forgotten as we held each other through the night. She stirs and burrows her face in the crook of my neck. I rub her bare shoulder, skin warm under my touch. I slide over the cluster of freckles, across her clavicle, landing over her heart.

"Hey," Bridget murmurs. Her eyes crack open. Already, they're bright and sparkling, the day yet to begin. "Merry Christmas."

"Merry Christmas. How'd you sleep?"

"Great. Really great. You're like a human furnace. I don't need to pay for heat when I have your thigh over mine."

"Glad to know why you keep me around."

"The glasses are a nice touch, too."

I chuckle. "I had an idea about the seventh tree."

"Did you?" She sits up, the sheet pooling at her waist. "What is it?"

"I want you to tell me if I'm being selfish."

"Doubtful. Let's hear it."

"My family and I haven't had a real tree since the accident," I explain. "It's what we did before, and I've found I categorize my life into two firm timelines. Before and After. I keep the Befores far, far away from the Afters."

Bridget shifts her position on the mattress, angling her body so she's by my side. Unfolding my hands, her fingers map out the lifelines of my palm, a trail she's trekked before. She doesn't rush me, patiently waiting for me to share more.

"What if we took it to my parents' house? Mac is there. We could decorate it all together, and invite your family, too. I know it'll only be up for a few hours, but this has been the season of new things. New traditions and new friends. New feelings. Maybe it can be the start of a new After, too."

She dips her chin to kiss the inside of my wrist, lips pressing four pecks along my pulse point. "I love it, Theo. It's perfect."

"Are you sure you're okay with this? You said you'd find a place for the last one, and the trees are your thing."

She moves to my lap, head resting on my shoulder. That's her favorite spot, I've learned. Tucked in my hold, safe in my arms, our heartbeats synchronized. "They're not *my* thing," she says emphatically. "They're *our* thing."

"Okay. We can stop by the store before heading over. C'mon, Boylston. We have a busy day of spreading Christmas cheer ahead of us."

❄

IT'S CLOUDY OUTSIDE, a gray and dreary fog in the air. Our drive to the store is gloomy, the beginning of misty rain falling from the sky. The avenue is empty as we turn onto the brick road, and we're the only car on the street. I park outside A Likely Story and cut the ignition.

I hop out of the car and walk to Bridget's side, opening the door and offering her my hand as she steps onto the sidewalk. Her feet splash into a puddle, water kicking up onto my boots.

"The tree is tucked away toward the back of the store, so we'll have to maneuver it around the other displays. It's in the stand, but not decorated. Will that be okay?"

"Yeah," I answer, hustling her under the awning. "That's totally fine."

"Okay, good." Bridget wrestles with the lock, jostling the key before it finally gives. I make a mental note to pop over her tomorrow and fix the knob. "Are there lights at your parents' house?" she asks as she opens the door and strides inside.

"Mhm. We have some."

"Okay, good, I bet there are–" She stops mid sentence and her keychain jangles to the ground. "What... what is this?"

I fold my arms over my chest and follow her gaze, already knowing what I'm going to find. The rolling ladder Lucas and I finished before the ceremony yesterday is attached to the shelf with a big red bow. Painted white, the wooden piece is fixed with wheels on the top and bottom. It's attached to a long metal rod running from end to end of the bookshelf, stretching over seven feet tall.

"Looks kind of like a ladder to me," I answer with a shrug.

Her head whips around, brown hair flying everywhere with the jerky motion. Her eyes tell me she's not pleased with my sarcastic answer, but her smile... *fuck*, that smile is perfect.

That smile is my favorite thing in the world.

"Is this for me?"

"Yeah, it is."

"Theo. Did you do this?"

"Maybe." I make my way across the floor. My arms loop around her waist and I drop my chin to the top of her head. "Lucas and I have been working on it for a while. Merry Christmas, Bridget."

"It's… Oh my god."

She's crying. I hear her sniff. I feel her shoulders shake, rumbling against my chest. I pull out a tissue from my pocket and hand it to her. "Do you like it?"

"Like it? You built me a damn bookshelf ladder," she squeals. "Of course I like it."

"Good. I'm glad. It also comes with a joke. Want to hear it?"

Bridget spins in my arms, looking up at me. Her eyes are watery and her brows are pinched, confused. "A joke?"

"Knock knock."

She huffs but decides to play along. "Who's there?"

"I love you, Bridget Boylston."

The admission catches her off guard. She blinks a few times. Her mouth drops open then closes, lips pursing together as she swallows. "What did you say?"

"It's not a doorknob aisle, and it's cheesy as hell, but I said I love you, Bridget Boylston. And I have for a while. Since Thanksgiving. Since the interview. All the way back when you told me what would make you happy and mustard stained my jeans. Definitely the Wednesday you pushed back, telling me I was wrong about your late arrival. This morning, when you were the first thing I saw when I woke up. Last night, with joy on your face and tears in your eyes." My hands cup her cheeks. "I love you so very much, sweetheart. You don't have to say it back. I just wanted you to know. My heart is yours. Keep it, please. Don't ever return it."

The words don't seem sufficient to convey how much I care about her. How much I plan to treat her right and how every day with her is the *best fucking day.* Nothing has ever compared. And with a twinkle of trees behind us and fake snow under our feet, I'm sure, for the first time in many, many, years about one thing.

I'm going to keep this woman until the end of time, and even that won't be long enough.

"I love you, too," she blurts out. It's a jumble of words, fused together to become a garble of syllables and sounds, but I hear her as clear as day. "I realized it a couple of nights ago. I'm glad you were early that Wednesday. I'm glad someone from your store entered the contest. I'm glad we got paired together, because otherwise I might not get the chance to say I love you so much."

"How much?" My nose brushes against hers and I catch a falling tear. "A shit ton? A fuck ton?"

She laughs, arms draping around my neck. "More. An infinity ton. And then some."

WRESTLING the tree into the bed of my truck in the middle of a rainstorm is far from enjoyable. Pine needles coat my arms and sprinkle into Bridget's hair. Water soaks the cuff of my jeans. Branches scratch our necks and hands, brittle wood coarse and leaving behind splinters. When we finally heave it in safely, we look like we've been through the ringer.

"Theo," she yells, pulling aggressively on the locked handle. "Open the door!"

"Not yet," I call back, holding out my palm. "Dance with me."

"What?" she laughs. Her hair clings to her face, bangs matted to her forehead. "We're soaked!"

"Exactly. What better time than the present?"

Bridget accepts my hand and giggles. Her head drops to my chest and I hum, rubbing up her back as we sway to the symphony of the storm. The howl of the wind. The cleansing of the earth. "I didn't peg you as a dance in the rain kind of guy," she whispers. Her eyes close and a smile, content and happy, stretches over her lips.

"I'm not," I answer. "It's on your list. It makes you happy, so we're doing it. I'd dance with you in the rain any day of the week, though."

It might be seconds. It might be days. Weeks and months might pass us by. I can't tell, and I don't care, because I'm too caught up in *her*. Her smile. Her mouth against mine. Her laugh as I dip her low to the ground. A million things I want to remember forever.

A new beginning. A new after. A new everything, with her by my side.

"MERRY CHRISTMAS!" Bridget announces as we walk through my parents' front door an hour later in dry clothes.

Ziggy jumps off the couch and runs our way. He barks at the six-foot tree we're holding. We're attempting to shuffle through the foyer and into the living room without marking up any of the walls. My mother would flip a shit if she found a scrape on the forest green paint.

"What's going on? Theo? Is that you?"

"Hey, Mom!" I answer. "Meet us in the living room when you can."

"Is this a good spot?" Bridget asks.

"Yeah. Watch your fingers, angel. There we go."

We set the tree on the beige carpet and step back to admire the position. It's to the right of the large couch where Mac sits every year to unwrap presents, near the center of the room and in the front window. Later tonight, it'll be visible from the street.

It kicks the ass of the four-foot artificial tree on a cardboard box standing pathetically in the corner.

"Dad!" Mac runs into the room, enveloping me into a hug. The affection is cut short when she spots Bridget, heading for her next. I watch them, the way Bridget strokes Mac's hair, pinches her cheek, and answers the half-pint's hug with a strong one of her own.

"Hey, Mac Attack. Merry Christmas," says Bridget. "Did you and Ziggy behave last night?"

"Maybe," she answers with a grin. "We definitely didn't stay up too late. We also didn't have birthday cake for dinner. Of course I didn't feed Ziggy half a pancake, too."

"You're trouble, kid," Bridget laughs.

"Theo, honey, what in the world is going on?" Mom's parked in the entryway, looking around the space.

"Merry Christmas, Mom. Bridget and I brought over a tree. A real tree. We thought we could decorate it together and open some presents."

"A *real tree*?" Mac asks. "Holy crap, it's been years since we had one!"

"Mackenzie Ruth. Watch your mouth," I scold. She and Bridget dissolve into a fit of giggles. I walk to Mom, crouching beside her. "Is this okay? Do you like it?"

"Oh, sweetie, it's more than okay."

"We'll probably need your direction for decorating, Mrs. Gardner. The tree Mac and I did at the story is pretty terrible," Bridget admits, slinging her arm around my daughter's shoulder.

"If you're going to be around for the holidays and dinners going forward, there's no more of this Mrs. Gardner nonsense," Mom chuckles. "Call me Maureen. Steve, get in here! Theo, can you get the ornaments from the attic? Mac, you and Bridget can transfer the tree skirt to this one. We'll move the presents after."

I stop by Bridget and Mac on my way to the attic. I lean down, lips ghosting against Bridget's ear. "I love you," I whisper.

She smiles, squeezing my hand. "I love you, too. Best Christmas ever."

"CAN WE PLEASE OPEN PRESENTS NOW?" Mac asks through a groan. She flings herself onto the couch. "We've eaten two meals so far."

"Yeah," I laugh. "We can open presents now."

"Okay, Mac," Bridget starts. She rifles through the large bag she brought inside. Plucking a rectangle box out, she hands it over. "This first one is for you."

She didn't share any of the presents with me, so I have no clue what might be inside.

Mac tears into the present as best as she can with one working arm, taking longer than years past to unwrap the gift. "A Kindle?" she gushes. "Holy cow, this is perfect! Thank you, BB."

"Now you can read all the books you want." Bridget nudges my ribs from beside me on the floor. "It'll help your wallet out, too."

We go around the room, distributing our gifts to each other. Mom, as predicted, bawls over the photo of Mac and me with the mall Santa. Dad winds up with a new meat thermometer. Ziggy gets a new toy. Mac grins at the new soccer cleats and autographed copy of her favorite book from me. I get a pair of work boots and Bridget gets a new set of Converse, complete with candy canes on them for next year's celebrations.

After unwrapping, Mac is showing my mom how her new Kindle works, setting up the device with all her book preferences. I need to remember to put in my credit card information for her. I stretch my arms over my head and scratch Ziggy's ears, so supremely happy with the way the day has unfolded.

Bridget kneels down between my thighs and holds out a picture frame. "I have something for you. I finished it last minute, so forgive the lack of wrapping paper."

"What is it?" I ask. I turn over the square frame and study what's behind the glass.

"Your original plans for the avenue. I found it in the pocket of your jeans the other night. I made a copy and framed it. I know it's important to you, and one day, when you accomplish the goal, I want you to look back and see where it all started."

I think my heart cracks in my chest. It splits wide open, a chisel to the organ, for the entire world to see. My fingers run over the etchings and blueprints I've looked over hundreds of times. My vision grows blurry and I push my glasses up my nose, hoping to deter any swell of emotion that's close to showing itself.

"This is... Bridget. *Fuck*. You're too perfect for a Grinch like me."

"Perfect?" she laughs and shakes her head. She puts her hands on my legs and leans forward. "I'm not. I'm flawed, just like you. I make mistakes, just like you. And we're going to keep working together to be the best versions of ourselves. With Christmas trees, a meddling teenager, hopes and dreams, and whatever contest the city decides to do next. Is that okay with you?"

"Yeah," I huff. I set the frame aside and pull her into my lap where she belongs. "Sounds great."

"Welcome home, Theo," Bridget whispers. She kisses my cheek and places her palm on my chest. "We've got a lot of Afters to look forward to. Together."

EPILOGUE THEO

Theo
Two years later

"FOR THE RECORD, I *hate* this whole secrecy thing," Bridget says. I tighten the blindfold around her head, making sure it's snug. "Is it really necessary?"

"Do you want the surprise to be ruined?" I ask.

"No," she grumbles. Her arms cross over her chest and she leans back in the front seat of my truck. "A blindfold and earmuffs, though? People are going to think I'm in a cult."

"Don't worry. I covered all our bases."

I spent weeks making calls and talking to people, explaining my plan and *swearing* the woman with me isn't being held against her will. It took a half a dozen trips to the airport, printed documentation and proof of identities until I finally got the airline onboard with my plan.

"It's going to be weird not spending Christmas at the house," Bridget sighs. "But change can be good, and I'm excited to see what you're planning."

I smile as my hand drops from her hair to her arm, thumb

rubbing over the tattoos she got three months ago. Every time I see the shapes, I grin like an idiot, a fool hopelessly in love. On her right arm is a muffin, complete with blueberries and steam rising from the top of the inked pastry. On the left is a soccer ball, Mac's jersey etched into one of the hexagons, proudly displaying the number four.

The agreement was I'd also get a piece of artwork done. So, I did.

A series of three paw prints on my shoulder, taking over the small sliver of space under my Bowie tattoo. And, the most special one I've gotten to date: a stack of books and a snow globe beneath a decorated Christmas tree, etched over my heart.

Bridget only cried twice when she saw them. When I walk around the house without a shirt on, she stops me in the hallway so her lips can press a kiss to my bare skin, reverently outlining the shape with her fingers. It's funny to think about the girl in the park, at the town hall meeting where our love story originated. The one who was afraid to get anymore ink on her body now proudly wears a symbol attributed to me for all the world to see, the two of us forever linked in this lifetime and beyond.

It's taken months of planning to attempt to pull this excursion off, and the next four hours are going to be the most difficult part. People are definitely going to stare. Between the bright pink earmuffs I purchased half-price at a thrift store, the cheetah blindfold (a gift from Bridget last Christmas that's been put to good use), and the obnoxious yellow shirt she's wearing that says: *I'm going to see snow for the first time and I have no idea, please don't ruin it Chandler it sounds stupid we need to pick something else* plastered on the front and back of the cotton, we're going to be the object of everyone's attention.

There was an obvious miscommunication with the printing company.

We bought a house together ten months ago. It's a ranch-style home on the outskirts of Park Cove, sitting on seven acres of land. Outside the back windows is a forest of trees and we watch the sun rise over a cluster of live oaks every morning, a chorus of birds greeting us with their wake-up songs. A wooden fence runs along the perimeter of our property line, a haven for Ziggy and his new friends to freely roam.

The first thing we did after we picked up the keys was head to the local shelter where we adopted two dogs. Add in a rambunctious teenager who has more energy than any human should, and it's practically a zoo.

Bridget as a parental figure is... amazing. She fell into the role easily, setting a firm boundary between her and Mac's friendship and an adult who scolds and praises. She helps with homework but also encourages Mac to problem-solve for herself. We've talked about more kids, maybe, but nothing in great detail. If it happens, it happens. If it doesn't, I'm still the luckiest bastard to walk the earth, the two greatest women by my side.

Business got out of hand when the holiday competition wrapped up, and exploded further when we sat down for an additional interview with *Travel Living*. I hired eight new employees after the features in the magazine brought an influx of customers from outside our city limits. We package and ship out hundreds of orders a day, nearly doubling our revenue in just a year. With Lucas's pestering and my staff's encouragement, I started doing a weekly video on our social media page, explaining how to do basic projects around the house.

Bridget cracks up at the comments.

In a crazy turn of events, we knocked down the shared wall between Gardner's Hardware and A Likely Story. It made sense; all our employees kept running back and forth between the two shops to socialize, and the demolition awarded us significant floor space to set up displays and demonstration tables. Plus, it gives me more opportunities to spend time with Bridget, sitting on the couch in her office and watching while she debates which book cover she likes best.

Bridget is working on securing a Book Bus of some sort. She implemented the Little Free Libraries throughout the neighboring towns and visits them twice a month to make sure they are fully stocked.

Mac is in high school and thriving. She made the varsity soccer team and splits her free time between reading in the library Bridget designed in our house, and hanging out with friends, rolling her eyes when we–I, really, because Bridget always falls for the pouty lips and doe eyes–remind her of her curfew.

My parents are doing well, and Mom took her first steps since the accident three months ago. It's been an extensive physical journey for her, and it's encouraging to see even small improvements. Therapy is still a weekly occurrence for me, and I've let go of the animosity and guilt I've held onto for years. I met Bridget's parents and siblings, and learned exactly where she got her zest for life and vivacious energy. Her family is bright and welcoming, treating Mac and me like we've been around for decades instead of only two years.

It's stupid and cheesy as hell, but I've never been happier. The days before the accident were never this *good*, and I'm constantly questioning how my ass wound up trading the scowls for smiles, grinning from ear to ear every morning I wake up with the beautiful brunette in my arms.

"Can I make a guess?" she asks.

"Nope. I'll warn you, though, it's going to be a couple hours until you find out."

"Hours? Are you out of your mind?"

"I'll give you one hint. It involves an airplane."

❄

THE AIRPORT IS a total shit show. I picked the worst day for us to travel. Thousands of people are flying out for the holidays, eager to get to their loved ones in different states. Hundreds of families are heading home from their theme park and beach vacations, shoulders weighed down by heavy bags of souvenirs that will end up in a coat closet sooner rather than later. When we finally make it through security and onto the plane, I breathe my first sigh of relief in hours. My head drops against the leather seat, enjoying a brief moment of peace.

A buzz in my pocket breaks the solitude and I dig my phone out of the denim. My free hand rests on Bridget's thigh, fingers drumming against the corduroy of her pants.

> Mac: Dad are you on your way? We're in the car!
>
> Chandler: I need someone else to get here. Lucas is driving me up a wall.
>
> Lucas: You know I'm in this group chat too, right? And sitting two feet away from you.
>
> Chandler: Yeah. I'm well aware.
>
> Theo: We're on the plane. I'll let you know when we land.
>
> Chandler: Someone hurry, please. Lucas just put on Christmas music and won't stop smiling at me.

I chuckle at their responses, feeling sorry for Chandler. Lucas isn't going to stop smiling at her anytime soon, and she's in for a long afternoon until the others join her. Plucking the earmuffs away from Bridget's ears, I kiss her cheek.

"How are you doing, sweetheart? Is anything bothering you?" I keep my voice soft to not startle her, and she smiles when she hears me.

"No, I'm good," she answers. "Are we on the plane?"

"Yeah. Didn't you feel me strap you in?"

"I thought you were just trying to get handsy."

I laugh, lifting the armrest between us so I can pull her into my embrace. "I'll always get handsy with you, Boylston. You keep me young."

"The gray in your hair says otherwise, buddy."

BRIDGET JOLTS when the wheels touch down, lifting her head away from my shoulder, the spot it's been for the last hour.

"I fell asleep." Stretching her arms, she fumbles with the window shade. "Are we there? It feels cold."

I wait until the flight attendant finishes the arrival announcement and pull the earmuffs away from her ears the final time. "Sort of. We have another forty minutes or so. The airport is small, so we should be in the car soon."

She's already smiling even though she can't see a damn thing. Zipping her fleece jacket up is a hassle, because she won't stop giggling and fidgeting, cheeks flushed pink with excitement. I pile her into the rental car with our matching suitcases and turn on the seat warmers, driving toward our destination in a content silence.

Yeah, I'm a matching suitcase guy now.

Next will be a minivan.

I finally understood what Bridget meant when she said she wanted a relationship where there wasn't a need to talk all the time. The quiet is beautiful, an expression of love conveyed through small touches and subtle glances instead of voices and declarations. Sometimes, when she looks up at me from across the couch with a book in her hand, the grin I'm awarded is more meaningful than three little words.

But I still tell her I love her every fucking day.

An hour later, after careful navigation over snow-covered roads and icy intersections, I park the SUV outside the cabin I rented for the week. The wrap-around porch is decked out in lights, roped around the railings and banister. There's a towering Christmas tree visible through the large front windows, frost fused to glass. Icicles hang from the roof, dangling precariously along the gutters and threatening to fall with any gentle billow of wind. The area around the cabin is a blanket of stark-white snow as far as the eye can see, no other buildings in sight. Smoke puffs from the chimney, a fire burning inside the cozy abode. It's still and serene, an ambiance of peace reaching through the car and welcoming us with open arms. An owl hoots. A crow caws. It's everything I thought it would be, and worth every penny.

A portion of my contest winnings went to this trip. The initial proposal of avenue accessibility no longer needs my monetary contribution. I had a meeting with Jamie, who turned out to be a nice guy, outlining the changes I wanted to see accomplished. He listened to my ideas, organizing a team to head up the project which includes curb leveling, additional handicap parking spaces, and street expansion. Once a month a group of us meet, discussing potential designs and firming up an exact budget needed for future tasks. It's an arduous process with a dozen moving parts, but the important thing is we're *working* on it, the dream slowly turning from a hazy outline to a sharp reality.

Renting the cabin in Steamboat Springs, Colorado was the only thing I wanted my money to go toward. I'm giving Bridget her white Christmas, and, lucky for us, a blizzard passed through two days ago. The whole town is coated in eighteen inches of fresh powder, a far cry from the 75 degree weather we left behind.

Bridget's going to be excited and appreciative of the gift, but she's a lover, happiest when she's surrounded by important people in her life. I knew she would be bummed spending the holiday away from our families, so I decided to fly them out, too. Lucas and Chandler only argued four times on the cross-country flight, apparently, so we're off to a good start.

It's all a carefully calculated plan. Chandler and Mac packed her suitcase. The store is closed for the week, with the promise of fulfilling all online orders when we get home. Her social media followers were understanding when Chandler accidentally revealed the news in a quickly-deleted post, saying they couldn't wait to see photos of the book nook I made sure the cabin had.

"Okay, angel. Ready for your surprise?"

"I've been ready for hours!"

"You remember the night we ate burgers together? After the Christmas tree lot? I asked what made you happy."

Bridget smiles. Her lips curl up and she fumbles across the car, searching for my hand. When she finds it, her fingers lace through mine. "You did. And you've delivered on every single one of them."

I have. The house, the dogs, dancing in a rainstorm. Making love in a field–our backyard on a rare night alone, under the stars with a crown of flowers in her hair–and fucking in the back of the truck on a weekly basis. We laugh *constantly*, the muscles in my stomach aching for endless hours from how much fun we have. She cries and laughs through the big, important parts of life. I wipe away her tears and hold her close, encouraging her to never stop dreaming, because she's going to succeed at anything she puts her mind to.

"Well, we're missing one. One I haven't been able to deliver yet. One that's taken me a long time to pull off."

I reach over and untie the blindfold, silk fluttering to her lap. Her eyes squint, vision adjusting to the light for the first time in hours. She peers through the fogged windshield and into the gray, dim outside world. Blinking, her mouth parts as she processes where we are.

"Theo," she whispers.

"Merry Christmas, Bridget. Here's your white Christmas."

"You're not serious. This cannot be real."

"Look at your shirt."

Her chin drops as she slowly reads the words out loud, voice turning choked and stilted as she struggles to get through the sentence. "H-how long have you been planning this?"

"Since the night you first mentioned it. Sap on my hands, pine needles in my hair, and a beautiful woman next to me, pouring her heart out to a guy who couldn't believe he was lucky enough to sit beside her."

Bridget unbuckles her seatbelt and launches herself at me, diving straight for my lap. I laugh and pull her into my arms. Her hands wrap around my neck, palms running up my back in small circles then down again. I feel the tremor in her touch, the emotions she's trying to steady. It's a losing battle she's fighting, a fresh batch of tears forming in her eyes.

"Don't cry, angel."

"I can't help it." She sniffs and wipes her cheeks. "This is wonderful. I'm so freaking happy. I waited so long for someone who got me, Theo. And you do. You understand me. You know how my brain works and what I need to feel fulfilled in life. Thank you so much, sweetheart."

I press a kiss to her forehead. "We talked about a lot of things that day. It was when I really saw how wonderful you were. I liked being with you. I liked my arm around your shoulder. My heart skipped a beat when you said nice things to me. It was the beginning of us, I think. Do you remember earlier in the night when you asked me about my favorite story? I told you I didn't have an answer for you."

"Yes," she whispers. Her voice trembles and I adjust our position to bring her closer.

"I finally figured it out. It's ours. Our story is my favorite. In every realm, on every page, I'm yours. The chapters with you are my favorite, and it's a tale I could read over and over again, never growing tired of it. You are the love of my life, Bridget Boylston. The reason I went through years of suffering, because whatever higher power out there knew I needed you, specifically, to be complete. And, fuck, are you not my perfect other half."

A sob, happy and thankful, rattles her shoulders. A laugh gets tangled in the sound, too, barreling dangerously close to hyperventilation. "I love you, Theo Gardner. I want to make blueberry muffins with you by my side for the rest of my life. I want to watch you try to find your glasses until you give up and ask for my help. I want to share a bed with you and too many animals. I want to fight with you and then kiss you senseless five minutes later, because you know I can't stay mad at you. I hate that you had to suffer, but I'm so glad the universe led me to you."

"That reminds me. There's one more thing. Close your eyes."

Her eyes flutter shut, tear drops clinging to the fan of dark eyelashes. I lift her gently, enough to dig into my other pocket. I pull out my wallet and turn her palm face up, placing the leather in her hands. Her eyebrows furrow and her thumb rubs over the weathered material.

"Why am I holding your wallet?"

"We might as well keep walking down memory lane. Remember the night I told you I was going to grab my wallet and you panicked, thinking there was going to be a ring after six minutes of knowing each other? Maybe you should check again."

"You didn't," Bridget whispers, eyes flying open.

"Guess you'll have to open it to find out."

She unfolds the accessory, rifling through the photos I keep tucked inside. The two of us in matching Santa hats from last Christmas. Mac and Bridget on our front porch swing, three dogs at their feet while they read a book. Mac in her soccer uniform, ball tucked under her arm. Reaching the end of the keepsakes, she pauses.

"Holy shit," she exhales. Extracting the ring, her hand shakes as she examines the diamond. A princess cut on a white gold band Chandler helped me pick out. It's nothing gaudy, just bold enough to let the world know she's mine.

And I'm hers.

As if the idiotic grin on my face doesn't say enough.

"I love you, Bridget. I can't wait to eat blueberry muffins with you for the rest of our lives."

I slide the ring onto her finger, over the snowmen painted on her nails and past the knuckles I've kissed thousands of times. Her hand—*fuck*, I love the feel of the metal against my skin—moves to my cheek and rests there, a boat anchored to the shore.

"I love you too, Theo."

I kiss her, and it's the first kiss of forever. Of a new part of our lives, and I savor it. I put every ounce of myself behind the press of my mouth against hers. The drag of her tongue against mine. The sharp bite of teeth sinking into my lower lip, and the chuckle I give her in response.

"We need to stop, angel. We have an audience."

I pull away reluctantly and adjust her jacket, dragging the zipper up toward her neck to hide the two hickeys I left on her throat last night. A mistake in the heat of the moment, but one I'm not mad about.

Bridget runs a hand through her hair as she climbs out of my lap. The waves are disheveled from our long airplane ride coupled with the blindfold and dry outside air. Brown locks hang down her shoulders, past her chest, nearing her waist. It's the longest it's ever been, and she's grown it out, planning to chop it short soon to donate to charity.

How the *hell* did this woman end up with me?

"Who's watching us? The trees?" she asks, needing clarification.

"One final surprise. Then I promise I'm finished."

I cut the ignition and jump out of the car, hurrying to her side. I offer her my hand and her fingers tangle with mine, palm warm against mine to ward off the dropping temperatures, the faint glow of dusk turning cold to frigid.

"I like you with a ring," I say.

Chandler and I bounced from store to store for days, searching for the right one. Losing hope and close to giving up, I saw it in a window at the eleventh hour and knew it was made for Bridget. Even Chandler teared up, nodding emphatically when I pointed out the beautiful piece of jewelry.

"I can't wait to show Chan. She's going to freak. We have to get a picture so I can send it to her!"

"Trust me, we're going to have plenty of pictures."

We climb the frozen steps carefully, a thin sheen of ice covering the surface. I can't even knock before the door flies open, a rush of heat, the flicker of Christmas tree lights, and nearly a dozen faces greeting us.

"Surprise!" Chandler bellows.

"Merry Christmas, you love birds," Lucas sings, clapping his hands together.

"Finally," says Mac. She clicks a photo—the first of many—on her phone, grinning from ear to ear.

Bridget is bewildered. Her mouth forms the shape of a

perfect O. Her eyebrows raise, disappearing under her bangs. "Is *everyone* here?"

"Yup. Your family. Mine. Chandler and Lucas. The dogs, unfortunately, were too difficult to bring. They send their love from daycare."

She jumps into my arms, legs encircling my waist. There's not a care in the world we're surrounded by an army of humans, her attention solely on me. "I can't wait to spend the rest of my life with you," she whispers against my lips.

"You're booked for the holidays for the foreseeable future, Boylston. Every last one of them. Because I can't wait to spend the rest of my life with you, either."

Lucas coughs and Mac giggles.

"Dad. Mom. Look up," she says.

My eyes drag to the covered roof. There, attached to a wooden beam, a cluster of mistletoe hangs above our heads.

"Well," I murmur. "We've had a good streak going, and I don't want to mess it up. We can't piss off the holiday berries."

"No," Bridget laughs. "We can't."

I kiss her again, and again, and again. I'm going to keep kissing her for the rest of my life. I used to dread the after, wishing I was still stuck in the before. Until I met her. Now all I do is look forward to tomorrow, another day I get to spend with her. We have thousands more left to live, and I know, even after two years of pure bliss, food fights in our kitchen, hugs and laughter, tears and triumphs, the best is yet to come.

"Best Christmas ever?" she asks.

I drop my forehead against hers, heart racing in my chest. Full of joy, full of cheer, full of love. "Yeah, angel. Best Christmas ever," I agree. "By a long shot."

ACKNOWLEDGMENTS

Thank you for reading my third novel. This one felt special, and of all the couples I've written, Bridget and Theo are my favorites. I hope you enjoyed them, too.

To my beta readers, Cassidy, Dani, Delaney, Jocelyn, Katie, Kelly, Sarah, Lauren and Athen: thank you for all your feedback. Thank you for talking out scenes with me and making sure body parts were in the proper locations. I appreciate y'all immensely.

To Beth and Lily: thank you for helping me with the Jewish representation in this story and telling me different ways latkes would burn! I'm grateful for your insight.

To Kristen: thank you for always being willing to read my writing at odd hours of the day and night (like when I'm not sleeping in London on my layover). I'm so glad we became friends!

To Haley, Katelin and Amanda: my MFers. I can't tell you how much I love y'all. You three are the best. There's no one I'd rather lie on the dock in Michigan with, searching for otters (and hot dads). You're stuck with me for life.

To Britt: thank you for your editing expertise. Thank you for being flexible with my short timeline and your comments and notes. They helped me SO much.

To Sam: Another cover down, and this one is the best one yet. I truly cannot figure out how to voice how thankful I am for you and your incredible artistic ability. Thank you for continuing to make my visions become reality. You are a true superstar.

To Tarah DeWitt and Hannah Grace: thank you for being

incredibly kind people and wonderful authors. Thank you for letting me use your creative geniuses in my story. I can't wait to read what y'all write next.

If you haven't read FUNNY FEELINGS or ICEBREAKER yet, what are you waiting for?!

To the Booktok and Bookstagram community: you all have made this year extraordinary. Never in my wildest dreams did I think I would write one book, let alone publish three in a year. But here we are. Thank you for every tag, every share, every review and message about how much you enjoy what I write. Y'all keep me motivated on the days I want to throw in the towel. I hope I can keep getting better as an author and share many more stories with you.

To my family: I love you all!

To Mikey and Riley: I love you guys. Thank you for always encouraging me. No jetskis yet, but soon. I promise I'll take a short break after this one. Maybe.

ABOUT THE AUTHOR

Chelsea Curto splits her time between Winter Park, Florida and Boston, Massachusetts, where she's based as a flight attendant. When she's not busy writing, she loves to read, travel, go to theme parks, run, eat tacos, hang out with friends and pet dogs.

instagram.com/chelseareadsandwrites

tiktok.com/@chelseareadsandwrites

twitter.com/creadsandwrites

goodreads.com/chelseareadsandwrites

amazon.com/Chelsea-Curto/e/B0B27CWPKK?ref=sr_ntt_s-rch_lnk_1&qid=1669506824&sr=8-1

ALSO BY CHELSEA CURTO

An Unexpected Paradise

The Companion Project